Escape f

Arson, corruption and vice. A story that will tug your heartstrings.

Toni Bolton

A 'Men of valour and women of steel' novel

ISBN:978-9998533-0-3

DEDICATION

To any person who had suffered emotional physical abuse and particularly Linda who was stalked and murdered on her doorstep

ACKNOWLEDGMENTS

To Steve who read this and printed and formatted it.

Prologue.

Kirsten felt as if a bell was ringing deep inside her head. Rough hands were shaking her awake, digging into her, bruising her. She tried to bury herself in the safety and security of her sleeping sub-consciousness; the obscurity of the darkness, wanting the anonymity.

The hands were around her throat groping her, choking her. A heavy body was suffocating her until the blessed darkness engulfed her. Her dream not over, she regained consciousness slowly, coughing and spluttering, still seeing those eyes above her; emotionless flat grey pebbles staring at her, while she cringed away from them.

She made an inhuman effort and pushed the hands back and woke up with a start; feeling sick as she fought the lethargy and sickness induced by the sleeping pill. It had only been a nightmare, thank God. Her breathing slowed down as she realised she was alone in the room but her phone was bleeping.

Oh God, have I been found here? she wondered, her heart jumping in her throat. Only three people outside of Indonesia knew her existence on this small island.

She fumbled for the light switch, ice gripping her heart. All the blood had rushed out of her face. She could hardly bear to look at the mobile, but peering with half-shut eyes at the face, she saw that thankfully it was her Aunt Freja's number. The sweat pouring out of her froze on her icy skin.

She got out of bed to wash herself and pulled on a robe. It was 23C in Indonesia but she was perishing cold; a reaction to the fear that had engulfed her. She made a hot chocolate, a comfort drink. It helped her overcome the shadows that threatened to envelop her, even in this isolated place where few people knew her.

Now her pulse was no longer racing and she was warming up she could concentrate on her aunt's phone call. Her aunt had given up ringing and finally sent a text. She had bedded down early, the heat making her tired. It was only 10.30pm. A night owl, her aunt would have expected her to be up for hours.

She read the text. "Kirsten Darling. I have something I would like you to check for me. A man wants to buy my house and is rather insistent I sell. He has phoned me five times and will not accept I don't want to sell to him. He now wants to meet me in person and visit the house today. Michael said he will stay with me while the man comes but I want you to check his background for me. I feel something is not quite right. The way he spoke gave me the shivers.''

She texted back, "Send me his name and anything you know about him Aunt Freja. I have an internet connection and can follow it up.'' She went back to bed to an uneasy sleep; her aunt having worried her. Freja was a cool lady with good instincts.

The next morning the details were in a text. She put the details into her laptop and pulled out what she could. The man who was pestering her aunt to sell was a rather seedy property developer who had made money during the bubble of the eighties and early nineties. He also had connections with some investors in banking and mining. She emailed a friend who had police connections in the USA. He wrote back stating the guy had a record.

The connection was failing. Storms had brought the feeble lines down and the island had suffered severe storm damage. Many of the women were leaving with their families until their homes could be rebuilt by their menfolk, aided by the relief agencies. It was the appropriate time for her to leave for England, earlier than she had agreed in her contract. She could do little here now and could follow up her leads much more efficiently in England than here in Indonesia.

Devil's Creek Florida June the 6th 2013.

Thick smoke enveloped the table she was leaning on. Putting a towel around her neck and mouth she coughed her way to the door and pulled the handle. It rattled but stuck.

"Stay calm Freja!" she told herself but panic was beginning to overwhelm her as the flames grew closer, the white heat almost burning her eyebrows and lashes now. Her throat and lungs felt tight as the black smoke invaded them, clogging them. She gave one more tug and gave up and tried to force herself toward the window.

A smash at the window attracted her attention. A towelled hand smashed the broken glass away until a man could force his way through. It was Michael. He climbed through with an unexpected agility for an eighty-five-year-old man.

He pushed his way toward her, through the gaps between the flaming furniture, stopping for a moment as the heat and intensity of the flames drove him back. His head was covered with a towel and he pushed his head like a bull and charged again, kicking the furniture away with his heavy boots making a pathway toward her.

She in turn didn't waste time and launched herself toward him ignoring the biting heat of the inferno.

"Freja!"

"I am here Michael!" she cried as he glimpsed her through the wall of thick black smoke. The towels were burnt off his hand and she could smell the sickening sweet smell of burning flesh but he continued to press toward her. She made one last push forward and was in his arms.

He put his arm around her and they headed toward the window. Too slow! A beam crashed and hit her on her head and shoulder and she almost collapsed to the floor. The old man caught her as she fell, and he half carrying her, they pushed forward and reached the window. He pushed her out of it, uncaring as she hit the hard ground.

She was safe now. He climbed over the sill and fell choking on the paving himself. His last thoughts to himself before he lost consciousness were, he would get the bastards who did this or his name was not Michael Defoe.

London, June the 6th 2013.

Kirsten took her mobile out and read the text her aunt had sent her late the night before. The urgency of the message stunned her. Her aunt was not a panicker, something must have really spooked her. She read the words again to herself trying to make some sense of the situation.

"Kirsten Darling. That man I texted you about is threatening me and searching my house. He is trying to get me to move out and sell the house to him. If you can get here I need your help. Text me please, Aunt Freja.''

She booked a flight that evening, paying through the nose for flying at short notice but she would economise at the other end. Her aunt's life was more important. She would not have contacted her and asked her to fly out unless she was in danger. She knew Kirsten wanted to remain anonymous and respected her privacy. Thank God, she had returned from Indonesia early and her work could be done online from anywhere providing there was an internet connection.

She packed and went to bed early but was woken by a phone call early in the morning.

"Ms. Gateman, this is Dr Brant from Devil's Creek Hospital. You were put down as the next of kin of Ms Freja Andersson.'' Her heart lurched at his words.

"Yes Doctor, how is she?''

"She was caught in a house fire and is alive but suffering from severe smoke inhalation. If you wish to come, I would advise it as soon as possible.''

"Will she survive Doctor?''

"I am afraid we are not sure at the moment.'' He left the rest of his statement unsaid. Someone would be needed to sort out her personal affects and house if she died.

"I am taking a flight later today, Doctor. My aunt contacted me last night and asked me to come.''

She finished the call and took a taxi to the airport. Counting the notes in her wallet she cursed her financial situation. She hoped her aunt would be awake and able to lend her some money when she arrived. Would the house be liveable in? She had little spare money to pay for living accommodation. The flight cost had absorbed most of her spare cash. Not for the first time did she curse the man that had condemned her to her present impecunious position.

Chapter one

The steward on the flight pressed the sign for the aeroplane's slow decline to the runway. Kirsten yawned and stretched her aching legs as she tried for the hundredth time to curl into a comfortable position. Limited funds meant she had to take the cheapest route and seats from Heathrow to Fort Lauderdale. She clipped her seat belt and closed her eyes for the descent.

A beautifully manicured hand gently touched her arm and a card was placed in her hand. ''From the gentleman in seat 5A in Club Class Ma'am,'' The card contained an elegantly printed name and telephone number in gold with the simple message, "Would you do me the honour of taking a drink with me before your next flight takes off?''

She remembered being messaged through a waiter whilst she had waited in the lounge after entering security. That time, a glass of the sparkling water she had been drinking and some canapés had arrived with the message, "I would like to make your acquaintance. If you are interested, I always book the seat next to me and keep it free. It is yours if you would like to use it!''

Her eyes had searched around the lounge but she could not pick out the man who had propositioned her in this way. It had been the same card. There was the name Joshua Rutland and a telephone number on it, as if that said all that was needed to be said; no other explanation of him needed.

She had returned the card with the polite answer, "Thank you for your considerate offer but my seat is already reserved.'' It was bad enough being propositioned by a stranger but worse when he did not even show himself. Her mind went into overdrive, thinking of the Boston Strangler and stalkers but she chided herself for her over-active imagination and left swiftly for the plane and her cheaper seat.

Why did the man think she was changing flights? He had guessed incorrectly. She was taking the bus, not a flight to her destination, to save dollars. She called the flight attendant. "The gentleman who sent me this card. Where is he flying to next?''

"An airport, three hundred miles from Fort Lauderdale Ma'am.''

"Thank you,'' said Kirsten guessing who had told the man her details. "Please give his card back to him!'' She had written, "Thank for your kind offer, but no.''

The attendant looked at her as if she was mad to reject his offer but she merely shrugged and watched the television. No strange man was going to pick her up at airports no matter how good-looking he was.

"Shame'' came back the message on another card. "Keep my card in case you change your mind.''

"Damn the man! What a cheek he had! Conceited twit! Thank God, she was landing in a few minutes.''

She got off the aeroplane and readied herself for the slow wait for her luggage. A natural curiosity could not help her wondering where the man was. She was regularly propositioned in bars and hotels but not in that quiet, assured way that was his.

Her heavy luggage arrived on the belt and she would have dragged it off but she was gently pushed out of the way and a deep masculine voice ordered, "Wait!'' as with ease he pulled the cases off and put them on her trolley. Grateful but exasperated at the same time she recognised the man from seat 5A.

''Thank you,'' she said, "they are heavy,'' and afterwards would have moved the trolley away from him.

"It was a pleasure Ms Gateman.'' She eyed him warily, feeling uncomfortable he knew her name. Had he had a chance to look at her case label?

"Excuse me Sir but I need to find a seat in this crowded lounge.''

"That is no problem,'' he said, taking hold of her trolley. "I have spare tickets for the Executive Lounge. There's no crush there.''

"A spare seat in the aeroplane and in the lounge. How convenient!'' snapped Kirsten. She tugged at it but he took no notice and pushed ahead, forcing her to follow him. She had no alternative unless she shouted for security and made a scene.

He pointed to the armchair next to him but she refused to sit down. "Do you usually expect people to conform with what you want?'' Her voice was laced with ice; cold tones cut like glass, intimating he was invading her privacy. Sea blue-green eyes faced him off, challenging him. Smiling, as if he were speaking to a child he explained, "I find I rarely have to ask twice.''

She believed him. Shrewd green eyes assessed her from a rather severe face that only lit up when he smiled. He was handsome enough to attract stares from most of the women he passed. A natural authority characterised him, as if he was used to getting his way.

"A drink and snacks?'' he asked her, waving to an attendant. This exclusive lounge had waiter service, a far different lounge from the crowded ones Kirsten was usually forced to use.

"No thanks,'' said Kirsten. She wanted out of this situation as quickly as possible. Her bus would leave in two hours and she must find somewhere else to sit out of his reach. He was beginning to give her the creeps.

"The drinks and snacks are included in the ticket price.''

"I am neither hungry nor thirsty.''

"You're kidding me! I know the food in Economy. It is barely edible.''

"Nevertheless, I need to go,'' she said taking her trolley.

"No stay, Kirsten,'' the man said enclosing her hand with his. "I have only just met you and you interest me!'' He pulled her gently but firmly on to the seat. He was the sort who would not take no for an answer.

"How do you know my first name?'' It was not on her label.

"Information can be bought easily if one pays the price Kirsten,'' he replied, softly. *Damn the man! He must have questioned the flight attendant for more personal information about her.*

Kirsten felt uneasy. Was this man a stalker? If he did not leave her alone she would have to contact the airport authorities. The last thing she needed now was a fuss and the notice of the police. She needed to get to Devil's Creek as soon as was possible and help her aunt.

"Mr. Rutland. You are Mr. Rutland I presume!''

He nodded. "At your service, Ma'am.'' His deep voice with its Southern twang reminded her of molasses and thick hot chocolate. Seductive and sweet, it promised hidden pleasures if she took up his invitation. His firm grip was at odds with his seductive voice. He had every intention of making her obey him regardless of the seductively gentle way he put his business.

"Why are you accosting me in this way? My name is my business as is my destination. Please respect my privacy.'' She rose, pushing his hand out of the way. He released her reluctantly but he still regarded her with that assessing look that made her feel she was under a microscope.

He stood up with her in his gentlemanly manner. He was the epitome of an old fashioned Southern gentleman, smooth and relaxed, unless one looked into those eyes which speared her with his emerald gaze. She felt like a rabbit trapped in the glare of a much fiercer predator; unable to tear her eyes away from this man.

"I thought it was obvious. I was attracted to you by your looks but now I see there is more to you. I would like to get to know you better.''

"Thank you but I am not interested.''

"Why not?''

"I don't go out with men who proposition me in bars and or airports.''

"Oh, so it is not personal then. If I met you in a legitimate social setting, a party for example, you would consider a date with me?''

"The question is hypothetical as I have no intention of meeting you again,'' she said, finally tearing her eyes away from his hypnotic stare; determinedly pushing her trolley away toward the door.

"I wouldn't bet on that Kirsten,'' she heard him say as she left the room.

What an arrogant creep. She was starving, the food in Economy being as inedible as he had said. She looked longingly through the window at the tables containing snacks in the executive lounge. Sighing, she grabbed a packet of biscuits out of her haversack and moved to the queue for the bus. She would have been unnerved if she had heard the conversation in the lounge which concerned her.

"Drakeman, I have a job for you," said Rutland into his cell. He looked through the window and saw Kirsten in the long queue waiting for the bus. ''There is a girl, Kirsten Gateman, I want followed. Get a man here to the bus line at Fort Lauderdale airport! I want to know where she is going and where she is staying. I want a full background check on her. No, it's not business. It's personal but I want this information yesterday!''

He closed the cell impatiently, irritated that he had taken his frustration out on one of his friends. He was normally the calmest creature one could meet; so calm and detached his enemies called him the 'Vulcan,' but this girl 'irritated him, no intrigued him,' he admitted reluctantly to himself.

It was not just pique. It was unusual for a woman to refuse to dine or spend the night with him but there was something else about this girl that interested him. It was if she was wearing a hands-off label as if she didn't welcome intimacy at all. An ice-cold blond one could catch frostbite from, Ms

Gateman would get a surprise later. He would not easily take no for an answer. He usually got what he wanted.

He watched her intently. A beauty, she could attract any man. She was standing there dressed in simple worn jeans, outlining her slim long legs which seemed to go on for ever. A thin loose jacket topped a flowing shirt which barely outlined her figure.

Rutland was definitely a 'tits' rather than an ass man and he admired her rack but when she bent to reach her cases her neat derriere kept his eyes glued to her. He became hard just looking at her tight ass when she bent to undo her leather haversack. She would stand out anywhere. She pushed her long flaxen hair out of the way of her sea blue/green eyes as she tried to stand comfortably in the slow-moving queue.

She looked tired now, her eyes tightly closed as if she had a head ache; the world a heavy burden weighing down on her slight shoulders. Rutland felt a strange desire to make life easier for her. He shook himself. He must be going soft. She interested him, intrigued him but that was all.

A one-night stand or a couple of weekends away was what he wanted from her, not a life-time; the same arrangement he made with all his ladies. A pay off with a diamond bracelet would end a perfectly amicable civilised interlude and then he would find another agreeable female.

A pout of perfectly painted lips or a shrug of a beautiful shoulder and the ladies he romanced usually moved out of his ambit, forgotten quickly but accepting of his dismissive attitude. They knew the score; moving from gentleman to gentleman until they found the man who would provide the lifestyle they considered their right. The arrangement suited him perfectly; no messy entanglements, no arguments nor temper tantrums. He laid down at the beginning what he was offering and the women took what they could and didn't expect anymore.

As she moved slowly down the queue she could not resist looking back and saw him watching her through the window. He raised his glass and smiled at her.

"Damn the man,'' she cursed to herself. He was quietly relaxing, a man at ease with himself, waiting for his next plane while she was tired and dreading a long journey on a bus with many stops.

Now she was safe from him she was curious as to what he would have offered her that evening. Drinks and perhaps dinner if her destination was close to his, followed by a night in a hotel room. He was clearly a player with the income to pay for what he wanted. Many women would be attracted by the power and confidence that exuded from this man.

He was dressed casually in denims, tee shirt and well-worn leather jacket and loafers but his clothes were of high quality and his watch was a Rolex. Standing straight and tall, at least five inches above most men, he had dominated the lounge with his presence. He looked like a football or hockey star, an athlete. He had the body of someone who worked hard to stay fit.

Yet she recognised the intelligence in his eyes. This man was not a jock. He assessed the world in a cynical way and with his computer like mind he made his mind up quickly. He had made his mind up about her in an instant when she had tried to pull her trolley away from him. Unfortunately, he saw her as his next conquest. She was a challenge to him, she realised her heart thumping. The last thing she needed now.

He had moved with the grace of a huge sleek cat, a dark panther. She recognised the look of a predator, eying up his prey when he looked at her. His eyes had run from her hat to her leather shod feet, mentally stripping her, making her feel naked and vulnerable. She wanted nothing to do with a man of his kind. She had met men like him in the past.

At last the queue ended and she purchased her ticket to a small town ten hours' bus ride from the airport. At least Rutland could not find her residence there. She had not booked a hotel to stay in yet, not knowing if her aunt's house would still be in a fit state and available to her to live in.

She parked her heavy suitcases by the hold and sat in the lumpy seat, trying to make herself comfortable and ignore the child kicking her in the back. *Sod it.* Tomorrow she would see her aunt and find out how the land lay. She would forget that arrogant twit when she was at her aunt's bedside. She had more important things to think about.

Rutland took a sip of his wine and relaxed back in his reclining chair as he read the email attachment. Drakeman had done a good job. He was now enjoying unwrapping the mystery that was Kirsten Gateman. She had clearly inherited her physical genes from her Swedish mother; her height, fair skin and those beautiful sea blue-green eyes. Her flaxen hair waving around her shoulders had made her look like a Valkyrie. He could imagine her snatching warriors and taking them to heaven and bliss.

He continued to peruse the file. Her father was a senior policeman, a superintendent but did not live with her mother. They had divorced when she was ten. She had attended a private boarding school until then but afterwards had attended the local grammar school. *A brain as well as a beauty.* A first-class degree from Cambridge and then she had passed her law finals with flying colours.

She had had one serious boyfriend, a friend of the family, a law student four years older than herself. Whilst studying for her law finals she had lived with him. She had been engaged to him for one year. She worked for three years in a law firm until she had disappeared for twenty months.

Her reasons for coming to the States had not been uncovered yet but Drakeman was thorough and would soon unearth that information. Rutland now had to rethink his strategy if he was to persuade this woman to dine with him. She was not the beautiful babe he had stereotyped her. He had taken the wrong approach. A drink, dinner and bed with a good-looking stranger was obviously not her style. He had misjudged her harshly; his money was not enough to attract Ms Kirsten Gateman, although looking at her clothes, worn luggage and economy ticket she looked as if she had fallen on hard times.

Rutland was expert at finding the things that endeared a woman to him. He would divine what drove Ms Gateman and manipulate her until she ached to enter his bed. Relishing the thought of seducing the young woman he hardened and his pulse raced. It was years since he had felt so aroused at the idea of taking a young woman. Beautiful women fell into his hands like fruit from a tree and he could cherry pick, taking the best ones until he became bored and looked for fresher fruit.

His plane landed. He would pick up his hire car and drive to Devil's Creek. This was a bitter-sweet visit. He had lived with his grandparents after his father and mother died. They had turned around a sulky sometimes violent boy who was picked on by the older kids in Miami who knew his mother's reputation and the way she had earned the money to pay the rent. It was his granddad who had persuaded him to stay on at school, to graduate and then later join the Navy where his intelligence and aptitude was recognised. Without his granddad, he could have joined the gangs in his mother's neighbourhood and ended up on the different side of the law to that which he had ended up in.

Now his granddad was in hospital and he had rushed here to find out how seriously ill he was. The thought of the old man dying made him cold inside. He and his grandma were the only good things to have entered his early life and encouraged him to turn into the man he was now. Strong Catholics, both, they had instilled the meaning of right and wrong in him. He had no illusions; he was not a good or kind man but he was a decent man and owed everything to his granddad and grandma.

He gunned the Mercedes along the road to the freeway. He considered Kirsten still hours away and wondered where she would be heading. He only had the address of the bus station she was heading to. Drakeman was trying to find out her destination.

Chapter two.

The officer opened the door to the remains of Rutland's Granddad's house. He had lived in it since he had given up the ranch when he became too ill to work it any longer. Rutland had enjoyed coming back to the ranch and later his Granddad's little house to unwind.

A short confidential email from the local Deputy suggested the fire was a sad accident and they were wrapping the investigation up soon. That and his Granddad's deteriorating condition had made Rutland come post haste. He wanted to make sure the investigation was tightly managed by a professional team; no hick lawman wanting to wrap it up fast without paying attention to the forensics.

His keen eyes saw evidence of more than an accidental fire. He had been a criminal lawyer for a couple of years and this case smelt of arson. He would have the hide of the small-town Deputy if he had neglected important evidence.

Thanking the officer, he left the house and took his cell out and called Drakeman. "I want the best forensic investigator flown out here immediately. He can name his own price. There is something odd about this fire and the local cops may not be very thorough. I don't want to take any chances.''

"And do you still want me to collect info on this woman Josh?''

"Yes, that is second priority now but important.'' He had forgotten temporarily about Kirsten in his thorough investigation of the house. "What else have you picked up about her?''

"She has lost contact with her parents. Has not talked to her father for years and is paying her student debts herself. There is bad blood between them. She last saw her mother two years ago.''

"Where did she disappear for twenty months?''

"No idea but she bought an aeroplane ticket to the States after she finished with her barrister's job. Not to Fort Lauderdale but to New York. She cleared her building society account. She has not touched the accounts she shared with her fiancé. It was if she just disappeared without wanting to be traced.''

"And the fiancé?'' Rutland had a personal interest in finding what sort of man had attracted the young Kirsten and what had caused them to break up.

"A hotshot lawyer, one of the rising stars in the legal profession in London, the son of a good friend of her father. Her father approved of the match and when she broke it off it caused a rift between them.''

"Was it an amicable break?''

"Not sure yet. For some reason, no one talks about the man, as if he is beyond criticism. There was a hint of a law suit against him by some woman but it seems to have been hushed up.''

"Find out Phil. It smells fishy. Offer what you need to get the information. And, I owe you one.''

"No problem Man, I'd like to meet this girl if she interests you this much. Pretty special, is she?''

"I would keep a lecherous bastard like you away from her. Find out if she treats all men like carriers of the bubonic plague or if it was just me. She treated me like the Boston Strangler when I offered her a drink.''

"A drink eh! Is this a fit of pique Man? Has the great lover been rejected at last?''

"She did reject me my friend but it was more than that. Something more than a reluctance to be picked up by a stranger. I bet my bottom dollar that she has something to hide. She doesn't trust men at all!''

"You think something in her past has frightened her off men.''

"Just so! There was more than mere distrust; a contempt and hatred in her eyes that went beyond dislike when I touched her arm and took her case.''

"And you want to bed this ice maiden?''

"I think there is something else below that frosty surface, a different woman who is worth getting to know.''

"Good luck then Mate. I'll pass on the info when I get it.''

"Thanks, and enjoy your weekend with Lucy, is it?'' replied Rutland, trying to remember his latest lady.

"Lucy was last month, keep up! This month is Samantha, blond and small and buxom.''

"Enjoy yourself.''

Drakeman was worse than himself, changing his women so frequently his friends couldn't keep up with him. A loner, like Rutland, he kept himself to himself, socialising with only a few friends and focussing on his work. He chose ladies who wanted as few commitments as himself and didn't delve too closely into his background or his work contacts. He was a closed book like Rutland.

The Deputy was a portly, portentous man who carried himself with an air of arrogance. "How can I help you Mr. Rutland?'' He fixed his beady eyes on this quiet man who carried an air of authority with him. He was not going to be pushed around by a big city lawyer. The Sheriff was out of town on a long course. He now ran the law around Devil's Creek!

"I would like to know the latest details about your investigation into the fire at my Granddad's house.''

"It seems to have been a regrettable accident; could have been prevented if the occupants had taken more care but you know these old folk,'' the man said regretfully. "They are not as sharp as they used to be and left papers and other flammables near the fire.''

Rutland looked at him sharply; angry at the inference his Granddad had lost his marbles. The old man was as sharp as needles; he could beat much younger men in his Saturday night poker game. Daniel had moved nearer to the town because his physical health had deteriorated but at eighty-five that was not surprising. This arrogant moron was pissing him off quickly and he decided to wrap the meeting up in his usual determined style.

"I don't think the fire was an accident. I am sending my own private forensic investigator over to help you, paid by me. He will report the circumstances and facts to me Sir!''

The man blustered, "You can't do that. You can't override my decisions!''

"I have no intention of doing so Sir. I want to help you and can afford to hire the best investigators. My friend is Police Chief of the County and will assure you of my best intentions. He will also send some men to help you if I think you are too short-handed to give enough attention to this case. I also have some very good contacts in the FBI.''

Mentioning his friend's status changed the Deputy's attitude from arrogant belligerence to a wary respect for him.

"Of course, we would welcome any help from experts providing they answer to us. There is no need for your friend to be involved. Please send the man to me and we will give him all the information he needs.''

Smiling, Rutland shook his hand and said, "We understand each other perfectly Sir.'' His friend had a formidable reputation for solving crimes and reducing little Hitlers like this to shivering obedient wrecks with a few curt words. It was the correct implied threat. He left and went to the hotel and tried to book himself in.

''Sorry Sir, there is an exhibition and all the rooms are booked,'' said the polite receptionist, smiling, all white polished teeth; a beautiful wide-eyed babe who looked up beneath long dark lashes, subtly, suggestively inviting him to ask her to dinner.

"Can you find me another hotel room?''

"The only other good hotel is being renovated and is closed. There is a b and b on Main Street, more like a lodging house but clean and warm and does a good breakfast. I can try to get you a room there.''

"Do that please,'' he said smiling his thanks at her. It was not her fault his day was going from bad to worst and she might provide a little sexual interest later if he took her up on her invitation.

"There should be a room free here in several days' time. The party has not decided yet when they intend to leave. I will reserve it for you if you wish.''

"Thanks,'' He passed his business card over. "If you would like dinner tonight or tomorrow please phone that number,'' he said, noting the girl's bright blue eyes light up in answer.

Picking up his cases he turned left for Main Street. Arriving at his destination he looked at the peeling paint on the b and b which had clearly seen better days. A pretty smiling middle-aged woman answered the door.

"You will be the guest sent over from the Girling then. I'm Gracie Grigson. "

"Yes, Ms Grigson, I am Joshua Rutland,'' he said shaking her hand.

"Well it won't be what you are used to but it is clean and comfortable here,'' she said, shrewdly assessing his worth by his Rolex.

"I am very grateful you have a room at all.''

He carried his cases up and lay on the bed. It was surprisingly comfortable and the room was spacious even if the fittings and upholstery were a little worn. He stood under the red-hot shower, allowing the streams of water to rid him of the aches from sitting in a plane. He had wanted a swim and workout in the fitness centre of the up-market hotel.

Wearing just a towel around his waist he answered a knock at the door.

A very young fresh-faced girl passed a message to him, her eyes widening with interest when she saw his state of undress.

"This was delivered by express, Mr. Rutland.'' Eagerly, he opened the envelope. It was the name, telephone number and address of the forensic scientist and more information on the Gateman woman.

He smiled, gave her a large tip in thanks, and shut the door quickly on her to show he wasn't interested. He was not attracted by gaol bait. He preferred more mature women who knew how to satisfy a man.

A cheeky message from Drakeman accompanied the information. "Good luck Romeo! Better you than me. She sounds a hard nut to crack!''

What was interesting was that she was heading to Devil's Creek that evening. What sort of co-incidence was that? It was unimaginable. Two strangers meeting on a plane, one attracted to the other and both going to the same destination.

Rutland decided he would meet the bus when it arrived and follow her to where she was staying. Perhaps she had friends or relatives to stay with. It was a small town where everybody knew each other. If his granddad had been well, he might have asked him about her.

He visited his grandad. He caught his breath when he saw him attached to an oxygen machine his face ashen. His hands were bandaged as if he had used them to beat away the flames.

"He is suffering from smoke inhalation and his lungs were damaged by the heat,'' explained the young nurse.

''I want him in a private room,'' demanded Rutland, "and the best specialist you can find. Get the consultant for me now!'' Urgency and grief made him speak more harshly to the nurse than was needed and he saw her draw back, uncomfortable. He immediately regretted his aggressive manner. His height and breadth intimidated people without any need to act the heavy!

"I am sorry I spoke in that tone,'' he apologised softly. "He took care of me when my Mom died.''

"I'll get the consultant but your Granddad asked to be kept next to his friend,'' she said, nodding her head to the next patient, a woman younger than his Granddad by about ten years.

"Is she important to him?''

"Very, so it seems She was the first person he asked about when he regained consciousness. She is his neighbour and her house was also burnt down in the fire.''

He looked at the woman lying there sleeping. There was something in her features that reminded him of someone, although her head was partly disguised by bandages as if she had suffered a fall or something. Her flaxen hair was tied in a plait around one shoulder and when she flickered her eyelids open he could detect blue-green eyes. He wondered what she meant to his Granddad. She had been a beauty in her younger days and despite her age her high cheekbones still set her apart from normal women. Even in her sleep she looked determined and a woman one would need to treat with respect. Like his Granddad she looked as if she knew her own mind.

The consultant arrived and Rutland said, "I would like both moved to a private ward at my expense. I am not happy concerning the details of this case. If it was not an accident, then someone might try to harm them if they know too much.''

"It can be done without harming their chances of recovery.''

Rutland asked the question he had been dreading asking, his heart falling to his boots for fear of getting the answer he didn't want. "Will they survive?''

"The chances are slim given the extent of smoke inhalation. The burns were insignificant compared to the danger of that for them but your Granddad and the old lady are very strong and may pull through against the odds. If you are here he may have the will to live.''

"I will stay here the night,''

"They are under heavy sedation and will sleep the night through. You will be needed tomorrow and should try to get a good night's sleep.''

"Will the old lady have visitors?''

"Ms. Andersson has a few friends but her relatives are not in this country. One has been texted and is coming over and arriving soon.''

Rutland noted the foreign name. Andersson sounded Scandinavian in origin. "What is her first name and what was she to my granddad?''

"She is called Freja Andersson and I think your granddad might have been intending to become engaged to her. They had become close since she moved here.''

"How long has she lived here?''

"Two years ago, a little less than your Granddad. She had small holding ten miles away but gave it up when she developed angina.''

"She has no family?''

"She is unmarried.''

Rutland remembered his Granddad talking about a new neighbour but as he hadn't met her he hadn't taken much notice. Now he wished he had come back earlier and spoken with her if she meant that much to his Granddad.

Two hours later Rutland sat outside the bus station. It arrived at last and the ragbag of exhausted passengers poured out, desperate to collect their bags and get home. His eyes narrowed at the descent of a tall blonde who waited patiently for the bags and lifted them wearily to the exit where she caught a cab. Rutland followed in the Mercedes, surprised the destination was not one of the hotels but instead the hospital. She leant in and gave the driver another destination and he left with her cases. Then she walked into reception.

Kirsten felt tired and ratty. She needed a good shower and her hair felt scratchy and itchy. Her head ramped from the noise of the boy in front of her who had played a radio at full volume, the driver not caring a damn. Her back ached from the kicks the kid behind had given her throughout the whole of the journey. She was close to pulverising the little buggar by the time she descended from the bus.

She thought maliciously of Rutland enjoying a fast journey plied with wine and good food. Why that man kept coming into her head she couldn't guess? She had been propositioned by men she didn't know in the past and had forgotten them easily.

Rutland was different. There was something about him that intrigued her. His self-confidence and assurance would have attracted her if she had met him before Justin but now she knew what sort of man Justin was and this man was of the same ilk. He was a man she should and would avoid if she wanted to keep her independence and sanity.

She must keep focussed. The only thing that was important was finding out how ill her aunt was and if she could help her. The final text her aunt had sent had been chilling following an email sent earlier. Kirsten could sense her aunt's fear.

"Kirsten, we are being threatened and no-one will listen to us as we are old. I don't know if you got my last text. Can you come over immediately and help us? I will send you the money for the ticket for the plane and bus."

The email had amplified the threat. Her aunt had received demands to sell her house and when she refused the demands had become more menacing. Her house had been searched and the old lady had been pushed roughly against the wall when she had interrupted an intruder searching the house again.

She had not been injured but a day later Kirsten had learnt about the fire. Kirsten's tears welled in her eyes as she thought of the feisty old lady who had come to her aid when she had left England months before. She had found her a haven when she needed peace and quiet to lick her wounds.

If the fire was malicious she would hunt the perpetrators to their grave. She had nearly asked for her father's help but Freja was estranged from him as she was and she must respect her wishes. She also feared her father would disclose her whereabouts to others.

She saw to her surprise the two-old people being shifted into a private ward. Her aunt couldn't afford this! Her health insurance would not cover these costs. If she was well enough and the house was in any decent shape Kirsten would nurse her back to health. She owed it to her.

She collared a young nurse. "Please can you tell me about the progress of Ms Freja Andersson? I am Kirsten Gateman, the niece you texted."

"The consultant has left now but will be back tomorrow morning to answer your questions in detail. I can tell you that she has suffered severe smoke inhalation and her lungs were damaged but she has lasted longer than we expected already and she is a tough old lady. We are still holding out a little hope but the chances are still very slim. They are moved now. Would you like to see her?"

"Yes, but who has paid for the private ward?"

"Mr. Defoe's Grandson. He has insisted he will pay for the private room and extra care of both patients." Kirsten knew her aunt would have rejected the help of the man if she had been compos mentis. She needed to see this man.

"Where is his grandson?"

"Gone to his hotel I think. He is coming back to the hospital when the sedation wears off his granddad tomorrow morning. He looked played out!"

Kirsten did not want a confrontation at the hospital in front of the staff. She would have to beard him in his hotel when she located him. For the moment, she wanted to see her aunt to ascertain for herself how ill she was. She was her rock, the only person who had cared for her. She could not let her go so soon.

She sat by the bed and took her aunt's thin hand. Wrinkled and brown, covered with age spots, it was the hand of a woman who had worked hard all her life. She had given her life to her animals, caring for them with little help when she gave up being a vet and turned her home into the animal shelter.

She had taken care of her skin and her beauty still shone through. Her beauty was rare both inside and out. She looked only in her sixties. Her hair was still blond with little grey and her slim figure was toned by the work she still undertook at another shelter two days a week since she closed her own animals' home. Kirsten gulped and her throat felt as if she could not swallow. Her eyes filled with tears at the sight of the aunt she loved like a mother lying there looking so weak and vulnerable.

She felt a prickle in her neck as if she was being watched by someone. Looking behind her through the open door she saw a tall figure disappear into the shadows of the corridor. She tried to identify the figure but it moved too fast. She felt uneasy and shivered. Someone hadn't wanted to be seen by her.

Kissing her aunt, she then got up. She felt human again, breathing in fresh air outside the hospital.. She had nearly vomited in that stifling hot atmosphere. She called a cab to take her to her aunt's house..

She was led in and looked around. She coughed dust out of her lungs, thinking of her aunt, terrified and trapped in here. Anger consumed her but she dampened it, determined to control it and direct it at her aunt's enemies. She could do no more here and exited the house. She would talk to the Deputy tomorrow.

She would have walked to her b and b to rest for the night but a hand grasped her arm as she walked out of the garden and halted her. She jumped and turned angrily to the man who had accosted and frightened her.

"What the devil do you think you are doing?'' She stopped when she faced Joshua Rutland. He was the last person she had expected or wanted to see!

"I was hoping to take you out to dinner,'' He pressed his fingers gently across her lips and tried to explain before she bit his head off again.

''This is not a pick-up line. Believe me, this is the last position I would like to be in when I ask you out for a date. This is strictly business! ''

"What business Mr. Rutland? I am not in the mood for any funny business, however amusing you may think you are.'' She pulled herself away but his sharp fingers circled her wrist again in a punishing grip again, intent on stopping her from striding away.

"My granddad was your aunt's next-door neighbour and he is on the edge of death in that ward with her. Now how about we work together and finding out what is going on around here.''

She stopped in her tracks. "Did your Granddad tell you anyone was threatening him?''

"No, did your aunt tell you any such thing?''

She looked at him, sizing him up, deciding if he was worth trusting. A shake of her head decided against his favour.

"I will talk to the Deputy in the morning Mr. Rutland. Please let me go to my lodgings and we can talk with the Deputy together if it is needed.'' She looked as if she would make sure such a meeting would be totally unnecessary. Suspicion and mistrust of him radiated from her.

He lost his patience. His Granddad had nearly been killed and she was withholding important evidence from him and possibly the cops.

"You had better come clean with me Kirsten Gateman. My Granddad was nearly murdered in that house.'' He tried to calm himself and reason with her. She was a lawyer in England. Surely, she could act rationally in these circumstances.

"I repeat, I will tell the Deputy what I know in the morning and I will not withhold anything from you. Now let me go please,'' she snapped, spitting fire at him from eyes that had changed from a light blue green to sapphire now. Her hair was now tied in a braid and she swished it around her shoulder like an angry cat. Christ, she looked so desirable there, defying him; he wanted to pull her into his arms and kiss her senseless.

He pulled himself together, ignoring her flashing eyes which attracted him so much. First impressions were wrong. Kirsten Gateman was not an ice maiden. She was fire and ice! The man who melted that icy cage would find a passionate woman inside.

He intended one day to be that man but for the moment he tried to concentrate on their business which should be upper-mind in his head. Christ! He was supposed to be after an attempted murderer, not intent on seducing the victim's niece. That could come later after he had found the perps.

"We are going to dine together,'' he said. "I need to put you straight about this Deputy. How can a meal with me harm you? Your choice! You obviously know the area?''

Recognising the same stubbornness in him that characterised her, she knew he would not easily let her walk away from him.

"If you stop your Neathanderdal tactics we can go to the Blue Dragon. It is five minutes from here.'' She gave him brief directions.

He nodded in agreement. Holding her by her elbow, he led her to the Mercedes thinking how fragile she was. She had barely any flesh on her bird-like arm, almost skeletally thin, her skinniness hidden by the baggy clothes. Instead of her thirty years she looked like a young girl straight out of uni. He insisted on opening her door for her as he a Southern gentleman should do.

"Forget his good manners Kirsten,'' she told herself. She felt the bruise already colouring her wrist where he had grasped her so hard. Under that polished veneer was a macho male determined to dominate and get what he wanted from her at any price. He was the same as Justin but with a different accent and looks.

His dark brown almost black hair waved down to his collar, slightly shorter than she would have expected in most modern men. She wondered if he had been a military man. He held himself in a certain way, very upright, as if standing to attention was normal for him. His profile turned away from her was severe but when he smiled a dimple appeared in his cheek, lightening his face and making him seem more human then.

He reminded her of Rhett Butler, smiling that seductive smile that could sway a naïve woman to his way of thinking. She shuttered her heart to him. She was no Scarlett O'Hara. She had given her heart once and had it smashed. No good-looking charmer was going to steal it again.

Rutland stopped in the parking lot at the restaurant. He opened the door for her and said, ''I haven't eaten here.''

"I am surprised if you visited your Granddad regularly.''

"He wasn't one for foreign food. Steak and burgers were more his style and I only came for flying visits over the last few years.''

"If you want American food there is a steakhouse near here,'' she said compromising. She did not want to put his back up unnecessarily.

"Chinese is fine,'' he said indifferently. He probably ate in the best restaurants and would slum it to get her on his side. He rested his hand on the small of her back; moving her swiftly through the crowds in the foyer to the hostess and demanding a quiet table away from the crowds. He palmed the girl with a large note to get what he wanted. The restaurant was simple with wooden tables with glass tops and menus placed under them to read. One ordered by number as he had done in his student days when Chinese meals were a weekend luxury from a carry-out.

''What do you recommend?'' he asked. ''Just order for us!'' He was not in the mood for negotiation over food. He had more important things on his mind and this woman's belligerent attitude irritated him.

''Yes Sir!''

She ordered sticky beef in black bean sauce, yuk sung, prawn chop suey and ribs to be accompanied by rice. The girl arrived with the prawn crackers and he noted she set to eating them with a vengeance.

"No food on the bus then?'' he commented. She looked embarrassed and ate more slowly.

"It was worse than the food in Economy. I ate some biscuits and would have eaten some sandwiches later in my room.''

Their dishes arrived and he dug in. "This is surprisingly good!'' he said, tucking into the sticky beef with relish.

"Su Lin has had this restaurant for fifteen years and its reputation grows every year. She is a friend of my aunt and we used to eat here regularly.''

"My Granddad only moved into town four years ago. He owned a ranch, fifteen miles from here, but gave it up when his health became more fragile.''

"What sort of ranch?''

"More of a smallholding really, a few cows and bulls and horses. He came from an immigrant family and made good for the grandson of a man who arrived here with only a few shillings in his pocket.''

"An Irish immigrant?'

"Yes, from County Cork. Granddad met my Grandma and charmed her in face of opposition from her wealthy family. He married her but her father disowned her. They stayed true to each other and Granddad worked the building sites until they could afford to buy a small ranch in their middle years.''

''That is a beautiful story!''

''Yes, it inspired me when I was a bratty adolescent who had a chip on his shoulder.''

''Did they have a large family?''

''No, one daughter and three sons one of whom was killed in Vietnam.''

''Your Grandma must have been bereft.''

''She was a tough old bird and coped but we knew sometimes she was thinking of her fallen son when she used to go down to the Creek where they used to play.'' Kirsten was surprised to see his green eyes slightly mist over when he spoke of his Gran. Perhaps there was a sensitive side to this severe man but well hidden, deep in his psyche.

''Were you brought up here?''

'No, I lived in Miami but when my Parents died my grandparents took me in until I graduated from High School. How did your aunt find herself here?''

''She trained as a vet in Sweden and came over here. She worked in a small town near here and then ran a small-holding looking after stray animals when she retired.''

''She never married?''

''Her policeman fiancé was killed whilst on duty and no-one else persuaded her to marry. I came over here in the summer holidays when I was a child.''

''Didn't she want to go home?'

'Her parents died. She didn't get on with my Dad, her only brother but she liked me. She was like a second mother to me.''

''Gramps and Gran were better than parents to me. I was a difficult kid who often got into trouble but they didn't give up on me. It was Gramps who suggested I joined the SEALS after graduating from High School and it was the best thing he could have done. It gave me direction and discipline and I gained scholarships to study for a degree in finance and my law exams.''

Looking at him she understood why he carried himself so straight and was so self-contained. Years of discipline was ingrained in him although she detected a rebellious streak hidden deep in his psyche waiting to be unleashed.

He had patiently tried to relax her but now he wanted her to spill the beans about her aunt and the fire.

''Your aunt. Did she fear someone hurting her?'' he asked suddenly.

Kirsten jumped. She had felt tired and was relaxing, the tension seeping out of her as she drank a beer and read the message in the fortune cookies placed before her. The bastard had merely been softening her up until he could pump her for the information she held.

Blue eyes speared him, sparklingly angrily. ''My information is for the

Deputy's ears only Mr. Rutland.''

''The Deputy is a pompous idiot, incompetent and will let the trail go cold. Tell me what you know and it will be acted on quickly.''

''I know very little but the authorities should know first.''

''Look, this is not like in England. Out here in the sticks the Sheriff and in this case his Deputy rules the roost, dominant in his little empire. We may need to get the County Chief of Police to pressurise him to act on any evidence he can find.''

''Why should he want to bury the evidence?'' asked Kirsten perplexed.

''Not bury the evidence but make us believe there was no malicious intent. He inferred my Granddad was too senile to take care with a fire and caused the fire himself.''

''My aunt was certainly not senile. She is as sharp as needles but has angina which is one other reason why she gave up her rescue.''

''That is one more reason why we should work together and find out who set fire to the houses. I believe it was arson.''

''What makes you think that?''

''I was a criminal lawyer for two years and saw many crime scenes. Granddad's house was turned over for something and there was damage to the desk which the fire couldn't hide. The perps were after something.''

She looked at him assessing him, deciding if she could trust him. Aunt Freja had talked about Mr. Defoe having a hot shot lawyer grandson who had made good in Miami but still came back regularly to visit his Granddad. He put his hand over hers and held it still. She tried to pull it away from him. He held her hand more tightly and said, ''We are stronger acting together than acting separately. Better than divide and rule you know!''

Her reaction was not what he expected. Instead of softening toward him she snapped, ''Take your paw off me Mr. Rutland. This is business not a seduction you know! Your words!''

Hoist by my own petard, he thought as she pulled her hand away as if she had been stung. He was shocked by the look of contempt in her eyes as she recoiled from him as if he had tried to trap her, a wild animal in his net.

Kirsten had begun to trust him but his hand trapping hers and his soft words reminded her of another time she had been seduced into trusting an equally charming man. Look where it had led her. Better to stay aloof and only trust the official police!

''I would like to go to my lodgings, Mr. Rutland,'' she said standing up ''Su Lin will call me a cab.'' Throwing some bills on the table he also got up. ''Over my dead body! I am taking you home!''

''That can be arranged,'' she said facing him off. She put her own bills on the table and tried to throw his over to his side. She was halted in her action by a hand holding hers tightly, cruelly, making her pick them up and stuff them back in her haversack.

Hurting, she dropped them and shut the sack, shaking her hand to allow the blood to flow. Why ever did she allow herself to get into this position again with a man much stronger than her? She had not been thinking clearly getting so physically close to him. She ought to have learnt her lesson a long time ago.

"When I first met you, I thought you were a bully Mr. Rutland," she said tersely.

"Call it Southern hospitality. My Granddad would have a fit if I allowed a lady to buy her own dinner," he replied ruefully.

"This is not the time of the Civil War. You are not Rhett Butler and I am not Scarlet O'Hara," she snapped back at him. He laughed at her.

"My Granddad would kill me if I didn't escort you home. The Doc thinks he was going to ask your aunt to marry him you know. We are almost family!"

She looked serious again. "I didn't think it had gone that far. I know she liked him."

"He is a very likable man. A man of great integrity!"

"I met him and I liked him. He was good for Aunt Freya."

"Let me take you back and we can continue our discussion in the car."

She hesitated. She didn't want to be in a small enclosed space with him. She had felt suffocated being so close to him in the car journey to the restaurant. Worse, still when he held her hand she had felt a shock go through her body, tingling up her arm.

He had noticed it as well but only his eyes showed it, narrowing, his pupils widening and darkening, showing he was aroused. The chemistry between them was almost tangible. She tried to ignore it but it was there tormenting them, enticing them; reminding her if she had met him before Justin she might have been attracted to him.

She felt unsafe with him. He was quiet, panther like, as if he was waiting for her to make the wrong move and then a hunter, he would pounce on her. She knew men like him; who forced women to be obedient to their demands, uncaring about the women's needs. She had lived with such a man and only just survived her life with him. She would not easily become trapped by such a man again!

Without waiting for her answer, he manoeuvred her through the restaurant. Recognising his determination, she cooperated reluctantly. They were already the object of curiosity, being regarded closely by the good citizens of Devil's Creek. Resistance would only muddy the rumours swirling around the little town.

"Where to?" he asked curtly. Her uncooperative attitude was beginning to more than irk him. He was on her side for Christ's sake! Just because he had made passes at her didn't mean she should treat him like a leper. When would she start acting professionally and work with him to solve this mystery?

"The Spring Flower Bed and Breakfast please. I have not booked a room but Gracie will give me a couch if she has no room spare until I can move into Aunt Freja's house."

"It will be a while before you are allowed back there. Have you anywhere else you can go? Your aunt's friends for example."

"No-one I know well enough to be comfortable with. The forensics should be finished in a few days. Anyway, I can't afford to stay anywhere else and I want to nurse Aunt Freja back to health. She can't afford the private room you put her in.''

''That is taken care of. Get in,'' With bad grace, she got into the car.

''You think you can push everyone around, don't you?''

''Only if I think it is in their best interests. Your aunt has only basic health insurance and may need to stay in hospital quite a while, not forced out before she has fully recovered. I want her alive and healthy. It is in my interests for her to recover quickly and solve this arson crime. If I pay, we are all winners!''

She could not argue with that logic. ''Fair enough, but as soon as she is well enough I will take her home and care for her.''

''Agreed,'' he said. At last they had made some compromises! He didn't want to fight this lovely woman. She still sat fuming. She felt she was losing control over her life to this domineering man who expected everybody to step into line.

Normally he quite liked a woman who didn't chat aimlessly while he drove but the silence was becoming oppressive. "I am paying a private forensic investigator to look over the house tomorrow and present the evidence to me and the Deputy when it is appropriate. You can also be at his presentation if you want.''

He must be loaded. She knew he was wealthy but he was clearly well out of her league, thank goodness. She didn't want to hang around with men of his wealth. They thought money could buy them everything; everyone had their price!

She bit back her misgivings. She needed this man's help even though she mistrusted him. ''Thank you. It would ease my mind if I knew an independent professional was investigating this case.'' He breathed a sigh of relief. He had hit the right note at last. She was coming around to his way of thinking.

''I heard nothing of threats to my Granddad. He kept his problems tight to his chest unfortunately. Was your aunt the same?''

''No, she was a more open character, very trusting of others.''

''Did she mention to you she was in danger?'' Kirsten thought she could tell him about the text. He would hear it from the Deputy anyway.

''She texted me before the fire telling me she believed she was in danger, being threatened, and asked if I would I come over to visit her.''

''Did she give any details?'' he asked, alert now, the sharp attorney, green eyes piercing her with their intensity.

''The names of some men who were harassing her. I investigated them and came back to London to access more information. She texted me saying she had disturbed an intruder. I booked my flight but the fire occurred before I could get here. She had named me as her next of kin and the hospital contacted me about her circumstances.''

''Is that all you can tell me or are you hiding anything?''

''No, that is all.''

''Once we have talked to the cops and the forensic scientist something else may be jigged in your mind. I wish I had come home at Thanksgiving and talked with Granddad. I might have prevented this happening.''

''Too much work?'' she asked, not really caring but trying to be polite.

''Yes, I was tying loose ends up so I could have a break for a while. I was coming here for a respite but I was too late.'' He had been intending to slow down a little. He could only make so much money and the deals he brokered were less interesting to him now. He needed something to inspire him, a new direction. He was too energetic to give up work completely and play on the golf course or go to the gym. He needed mental stimulation.

''And you?'' he asked. ''What have you been doing?'' She looked at him, her head on one side, watching him shrewdly. Not much would pass Ms Gateman. He'd bet his hat on the fact; she would have made a hell of a lawyer in and out of the courtroom.

What harm could it do to tell him something about herself? He had already had her investigated, that she was sure of. He knew where she was going. Men of wealth and power always investigated the women they dated. She knew that from her own family and the wealthy clients she had represented.

''I was a lawyer like yourself. I worked three years after my finals and then I left. I came over here for two months to visit my aunt and then worked in Indonesia as a VSO volunteer.''

''What area of law?'' he asked but wondered why she had given up a good law position. Nothing fitted but he would wait to ask that question. Wait until she trusted him more.

''Employment. Mostly tribunal cases for individuals. Then later corporate financial law.'

''Did you enjoy it?''

''I loved it but it was the wrong job at the wrong time and the wrong place!'' she said with finality, wanting the subject closed. ''Why did you move from Criminal law?''

''For the worst but most obvious reasons. The money! I recognised I could earn more as I had taken a finance degree and could deal with acquisitions. Corporate law pays more than private criminal law unless one represents some shady individuals.

'I also worked on building sites to pay my lodgings and food bills through uni and saw opportunities in the Florida property boom. 'I competed in swimming competitions and the sponsorship and prize money enabled me to start my own business in construction. I also had a mentor, a very kind man who also lent me some money to get started. Gramps couldn't help me as Gran was ill and he had to pay her medical bills.

'I enjoy engaging in business and start-ups. Now my companies cover a wide number of industries and my work is stimulating.''

She assessed him again. He could not be much older than forty but from what he had said he had built an empire. Where had she heard the name before. He answered for her.

''Rutland is my family name but my companies fall under the corporate name of Defoe Holdings.''

Christ! The company owned a large section of real estate in Florida and neighbouring states and he had decided to hit on her! He must be slumming it a bit! She knew she was attractive, some men had called her beautiful but she was too slim and stroppy for most men, unwilling to keep her mouth shut. She had always attracted the interest of men but only a few men had really liked her, the others wanting to tame her. *Joshua Rutland was like that*, she thought; *dark and dangerous, a barracuda waiting to devour her whole.*

Stopping outside of the b and b Rutland opened her car door. He took her small haversack from her and led her into the house.

''Mr. Rutland and Kirsten, it's great to see you,'' said the owner, barely hiding her interest in seeing them together.

''Mr. Rutland and I met when I visited Aunt Freja, Gracie. His Granddad was in the fire as well.''

Gracie had only moved into the town long after he left for the Navy. On his flying visits, he had barely visited the town, eating only at two establishments. A sulky arrogant boy, he had not made many friends among the local kids, using his fists more than words to win arguments. He only remembered one good local friend who had joined the Navy with him but had been killed in Afghanistan. A few more of the girls would remember him as he had cut a swathe through them in High School. He had found his looks, height and brooding manner had attracted the wrong sort of girl and earned the disapproval of his Grandma.

Very few people would remember him with fondness and Gracie would not be expected to know him at all. His company helped charities but not in this town, *something I should rectify soon,* he thought. The hospital was trying to save his granddad and many of the town-folk had already visited him leaving cards and flowers. He owed this town something for the loyalty shown to his Granddad over the last few days.

"What time will you go to the Deputy tomorrow?''

''Only after the forensics expert has reported to me. Please come with me. First, I want to visit the hospital at nine o'clock. I will take you there with me if you want. You don't have transportation, do you?''

''Only Aunt Freya's car when the police release it to me. I am on her insurance so they know my use is legit.''

''That will take a few days as the perps may have left prints on it if they entered the house by the garage.'' He thought quickly and decisively. ''We will breakfast together at 8.30 and then go to the hospital together.''

She looked puzzled. ''You needn't breakfast with me. You can pick me up at 9 a.m. Or I can walk to your hotel.''

''Not tomorrow. I am here until a room comes free at the Girling and then I will switch to there. I need to use the hotel's business facilities.'' Not to say the swimming pool and gym. The air-conditioning was unpredictable in the b and b and he was baking.

Christ! It was bad enough being near him in the hospital or car. She now had to be in close proximity to him for several days in this small establishment. She would stay in her room when she wasn't at the hospital or the Deputy's office. She had some legal work she had brought with her.

She had intended to start working from home as a legal secretary. Her account was so empty these days she had to take what she could. She couldn't work easily as a barrister whilst she was trying to remain anonymous but this work she could do over the net and through the post. One day she might return publicly as a barrister when she felt safe but for now this would have to do.

"The lounge is comfortable and there is an honesty bar," said Gracie.

"Wonderful! I could do with a scotch on the rocks. Coming Ms Gateman?"

"No thanks. It was a long journey. I am going to my bed." He raised his brows as if he did not believe her excuse but let her go.

"Damn the man." He knew the affect he was having on her. She felt uncomfortable in his presence. Was he enjoying winding her up?

Rutland was not enjoying himself. He felt strangely lonely in the lounge and drunk his scotch quickly, instead of savouring it as he usually did. He missed her barbed comments and had enjoyed trying to remain one step ahead of her. She was an enticing bundle he would enjoy unravelling.

He went upstairs and undid his laptop. She had left England after breaking her engagement and then crossed the ocean to Indonesia. Was it to forget the fiancé or to hide? He emailed Drakeman asking him to find out what the case concerning her fiancé was about. His eyes widened as he scrolled through the attachment he received back.

Justin Grayson hailed from one of the most prominent legal families in England. 'From the top drawer,' as the English would say. Brilliant! A double first at Cambridge and had taken silk much earlier than most barristers. He was the darling of the legal profession. His father was the best friend of Kirsten's father and the families were very close. They had spent holidays together before Kirsten's parents had split up.

Drakeman still could not find a lot about the case that had nearly been taken against Grayson. It concerned a girl he had lived with before shacking up with Kirsten.

Another attachment concerned her father. A superintendent, he was not however the epitome of moral turpitude. The bastard had several families spread over the country. Kirsten had five brothers. She had been pulled out of private school at the age of ten. Her lifestyle was abstemious, her mother making ends meet by teaching piano privately until she married again.

His image of a spoilt privately educated girl with a cut-glass accent was far from the truth. She spoke like a lady from a private school and her manners were delicate but she had worked Saturdays in retail and on her aunt's ranch in the summer to pay her way through school and college. Her life had nearly been as ruptured and turbulent as his but she had knuckled down like himself to build a life and career for herself.

All he had to find out now was what had made her leave her well paid barrister's position. Drakeman had found out she had been sorely missed and would have been offered a senior position within the business if she had stayed.

He would bet his last dollar it was because of Grayson's behaviour. Kirsten Gateman was running from something or someone. In his bones, he felt she was not a natural runner. Something must have really spooked her.

Chapter three.

Rutland woke early. He was sweltering hot, the humidity uncomfortable. Running would concentrate the mind and enable him to plan how he intended to manage the meeting with the official. He set off for his six-mile run, determined to keep focused on the job in front of him. He would not be distracted by the thought of his unwilling breakfast partner who last night had been as jittery as a rabbit who had seen a wolf.

Kirsten had been woken by her nightmares. Giving up on sleep she stood in the garden and watched him leave the establishment, pounding the track; a dynamic man, his arms moving like pistons, his biceps bulging as he pushed up the speed, his muscled thighs powering him forward. He moved fluidly as if running at speed was as comfortable as breathing, a streamlined machine.

He had the physique of a man who had the broad shoulders of an athlete but a slim build for a big man and narrow waist, unlike the football or hockey jocks. Muscled, he had little fat on him; his was not the form of a bulky man who worked out daily on machines in the gym. She guessed running and swimming were his main sporting pastimes living in Miami. She had watched him doing squats and push ups before his run. He was in peak condition, as if keeping fit was important to him. His expression was grim; eyes like green marbles, his firm chin set hard as if he were totally focused and determined to achieve his goal whatever that might be.

A hard man to cross, she thought, shivering at the possibility of another confrontation with him over breakfast. Neither had won their confrontation last night, both assessing each other warily, neither totally trusting each other. They needed each other and were willing to work with each other, subject to careful boundaries.

Now as he vanished into the distance she appreciated his male form; enjoying watching a supremely fit and dominant male in his prime. Kirsten recognised another dimension to their relations which she had to keep under control. She had recognised her own positive reaction to a gorgeous male last night, disguising it with contempt and an icy reserve to keep him at a distance. He was the sort of man who would have attracted her years before she had settled down with Justin; cool, charming and with a powerful intellect. His humour and his concern for his Granddad and generosity to Freja had surprised her and attracted her to him

When he had gripped her arm last night she had felt shivery inside, her pulse and heart-beat quickening, her body recognising the chemistry that sparked between them, that her mind refused to acknowledge. She had not deceived him. A man experienced in reading the body language of women, he had read her interest in him. He had not exploited it which had surprised her; he was more gentlemanly than she had thought.

The cynic in her believed he would wait his time until he had got the information he wanted from her and then he would strike, using his charm on her to try to get her in his bed. He was devious like most rich and powerful men, exploiting women when they were at their most vulnerable, to achieve his aims.

She would raise her barriers to him, ignore that charm and charisma. He was too dangerous for her to let him close to her.

Rutland came back, slowing down, then stopping and breathing heavily, bending over and stretching as he tried to regain his breath. As usual, he had pushed himself to the limits. He was no longer sleepy, his mind now clear and he was raring to go; ready to face the Deputy.

He had seen Kirsten watching him. She could not disguise her interest in him, her pupils darkening and widening as she had watched him as he built up speed. She enjoyed watching the male body. She was as appreciative of a male body as any other young woman despite her pretence to be an iceberg.

Interesting and something to pursue later when this case was solved. He moved to his room for a quick shower, looking forward to meeting her again.

Breakfast started uncomfortably. Dark shadows under Kirsten's eyes told Rutland of her disturbed sleep. He had slept like a log aided by the Scotch. Years of sleeping on a hard floor or bare earth on manoeuvres had inured him to hardship. After the horrors of war, nothing gave him sleepless nights bar the nightmares when he remembered a close friend dying from a roadside bomb he himself had missed by seconds.

She barely spoke to him at first; suspicion and wariness in her eyes. He broke the ice. He needed to develop trust between them. "We need a common agenda for when we meet the Deputy. I am not going to let him weasel his way out of responsibility for this case?''

''I will say Aunt Freya feared someone was threatening her and I have the texts stored to prove it!''

''Good Girl.'' He took her hand and squeezed it encouragingly. For some reason that irked her she glowed with pride at his praise. Damn the man! She didn't want his approbation. She had begun to soften a little toward him the night before when he showed his tender side, caring for his Granddad's welfare. She needed to harden herself to his charm. He was still the man who had tried to pick her up and had taken her cases against her will.

He explained his position. "I will say the house showed evidence of being turned over before the fire had been lit. I worked with arson cases in the past and know the signs. My forensic investigator will arrive later today. It is imperative no-one is allowed into the houses who could disturb or corrupt the crime scene before he arrives.''

''I saw one desk that had not burnt out. It looked as if a lock had been broken.''

''Even better! If both houses were searched and ransacked the Deputy cannot ignore the evidence. It is also important that the old couple are not portrayed as senile.''

''If my aunt recovers she will have the Deputy for mincemeat if he patronises her.''

''A fierce old bird, is she? Like my Granddad?'' he enquired, smiling at the memory of the single-minded, at times, cantankerous old goat.

''No, she is feisty but logical. Get on the wrong side of her and you will know it. I have never known her to bear a grudge but she doesn't tolerate fools easily.''

''She sounds as if she would be a good partner for my Granddad. He would tear a strip off anyone acting in a condescending manner to him or my family.

'I also have another card to play which the Deputy knows of. My friend is the County's Chief of Police and he and I have friends in the FBI. I have only to suggest to Lance there may be evidence of some Grand Larceny or corruption and he will refer the case to the FBI.

'We are agreed then. May I take the lead after you have given your evidence to the Deputy? I want to make sure my investigator is briefed and given the force's cooperation.'' She nodded reluctantly. It was the most logical approach although she didn't want to hand over control to this man. He had the resources and the power to manipulate the Deputy's department.

He sighed with relief. It was like pulling teeth negotiating with Kirsten Gateman. What would make her trust him?

''Come on let's go to the hospital and talk with the quacks. I will meet you in the lobby in five minutes.'' He noted she had only picked at her food. That and her red-rimmed eyes told him she had cried during the night and was still distressed.

''Please God, make the old couple fighters and survive this attack!'' He wouldn't want to have to handle Kirsten Gateman's distress if her aunt died. She was clearly closer to the old lady than she was to her parents.

Chapter four.

They arrived at the hospital and were let into the private ward. Two beds were separated by a wall and a curtain giving privacy to the couple. The doctor approached them.

''Your Granddad woke and asked for her immediately. She is just waking. He was burnt more on his hands trying to get to her but she inhaled more smoke.''

''That's a good sign isn't it, him asking for her?'' said Rutland.

''Very,' he said. 'He can't talk much. His throat is burnt but he said it was arson.'' Rutland nodded content, his suspicions were confirmed.

''Will they make it?'' Kirsten framed the question that was on Rutland's lips. She was clearly a woman who faced the worst head on; a brave woman he was beginning to respect more, not the vacuous beauty he had labelled when he had targeted her at the airport.

''We are still not sure but the fact they have survived the night is good news. If they survive the next forty-eight hours they may have a good chance.''

Both Rutland and Kirsten expressed sighs of relief. They had both been holding their breath. Rutland let go of the hand he had unconsciously grasped, giving and needing reassurance. He noted she had not removed her hand from his, subconsciously wanting that gentle intimacy, recognising they both cared for this old couple.

More progress. She is trusting me a little.

''Can they be questioned? It is vital we find out information before the leads go cold.''

''For a few minutes' only.''

''Is it better to wait for the investigator?'' asked Kirsten.

''I don't know for certain. I think we can ask general questions and then get him to come back and ask more detailed questions later. I want a cop outside this hospital room. The perps might come back and try to finish the job. I am going to put out through the media the old couple haven't regained consciousness and are in comas.''

She nodded looking white. She had thought the same. *Clever girl. Not much would get past her. She would be one step ahead of the perps if she was prosecuting them.*

''Shall we start with my Granddad as he is more awake?'' She nodded following him. He was beginning to win her respect, she admitted grudgingly. He had consulted her and treated her with respect, as if she was a professional, not the pretty girl he had propositioned at the airport.

Some progress. If he resists propositioning me we might work well together.'

They sat down and he stroked the old man's hand until his eyelids fluttered and he opened tired but sharply acute eyes.

''Joshua, you got here? I thought you were here last night,'' he rasped. He coughed and Rutland lifted him up and gave him a sip of water, gently placing him down on the pillow where the old man's breathing settled slowly.

Rutland held the old man's still strong hand and gripped it tight. ''I was here last night. You were asleep but your sub-conscious must have identified my voice when I was talking to the Doctor. Freja's niece is here as well to see her aunt.''

''That pretty young girl was here last year. She's a good girl; cares a great deal about her Aunt!'' Rutland was surprised to see 'that pretty young girl,' blush at the compliment. She was clearly unused to or uncomfortable being complimented.

''Strange!'' he mused. Most beautiful girls took compliments as expected. Another thing for him to catalogue in his mind for the future. She was a Pandora's Box waiting to be opened!

He turned his mind back to the matter on hand with some difficulty. ''You need to tell us what happened. I have a forensic investigator coming as well and he will need to talk with the both of you quickly to avoid the trail getting cold. I want to nail these bastards who did this to you.''

''Hey boyo, there is a lady present. Watch your language! Your Grandma didn't bring you up to cuss in front of ladies.''

''It is perfectly ok. I have heard considerably worse in my profession,'' said Kirsten wanting to deflect the fire in the old man's eyes when he regarded his Grandson.

''You won't have heard it in my house,'' said the old man firmly. ''We brought this young man up as a gentleman around ladies. His Grandma would turn in her grave if she heard him use that word.''

Changing the subject Kirsten said, ''My aunt indicated she was being threatened. Do you know anything about it?''

''A son of a bitch named John Thirman was pestering her and intimidating her with letters and a threat of a court case.'' Kirsten smiled at the old man who in anger forgot he shouldn't cuss in front of a lady. He clearly cared for her aunt.

''Why was he threatening her?'' asked Rutland.

''He wanted her house. He started gently, trying to sweet talk her but later the letters and visits became more menacing. She was more than a match for him. Threatened him with her shotgun even and peppered him around his feet but he retaliated. First, it was silent phone calls, heavy breathing; you know the sort of thing.''

Rutland's chest was tight; his breathing shallow as he imagined the fear the old woman must have felt. If he got hold of this scum he would choke the breath nearly out of him and make him feel what the old girl must have suffered. He had the skills to hurt this guy badly, courtesy of his period in the SEALS and he would enjoy inflicting pain and fear on him.

''It got worse. Threatening letters, a man entering the house, the drawers searched. She knew someone had been in the house but there was not enough evidence left to show the police. They thought it was her imagination, the product of a wavering mind of a batty, senile old woman.''

''Didn't my aunt show the letters to the police?''

''They disappeared when the intruder came into the house. The phone messages were wiped off the answering machine. Even when she was pushed against the wall, when the intruder escaped, the cops didn't believe her. I wasn't there when Thirman and his thugs came to the house. It was hearsay on my part. The Deputy said there wasn't enough evidence to investigate Thirman.''

''Is he close to Thirman?'' asked Kirsten.

''Is he in the pocket of Thirman?'' asked Rutland. Clearly the idea of a corrupt cop had passed through both their minds. They were on the same copy!

''No idea but he thought we had lost our marbles and wouldn't take us seriously. You could investigate his connections to Thirman.''

''We're on to it,'' Rutland trusted Kirsten to ask any more pertinent questions. The nurse came to terminate their interrogation of his Granddad. He moved to the corridor where there were no eavesdroppers and it was safe to use his cell.

Drakeman answered immediately. ''Got anything for me Man?''

''A name, John Thirman. Put it through the computer please. He wanted the old girl's land enough to buy it and then search the property. She refused and then the phone calls and the searches of the property began. Next, a visit and all the evidence of the intimidation was stolen. The old girl was pushed roughly against the wall when she disturbed an intruder. Finally, the fire!''

''The investigator should be there this afternoon. Name of Claremont. Not local; from Kentucky but has a record for being thorough and a tough nut. Blakely recommended the person. Doesn't bow to pressure apparently. What you need.''

''Thanks, Man. There is more. The Deputy is a gutless weasel but he may be too close to Thirman to make sound judgements. He may also be in the pay of Thirman.''

''Onto it Joshua. And how is it going with the beautiful blonde. Any progress there?''

''Softly, softly catchee monkey and all that crap. She is a jumpy as a jack-rabbit.''

''Your Southern charm not working, Casanova?''

''She still regards me with suspicion but is opening up to me slowly and working with me now. Have you found anything more about that fiancé yet?''

''Nothing yet. I fancy a trip across the Briny but I wondered if you need me there.''

''I may need you to bring your scraggy ass here so don't think about gallivanting across the Atlantic yet.''

''You are a hard boss, Mr. Rutland.''

''See you soon Pal and thanks.'' He laughed but knew his irreverent friend would come to guard his back if he needed him. Their connection had developed in Iraq and consolidated in Afghanistan. Friendships develop in war, solidified and rarely broke in peacetime.

This damned fiancé was bugging him now. The cool professional attitude of Kirsten didn't fit with the nervous woman around a man. She was confident in her investigative role but if he moved out of his professional role she looked at him as if would jump her. She seemed to fear self-assured men who were at ease with their sexuality. He was sure that was the problem. She respected him as an attorney but feared him as a man.

He went back to Kirsten who stood at the door. ''He is sleeping. Our questioning has used up all his strength but he said he was glad to get it off his chest. He can rest peacefully now. He is tough and I think he will make it.'' He took her arm. ''Let's get a coffee and visit your aunt now.''

They went to the old woman's bed and saw she still slept deeply. The Doctor explained, ''She is not to be disturbed. She was in pain and has been given some sedation. She should wake up in a few hours and you can talk to her then.''

''Did she have her cell with her when she was brought in?'' asked Rutland.

''Sure, but it was taken by the police as evidence.''

''Damn!' He called Drakeman again. ''The cops got hold of the old girl's phone. I may need to get to the court for a subpoena to get it back again. I want a legal secretary onto it.''

''Done.''

''No evidence from the old girl. She is under sedation. I am going with Ms Gateman to the Deputy now. If you hear an explosion, you'll know the Bastard hasn't cooperated.''

"I wouldn't be in his shoes,' said Drakeman. 'Don't hurt him too much!''

''If he has harmed this case in any way his career is toast. Bye for now!''

''Ready for the Deputy now?'' he asked Kirsten.

''Yes,' she said but embarrassed she heard her stomach rumble.''

''The cafeteria first I think. You ate like a bird at breakfast. I did it justice. As you stated Gracie's breakfast was out of this world''

''I felt a little under the weather,'' she admitted.

''It is hardly surprising the stress you have been under. At the counter, he asked, "French toast or muffins?''

''A B.L.T please. I love crispy American bacon.''

''A girl after my own heart. Two BLT's please and one Latte and one Americano.'' He had noted what she had drunk at breakfast. She watched him demolish his sandwich and coffee and then order a round of pancakes with maple syrup. Her eyes wide, she wondered where he put it all after the enormous breakfast he had polished off at Gracies. He had not a spare ounce of fat on him.

She could see how powerfully he filled his polo shirt, his biceps showing when he flexed his arms. His broad shoulders and his six-pack showed he must exercise regularly. A leather jacket hung negligently across one shoulder. He was dressed casually but smartly to impress the Deputy. Without trying, he was one of the most masculine men she had met. He was raw potent masculine sexuality and he scared the hell out of her.

''Now to beard the Deputy in his cave.'' Watching her, he said, ''I like a woman who is not scared to eat. Too many of the women I have dated resembled stick insects, scared of putting on a lb. You look as if you enjoy your food.''

She looked defensively at him but saw he was smiling and telling her the truth. Justin had said he loved her slim figure and had hated it when she had put on two lbs. He had called her a 'lazy fat cow' and other horrible things and insisted she dieted.

She shook his image out of her mind and followed Rutland to his car. In the last eighteen months, she had put on half a stone, even in the hot Indonesian climate. Her aunt had had a fit when she had seen her; scrawny, nearly emaciated, a shadow of herself. She had lost weight to please Justin when nothing else she did seem to please him. When her health had finally suffered, it was one of the reasons why she had plucked up the courage to leave him.

She was still not yet satisfied with her weight and body image but she no longer felt guilty finishing her plate of food. The doctor in New York had said she was borderline anorexic but she had recovered quickly, her mental health improving when she was away from the invidious dominating presence that was Justin. She had control over her own body and her life now and would not give that up to any man again.

Rutland watched her while she ate. She was relaxing again at last. Dressed in a crisp white blouse and smart navy chinos she looked casual but elegant. He noted she dressed to distract men away from her figure. Her buttoned up look, with shirt done up to the top of her neck, looked almost school-mistressy. She would fit well in a classroom or a library. Even at the airport she had worn light loose clothes to cover her slight curves although she could not disguise her long slim legs. His mind did somersaults, thinking of those legs curled around him if he could get her in his bed.

''Stop that!'' he remonstrated to himself. Part of the fun in dating women was the chase but he had never stalked an unwilling woman. If she really didn't want him he would reluctantly back off.

''Let's get to the Deputy and we can try to make the dept. release your aunt's car.'' He had gleaned enough intelligence about Kirsten Gateman to know she would cooperate more with him if given the freedom to choose to work with him.

Chapter five.

The deputy was more welcoming, even sickeningly obsequious since he had found out Rutland's financial status and had listened to Rutland's friend's sharp but telling call that morning suggesting this could be a case for the FBI. The Police Chief would formalise the forensic scientist's role as a consultant for his department. Under the pay of the authority, no one would question his authority and right to demand evidence.

Deputy Brune didn't want any sharp FBI brains nosing in his town. He had his fingers in too many lucrative pies and didn't want any feathers ruffled. He would cooperate with Rutland and sacrifice Thirman if need be. There were much more powerful men to keep happy than that loaded but greasy jerk. He smiled a grimace that looked as if it had been nailed in place on his plump face.

''Now how can I help this little lady?'' he directed at Kirsten. Kirsten smiled and ignored the urge to roll her eyes at Rutland. She had dealt with worst chauvinists in the City of London. Biting back her contempt for him she explained quietly, "I want to give you a copy of the text messages my aunt sent to me. It confirms my fears she was being threatened and the fire was indeed arson.''

She gave him a copy of the texts she had printed on her laptop. "*Thank God for modern technology!*'' The Deputy took the copy and said, ''She was rather vague before the fire you know.''

Rutland intervened before Kirsten could respond waspishly to the insinuation her aunt was losing her marbles. It was time for him to take charge. He had noticed the Deputy's change in attitude toward him since the previous day. His friend's call and his elevated status in the mind of the Deputy would make the little shit cooperate with him now.

Placing a restraining hand on Kirsten's arm he stated, ''My Granddad said, Ms Gateman's aunt had been suffered threatening phone calls and letters and her house was searched before the fire.''

''But there was no formal evidence of this when she asked us to investigate. It had disappeared like magic,'' replied the Deputy, moving his hands in the air as if the papers had vanished in a puff of smoke. Kirsten would have intervened but a grip of iron around her wrist made her wince and shut her mouth. Glaring at him, she tried to move her arm from his grasp; without success.

''I have witnessed several arson scenes whilst I was a criminal attorney and it is clear to me that locks have been broken in my granddad's house. One desk was rifled. My forensic investigator will report to you but I hope prints have already been taken by your officers.''

''Indeed, they have and are being matched by computer as we speak.''

''Then we will leave you until my investigator reports to us this evening,'' said Rutland shaking his hand. He directed Kirsten out of the room, with a possessive hand on the small of her back.

Out of the office she turned her anger on him, blasting him angrily. "Why didn't you let me speak? He implied my aunt had lost her mental capacity to make decisions or give evidence! He inferred she was senile!'' she snapped.

''Well little lady,'' he said mimicking the Deputy's accent and condescending manner perfectly, "Our puffed up and intellectually challenged Deputy has you marked as a blond bimbo. He would not have cared what you said!''

She acknowledged mentally what he said was accurate. *Damn the man, he was right.* He had not wasted time with that moron.

''So, what do we do now?'' she asked. She stood subconsciously rubbing her wrist where a bruise was forming; his grip had been so hard. He took her hand and rubbed her wrist. His thumb moved lower and grazed the palm of her hand gently, soothingly. Designed to reassure, it was nevertheless the most erotic gesture, awakening senses she had thought she had long forgotten. Her hand trembled.

He said nothing but his eyes narrowed, darkening in their intensity as he silently acknowledged the spark between them. ''I am sorry, I do not always know my own strength.''

She pulled her hand away, trying to ignore the heat passing between them. There was some indefinable link between them she must not acknowledge if she was to remain safe and sane. Rutland pushed her towards the car.

''Get in please,'' he said, more impatient than he should have been. He was irritated by her obduracy. Why could she not admit they were attracted to each other? He struck sparks off her whenever he touched her.

''We will go back to the b and b and see if our investigator has arrived. He should be here soon.'' He fired the engine and made a note to ask Drakeman to drive his Aston down if he came. He might as well enjoy driving around here. If he had known, he would be here a while he might have brought his bike. In this weather, a few rides across the coast in his spare time would clear his head.

''Your guest has arrived Mr. Rutland,'' said Gracie. 'In the lounge!' The way she narrowed her eyes and looked sceptically at him made Rutland immediately suspicious. What was up? He and Kirsten went into the lounge and he was floored. Instead of the masculine investigator he had expected a petite brunette was curled up in an armchair tapping on her laptop. She looked up in surprise and smiled; a beaming smile that lit up her face. She uncurled herself like a sleek cat.

''Ma'am,'' he said shaking her hand. ''I am Joshua Rutland and this is Ms Gateman.''

''Nice to meet you Ms Gateman and Mr. Rutland. I am Elisabeth Claremont.'' Business like she collected her laptop and asked, ''Can we visit the crime scene now please. I don't want any evidence to be lost.''

''This way,'' said Rutland, liking the way she took charge. She would not be bullied by the Deputy. Kirsten briefed her about the phone call. ''The Deputy is trying to make my aunt appear senile. She is as sharp as a needle.''

''Does the Deputy have an axe to grind?'' asked Elisabeth Claremont, her nose wrinkling as if trying to analyse a puzzle.

''We are not sure if there is incompetence or corruption yet,'' said Rutland. ''Keep an open mind until you have more evidence.''

''Of course,'' she said, piercing him with steely hard brown eyes, as if she resented him reminding of her need to remain unpartisan. Rutland took a mental step back. This woman was as prickly as Kirsten Gateman. Just his luck to have to work with two feisty women! So much for an easy way forward! He must be losing his touch with the ladies.

The two women walked ahead of him, assessing each other and liking what they saw. Opposites in looks, Kirsten a tall slim blond and Elisabeth a smaller voluptuous brunette, they nevertheless both shared the same steel and determination, professionalism and integrity.

Elisabeth outfitted them with plastics and they entered Freja's house. The acrid smoke was barely noticeable now and they could breathe easily. Kirsten shivered, imagining how her aunt had felt in the inferno, trapped in this house. Rutland put his hand gently on her shoulder and she looked up at him, surprised at the concerned look in his eyes when he regarded her closely.

He took his hand off and pushed her into the lounge where the fire had started. Elisabeth was all business, making for the point where she believed the blaze had started; taking finger prints from the furniture which had survived. Smudged and blackened with dirt; Kirsten thought they might not be of use, but there were some on the inside of the safe which had survived.

The intruder had removed his gloves to feel the tumblers and hadn't wiped them clean enough. This guy was not as professional as they had believed or he might have been disturbed while searching the safe. This might be his first mistake and their lucky break.

After a rudimentary examination of the place where the fire started Elisabeth said, "It was arson. There is evidence of accelerants used. The desk was broken into as well. They left a hell of a mess, papers around it, which probably made the fire burn faster."

"Have you enough evidence to talk with the Deputy yet? He is a chauvinist and you need to be able to back up your statement."

"More than enough. It is a classic case of arson but not well carried out. You can add to it attempted murder as well. Those doors were locked from outside and the window was made deliberately difficult to open from the inside. It was designed as a death trap. Someone wanted your aunt to die Kirsten!"

Kirsten's face lost its colour and she felt slightly sick. It was one thing to believe her aunt was meant to die but another to have it confirmed in black and white by an expert. A few minutes more and her aunt could have been toast!

Rutland rested his hand on her shoulder, unconsciously rubbing it, trying to give her some comfort and moral support. Kirsten found it soothing but moved away, not wanting to rely on this man. Men pretended they were your friends and cared for you and then took your freedom away when you were most vulnerable. Joshua Rutland was particularly dangerous as he was most appealing when he was acting so tenderly and kind.

Elisabeth moved to the door. "I am going to the other house to see if that was designed to be burnt or merely caught fire as it was adjacent to this one."

Rutland said to Kirsten, "Everything is falling into place. We will leave Ms Claremont here and go to the hospital. Ms Andersson may have woken up by now.''

''She seems very thorough.''

''Drakeman would only have selected the best. Let us hope the Deputy doesn't treat her the same way as he did you.''

''I think she is more than a match for him. She will baffle him with science. He didn't seem to be the highest creature on the food chain.''

Rutland called Elisabeth. ''Can we leave you for a few hours please and then collect you and take you to the Deputy later? We want to visit Ms Andersson at the hospital.''

''Sure, two hours is about enough time for me to do a cursory first examination of both houses. Both were intended to burn but the fire was intended to be restricted to certain areas as if the perps might comeback. It is now two cases of attempted murder if we can prove they knew the vics were in the house.''

She was delighted he was leaving. He would not be breathing down her neck. She watched them exit, his hand proprietarily on Ms Gateman's arm. She sensed the other woman's discomfort with his hand on her body. Kirsten Gateman did not want any intimacy with this man.

Rutland, she believed felt differently. She had watched him when Kirsten's face had changed when she Elisabeth had told them it was attempted murder. He looked like a man worrying for a woman he cared about. She wondered what there was between them. He looked as if whatever there was he wanted more.

Kirsten and Rutland left for the hospital and she asked to talk to her aunt on her own. He could hear a lot of their conversation through the curtain. She sat down and held her aunt's hand. Freja could whisper and Kirsten sat closer to her as she seemed agitated and determined to put her points to her niece.

''Gave my evidence to that Deputy but he didn't believe it was arson Kirsten.''

''I know Aunt Freja, but Mr Rutland has an investigator working on the case and told the Deputy he recognises signs of arson from his former criminal cases.'' Her aunt held her hand tighter, so tight Kirsten winced.

''He is a good man,'' she said gasping and nodding her head to emphasise her words. ''His granddad says he puts on a hard front but underneath he is kind and caring.''

''He is certainly domineering and wants to control the investigation.'' replied Kirsten grimly.

''He had a very uncertain childhood and he needs control in his life. Trust him Kirsten, He is like Michael and will not let you down.''

"He suffocates me. Tries to control me!''

''He is no Justin. Michael says he just wants to tie everything up so the Deputy cannot ignore any evidence.''

''I'll take your word for it but I will keep my distance.'' There were too many similarities between the men and parallels between their situations for Kirsten to give her wholesale trust to Rutland but she would try to keep an open mind.

Rutland came in. He had heard her aunt pleading his case but saw Kirsten still stiffened when he sat close to her. Her lack of trust in him irritated him. Women were usually drawn to him by his easy manner. He was certain now; something he could not put his finger on, was not quite right about her attitude to men. She was equally polite and distant to Phil who had not made a move on her. It was more than merely a mistrust of men, she appeared disdainful of the male gender as if they were lesser beings, dangerous, to be avoided at all cost.

He revised the evidence the police had taken from Freja in a short interview the night of the fire. Checking every detail with his usual thoroughness, he impressed Kirsten. Her aunt's case was in good hands. There was little she need do with this experienced former criminal attorney working for them. They said goodbye to Michael and left to find out what progress Drakeman and Elisabeth had made.

Chapter six.

Elisabeth had started a deeper investigation. She was deep in thought, on her knees on the floor, when she sensed someone behind her standing close and quiet. She jumped up, swivelled round on her heels and the man stepped back.

''What the hell were you doing frightening me like that?''

''Sorry Ma'am. You seemed engrossed and I didn't want to disturb you.

'Philip Drakeman of Drakeman Security,'' he said taking her hand in a firm grip. ''I was the guy who hired you on behalf of Joshua Rutland.'' He was assessing her, running his eyes from the top of her head to her feet. He looked as if he liked what he saw. ''I guess you have met Joshua Rutland.''

''Yes, he has briefed me and gone with Ms Gateman to talk with her aunt.'' She regarded him with professional interest. She knew of this man. Like Rutland he hadn't been born with a silver spoon in his mouth and had worked his arse off for years to develop one of the biggest security and investigation firms in the USA after a short spell in the FBI. She wondered why he had come to this backwater.

''Is he picking you up later or may I have the pleasure of escorting you?'' asked Drakeman, his Southern drawl making this sound more like an invitation to go to bed than a drive to a professional meeting. She met him stare for stare. He was so self-confident; this tall blond man whose quiet assurance spoke volumes about himself.

Dangerous and seductive, a man to avoid.

''Mr. Rutland is collecting me to take me to the Deputy's office,'' she said, "but thanks for the offer Mr. Drakeman.'' She emphasised his surname, deliberately creating more formality between them. He smiled and said, "Would you mind if I looked around?''

"Not if you put plastics on. I don't want the crime scene to be contaminated.'' She took another uniform from her case and threw it at him. He took off his coat revealing broad shoulders and developed biceps; too distracting for a professional woman wanting to concentrate on work. Damn the man; he oozed sex appeal and he knew it.

''Can I help?'' She knew he could be trusted having worked with criminal cases during his spell with the FBI. No one would know he had helped. ''You can take samples of the ash in this room please?'' He nodded and got down to work, watching her closely when she had her back to him. Beautiful and cautious she moved carefully, not leaving an inch of the room uncovered.

He noted the way she had withdrawn from him, snatching her hand away as if she had been burnt. Elisabeth Claremont was a lady he would like to get to know better. Suddenly, this case was beginning to become more interesting.

After crawling about the floor and crevices both Drakeman and Elisabeth were grateful when they heard the other pair arrive back.

''Great, they are back,'' said Drakeman as he straightened up and stretched and grimaced.

“Getting old Mr. Drakeman,'' tormented Elisabeth. She admitted to herself she enjoyed getting a rise out of this confident man, trying to put him off balance.

He raised his brows, ''Are you challenging me, Ma'am?''

''Not at all!'' she said, backing off quickly as he moved toward her. ''I was merely enquiring about your health. When one reaches a certain age, one isn't as flexible as when one was young.''

He took another step toward her, spearing her with his steely blue grey eyes. “Would you like to test my agility and stamina Ma'am?'' She shook her head, not liking the wicked gleam that appeared in his eyes. What he would have done next, she didn't find out because Kirsten and Rutland walked in but there was mischief in his eyes that played havoc with her senses.

''Saved this time!'' he whispered in her ear as he stood next to her. ''Next time you won't be so lucky.'' She shivered at the implied threat in his words. She had better not tease him again; he was the type of man one didn't challenge. She just hadn't been able to resist winding him up. He was too self-assured for his own good.

Drakeman backed off physically and mentally but he would take up the challenge with Ms Claremont sooner or later. She might try to deny she was attracted to him but physically and mentally she was drawn to him and him to her like moths to a flame. He had seen the spark of interest in her eyes when he had walked through the door and teasing him was a preliminary stage to flirting with him. He had the hots for this little brunette and he would bet his hat she was equally as smitten by him.

Moving to his friend he patted him on the back and asked, ''How did you get on at the hospital, Man?''

''Ms Andersson was awake and coherent. She couldn't speak much; her vocal cords are damaged but she confirmed what we thought. She had disturbed the intruder two days before the fire. She couldn't identify him. He rushed passed her and he was masked. She could only give a limited description. She mainly confirmed what my Granddad had told us. We will try to ask her more tomorrow.

'I am pleased to see you but what brought you here? I thought you might be going abroad.'' He raised one brow to warn Drakeman not to mention London in Kirsten's presence. She was as sharp as a needle and would guess he was checking up on her.

He could not take any more of Ms Gateman's wrath. He could sense she was containing an anger around him and he couldn't guess what he had done wrong. Apart from holding her hand and trying to reassure her with his hand on her shoulder he had avoided any intimate contact with her, He had treated her like a friend or colleague. One minute she seemed to respond positively to his gentle treatment of her then the next she withdrew from him, regarding him suspiciously, as if he were the enemy instead of Thirman. He couldn't work the damned woman out and he was beginning to lose interest in trying.

''I found a friend there who is working on the problem today for me. Saved me a long trip and I thought you might want some help. I drove your

Aston down for you.''

''Great, you can have the Mercedes.''

''Your bike will arrive tomorrow. You seem to be here for a while.''

Kirsten saw Rutland's eyes light up when he heard of the bike and car coming. He was a petrol head then. Until now he had barely showed any emotion about anything, little ruffling his calm state; he regarding his surroundings with the Vulcan-like detachment which characterised him.

Now, his emerald green eyes sparkling, she could imagine him on a powerful bike; his strong arms manoeuvring the bike wickedly fast round tight bends, holding the machine to the road. In leathers, he would look like a dark knight, carving a path and destroying anyone who stood in his way.

She had known he was handsome but had not realised quite how attractive he was until he greeted his friend and grinned at him, that smile warming up his handsome but rather severe face. With a smile like that he could charm the birds off the trees. When he directed his smile at her she found her pretended indifference toward him melting. She had googled him and now knew he was a player but she could see how he had got his reputation. That smile could melt the iciest of hearts. She would have to create more barriers to this charming, Joshua Rutland.

''The Deputy now, Ladies and Gentlemen,'' said Rutland moving toward the door and his car. ''Let's hope he is more than cooperative.''

The Deputy was as pompous as before but showed more respect to Kirsten than on his previous occasion. He looked at the female forensic investigator with scepticism in his eyes but Drakeman's reputation had gone before him. The Deputy eyed him warily and listened to his opinion about the crime being arson.

''Ms Claremont has already found that the desks and safe were tampered with. Some prints were taken from the safe. It looks as if the intruder was disturbed while he was tampering with the safe. The locks on the desks had been broken also.''

''How do you know these situations are linked?''

''It seems too much of a co-incidence Deputy, for them not to be linked,'' she replied firmly.' 'The dust on the prints links to the time the safe was cracked. The accelerants I have taken samples of in the ash show it was a deliberate fire.''

The Deputy gave in sighing. ''If it was arson and I am not saying it looks like it is; what was the reason for destroying the building?''

''We think it was attempted murder as both houses were searched and then deliberately set fire to.''

''Why would the perps want to murder two old people?' Neither were filthy rich?''

''A man called John Thirman was trying to buy Ms Andersson's house. You need to find out what was so important about her house that he would want it so much,'' said Drakeman.

''I will get my men to look into it and now little lady will you pass your evidence over to my men?'' he said turning to Elisabeth.

''I still must work on some of the samples tonight but I would be delighted to pass on anything tomorrow morning.'' Displeased, the Deputy shrugged and dismissed them.

''So much for Southern hospitality,'' commented Kirsten when they got out of his office." He was as friendly as a rattlesnake.''

Rutland could see the strain on Kirsten's face. A little relaxation would do all of them some good. ''If you want some Southern hospitality Phil and I will show you two tonight how Southern boys like to treat their ladies. Dinner and dancing at the best hotel in Devil's Creek. Ok, with you Mr. Drakeman?''

''Delighted Mr. Rutland,'' said his friend, smiling at the way Rutland was persuading these cantankerous women into spending the evening with them.

''Thank you but I must work on these samples,'' declined Elisabeth, ''And I have some legal work to prepare in my room,'' said Kirsten.

''Well the offer is open Ladies but I insist you let us take you to dinner. We need to discuss our strategy for tomorrow and I am moving to the hotel as soon as a vacancy comes up with Ms Claremont and Philip if he wants. Ms Claremont is in the b and b tonight I am afraid and Drakeman if he hasn't already found a room. The air conditioning is lousy but the beds and breakfasts are first rate.''

The woman gave each other looks and a silent message passed between them. Together, a combined force, they would be safer than alone with these dangerously seductive men. They would cover each other's backs and make sure they stayed in each other's company until they were safe in their own beds. These powerful charismatic men sucked a woman's will power away with their looks and smiles.

''Dinner then,'' said Kirsten, ''but that is all.''

''What else might you be thinking of Ms Gateman?'' asked Rutland, smiling that breath-taking smile again at her. Her heart lurched and she tried to control that unruly organ. He was melting down her resistance again with that Southern charm.

''Dancing, as you mentioned Mr. Rutland.''

"I don't think it is dancing you are afraid of Ms Gateman,'' he whispered as she squeezed past him into the car. ''We will have to explore why you are so afraid of being alone with me on another occasion!''

''Don't kid yourself Mr. Rutland,'' she snapped back. ''If your ego is so big I am sure you can cope with some rejection.''

''I am distraught Ma'am!'' he mocked.

She glared at him, refusing to let him bait her anymore; waiting for him to start the car while Drakeman and Elisabeth smiled at their verbal combat.

He drove them to the b and b and Drakeman and Ms Claremont registered. Drakeman wiped the sweat off his forehead. The heat of a Floridian summer was reaching its peak. ''What I wouldn't give for a swim tonight?''

''You can go skinny dipping in the creek like the kids,'' suggested Rutland.

''With half the teenage nubiles in the Creek watching?'' grimaced Drakeman. "No thanks. I don't want to offer the girls free entertainment. You know I prefer my ladies more mature than that!'' he said looking at Elisabeth who blushed. She thought, that *man sure knows what he wants and pursues it like a shark!'*

''I'll wait for the hotel pool tomorrow if we are lucky enough to get a room.''

''See you in an hour Ladies, in the foyer,'' said Rutland as the men headed up the stairs together.

''Like a pair of barracudas, aren't they?'' said Kirsten. ''Waiting for their prey to pass by!''

''More like wolves but they are gorgeous in a bossy sort of way. Particularly Drakeman!''

''If you like domineering men,'' said Kirsten. ''You can keep that sort of man. I am finished with that type!''

Elisabeth gave Kirsten a queer look. Kirsten's voice betrayed more than a little bitterness toward men. She was scornful, almost, showing a dislike and contempt of them. She was a beautiful woman who would attract men like bees to a honeypot but she dressed older than her age; hiding her wonderful body, studiously avoiding Rutland who was clearly attracted to her. There was something odd in the manner in which she spoke to these two wickedly attractive men, as if she tried to repulse them physically, expecting them to harm her in some way.

Drakeman and Rutland sat in the bar. They had it to themselves and could speak privately. ''So why did you come then?'' asked Rutland. ''Spit it out!''

''I thought you might need some help with the investigation. But I also wanted to see this woman who had captured your imagination. It is years since I have seen you so interested in a woman!''

''What did you think of her?'' Rutland was interested in hearing his friend's opinion of her. He was usually a sound judge of character, especially of women.

''If you want the truth. she is a bit too cold for my liking. Too much ice surrounding her!''

''She is a particularly interesting woman but there is some mystery about her. I would describe her as ice and fire. She is cold and detached, polite, almost indifferent and dismissive to me most of the time. But get her angry and a warm passionate creature is hidden under that ice. The man who could breach her defences could find a caring loving woman there.''

Rutland remembered the hospital where Kirsten had sat holding her aunt's hand, giving what comfort she could while tears streamed down her face. When she left, she had hugged and kissed the old lady, promising her fiercely, ''We will catch these men Aunt Freja and make them pay for hurting you!'' That was a woman who cared passionately about another. There were hidden depths to Kirsten Gateman he had yet to divine!

''Smitten eh?''

''Let's just say more than a little interested but I am sick of being rejected. This Elisabeth Claremont seems to be worth getting to know instead.''

His friend gave him a look out of narrowed eyes and frowned a little.

''You after her yourself? I thought tall skinny blondes were your type, not small curvaceous brunettes.''

''A man's taste can change, particularly if the lady in question is as feisty and intelligent as this one. If you are interested let the best man win.'' He gave him that look which said he was sure he would be the victor. Drakeman was intensely competitive when he set his mind on a goal.

''I am clearly not as interested as you. She would have been only a diversion from the lovely Kirsten. The field is clear for you.''

''Thanks Man. I think I am going to enjoy the chase!''

'' Did you find out any more about Kirsten?''

''A little more is unravelling. Can't find out more about the fiancé yet but the girl did VSO in Indonesia after two months with her Aunt Freja. Where they stayed, I don't know and where she lives in England I cannot trace. She has hidden her trail. All I can find out about are the airline tickets she bought to get to Florida and then to and back from Indonesia.''

''What about the name on the lease? She must have rented somewhere.''

''No joy. She must have stayed with friends or rested somewhere where they were not keen on maintaining the legalities.''

''Or were protecting those who lived there under an anonymous name. Was she hiding from someone?''

''You think her fiancé?''

''Possibly. He is the only one who fits the puzzle. Dig deeper Phil. Something tells me he is this answer to this puzzle called Kirsten Gateman.''

''What do we do next?''

''Dine and try to use our Southern charm on these lovely ladies. Perhaps, change their mind and have a dance or two. I want Ms Gateman to move to the hotel with us but I suspect she will reject the idea out of hand.''

''Why move her there, apart from getting her closer to you so you can have your wicked way with her?''

''Call it instincts Friend, but something is not quite right around here and she could be in danger. The perps may think she knows more than she does and try to persuade her to spill the beans.

'I think she is like a wound-up spring. She may end up trying to solve this case herself by her own methods. I'd like her near me to prevent her getting into trouble. She has a damned independent streak and is as secretive as hell.''

''Perhaps she doesn't trust you as you tried to seduce her? Do you blame her?''

''No, it runs deeper than that. She jumps if I touch her and would run a mile if I tried to become intimate with her.''

''Rather you than me then. I prefer Ms Claremont. She can torment and flirt, that woman. You would think she is Southern born.''

''She is a warm and talented woman,'' replied Rutland, certain Drakeman would have Elisabeth Claremont soon. He had set his heart on having her.

Drakeman thought of her talents and they went much farther than her abilities in the lab. He wondered if her skilful fingers could entice a man to ecstasy and if she would enjoy being dominated in bed. He would love to tame that sassy mouth of hers and make her come and call his name out time and time again.

The next morning, they were up bright and early. The men were clearly morning people and conversed easily between themselves. As usual Rutland took control of the agenda.

"Ms. Claremont needs to investigate the crime scene again and Phil you need to find more about Thirman's team. Ms Gateman and I can talk to our victims again and do some admin. I want to check some of the facts the Deputy has given me."

"I must visit the house and the pound where her car is being kept. I must also go to the bank. I have Power of Attorney over her affairs."

"I would like to take you to the pound and the bank and see if the Girling has vacancies yet. I need some business facilities for us. Will you come? We can collect the car and you will gain some independent transport."

"Thank you. I need to check out Aunt Freya's cat. She is with neighbours. I may have to put her in a cattery or get her rehomed. I will stay at Gracie's but everyone else can move out to the Girling."

"What is wrong with a little luxury?" He decided to put her on the spot. "Or is it the company you dislike?"

Why did this man always have to try to put her in the wrong, make her feel immature and ungrateful when she just wanted to be her own person and make her own way in life? She shrugged, "I just like my own company. Don't take it the wrong way!"

"Why do I think you are hiding something?" he asked, puzzled at her reaction. Why did she always retreat into her shell if he tried to get her on her own? He hadn't made a move on her again. She was this obsessive loner with Phil and him but opened up to Ms Claremont as if the woman was an old friend. Were men the problem?

She retorted resentfully, "Why do you have such a suspicious mind? Just accept that some people want their business to remain private and don't mix well with others." He recognised he had lost the argument. She was like a bloody clam again.

"I don't believe you Ms. Gateman but we will leave this subject for a while."

He settled the bill and took her arm and led her to the Aston, opening the door for her. He drove silently, the atmosphere heavy between them as if waiting for a storm to break out.

What drove this woman's anger, he wondered? It was festering and simmering beneath the surface, waiting to break out if she lost that icy control.

What would make her break her silence and let him behind her barriers? He would leave her alone for a while and then push her buttons and assess her reaction to him. He hated festering wounds. He was a man of action who would burst the infected area and cleanse and purify it.

The bank business was settled efficiently. Phil and Elisabeth would drive the car to Gracies and check it out for any evidence of it being tampered with. The cat was the 'fly in the ointment'. The neighbour who was looking after it needed to visit her ailing mother.

''I have asked around but no-one will take it in Kirsten. They are all dog-loving households and fear mayhem with this feisty beast.'' The beast in question scowled at Kirsten and scratched her with an outstretched paw, claws ready to reject anyone who tried to take her from this woman's arms. Green eyes balefully regarded Kirsten through slitted lids and a hiss made her views clear.

Kirsten said, ''I will have to find a temporary rescue or cattery for her. She will be difficult to rehome. She is a one-person cat and hates other animals. She adored Aunt Freja but rejected me.''

''Give her to me please,'' asked Rutland. He grasped the cat around the scruff of her neck and under her behind, ignoring the evil snarl and hiss and wails that greeted his attempt to hold her still. The cat wriggled and then recognising fighting was futile she went as stiff as a board until he relaxed and then she turned in his grasp and sunk sharp fangs into his hand.

''Shit!'' he exclaimed, holding for dear life to the animal who hissed and tried to escape his arms. He then apologised to the women. Kirsten took her cardigan and wrapped it around the offensive animal Ali Baba style until the cat couldn't move and stared at her angrily.

''Well done. Phil has an assistant who will find a place in a rescue for us.'' He texted Phil and thanking the neighbour he drove them to a pet shop whilst Kirsten struggled to hold the wriggling animal on her lap.

''Bloody feline had better cooperate or she is for the chop,'' he said taking the animal and shoving it into a basket he bought. The animal safely in the basket he relaxed and inspected his wound.

''You need some antiseptic on that.''

''I didn't know you cared Ms Gateman.''

''I will just enjoy watching you squirm when I put it on you,'' she replied. She bought some salve and rubbed it in his wound watching him wince a little.

''Men should be able to take their medicine without flinching,'' she mocked. ''Not used to battle wounds?''

''You are a hard woman Ms Gateman.'' He read a text. ''Phil has found a place for the cat. It is a rescue that asks for donations.''

''If it is local my aunt used to volunteer there. I will send some money. They are always on the point of closing due to lack of funds. Aunt Freya gave her vet services there for free.''

''A decent woman.''

''The best. They won't put a healthy animal down.''

''We will take her there now Phil,'' texted Rutland. ''If the house had been habitable Kirsten could have stayed there and fed her but the police still want it locked up.''

The cat was duly imprisoned in a cage at the rescue and sat sullenly in her new home. Kirsten put a substantial donation in the box which Rutland suspected she couldn't afford. He put his own in but intended hers would be refunded later. Her worn baggage and lowly paid job indicated this flight had taken most of her funds. She was suffering enough already with her aunt at death's door. He didn't intend to let her obstinacy and need for independence cause her to deny herself anything while he was there to help her.

Kirsten received a phone call from the rescue thanking her for persuading Rutland to make a large donation which could keep the establishment in funds for the rest of the year.

''I don't understand,'' she said.

''Oh, didn't Mr Rutland tell you? He told us to keep it secret from the press but he arranged a donation from the animal charity he supports.'' The sum she mentioned gob-smacked Kirsten. She was delighted the charity would carry on but wondered about Reynold's motivation. Was it to impress her?

Rutland rang her to meet him in the lounge. "I am going to see Granddad again. Do you want to come and have a late lunch/afternoon tea afterwards with me?'' She wanted to visit the old couple but the donation had unsettled her. Was his trying to buy his way into her loyalty?

''I would love to visit my aunt and Michael but I am unsure about lunch. I was going to grab one of Gracie's sandwiches in my room.''

''You can hardly compare a sandwich with a lunch at the Girling.''

''Ok, thanks'' she said letting him lead her to the car. She still felt very suffocated in that car so close to him. A powerful man, he drove the machine as if he were one with it, smoothly edging his way through the traffic to the hospital.

Kirsten feared her aunt may have worsened but she was sitting up talking to Michael her voice still hoarse. She looked pale and feeble but kissed Kirsten and hugged her fiercely. "What have you been doing this day, my love?''

''We arranged for the car to be transferred to my name and your cat to be put into Hillfield Rescue. It bit Mr Rutland viciously but is sulking in safety now.''

Kirsten turned around and challenged Rutland to tell the truth. ''Mr Rutland has secured the future of the rescue by donating a large sum Aunt Freya.''

Rutland looked annoyed. ''Damn those loose-mouthed staff.'' He had specifically asked them to say nothing to anyone for two months until the details were tied up and monies put in place. Now it could appear he had donated the money to impress Kirsten. Not so. He was animal mad and wanted to help this town that was helping his Granddad.

''The Defoe Foundation has a small animal charity allied to it that has a little money left over this year and the rescue could benefit from it.''

''A little money. $50,000. Hardly small change!''

''It is to Defoe Holdings. Supporting charities is good PR for an industry like property development that is traditionally unpopular with the public. Every bit of good publicity helps.''

''I hear you have some strays at home Joshua,'' said her aunt, dismayed. Josh was trying to help them but Kirsten appeared hostile to him.

''Yes, a dog and cat looked after by pet walkers. Neither could keep a home due to their bad behaviour but they have settled in after a shaky start. They never will be model pets but are improving when they don't steal or break things.''

Kirsten listened carefully to this. Perhaps his motivations were genuine after all. ''How long has the charity been running?''

''About five years since my cat was run over and a rescue saved it. I set up my own charity that helps rescues that don't put healthy animals down. Too many see euthanasia as an easy solution.'' He turned to her aunt. His ethics were never open to discussion if he could help it. Kirsten could believe him or not.

''Now Ma'am, do you remember anything else that could help us?''

''The only thing Thirman seemed to think was important was asking me if I had met the previous occupants who had lived there. Several times he asked me if I knew who had lived there before as I had known Michael for years before I bought this house. I met him when I stayed with a close friend a few doors away. The occupants were not friendly and I hadn't crossed the threshold until the realtor showed me the house just before I bought it.''

''That might be relevant Ma'am.''

He moved to his Granddad and shut the curtain. Her aunt rounded on her. ''What's up Kirsten? You were almost rude to Josh then. Hardly polite when he is helping us!''

''I don't trust him Aunt Freya. He can buy anything. He thinks everything has its price.''

''I think you are wrong in this case. Josh is an animal lover. He sent some money in the past for his Granddad to kennel some animals temporarily that the rescue couldn't house.''

Josh had had enough. Out of hearing of the old people, he asked sardonically, ''Ready Ms Gateman? That is, if you can bear to take a lift back with a social pariah who buys his way into other people's good books.''

''Certainly,'' she said leading the way to the car. He opened the door and held her arm. ''I don't give a damn what you think of me. I am the only one who judges my actions.'' Pushing her in, he thought, *'you can like it or lump it my girl.'* She had the grace to look shamefaced and sat quietly until they reached the bed and breakfast. She realised now, she only looked for bad things in men instead of looking at their good points. When had she grown to be so suspicious and cynical?

''Dinner is at eight. We need to discuss our progress for the day with Phil and Ms Claremont. Meet me in the lounge please.'' He stalked off. She knocked on Elisabeth's door glum faced.

"What is wrong?''

"I have just bitten the hand that feeds me. Mr Rutland made a $50,000 donation to the rescue that took in Freya's cat. I found out by accident and implied he had done it to impress me; to buy his way into my good books. He is insulted and has gone off in a mood."

"What do you expect when he is generous to a fault and has his generosity thrown back in his face?" She looked exasperated at Kirsten. "Honestly Kirsten, he is filthy rich and can afford to be generous. Phil says he enjoys spreading his money around and you dispute his decency. What more can he do to show you he is a decent guy."

"I don't know. I just cannot trust him. I have met other men who use money to trap a woman and then show a different side to themselves."

"Well make up your mind about him because you are going to hurt him otherwise. Phil says he is genuine. Joshua seems to like you very much even after you have insulted him.'' Kirsten had told her about the incident at the airport. She regarded her colleague who looked unhappy and lost.

"You don't look any happier either. Start over again and give him another chance. He has tried to wipe the slate clean."

"I will try this evening,'' said Kirsten.

'We may enjoy this dinner then!''

The dinner passed quickly. Joshua was quiet and Phil and Elisabeth did most of the talking, briefing them about the state of the houses and the samples that she had sent for examination in an independent lab.

"Little was damaged. The fire was designed to develop as much smoke as possible to kill the occupants and then be put out quickly. The perps must have been desperate or inexperienced to have taken the risk of damaging what they were looking for. The loft is untouched. We may find something of value there that Thirman wanted."

"We start as soon as the Deputy hands over the house to us for a full search. So far he has limited us to looking at the way the fire was started and damage done."

Rutland looked at his watch. He was tired and fed up. Kirsten was pushing him away and rebuffing him; all the trust he had earnt now lost because of that bloody stupid cat and the cheque he had given.

"Let's go up. I need an early night. Tomorrow we may get rooms at the Girling. You may stay here if you prefer your own company Ms Gateman. I can assure you, you will not be missed."

He got up, Phil following, eyebrows raised in question. What had got into his friend? Elisabeth shrugged her shoulders and Kirsten ignored him. They finished their drinks and Kirsten suggested they went to bed after Elisabeth retrieved her cases.

Rutland went for his shower. His cell rang. Coming to it immediately, he slung a towel around his waist, drying his hair with another quickly, his cell rested against his ear.

"Rutland."

"Can you come to my room with Mr. Drakeman please?" asked Kirsten. There was a slight tremor in her voice as if she was uneasy.

"Straight away!"

He threw on a pair of khakis and moved across the landing to Drakeman's room. Hammering on the door he yelled, "Kirsten's room, she needs us urgently." Drakeman opening his door, raised his brows, hearing about her request. Rutland read his mind. *Was she playing some kind of game after rejecting Rutland so forcefully?* Rutland shook his head. He moved to Kirsten's room at top speed, his heart thumping. She was not the sort of woman who would ask for help unless she was in real trouble.

As he knocked on the door it opened. Her eyes wide and pupils darkened she nodded him in. She had a gash on her forehead and a lump developing.

''What's up?" he asked holding her shoulder to comfort her. She was trying to hide it but was trembling. She moved away from him; taking back her personal space.

''I disturbed someone searching my room. When he saw me, he shoved me aside and climbed out the veranda and dropped on to the terrace below."

"What happened to your head?'

'When he shoved me, I fell against the dressing table and banged it"

Rutland burned inside with anger. He could willingly kill the asshole who had hurt and frightened this already upset and vulnerable woman. Usually totally unemotional, strong feelings like these were alien to him and inexplicable. He really must get his emotions under control if he were to investigate this case efficiently. There was no time to waste on anger.

"It is barely noticeable but my papers have been moved," she explained, wanting to get away from the personal topic of her injury and feelings. She did not want to share her feelings with him; to feel his empathy and sympathy. That would mean she felt close to him!

"Were any stolen?"

"None but they could have been photo'd."

"Quite possibly! Was your room searched Ms Claremont?"

"My cases were in the car until I brought them up with me a short while ago. I merely used the lounge and didn't register until you brought me here this evening. No one has had a chance!"

She retrieved her examination bag from her room and wiped Kirsten's forehead with antiseptic wipes and put a Band-Aid on it while Drakeman started to search the room for evidence of a break-in.

Rutland decided, "We will all move to the hotel tomorrow. I've checked, there are rooms spare."

'No arguments!'' he said to Kirsten who was bristling at his authoritarian manner. "We cannot afford to lose any information and someone may try to kidnap you if they think you know something your Aunt Freja told you. Use your head Ms Gateman and help yourself and your aunt.''

''Well as you put it so nicely Mr. Rutland, I will take you up on your charming offer.'' Rutland breathed a sigh of relief. She was being reasonable and logical for a change!

She gave him that look of contempt again as if he were an insect to be trodden on. He lost his patience entirely with her. He had rushed dripping wet from the shower and was uncomfortable, his wet body clinging to his now damp clothes.

For Pity's sake! He was trying to keep her safe. He was giving his time free and paying for Ms Claremont's time and she mocked him. The urge to put her over his knee and discipline her competed with the desire to take her into his arms and kiss her.

As he walked beside her he spoke softly to her, ''One-day Lady you will regret your sassy manner toward me!'' She gave him a haughty stare and tossed her head and walked in front of him.

''Remember payback time is near,'' he threatened as she ignored him. His patience snapped!

''Ms Claremont and Phil, take the Mercedes after you two have examined this room for evidence. We will meet you in the foyer at eight thirty for dinner.''

Holding Kirsten's arm in a steely grip, he manoeuvred her across the landing and into his room. She tried to tug her arm away. His grip was relentless, pushing her in front of him through the door, into the room. It was time he had a reckoning with this lady. *Bloody woman! She would be the death of him!*

Her sassy manner and verbal challenges were winding him up like a tight spring. She raised his blood when she met him stare for stare. He wanted to wipe that sassy smile off her face and kiss her senseless in his bed until her icy control cracked and she admitted she wanted him to take her over and over again!

''I just got out of the shower and need to dry off and change my clothes. Wait for me there,'' he said as he pushed her firmly on a seat. Gracie had given him one of the bigger rooms with a small kitchenette and a couch placed by the window. ''I will drive us in the Aston."

Kirsten did not want to be near this very masculine man. He was wearing his khakis half-buttoned and his feet were bare. His body was still damp, rivulets of water from the shower running down a muscular chest covered with dark hair. His hair was damp and ruffled as if he had pushed it away from his forehead in haste.

He had the determined look of a man who had identified his prey and had set out to trap it; a dangerous man! He pierced her with his emerald green eyes, assessing her. She felt as if she was an insect under a microscope so closely was he regarding her.

Something had changed in the way he watched her. The atmosphere in the room had become thick with sexual tension. Hours before he had behaved gentlemanly, treating her like an acquaintance but now she sensed his manner toward her had changed. There was no longer any pretence. He behaved like a man who had chosen his mate and wanted to secure her for himself.

She sat warily, watching him move about the room with precise careful movements. He dried his torso quickly and tamed his wavy hair. Gloriously masculine, he prowled the room picking up a fresh pair of boxers and smart pants. A quick change of clothes in the bathroom and he moved back to face her.

She drew an intake of breath, wanting to ignore him but she could not take her eyes off him as he pulled on his shirt over a muscled torso. Fully clothed, he maintained a veneer of respectability over that raw masculinity he could not easily disguise.

''Like what you see?'' he questioned, green eyes pinning her in place.

''I have seen other handsome men dressing before. Don't kid yourself you're something special," she bit out. He smiled bitterly. He could see the affect he had on her. She was aroused and interested in his body. A sexual creature, she appreciated a man's torso. What had turned her from a warm passionate creature to this icy imposter inhabiting her body?

Kirsten was tired of battling him. Rutland was one of the most sexually exciting men she had encountered. She shivered when he turned those deep green eyes on her, a hidden promise in them. He was a handsome devil and before she had loved Justin she would have enjoyed flirting and possibly kissing him.

When he called her Kirsten, Rutland's Southern accent sounded like smooth hot chocolate, almost seducing her into making the first move and kissing him. He was sex and sin on legs and he wanted her! He knew she also wanted him but she was too frightened to take up the challenge he presented and risk her health and sanity.

''My lovely Kirsten,'' he said, moving toward her having finished dressing. She moved back toward the kitchenette, not wanting close proximity with him. They moved slowly as if in a dance until he trapped her against the kitchen cupboard and there was no escaping him.

''Payback time is here Kirsten!'' He took her chin in one large hand and stared down into her eyes; such intense blue green pools he could drown in. He lifted her chin and bent down swooping, taking her in his arms, holding her so tight she could not move an inch.

At first, he moved his lips gently over hers, nibbling her lips, enticing her to open her mouth, almost conquering her fear of him. Then, when she succumbed to his touch, his lips became demanding. Her eyes opened wide and her pupils narrowed. Suddenly, his hold felt suffocating and she could not breathe. She felt as cold as ice and her heart lurched in an unpleasant way. Trapped in his arms, all she wanted to do was escape from this strong man who demanded more than she could give.

She pushed him as hard as she could within the constraint of his iron grip. Rutland smiled a smile which did not quite meet his eyes.

''Come Kirsten, this is what you have been wanting from me for ages. Don't play the tease!'' She managed to turn her head from him as he bent his head to kiss her again.

''I am not a tease. Let me go please.''

''Kirsten, you don't know what you want. You make sassy remarks to me, issuing challenges no red-blooded man would ignore and then you withdraw. If that is not a tease, I don't know what is. Be careful when you play with a man or you may get more than you bargain for!''

He pulled her closer, tightening his grip on her again. Panic overwhelmed her. Her heart lurched again; she felt as if she was going to vomit. She felt dizzy; a blackness was engulfing her. She had to escape from him before she fainted and was in his power, helpless!

She pushed him so hard this time he stepped back releasing her. She grabbed behind her: her hands sliding across the work surface until she grasped a kitchen knife and gripped it for all she was worth.

"If you don't leave me alone I will kill you," she said, stabbing forward with the knife, making him jump back. "I don't want anything from you especially your kisses! Men like you just want to dominate, to take and exploit!" she spat at him.

Rutland read hatred and terror in her eyes. She meant what she said! She would stab him without a moment's hesitation. Her eyes narrowed, she stared at him, like a snake watching a mongoose, waiting for the predator to strike. He was her enemy and he had to disarm her before she considered him a threat so deadly she would stab him. There was no rationality or reason in those eyes. She was so consumed by horror she would not think before she struck.

He had underestimated her fear before. This girl had not been teasing him nor deciding whether to be an easy lay. This was a woman who was terrified out of her mind and feared strong dominant men. Impatient and lustful he had ignored the warning signs and played his hand badly instead of waiting to find out what was wrong and earning her trust. She was damaged! He intended to find out who had injured Ms Gateman and hurt the bastard. He could feel her hurting as he stood silently in front of her waiting for her to calm down.

"Put the knife down Kirsten. I will not hurt you or touch you again unless you ask me."

"Move away you lying Bastard," she shouted, loud enough for the occupants of the other rooms to hear her distress, if not understand the words. She would have Gracie up here if she did not calm down.

He had to act quickly before she did either of them some damage. "You don't want to hurt either of us Kirsten." She stared at him; no trust in her eyes, unheeding his words.

"Please put the knife down," he said lowering his voice as he had been trained to do when faced with the enemy. "Please."

He did not take his eyes off hers for a second, trying to keep eye contact with her. Her eyes still stared at him, blankly now, as if she didn't recognise him; as if she were talking to someone else, someone else in her memory. They narrowed; now cold blue like chips of ice and focused again as if something had jerked her back to reality.

That look of hatred speared him as she cried, "Back off."

He moved as if he would back away but a lightning blow from his right hand came under her arm and knocked it, sending the knife spinning into the air to her side. His other arm came around her waist holding her tight until both arms were pinioned behind her, immobilising her.

She screamed in panic, "Please don't hurt me!" He rested her head on his shoulder and with his now free hand he caressed her hair gently, trying to ease her fears. She was still struggling but gradually became passive and stood stone still. His tenderness stunned Kirsten. His kindness overwhelmed her. Where was the macho man who wanted to dominate and subsume her?

For a moment, all Rutland could do was rock her gently. He crooned nonsensical words, and endlessly, soothingly, stroked her hair. Somehow, giving her tenderness, soothing her spirit contented his soul.

For once, giving instead of taking from a woman made him feel good, something he hadn't experienced in a very long time. The cold harsh mercenary relationships he had engaged in had given momentary physical pleasure but had not soothed his lonely soul. He had given little thought to the haunting, less tangible needs of his heart; had buried these since his betrayal by Vanessa.

The door opened and Drakeman and Elisabeth rushed in having heard the screams.

''What's up?'' demanded Drakeman. He saw the knife and took in the scene.

''Ms Claremont, could you comfort Kirsten please,'' asked Rutland reluctantly, wanting to prolong the intimate moment. "A man is not what she needs now.'' He gently pushed her toward the couch and motioned Elisabeth to sit down with her. The other woman put her arms around her and held her while tears streamed down her face.

"In your room, please Philip," said Rutland, not liking the look Drakeman was giving him. He was not a freaking rapist for Pete's sake. All he had done was kiss her, a misjudgement perhaps but not a capital offence. Other women had pretended they were not interested but after a long chase had succumbed to his charms

Elisabeth held Kirsten until she stopped shaking. "It is all right Sweetheart. You are safe now. What did that bastard do to you?''

Kirsten shook her head. 'He only kissed me and I let him for a moment which encouraged him to become more passionate. I panicked when he held me tight.' She shook and started sobbing again. It took her several minutes for the shakes to stop and then she gulped, blew her nose and tried to explain what had happened.

"I asked him to let me go and he called me a tease. He would not let me go until I pushed him back. I was so terrified he would hurt me I threatened him with a knife. He tried to persuade me to put it down but he struck it out of my hand in the end."

"Oh Kirsten, he should have let you go straight away. It is he who was at fault. Don't you blame yourself." Elisabeth regarded her carefully. She still looked as if she were in shock. Her face was drained of colour and a quick movement by Elisabeth made her jump.

This fear of men is not normal. Has she been raped?

"Have you been harmed by a man before Kirsten?"

Kirsten wanted to tell someone, to let the fear drain away, to feel safe again. She replied, "My ex intimidated me and hurt me." Elisabeth hugged her, rocking her until she stopped sobbing and felt safe again.

Sitting down in Rutland's room Drakeman said, "Come on, out with it then! That was not the complaint of a woman suffering maidenly outrage. She was terrified of you. What did you do?'

"I was impatient, a damned fool. I should have waited to find out what her fiancé had done to her. I kissed her and she responded at first but then froze and pushed me away. When she asked me to let her go I called her a tease and held her tighter. You can see the response."

He snarled at his friend, "Don't give me that look. I am not a freaking rapist!'' but he was secretly ashamed of his own behaviour. He thought back to the woman he could still hear sobbing in the other room.

''I think she is terrified of any intimacy with a man and thinks men will hurt her if she responds passionately. Someone has hurt her very badly in the past and I think it was her fiancé. I intend to find out what he did and punish him badly for hurting her.''

''Perhaps Elisabeth can get something out of her. They seem to have connected like friends.''

''In some ways, they are very similar. Kirsten has just developed a shell around her. I am going to ask them if they want dinner out or a carry in.''

Drakeman recognised the signs of a man disgusted with himself, who wanted to do something to keep his mind busy. Rutland might be a player but never a bully or stalker of woman. He was castigating himself.

Under the hard-bitten ex-military man was a sensitive man who had suffered when his father had died and his mother had become an alcoholic and a whore. He had turned wild and bitter and only his gentle but firm grandparents had drawn out a softness that might have been hidden for ever.

In his business dealings, his softness never surfaced but Drakeman had seen it appear when Rutland had financed his philanthropic charities. An old ratty cat or scruffy dog and an orphaned girl brought out an inner glow from him when he was given a lick or a hug. Drakeman believed he was merely waiting for the right woman to unleash his kinder self. He hoped Kirsten might be the one for his friend had fallen hard this time.

Rutland went back to his room. Knocking, he waited for a request to enter, all his arrogance knocked out of him. He felt flat, sick of his behaviour. He was kicking himself. He might have destroyed the only chance he would have with Kirsten. He the great lover, the stud, the man of sophistication, had hit on her like a caveman. He had never experienced such a powerful, overwhelming attraction to a woman. He had let lust cloud his brain. Selfishness and the desire to bed her had made him ignore the signs. The dislike of physical contact, the defensiveness, and the withdrawal into her shell should have convinced him she was not a tease but terrified of men.

Elisabeth pointed to the couch where Kirsten still sat huddled, covered by a comforter.

"Do you still want to eat in the hotel or should I order a carry in?"

Elisabeth went to the couch and held Kirsten's hand. ''Can you manage eating in the restaurant Sweetheart or should we eat in?'' Rutland noted the relaxed relationship she had with Kirsten and wished not for the first time he could talk with such ease to this woman.

Kirsten realised even in her dazed state she needed to move out of Rutland's room and shower. She had frozen cold and then sweated like a pig, her hair now covered and damp with perspiration. She looked and felt a wreck, not fit for company but she had to hold herself together for her aunt's sake.

Rutland stood at the other side of the room, not wanting to distress her again. He still looked larger than life and threatening but now she was thinking rationally she recognised he had never been a threat to her safety. The menace had been in her mind. He had not behaved much worse than other men she had met. Before she had slept with Justin a few other men had hit on her just as hard as Rutland and she had destroyed their advances with a few harsh words and a hard push away.

He was a player, over assertive and domineering but he would have let her go without her having to threaten to stab him if she had not allowed him to kiss her at first and had really asserted herself from the beginning. She was still angry with him for calling her a tease; for denying her the right to choose whether she wanted him or not but she had over-magnified the danger from him.

She had felt threatened and had overreacted. When she got back to London she would have to meet a shrink again. She had not made as much progress psychologically as she had hoped, after the short two months of therapy.

Justin still haunted her and until she came to terms with his brutality and her own sexuality she would not be able to develop a full relationship with a man again. She now felt embarrassed and sickened with herself. If Rutland had come much closer she would have killed him, she had feared him so much.

She had not been able to contemplate letting a man touch or kiss her since Justin. Then Rutland appeared. He had awoken feelings buried deep inside her. Fear of acknowledging those feelings made her defensive and angry. Survival meant rejecting him; ignoring her body's positive reaction to his sensuality and his kiss. In her distorted, terrified mind, kissing him implied giving power to a man over her again, losing her freedom to say no to him. She had reacted like a tortured animal fearing brutality; rational thought processes pushed away. Mindless fear had driven her.

It was time to take herself in hand. She no longer wanted to live in this frozen no-man's land, ignoring the sensations any virile man provoked in her; pretending she wasn't aroused by him. She wanted to be able to enter a relationship with a man; to love and live life to the full. She wanted to share a man's bed without fear of violence or humiliation.

She admitted to herself when she rejected him she was also rejecting a part of herself, because despite her denials she had begun to like him just a little. She had seen the tears welling in his eyes when he had held his Granddad's hand and stroked his head. He had treated her aunt as if she had been gold-dust; paying for her special treatment, making her feel more comfortable and speeding up her recovery. He had rescued her aunt's cat and secured the future of the rescue.

Under that harsh exterior was a gentle and caring man. Exempting his sexual advances to her he had treated her like a gentleman. Even when she had tried to kill him he had merely disarmed her and hugged her. She had misjudged him badly.

He did not understand her history. Despite her mistrust of him she yearned to tell him all. Of her loss, her despair, her confusion and need. Of her rage against life and her anger with men. Would he understand? She could not take the risk. Not all men were like Justin but there were too many out there pretending to care whilst waiting to harm.

"If I can have a half an hour I will shower and dress," she said getting up.

"That's my brave girl," said Rutland surprising both her and Elisabeth. He had seen grown men shake after being injured and tortured. Hard battle worn men turned into shadows of themselves in Afghanistan, after suffering stress from the trauma and shock of continual combat. This girl may not have suffered the ills of war but what had happened to her had left the same traits in her as he had seen in the men who had suffered in battle. It was a testimony to her strength of character that she would still dine with him and go out in public instead of hiding in her room and licking her wounds.

She blushed, discomforted by his kind words. She was not used to gentle words from men; her father and step-father both being men's men and rarely given to making compliments or praise. Criticism and goading a person to achieve harder were their distinctive ways of 'motivation'.

Rutland took a risk now she was no longer sending sharp glances at him. As she passed him he said, "Whatever you have suffered, you should not blame yourself. If any bastard has frightened or hurt you, it is he who is at fault. I am sorry I didn't realise you had been hurt before or I would have moved at a slower pace with you."

Tears flowed down her face again. Elisabeth watched as he took his handkerchief out and gently mopped them away. He put his hand out hesitantly and lightly caressed her hair, barely touching her, waiting for her to pull away from him. Instead she smiled and tried to stand still and bear his touch, showing him, she knew he would not harm her.

"That's my girl," he said softly. "You are much stronger than you think!"

"I will see you both later," she said and walked away leaving him with Elisabeth.

"Did she give you any idea of what has happened to her? Anything Drakeman might follow up?"

"Only the words, 'my fiancé intimidated and hurt me.' I don't think she would have told me that if she had been thinking clearly."

"That is enough," Rutland spat out, his knuckles white, cracking the glass he had picked up; his anger uncontainable now. Elisabeth mopped the blood and tweezered fragments of glass from his hand, rubbing anti-biotic crème in from a compartment in her examination bag.

He breathed deeply. He had to get himself under control. If he had that Justin before him he would squeeze his last breath out of him. The girl Justin had allegedly assaulted had been photographed with a broken arm, busted lip and a black eye. Rutland's stomach had turned over. The girl was slim like Kirsten and fragile. Why had the bastard done this to her and had he touched Kirsten like that?

He hated men who beat women. His father had turned his mother into a woman with no self-esteem. While his father was alive she had tried to hide her bruises from her son, not admitting to him what type of man his father really was. She had looked to other men and the bottle for succour and finally turned to whoring to keep a roof over his head when his father died. Taunted by other kids about her way of keeping a roof above their heads he had blamed her, not understanding how she had suffered until after she had died and his granddad had told him about her suffering.

Chapter seven.

Kirsten washed her hair until it was squeaky clean and for once un-braided it, curling it into waves. She layered make up, covering her red-rimmed eyes with mascara until no-one would recognise the sad woman earlier. She had been shocked when Rutland showed no anger with her and called her 'brave.' She was perplexed. He behaved as if he cared for her after she had stabbed at him. He must be mad!

She picked her clothes out carefully this evening. She didn't want to give him any encouragement to chase her but wanted to appear feminine and relaxed. She also didn't want to feed the gossips with anything they could twist around in this little town. It was bad enough they were staying at the b and b together and Gracie's waitress was a bad gossip, knowing and spreading around everything that went on in this little town.

She always wore casual tees and jeans in her aunt's house like any other woman of her age. She decided to wear a long peasant blouse and flowing skirt with high heeled sandals. Feeling feminine and attractive she met the others in the foyer.

Elisabeth had dressed to kill in four-inch heels and a pant suit with a low necked sweetheart neckline and wide legs. Her hair was up and long loopy amber earrings were hanging from her ears. Her brown eyes looked enormous in her face.

Drakeman looked stunned when she walked down the stairs. She had made an entrance, holding out her hand for him when he took it and kissed it Southern style. Kirsten smiled. At least these two knew what they both wanted and were not afraid to show it. Elisabeth had been a good friend to her, holding her tight while she wept her eyes out. Kirsten wished them happiness.

Rutland held his arm out and she took it. ''Two beautiful ladies, our luck is in tonight,'' he said winking to Drakeman who already had his hand pressed into the small of Elisabeth's back proprietarily, showing to others whose companion she was for that evening.

Elisabeth seemed content with his manner although Kirsten thought he was slightly over-possessive. She preferred Rutland's more formal but less intimate way of walking beside her, his arm engaged under her elbow.

He whispered gently, "You look like a water-nymph tonight or a Lorelei, Kirsten."

"I am not going to send any men to their deaths!" she said, "You are both quite safe," blushing, remembering their episode with the knife.

"My heart may not be," he said gallantly, flirting with her with his eyes. Flirting to him was like breathing. She turned away from him, wary. He was becoming too bold again. She did not know what to say to him. She moved toward the Mercedes. Rutland had changed his plans. She could be discomforted if she went solely with him in his car.

He followed her quickly to the car, looking around him for the men who might still be waiting to finish the search of her room. His military instincts told him she was in danger. He was no longer willing to play games with her; he wanted his relationship with her defined and on the straight and narrow. He could no longer deny his feelings for her. She was no longer an easy lay he would pick up at the airport. He cared for this woman in some indefinable way he could not explain. He would explore those feelings with her later if she could feel the same for him.

She enchanted him, looking like a slim will o' the wisp, a feminine look instead of the 'school mistress' or 'librarian look'. His imagination went overtime thinking of what she would look like if he peeled that blouse back over her creamy shoulders and wound his hands through her wild locks. This was the real Kirsten, not the buttoned up straight-laced woman she had been pretending to be.

Sitting in the dining room listening to the jazz band brought Kirsten's previous life back. Dressed, to kill she would always accompany Justin to his dinners. As well as being a top lawyer he also had his finger in many financial pies, being a director of his late father's business empire. He had always said she looked regal and elegant in evening dress, presenting the perfect image of a financier's future wife; making his business contacts relaxed before he took care of the business details in his killer manner.

She had wanted to please him having fallen in love with him when she was just seventeen. Eight years older than her, he had always been there, a friend of the family, at her home in the holidays and at weekends. Her father had largely ignored her and despised her. She was neither wanted by her mother's new family nor her father's issue from his illicit relationships. A nuisance and an embarrassment to her parents she moved between them, not fitting in and feeling left out by her brothers. Justin had treated her as a friend and she had liked his company when he had paid attention to her.

When she arrived at Cambridge he became her first and only lover; adored by her, until he had started to change, controlling her. At the beginning of her second year he had begun to show his jealous possessive side, demanding to know where she had been and with whom. Young and foolish she had been impressed, thinking his jealousy meant he cared for her a lot. Later, she found it meant something completely different.

Dinner went smoothly, the two men dominating the conversation, ensuring there were no silent uncomfortable gaps. She was surprised they did not turn the conversation solely to sport or cars like other men but engaged in topics both she and Elisabeth might want to contribute to. These were gentlemen and not as self-obsessed as she had thought. The topic of her aunt and his granddad barely come up. Rutland deliberately changed the conversation to lighter topics, determined to put her at ease after he had upset her earlier.

Drakeman thought his friend was falling for the first time for a woman since his ill-fated engagement to Vanessa; a beautiful young associate who had been his fiancé for eighteen months until he had found her in her flat in bed with another partner from a competing firm.

Defensively, she had gone on the attack. ''Í want a man not a machine; a workaholic who only fits me around his work. You cannot give a woman what she wants Joshua, a man who cares for her. Makes her feel his world revolves around her!''

A high pay-off and another post in the competitor's firm had persuaded her to leave and she had married the man she had slept with; her parting comments to Rutland being he was a better lover and was not as devoted to his work as Rutland.

Rutland took the break up hard but developed a harder shell pretending indifference. He had buried himself in his work, much to the distress of Drakeman who thought he was lonely and worked too hard already. In less time than most he built a business and legal empire but Drakeman recently feared he was burning out. He trusted few people and women not at all.

Women were now merely toys to play with. He used escort agencies to provide suitable women for business functions or arrived with the daughters of associates who knew his reputation as a player; a man who wanted no commitment. Other women he met in hotels or bar. Women who accepted jewellery or a weekend away in an exotic resort in return for a short fling suited his needs.

Drakeman was not as wealthy as Rutland but had a more balanced lifestyle and recently predicted Rutland would have a heart attack much earlier than him. Rutland had laughed his prediction off but had great respect for the judgement of his easy-going and less driven friend. Secretly, he had slowed down and had taken his doctor's advice to spend more time at the gym or in the pool instead of in the office.

His trip to his Granddad was the first attempt to create more balance in his life. He admitted to himself he was lonely at times and wanted more time with his friends. He envied those men who had a partner for life, something he had tried to achieve but had failed in his attempt to keep his fiancé happy.

Drakeman looked at the dance floor. He excused himself and went to the restroom but on the way, he tipped the band's leader and a short time later slow music began to be played. This was his opportunity to take Elisabeth in his arms and hold her warm soft body near to him. He wanted to feel those luscious curves and touch that luxurious hair which smelt of vanilla and sandalwood. She did not wear a heavy perfume like many women. She was as fresh as a daisy like Kirsten, the two of them standing out from the crowd.

"Can I entice you on to the floor for a short while? It is still only ten o'clock!' Elisabeth watched his eyes twinkle and a dimple she loved appeared in his cheek. This man not only oozed sex appeal but his charisma left her breathless.

''One short dance then,'' she said hoping she would not regret it later. Kirsten raised her brows but did not intervene. Elisabeth was a grown up. Just because she, Kirsten was a coward with men did not mean Elisabeth couldn't take a risk on a sexy hunk of a man. Let her live her life a little.

Drakeman put his hand possessively on the small of her back and guided her to the floor while Rutland and Kirsten watched them meld together as one and glide across the floor, her head on his shoulder and his head resting on hers.

''I think Ms Claremont has made a conquest,'' said Rutland.

''The feeling seems mutual. They seem made for each other, love at first sight if you believe it exists,'' she said rather embarrassed.

''Don't you believe in it? Some of my friends said it happened to them and I have no reason to disbelieve them.''

''Yes, I believe it exists but only a few people are lucky enough to experience it.''

''Let's hope it lasts for them,'' said Rutland. ''He is a decent guy and would make a good husband and father.'' He changed the subject. ''Would you be offended or frightened if I asked you for one short dance? I think our colleagues intend to dance another after this. They need to be surgically detached from each other.''

Kirsten looked at the other couple who were gazing into each other's eyes dreamily, as if only they existed. The rest of the world was outside of their ambit, so wrapped up in each other were they. Kirsten's eyes misted as she saw Drakeman pull Elisabeth closer to him and gently caress her hair. It was so romantic, like a soppy teenage movie come true.

Rutland reminded her gently where they were. ''They make a wonderful couple,'' he said, still waiting for her answer. She hesitated. He had played the gentlemen during dinner but she still felt uneasy; her heart leaping, her throat dry at the thought of being held tightly by him.

He saw her rejection in her eyes and said wryly, ''Forget it. I am going too fast again. Perhaps tomorrow you may feel more comfortable with me and stop thinking I am the reincarnation of the Boston Strangler.''

''I am sorry I cannot dance intimately with any man while I feel like this.'' She was grateful he was behaving so sensitively although she guessed he was not a naturally patient man.

''Kirsten, who did this to you? Was it your fiancé? That is all I need to know for the present.''

She nodded. "Justin put this fear in me but I can't talk about it to you. I had two months of therapy but I am going to go back for more.''

"I am prepared to wait for you Kirsten," he said to her surprise. Her eyes widened as he took her hand and kissed her fingertips. He had surprised himself. Suddenly, he realised he meant what he had said. This was no pick-up line meant to dupe and seduce a woman into his bed. "You mean much more to me than just a pick up at the airport. Remember that when you are upset with Justin and the world."

"Look,'' he said changing the subject, ''the lovers are returning to our table. Are we ready to go back to the b and b and a good night's sleep?''

Drakeman answered for the couple although sleep was not upper-mind in his head. The thought of Elisabeth in his bed moaning as he made her come obliterated the thought of sleep. ''We are ready but a drink in the lounge would end the night well.''

Rutland had given up the idea of dancing with Kirsten that night. A night of lust filled dreams awaited him. He felt like going skinny dipping in the creek but knew the tale of his swim would be spread around the bars and cafes the next day.

Celebrity status brings more grief than enjoyment, he thought, *in these small hick towns.* He much preferred the anonymity of city-life, never liking gossip about himself and his family. He would be the first to admit he had had more than his share of casual sex and one-night stands and deserved his notoriety but wished he could be given a break when he needed time to himself.

A couple of bourbons for the men and cocktails for the women cemented a pleasant and relaxed evening. Drakeman said, ''I think I will retire for the night. It was a long drive, even in that mean machine.'' He looked at Elisabeth, an open invitation in his eyes.

Elisabeth looked up at him, smiling seductively at him. ''I have several hours work still to do.'' She kissed him on the cheek. To his surprise and chagrin, she said, "Sleep well. I will see you in the morning,'' and turned to Kirsten. "What time are you breakfasting in the morning? I need to be at work by eight.''

Kirsten was amused at the astonished look on the face of the dismissed Drakeman who reluctantly moved to go up to bed.

"Drakeman and I will join you ladies then at breakfast,'' said Rutland. "With his early night, he will have had enough beauty sleep." He would like to hear Drakeman's assessment of the way the night went. He suspected it would be filled with filthy curses.

Elisabeth's eyes followed Drakeman as he went up the stairs. She looked a little sad as if she wasn't sure about her decision.

"Why didn't you sleep with Drakeman?' asked Kirsten. 'I am just curious, you know. You seemed made for each other."

"Because he expected it and I am not so predictable. He thought because I think he is devastatingly attractive I would fall into his arms. He is wrong! He is going to have to work harder than that if he wants me. I doubt few women have rejected him before.''

"Good for you, girl,'' replied Kirsten. ''Both these men are players and can pick their choice of women."

''Oh, Kirsten it was hard to deny him; my stomach twists in knots when he smiles at me.''

''If I was a betting woman I would bet you have the same effect on him. Keep him guessing and he will come chasing you.

'Come on, we have work to do. We are not billionaires like those overgrown kids. We have to work for a living.''

They each went to their own bed, Elisabeth dreaming of a blond-haired man with twinkling blue eyes and Kirsten longing for a peaceful night uninterrupted by nightmares. The recurrence of her nightmares had made her need her sleeping pills again if she wanted to face the Deputy and Rutland after a decent night's sleep.

As they got up a knock came on the front door. Gracie came in and said, ''I am sorry it is late but the Deputy has sent some men here. They want to search your room Kirsten. They have a warrant.'' Kirsten went white, the colour draining from her face.

''Of course, you may search my room Officer but what are you looking for?''

''I am not at liberty to tell you that Ma'am but we will make it as quick as possible.

'Lead on please.''

She unlocked the room. Elisabeth was permitted to watch as witness. It did not take the men long to find what they were looking for. An officer pulled up the mattress and found a plastic bag full of white powder.

''Do you know where this came from?'' he said sniffing it.

''Absolutely not,'' said Kirsten. ''What is it?'' she asked, already knowing the answer. The searcher of her room must have placed the cocaine under her mattress. She had been stitched up! Someone wanted her reputation to be damaged; for her to be put out of the way where she couldn't help her aunt.

''Cocaine Ma'am. Please come with us.''

''Can I pack a small bag please?''

''Certainly Ma'am!'' She packed her haversack and laptop and stood while he read her rights and then cuffed her hands behind her like in some corny American cop show.

Elisabeth was on her cell. ''Mr. Rutland. An officer has arrested Kirsten for possession of cocaine and is taking her to the gaol.''

"What the hell?'' he exploded, imparting a few extra choice expletives while collecting his briefcase and cell. "I will meet you there in a few minutes with Drakeman. God, that girl attracts trouble without trying. Make sure you go with her."

Cursing the Deputy, he asked Gracie to call a taxi. Being prosecuted for drink driving was the last thing he needed. The Deputy was just waiting for him or his team to step out of line and they would jump on him for any tiny misdemeanour. Anything to discredit his case and reputation.

Chapter eight.

The Deputy had the white powder in front of him and had tasted a sample. "Yeah this is the real stuff. Cocaine. What have you got to say for yourself Missy?"

"It is not mine and I don't know how it got there.'' Other than that, she knew to keep her mouth shut. Rutland would get her out of here. She had read about him. She knew his reputation in the courtroom was fierce and uncompromising if his clients were innocent. That determined chin, the blazing eyes, the deep voice, would convince a jury if the evidence was on her side.

Who had framed her though? Thirman or others? The Deputy clearly believed her guilt or was in on the plot to stitch her up. Either way, he made a bad enemy, clearly enjoying presenting the facts of her guilt to her, smirking at her, his piggy eyes not leaving her face for a minute.

''Is that Mr. Rutland representing you?''

''I should imagine so?'' she said. She would not be intimidated by this little creep. After facing off a dominant man like Rutland she could easily handle this depressing little man whose ego was probably bigger than his genitals. She thought of him sitting naked in front of her, a tactic she had used when interviewing dominant macho males in court. It always worked and she could not suppress a giggle which irritated the Deputy beyond imagination.

"What are you laughing at Missy?" he cried angrily. He had expected her to cower before him once he produced the cocaine.

"Nothing important,'' she said. ''Just a joke I heard.'' *'The last laugh will be on you,'* she thought, *once Rutland gets here.* He would make sure his friend destroyed this little Hitler's career. He was the sort who ate mediocre people for breakfast! She was glad he was on her side! She would not like to be on the opposite site of the courtroom to him. She had seen his sort in London courts. Justin was made from the same mould; he had that killer instinct that would screw his opponent to the ground.

Rutland appeared at the door and she breathed a sigh of relief. "Are you alright?'' he asked sharply, not wanting to touch her in front of the Deputy now he would have to represent her.

''Perfectly,'' she said getting down to business. "White powder was found under my mattress.''

He turned to the Deputy, wanting to wipe that smug expression off his fat little face. ''As it was clearly planted there this makes the investigation about her aunt more peculiar. Someone is framing Ms Gateman.''

''Delighted you are here Mr. Rutland,'' the Deputy said with exaggerated Southern courtesy. ''I can tell you the case against Ms Gateman is more serious now. Ms Gateman is going to be charged with conspiracy to murder her aunt and your Granddad and arson now, in addition to possession of cocaine!'' He smiled again, relishing each word as he broke the news to the shocked Rutland.

Rutland kept his cool and looked at Kirsten for answers. She shrugged her shoulders saying, "I am as much in the dark as you are! He just sprung the charge on both of us.''

Rutland took the seat offered to him. He demanded, "The papers please,'' and read the charges outlined and then tossed them over to Kirsten to read. Not bothering to hide his irritation he muttered, ''What utter crap!''

''It may be crap to a big city lawyer like you but murder is an important charge around here, particularly, first degree murder planned in advance.''

''I understand the words intent and intentional,'' snapped Rutland. ''Where's your evidence against Ms Gateman, who is now officially my client?'' He looked at Kirsten who didn't argue. He was the best and she would not reject his help when she was in big trouble.

''Well!'' the Deputy said slowly, deliberately, drawing the suspense out as long as he could. He was enjoying being the star of the show and wanted to make Kirsten wriggle. Kirsten stayed still and listened quietly, impassively; no expression clouding her face. No-one would know she had butterflies dancing in her stomach and she felt sick.

Someone wanted her out of the way for a long time. More than that; they might want her dead if a first-degree murder charge could be proven. She had upset someone badly but the rationale side of her brain told her that the thing the perps had been looking for must be very valuable to put them to all this trouble. She must find out from her aunt what could be of value in her house.

Rutland got straight to work. ''I want her arraignment tomorrow and bail granted for Ms Gateman.''

''Who will stand bail?''

''I will,'' said Drakeman. The Deputy regarded him disdainfully, looking at his old jeans and worn boots. ''It may be high for someone like you!''

Drakeman merely put his business card down on the table and waited for the Deputy's reaction.

''Are you?''

Drakeman interrupted him peremptorily before he could finish his question. *Anal moron!*

'Yes, I am the CEO. Rutland's friend, the Police Chief will vouch for me if you have any reservations although my credit has always been good around here in the past.''

Drakeman's determined set jaw and eyes as cold as pebbles defined a man who would not compromise. His military background shouted out at the officer; the way he stood tight and straight, lips tight, fists clenched; holding in a cold contained anger; ready to erupt at any time at the way the cops had treated this vulnerable woman. He would enjoy watching his friend making this inadequate squirm when they had some evidence to examine. Until then, both would keep their cool even if they wanted to punch his teeth down his insolent throat.

''What evidence have you got to substantiate these charges?'' asked Rutland.

''Witnesses to a conversation between this little lady and another, plotting to burn the house down. She had also sent men to search the house for something but what we don't know yet.''

''So, I am the one who is supposed to have been behind Thirman's intimidation of my aunt? What a load of baloney!''

''Ms Gateman,'' warned Rutland and she subsided. He was right. Silence was her best weapon at this moment although she wanted to punch the Deputy's eyes out. The pathetic prat!

''The evidence?" Rutland repeated. His look could have shrivelled a harder man than the Deputy who nervously bought time by opening and shutting a file on his desk.

''A Mr. Miles Cooper who is in the County Prison. He has sworn he overheard the conversation in a bar three weeks ago.''

''Drakeman?'' said Rutland.

''I am onto it. Do you want to come?'' he asked Elisabeth.

''No thanks.'' She beamed a smile at him, ''But thanks for asking me. I am going to examine fire evidence tomorrow and send more samples off to a lab.'' At least he hadn't taken her rejection of him badly. He had bounced back in his bubbly courteous way.

''Ms Gateman will be enjoying our hospitality this evening,'' said the Deputy, smiling his alligator smile.

''Not for long,'' said Kirsten. ''I have every confidence in my attorney getting me bail tomorrow.''

''A dangerous criminal and a charge of murder and arson. Unlikely I think. While your attorney is looking at the evidence you can spend the time in a nice little cell.''

He got up and took her by the arm, enjoying her discomfort as he slid his paw up her arm, a little too slowly for Rutland's taste. The creep was 'feeling her' up! He contained inside him the desire to punch the fellow's daylights out and contented himself with the knowledge he could have him screaming with just one touch of his fingers in a delicate place. If he was corrupt and they could prove it, he Rutland would enjoy a few private moments with this scum and make him rue the day he 'touched up' Kirsten Gateman.

Kirsten gave him one resigned look and went with the creep where he put her in a cell with other females. ''We only have one cell for ladies,'' he said.

Kirsten would not necessarily have described her all her cell-mates as friendly or companionable or even ladies. One meatier woman wearing tattoos and chewing gum had been charged with aggravated assault and enjoyed flexing her muscles in an intimidating manner near the more fragile Kirsten.

"You got some cigs?'' she demanded towering over Kirsten.

"I don't smoke nor use anything else'' snapped Kirsten.

Another more feminine, prettier girl was accused of soliciting near the hotel and spent the time playing with her cell she had hidden down her F cup bra. A third girl, rake thin and with pale almost bloodless skin was in for substance abuse. She looked so fragile she could be blown over by the wind. Vulnerable and starting to shake from withdrawal symptoms she needed a doctor.

Kirsten wanted to ask for aid for her but she held back. The Deputies were watching her from their desk. They might trump up another charge against her with this girl as witness if she got too close to her.

''What are you in for Lady?'' asked the meatier one.

''Alleged arson, possession of cocaine and conspiring to murder.''

Delia's eyes widened at the mention of murder. Her aggressive and contemptuous manner toward Kirsten slowly changed to respect. She moved back and held herself at a distance from her. Kirsten deliberately raised herself to her full height and stared her in the eyes, challenging her; knowing if she showed fear the woman would take the advantage and try to bully or hurt her.

"Í am going to try to get some sleep now." She lay on the only unoccupied bunk and covered herself with a rough but adequate blanket. She was scared shitless by this bully and pretending to sleep gave her some peace from this woman. The Deputies had deliberately paid no attention to the woman's attempt at intimidating her. She knew she was on her own. She had to look after herself in this hole. The Deputies wanted her frightened and passive, in the right mood to be intimidated when she was questioned by the prosecutor.

Rutland left the office and despite the late hour he went back to the hospital. Freja was awake and could talk more fluently and coherently now. She still gasped and coughed if she spoke too long and the nurse hovered in the corner, ready to move him out if he tired her.

"You have ten minutes and no longer Mr Rutland.".

"Evening Ms. Andersson.''

''Good evening young Man. What are you doing here so late?'' Her eyes held the same wariness as her niece. Was a suspicious nature a family characteristic or had a hard life had made her as cautious as her niece?

''I need to know why Thirman's team wanted your house and were trying to crack your safe.''

''There is nothing of value in my house except for a few valuable jewels and paintings inherited by me from my mother when she died.''

''Think hard Ma'am. There must be something. It may not be tangible but it could be a word or description, even an emblem or a key to something more valuable.''

''Í have nothing of the kind nor heard of anything like that.''

Rutland ground his teeth in despair. If she did have the answer to this puzzle she did not understand its relevance to the mystery. Truth shone from her eyes. She was no dissembler.

He was amazed at the family resemblance. Still quite beautiful in her senior years; he saw an image of what Kirsten would look like in forty-seven years' time. With good genes, she would grow old gracefully and elegantly. He saw an image of himself, walking with her on a beach growing old with her.

He shook his head. This idea was alien to him, the master of no commitment! He usually ran a mile from women who grew too attached to him and she had shown no interest in the long term with him. Any mention of commitment from him and she would run for the hills. He had only known her a few days and he was considering sharing his old age with her. He must be growing soft!

"Perhaps you could think about it for me and contact me on this number if you remember anything.'' She nodded but then asked, ''Where is

Kirsten?''

"At the police station. She is safe.'' He didn't want to upset Freja and damage her recovery. She could wait later to hear the truth when she was stronger.

He moved around the curtain to his Granddad. Michael was recovering more quickly, his burns being fiercer but not having inhaled as much smoke as Freja. Colour was now in his cheeks. He could not shake his Grandson's hand but he smiled and raised his bandaged paw at him.

''Well how far have you got with processing this case?'' he demanded. ''You were a criminal attorney so it should be second nature to you!'' Rutland grimaced. His Granddad always expected more of him than other people did.

''Do your best and do your damnedest,'' was his Granddad's motto. That was how he had pulled himself out of a slum and had worked hard enough to buy his own ranch. He had won the heart of the most beautiful girl in the county and swept her away from under the eyes of her hard-hearted father.

Michael looked at Rutland. He saw a younger image of himself. It was to his chagrin that his grandson had been bitten and hurt hard by that gold-digging, ambitious bitch who wanted a partnership and her lover more than him. He had seen a sensitive and already damaged young man build a barrier around himself and hide from the world outside, developing a hard, icy shell that no woman could penetrate.

He wished his Grandson could find a woman who would love him as deeply as his own wife had done. It would be the making of him and save him from a lonely life devoted to work and making money.

''I am working on it but the Deputy is depriving me of evidence. My own investigator will help me solve the case of the fire if there is any scientific evidence. You would like her. She won't take notice of that snake.''

''He inferred I was senile you know,'' growled the old man indignantly.

''He will regret it later. I intend to have his arse on the line when I am through with this case.''

The old man smiled with satisfaction. Rutland continued. ''I have asked Ms Andersson to try to remember what the perps wanted from her house. Can you think of anything even if it is intangible?''

''I thought we were looking for some papers or a key.''

''I think the clue is more sophisticated than that or they would have found it.''

''What makes you think that?''

''Ms Claremont rang me a few minutes ago to tell me that someone entered the house and searched it again. They were still looking for something.''

''Can she tell that?''

''Without doubt. The dust was disturbed and some dirt off a boot was found by her near some cupboards. The perp seems to have entered the house last night during the cop's break.'' That was another thing he would have the Deputy's hide for. He ran his department loosely. Without Ms Claremont, only God's knows how much evidence would have been ignored or lost.

“How is Kirsten? Her aunt expected to see her here today.”

“She is as well as can be expected. The Deputy is being difficult and questioning her still.”

“She is a good girl. The only one in the family worth talking about. She came here every summer to work the break on her aunt’s ranch. Her aunt paid for the air-fare. Her father wouldn’t or couldn’t pay and Kirsten wanted to get away from her family who neglected her.”

“Does her aunt know anything about a fiancé?

“

You should ask her that! Where Kirsten is concerned Freja plays her cards close to her chest.”

“It is quite important I know Granddad! It may be relevant to the case. I can’t find out information about where she was during the last two months after she left Indonesia and the Deputy is asking where she was during the last six weeks.”

“Ask Freja. She will know. I know the fiancé was a bad lot and hurt and frightened Kirsten. She had to run and hide from him.”

“I will,” said Rutland, satisfied he was near the truth at least. He went back to Freja’s bed knowing she had heard some of their conversation.

“Sit down young man. I heard part of your conversation with your Granddad. Why do you want to know about Kirsten?”

“I think someone has hurt her badly in the past Ma’am and I would like to find out how. So, I may help her.”

She looked at him through hooded narrowed eyes, resembling an old shrewd owl. “What is she to you, young man?” He felt he was back at school being interrogated by his fourth form mistress, so severely did she regard him now.

“I care for her as well Ma’am,” he said, admitting it to another person for the first time.

“In what capacity do you know her?” asked Freja making him wriggle mentally. She was fierce, this old bird, determined to protect her cherished niece from any more danger.

“I met her at the airport and was attracted to her but she disliked me on the spot and rebuffed me. By co-incidence when I came to the hospital I met her again and I have been helping her solve the mystery of the fire.”

“What are your intentions toward my Niece?” she demanded in an old-fashioned way.

Jesus! Her attitude was almost feudal, so protective of her niece was she. He decided honesty was the best policy and tried to appeal to her better nature. He hesitated, not wanting quite yet to admit or commit himself publicly to a relationship with Kirsten. He did not understand the depth of his own feelings yet toward her. He just knew he wanted to protect her from any harm.

“I don’t know yet, Ma’am,” he replied softly. “I know I care for her more deeply than I would a casual female acquaintance but how deep my feelings are yet I don’t know. I will not deliberately hurt her, I promise that!”

She appraised him. His face was an honest if guarded face, severe and serious; too serious even but the face of a decent if secretive man. ''I will help you but if you hurt her I will hang your balls up for breakfast, I promise you that!''

He smiled at her frankness and use of slang inappropriate for a well-brought up lady of her age. He could see what had attracted his Granddad to her. Her bolshie, take no prisoners attitude matched his Granddad's no-nonsense attitude to life.

He wondered if this was the mirror image of Kirsten before she had been hurt by her fiancé. Those flashes of spirit when he smashed that icy calm spelt out a passionate woman ready to be enjoyed by the right man. He was determined to be that man but for how long he did not know.

''I want to help her Ma'am.''

''Then tell me the truth. Why is the Deputy still questioning her?'' He sighed, not much got by this old girl. She was like his Granddad, tenacious to the point of cantankerousness.

''The Deputies searched her room in the b and b and found cocaine. They then accused her of arson and conspiracy to kill you and my Granddad.''

For the first time Freja looked stupefied! ''How did they get those crackbrained ideas in their mutton-brained heads?''

''I think someone is framing her. My money is on the Deputy but why I cannot fathom out yet. Can you?''

''That man has delusions of grandeur. He has his fingers in many business pies.''

''Does he have links with John Thirman?''

''That little rat! I don't know but Thirman is thick with many of the councillors around here. You need to investigate his connections Mr. Rutland''.

''I will do so; you can be sure of that. My mission is to get the charges dropped and Ms Gateman released as soon as possible''.

She took his hand. ''I know she couldn't be in better hands. Your Granddad always speaks highly of your courtroom skills.''

''I hope he has not overrated me Ma'am.''

He moved back to the matter that dominated his mind after the arson case. "What happened to Kirsten, Ma'am?'' he pressed. ''She seems suspicious and terrified of any sexually interested man. She has the look of a woman who fears intimacy with a man.''

Damn the man. He was like a terrier after a ferret, she thought, *unwilling to let go of his prey.* He shared the same characteristics as his bossy, nosy Granddad. She could see how he had frightened off her niece.

He was too much like Justin. Both were dominant focused men and yet she felt she could trust Joshua Rutland. He was not the type of man who needed to control a woman's every action, to prove she loved him. He was too secure emotionally for that. He didn't need to use his fists to prove he was a man either. Kirsten would be safe with him once she trusted him.

"Kirsten was very lonely as a teenager. Forced to leave a very safe private boarding school, she was neglected by an indifferent father who barely gave her a second glance because she was a girl.

'Her mother could not relate to young children and no bond developed between the shy and under-confident Kirsten and her socially conforming mother. She was gauche and clumsy, an embarrassment to her mother, saying the wrong things; too intelligent for her years.

'Her mother buried herself in her books and her teaching and dulled her senses with barbiturates until they divorced and she remarried. Kirsten found herself living with a harsh stepfather who resented her being there but he tolerated her and recognised her aptitude for learning. He paid for her to be tutored to get into Cambridge when her school said she had potential.

'Justin was a friend of both her father and mother. He spent holidays with her father when Kirsten went to see him and later he visited her mother and was treated like the son she had never had. She grew up with him and trusted him.

'When Kirsten was seventeen he started to groom her as a future lover rather than a friend. He was her hero, her knight in shining armour, complimenting and flattering her, unlike her critical mother and father, and she fell in love with him. He also met her on an intellectual level unlike other young men. When she went to Cambridge he became her lover. She thought he was the perfect boyfriend.''

''But you didn't?'' guessed Rutland. She was a good judge of character, this Aunt Freja.

''No, I didn't,'' affirmed Freja. ''He was too smooth and snakey for my liking, always giving the answer, one wanted and expected. Creepy, charming old female clients too much.'' Rutland thought, *he wouldn't be able to charm you!* She was too astute for that.

''I disliked him on sight and he knew it. He tried to get Kirsten to stop visiting me but I invited her here to my home during the holidays to try to break them up. He was too much like my brother, his father's friend, too domineering and wanting always to be right.

'I realised too late he was a misogynist, despising women. He wanted a trophy wife, intelligent but a marionette who would dance to his tune; to be wheeled out and displayed for functions when he wanted to impress clients. She wasn't allowed her own opinions. He began to quash her personality when she finished at Cambridge. He was grooming her to be the perfect lawyer's and financier's wife. He wanted a clever wife who would hostess his dinners and accompany him to legal banquets without boring or embarrassing his associates.

'She loved employment law but he wanted her to move into corporate work like him. He had got her the position and she felt she owed him loyalty for that and changed direction, helping him as his associate. He was tying her more closely to him socially and at work. He controlled her livelihood now as he had been made senior.''

"A web'' Rutland thought out loud.

''Quite right! A silken web, cleverly woven until she had no escape route. He owned her house, controlled her income and job and dictated who she spent her social life with. She began to feel suffocated. Even at Cambridge she had admitted once to me she wanted a wider social life than he would allow her and felt he was trying to get rid of her livelier, more independent female friends.

'He always criticised her flatmates and other friends. Gradually he took over all her spare time, isolating her from them until when she finally left their communal flat she didn't meet them again socially. When she needed friends later she had no-one to turn to.''

''And other men?'' This man was beginning to fit the profile of many abusers he had met in his short career dealing with the criminal law; isolating a woman, making her financially and socially dependent on him and then abusing her physically. This was a general pattern these types of men fitted.

"He started becoming jealous of other men when she went to dances at Cambridge. At first, she was flattered he was jealous. Later she disliked him interrogating her about the men she had danced with when she went out with her friends in the evenings.

'She broke off with him but he cleverly pretended to go out with other women and appeared less possessive and she took him back again. He seemed less possessive and dominating for a few months but when she shared his town-house his possessiveness started again and worsened. It was as if he had been playing a role to get her back again and now he had her he ceased acting that role.''

Rutland began to hate this man with an intensity he could not have believed before he had met Kirsten. He must be a sick, insecure bastard to treat Kirsten like this. He knew there was worse to come and sat quietly waiting for Freja to end her story.

"He gradually began to tighten his grip on her, criticising her dress sense and then her weight, saying she was putting on pounds and was less elegant. Kirsten had always been too thin, living on her nerves as the saying goes but she was filling out as young women do. He hated it, wanting her to remain like a stick insect. He suggested she accompany him each evening after work to the gym. She lost weight but it wasn't enough to please him.

'She visited me and I was shocked at her looks. She looked emaciated and felt guilty eating healthy portions. When I questioned, her she said she felt unhealthy and tired and was going to eat properly and cut the sessions at the gym and stand up to Justin. Her tiredness was affecting her concentration at work and she didn't want to make mistakes. Justin always checked her work thoroughly as her supervisor and made sure errors didn't pass through. He had wanted to set the date for their marriage but she felt uneasy about marrying him as he had changed and she was putting the decision off.

'The situation worsened when she tried to change her line of legal work. He could not cope when she stood up to him and began to have violent rages. She placated him but after that she made efforts to find a new job. She started to go to a new gym during the evenings, without him, where there was a programme there to help women who were suffering from the early stages of anorexia, a condition they thought she might be suffering.

'His violence escalated over the next few months and he physically abused her and she flew to New York where I met her. She stayed in a clinic under an anonymous name, her real name known only to the doctors who treated her. Then she moved to Indonesia where she taught for VSO again under an assumed name. Her friend from uni was the VSO co-ordinator and provided the false identity for her when she arrived there.

'Safe there, she was able to relax and rehabilitate. The men there deferred to her as if she were a qualified teacher, respecting her as a professional. Gradually her self-esteem grew again and her confidence developed until she came back and lived in a hostel for abused women. She took some legal secretary work via the internet and began to earn a living again.''

''I thought she seemed unnecessarily broke for an ex-barrister even in training.''

''Justin made sure her salary went into his account and allowed her only a paltry sum to spend each month. Pin money!'' her aunt spat out; "As if she were a 19th Century woman tied to her husband, his chattel only, servile without any rights.

'She still has to pay her professional course fees. Her father gave her nothing toward her fees and her stepfather thought he had helped her enough so she was reliant on the income Justin allowed her.

'She needs a good barrister's job but is too scared to take one for fear he will find her. After she left the job he came to my house in Florida to trace her. Michael sent him away with a flea in his ear and denied knowledge of where she was.''

Rutland could imagine his Granddad seeing the man off with his favourite shotgun in his hand, a few choice expletives on his sharp tongue, encouraging the younger man to hotfoot it away from Freja's house.

''Can she not get an injunction preventing him from coming near her?''

''She was so tired and sick she didn't get any proof from the hospital or police. He didn't break anything although she feared he would injure her badly which is why she was driven to leave him eventually. It would be her word against his, a respected lawyer and financier. She is scared to take the chance. If the injunction wasn't granted, he could find and really hurt her this time. She is in a no-win situation.''

Rutland had met abused woman in his time as a criminal lawyer and knew their mentality; the way men 'knawed,' at their self-esteem and confidence until it was reduced to the point where they saw themselves as having no value or worth and could not make clear judgements. They were so beaten and undermined, often suffering depression, they could barely think of how to eat, let alone decide to go to court.

He hated thinking of Kirsten in that state and swore he would hurt this Justin very badly. He had to do it without incurring the wrath of the law on himself and his keen mind was already speculating on ways to achieve this goal.

''I will help your niece avoid this man and start a new career if she will let me. I have enough money to help her.''

The old woman looked sceptically at him. ''Kirsten is too proud to accept money from you.''

''Perhaps she can pay me back in kind then. I can let her work in my offices as a legal assistant for a while and she can get some experience of

American law. It will be corporate law at first but I have friends who may provide employment law experience for her later. Believe me, this Justin will not hurt her if I employ her. I will make him too scared to touch her.''

She looked at him. His set mouth and determined chin spelt out a man who would not let any other sway him easily from his goal. His eyes were as cold as emeralds, no feeling in them. He had staked his enemy out and would trap him and punish him.

She realised now Joshua Rutland had deeper feelings for her niece than even he knew and would cherish her and protect her. She was satisfied and hoped Kirsten would recognise he was the kind of man she needed to care for her. Her niece was a calm but passionate woman who had buried her emotions deep to protect herself. That icy barrier she had built could be melted by the right man but he would have to build her trust in him, a task that would be horrendously difficult in her present state of mind. Men were enemies now in her niece's psyche.

She pitied her niece. She was not a shadow of herself but was like a whisper is to a cry, muted and scared to shout out loud for fear of being heard by the enemy. She would stay quiet and anonymous, pretending she didn't exist to the world; unless Joshua Rutland could break through that shell and make her want to proclaim to the world that she was the woman she used to be before Justin tried to destroy her.

''Thank you for trusting me. I now need to work and try to get your niece off these charges. Try to think of anything of value the perps were looking for in your house please.''

To his surprise, she bent toward him and kissed him on the cheek. Her beautiful green blue eyes that reminded him so much of Kirsten looked tenderly at him.

''Keep my girl safe, young man!''

''I will Ma'am. I promise you I will,'' he said, reluctantly leaving her.

Kirsten stood waiting for the judge to come in. Her hands gripped the bar nervously, all colour drained from her face. She had thankfully survived the night without losing any jewellery or suffering an assault by Delia. Rutland had met her at the court and had smiled and gently squeezed her arm to give her support. He had little of hope of getting her bail with the present presiding judge. His Honour was a supporter of the death penalty. Rutland was trying to get the charges of conspiracy to murder and attempted murder dropped. He would deal with the charge of possession of cocaine once he had shown the other charges had no validity and thought the Deputy would drop it willingly.

He had read the evidence shown him by the Deputy. A convicted criminal had heard Kirsten in a beach café discussing searching her aunt's house. She had agreed more serious methods could be used if the old woman did not cooperate. John Thirman's name was mentioned. It would seem to an outsider that Thirman was being employed by Kirsten or was an accomplice in the conspiracy charge.

No-one could put a finger on the reason the house was being searched and what the searcher was looking for. Thirman had been questioned about his interest in the house because Freja had told others of her fear of him and of his intimidating tactics. He had said he merely liked the house, it being old and having unusual architectural features. After all he was a property investor. He had offered well above the usual price of such a house because of its unique features which he would willingly explain to the law officers if he could show them around it. He also said he had met Kirsten several times before.

Rutland wondered if he was being paid to do time alongside Kirsten. Was there someone who would pay enough to the man for him to sacrifice several years of his life in prison? What was so important or valuable in this house that they wanted to sacrifice Thirman and Kirsten?

The court attendants stood for the judge and Rutland breathed a sigh of relief. It was not Judge Cope, the religious doctrinal judge he was expecting. Judge Green was a much more malleable and reasonable man, not a weak man or a fool but one who would listen to a rational argument. He had met Rutland before at Josh's Granddad's ranch and knew his reputation as a straight talker and one of the most honest attorneys in Miami. Kirsten was lucky for once.

The judge looked through the evidence after prosecuting counsel and Rutland had made their cases.

''So far there is enough evidence for Ms Gateman to be brought before a future court. I set the first hearing in two weeks' time.'' Kirsten's face fell but it was what she and Rutland were expecting. He turned to Rutland and said, ''Now Mr. Rutland what else are you petitioning for?''

''Bail your Honour for Ms Gateman. She has no criminal record, an impeccable legal career as a barrister for three years and has done eighteen months VSO. There is no real evidence to connect her with this crime, just hearsay.''

''Prosecuting counsel thinks he has evidence connecting her with the arsonists and a man who Ms Andersson claims was threatening and intimidating her.''

''Ms Gateman denies any connection with this man and claims she can prove it if she is given the opportunity.''

''Conspiracy to murder, attempted murder and arson are serious crimes. Possession of cocaine as well.''

''We think the latter was planted in her room to make the authorities suspicious of her and to distract them from the real criminals, your Honour.''

''Who is prepared to stand bail and ensure this young woman will not bolt?''

''Mr. Philip Drakeman your Honour. He is prepared to stand bail and Ms Gateman will stay in the hotel suite with him. He as you know is trained in guarding criminals as he worked for the FBI. Ms Gateman will not be able to leave her room without passing through his.''

Drakeman's reputation was well known to Judge Green. ''It is rare to allow such a defendant bail but Mr. Drakeman is a man of integrity. You are lucky Ms Gateman to have such a distinguished man stand bail for you. Bail is granted. $750,000.''

Kirsten gasped at the sum but Rutland merely said, ''Thank you your

Honour,'' and guided her to the car where he would start his questioning of her. Nothing added up yet and she had better start cooperating with him or she would end up in the gaol again. She must know something she was hiding from him. So far it looked black for Kirsten and until Drakeman arrived back he could not easily clear her name.

True to form Rutland wasted little time on small talk. "There are photos of you in a café talking to a man who the authorities claim was involved in the arson attack and the search of your aunt's property. You were also overheard conspiring with Thirman to intimidate your aunt. We will look at the photos back at the hotel. What are your answers to these charges?''

''I have never spoken to Thirman nor conspired with anyone at any beach café to hurt or frighten my aunt. It must be a case of mistaken identity.''

''Can you prove where you were during the last two years?''

''Absolutely!''

''Did you leave Indonesia for any period?''

''No, but I came home a month early to investigate John Thirman. The island was hit by a storm and floods and the internet connection was too weak at the VSO office.''

''Damn. They may be able to pin something on you if the dates fit. I suspect they know the dates you left Indonesia if they are determined to frame you. What were you doing investigating Thirman?''

''I was trying to find out if he had any criminal connections or reasons for wanting my aunt's house. I didn't find anything I thought relevant but the things we know now may shed a new light on what I found.''

''Copy it to me please when we get to the hotel. I managed to get your laptop back for two days to look at. I will look through your cell records as well. The cops have copied them for me after I twisted their wrists.''

''What about the cocaine charge?''

He shrugged. ''I can't do too much about that. I suspect the court will drop it if the other charges are dropped. We will work in the lounge next to Drakeman's room. As we promised neither I nor Drakeman will let you out of our sight unless you are in your bedroom.''

''I would like to help you do some research. I feel helpless at the moment.''

''Fine,'' he said but still looked harsh and worried. ''At last!'' he said getting to the hotel and taking her arm, he guided her to the restaurant. ''Food?''

''Oh please, I had only some damp cornflakes and milk this morning and a greasy burger and chips the night before.''

''You should be glad you had something,'' he snapped tersely. ''In your situation, you could be in the County Prison now if the judge hadn't been substituted and granted you bail.''

''I am grateful for Mr. Drakeman's promise to stand bail for me.''

''He is a decent man. Make sure you don't let him down by bolting.'' The curt way he said those words spoke volumes. He was beginning to doubt her side of the story.

''Can we see the photos please and the telephone records?'' She wanted to set the record straight.

He sat down on the sofa and threw a package on the table. He seemed reluctant to open it but after a moment's hesitation he tore it open and looked at the contents. He screwed up his face and placed the offending photos on the table side by side.

''Well you seem to be at the first café,'' he said as if resigned to the fact. "That is your face. What do you have to say to these?''

She squinted at the name of the café. ''I have never been to that place. Where is it supposed to be?'' He seemed to be reluctant to tell her. Was he trying to trick her into telling him the name if he thought she was guilty of planning the arson attack?

''You looked very happy and relaxed,'' he said. *I did*, she thought; a woman on holiday and staring into the eyes of a man who was holding her hand. She was also wearing a very revealing bikini kept together by two tiny chains and slips of cloth. Her hair was down around her waist.

Rutland knitted his brows when he looked closely at that photo. ''That wasn't your fiancé, was it?'' he demanded.

''Good God, of course not. Justin was fair and this man is dark haired and swarthy skinned, his opposite in looks. I have never met this man!'' She matched his sceptical stare, stare for stare. The look of contempt on his face chilled her. He did not believe a word she had said. She bit back the tears that threatened to swamp her face. While he believed her, she had had hoped she could prove her innocence but now she feared the worst.

''When am I supposed to have been at this place?'' she demanded.

''It is of little issue if you are in these photos,'' said Rutland, putting them away hastily in the envelope. ''The evidence is pretty damning. You are supposed to be the ill-treated ex-fiancé escaping a brutal man, in hiding and in fear of your life and here you are holding the hands of a man who intended harm to your aunt. The pictures paint a story that will condemn you in court if you can't explain them away.

'This man is a hardened criminal Ms Gateman but you seem very close to him, even intimate!'' He deliberately emphasised the word intimate, as if he detested the very word and had to bite it out.

''I am telling you I didn't meet him. It is not me in that picture. The photos could be doctored.''

''True but to what point?'' he said pinning her with a fierce stare.

''Discrediting me. I must have been getting nearer to the truth than I realised. These men must be more powerful than I thought if they traced me to Indonesia. I believed I had covered up my tracks well.''

''Any information can be bought if one offers enough money. Drakeman can find out anything about anyone if he wants.''

''Oh yes! I remember he did a background check on me for you!'' Rutland's comments during the last few days had shown he knew far more about her than was normal in these circumstances.

''It goes with the territory, Sweetheart.''

Labelling me a potential gold-digger, thought Kirsten. *Cynical bastard!* This man had serious trust issues with women. She bet he knew the contents of her bank account to the nearest penny!

Rutland got up and paced the room, clearly discomforted by the photos and her words. He had the air of a man who was confused and didn't know what to believe. Kirsten squeezed her eyes shut, preventing the tears from welling in her eyes. She felt cold and bereft again, the realisation that his opinion of her meant much more than it should have done. She stupidly wanted this man's approval. She wanted him to believe in her innocence. He was gradually winning her over, persuading her he was a nice guy at heart under that fierce hard womanising exterior.

He heard something and went to the window. ''At last, Drakeman! He may be able to shed some light on this conundrum.''

He smiled. The bastard had borrowed his Aston without permission. He couldn't blame him. The road had little police and it was safe to speed if one picked one's times. Drakeman was giving his valuable time free for his friend and was enjoying the perks. He would still wind him up though and enjoy getting a rise out of him. He had had little time for humour during these last few days. This lovely girl seemed to be up to her neck in trouble and he no longer believed everything she said.

''Please God, Drakeman has some positive news,'' he prayed.

''What have you found? We have photos incriminating Ms Gateman.'

''I interviewed the little weasel in the County Prison. He is in for extortion so his evidence may be easy to discredit.''

Rutland threw the packet of photos at him. Drakeman gave them a cursory glance and said, ''Yeah, these are the same ones he claims to have verified. He says Ms Gateman was there and he overheard a conversation between her and a man called Musquato, a pretty nasty character. I have other photos with Ms Gateman and John Thirman together at a table in another restaurant in another resort.''

''Which resorts and when?'' asked Kirsten.

''Don't answer that,'' said Rutland harshly. Drakeman looked perplexed. ''Why not?''

Kirsten gave Rutland a stare that would have shrivelled a lessor man. ''Because Mr. Rutland thinks I am guilty. You seem no longer interested in my trying to prove my innocence Mr. Rutland.''

''On the contrary. You are digging yourself deeper all the time you talk with me.''

Kirsten didn't understand his reasoning. He was allowing his prejudice against her to cloud his judgement now. She made a snap decision. ''I no longer want you as my attorney Mr. Rutland if you do not believe in my innocence.''

He shrugged his shoulders, as if glad she had made the decision for them both. ''And who is going to pay for a new attorney Ms Gateman? I was working for free as you were well aware.''

''I would have paid you back Mr. Rutland if it took for ever? I have no intention of being indebted to a man like you.''

''I am not interested in the past,'' he snarled. ''I am interested in how you will pay my existing bill and any future attorney?''

''That is my business. You are fired Mr. Rutland. Mr. Drakeman, I will represent myself in the future.''

The atmosphere in the room could have been cut with a knife. Bitter barbs were shot across the room at each other whilst the parties assessed each other. This conflict was doing no good for their cause. Rutland was hurting badly, remembering his fiancée, thinking a woman was making a fool of him again.

In Kirsten's mind, he was preventing her proving her innocence. He was now as guilty as the guys who had framed her. She was desperate!

Drakeman intervened. ''Please Ms Gateman. Joshua is the right man to represent you. You need an experienced attorney at this level and with these counts against you.''

''I am sure you and Ms Claremont can point me in the right direction and I can handle the law. I cannot afford another attorney.''

''I have no desire to represent a cold-blooded murderer and a blatant liar.

'But you are a fool if you don't employ an experienced attorney. You will be decimated in the courtroom no matter how good you were.''

''I don't want your advice Mr. Rutland,'' said Kirsten facing up to him, her shoulders pulled back.

''Go to hell,'' she snapped.

He thought she looked magnificent in her anger, her breasts heaving and breathing heavy and laboured; her eyes flashing bright blue barbs at him. This would be how she would look and feel if he raised her passion in bed!

God, how he wished he could believe her story! Everything so far proved she was guilty and he wouldn't be made a fool of again. He remembered the last time he had been made a fool of; the dirty whispers and unfounded rumours he had heard behind his back. He had sworn no woman would ever trick him again in that way and Kirsten wasn't going to make him break his oath to himself.

Nevertheless, he still wanted her. His desire for her was like a malady, a sickness he could not rid himself of. She was in his blood. The only way he would rid himself of her was to have her in his bed. One day he would have her, even if he had to wait until she was released from prison. Then he would enjoy having her submit to him, admit she had lied to him, but still wanted him as much as he did her.

He could tell she desired and wanted him. It was in her eyes that challenged him and her raised pulse he could almost feel from where he was standing. He grabbed her and pulled her into the next room to the consternation of the other two watching. He did not care.

''Drakeman, butt out! You too Ms Claremont. This is between Ms Gateman and me, isn't it Kirsten?'' he said, shutting the door on them and locking it. He was beyond rational thinking now. His emotions and senses pushed his common sense away. He was only raw male pride, hurt and wanting retribution. Forgetting her fear of men; he merely wanted to punish her for making a fool of him again.

''You dare to challenge me Ms Gateman! Your eyes and body language challenge me and I am taking up the challenge,'' he said, taking her into his arms, holding her so tight she could barely breathe. He felt her freeze again but ignored her rejection. He was past self-control, anger consuming him.

''I am a dangerous man to challenge Kirsten! Be careful you do not bite more off than you can chew! I am no gentleman when I am misled!''

''You pretend you are frightened of men and yet you still let that perp touch you intimately. You are a slut,'' he accused, not knowing what he was saying, so betrayed did he feel by her.

''Don't you dare accuse me of being a liar and a slut! You live by double standards, you hypocrite! You toy with women, bed them, you filthy lecher!'' Goaded beyond endurance, she turned to him and slapped him with the full force of her hand across his face. He grabbed her wrist tightly and immobilised her against his taut and angry body.

She had seen him contemptuous, arrogant, charming but not blazingly angry as he was now. ''That was foolish Ms Gateman,'' he said, softly, menacingly. ''One day I will make you pay for that. You will demand I take you over and over in my bed.'' He kissed her hard.

He said testily, ''If I had not represented you I would be taking much more than a kiss and you would not prevent me. You want me as much as I want you, my seductive little liar.''

''To hell with you!'' she said but didn't try to break free. It was useless fighting him. She tried to regain her dignity. He gave her one more kiss as she remained passive. He said, resigned. ''For my sins, I still care about you Ms Gateman even if you are a damned liar. I will make sure you get a good attorney.''

Then disgusted with her, he released her so suddenly she fell against the wall. She had not felt afraid this time he had held her. She knew he would not hurt her physically. He was too much of a man to beat a woman, even if she had provoked him. Instead, she was furious with him, a much healthier emotion. How dare he insult her? Yet despite her anger, she recognised a man whose self-control was being tested to the limit. He was so eaten up with anger he burned inside.

He pushed her back through the door to the waiting Elisabeth and Drakeman. ''Drakeman, arrange for an attorney and send me the bill. I will stand the rest as well, as I promised. I am not a liar nor do I break promises Ms Gateman, unlike yourself.''

''Go to the devil!'' She cursed him as he left the room. ''I will not take penny of your money or your help.''

''Enjoy your spell in gaol then Ms Gateman, with other criminals like yourself!'' He walked to his room and grabbed some trunks and a towel and ran down to the pool where he proceeded to make length after length, trying to exorcise her from himself.

Bloody woman, where was the passive Kirsten her fiancé had made of her? She had too much bloody spirit for her own good. He would take no notice of what she said and Drakeman would pay her costs for him and send him the bills. Despite her talent, she would drown under the volume of law she would have to learn in two weeks and one mistake could cost her liberty. With a good attorney, she still might get off.

He still did not want such a beautiful creature to lose her freedom if he could help it despite despising her lack of morals and ethics. Her morals had been eroded by a vicious and depraved man. He wished he could have met Kirsten Gateman before she had been corrupted by her fiancé. He might have saved her from herself and saved her aunt from the disappointment she would experience in her niece.

Drakeman took Kirsten in his arms This was not the time for formality as she trembled violently and sobbed onto his shoulder. ''You must not judge him harshly. He has had a hard life and bad experiences.''

''He is a hypocritical bastard and judged me and found me wanting before assessing the evidence. Where is his professionalism?''

''He cares too much for you to act rationally. He is always overprotective when a person he cares for is threatened. He will be back once his temper is calmed.''

Drakeman knew if he really cared for Kirsten he would be in the background advising her new attorney, distancing himself; scared of showing he cared too much for this lovely girl; fearful of being hurt again by a dishonest woman, but wanting to be proven wrong about her guilt. Rutland was frightened for the first time he was going to lose a woman he really cared for and it scared him rigid. He had believed he loved his fiancé but that had been an infatuation compared to the way he now reacted to Kirsten's alleged betrayal. The sensitive man was responding in the only way he knew, retreating into his shell where no-one could hurt him.

He looked out the window hearing a splash and saw Rutland spearing the water and then coming up, carving through the water, emptying the pool of more amateur swimmers. He would swim now until he had regained his usual calm and could talk without anger.

''Let's look at the photos again. Ms Claremont and I might find something which can help us.'' He sat her down and perused the photos, knitting his brow. ''Ms Claremont, cast your scientific eye over these and tell me what you make of these.''

Kirsten said, 'It could not be me. I am wearing a bikini. I haven't been able to wear one for over twenty months. That is why I wanted to know when it had been taken. I had a birth mark removed two years ago, and it isn't there in the photos.''

''It could have been covered by professional makeup.'' said Elisabeth. ''Sorry Kirsten, it isn't enough to prove the date of those photos.''

''This will be!'' said Kirsten and opened the ribbon of the peasant blouse. This was no longer the time for modesty. She peeled the loose blouse off her shoulder to reveal deep weals, no longer red but standing out from the skin. Elisabeth drew a gasp of breath.

''Cover yourself up now Ms Gateman,'' said Drakeman. ''Where else are the weals?''

''Over my back, down to my waist. My fiancé whipped me a week before I left him. I had these looked at in New York at the rehabilitation clinic. The doctor will verify how old the scars are. I could not be the person in that photo if they were taken in the last twenty months.''

''I believe you and so will the judge. We now must destroy the evidence about the conversation,'' he said, happy at last he had something he could work with.

''I think the photos could have been doctored,'' said Elisabeth. ''If these are sent to the FBI or police lab we could find out for sure.''

''It is time you flew them out,'' said Drakeman. ''I would not trust them to the cops' courier!''

''I will book my flight,'' said Elisabeth. ''Go to bed Kirsten. You have had a hell of a night and day!''

Kirsten dragged herself to bed and fell asleep immediately. Elisabeth looked in at her and observed her sleeping deeply.

''She is looking better now. When will we tell Rutland about the evidence?''

''Let him stew a while. It is unlike him to act irrationally. He will be ashamed of himself when he finds out the truth. He really cares about the girl. I haven't seen him so interested in a woman in years.''

''Will you find a good attorney?''

''Not as good as him but he will not desert her. He will be interfering, giving any young attorney unwanted advice. I know Rutland. Now he has got his teeth in Kirsten's case he will not let it go, especially when I tell him the new evidence. We must compare the dates tomorrow when she has had some sleep.''

He turned to her and said, ''And now my love I want to complete our unfinished business we left the other night.'' He took her chin in his hand and gently kissed her until she responded with as much passion as him, putting her arms around his neck and pulling him closer to him. His kindness to Kirsten and his integrity was gradually winning her over. A player he might be but he was a caring man whose company she wanted to share that evening while Kirsten slept.

Her flight was arranged for two hours later and they ate a light dinner in the room, holding each other tightly, talking quietly about nonsensical things until she had to leave. They still had not slept together but she had felt intimate already with this man and the headiness of their still young relationship was enticing her, seducing her into his web. When she got back from the lab she would decide if she wanted to bed this seductive man and consolidate their relationship further. She rather thought she might!

Rutland came out of the water. Kirsten thought, *he was like Mars; a dark avenging God, angry at the world.* In this case, however he was just angry with her.

He climbed out and towelling himself dry he looked up and saw her watching him. He raised his eyebrows at her but she refused to remove her glance from him. She would not allow him to intimidate her. He was in the wrong and would find out later!

She enjoyed watching him pull on his robe, flexing his muscles as he shrugged it on. She had felt how strong he was when he had held her tight. As she fought against that massive chest, she had felt small and fragile for a change, instead of the unfeminine Amazon Justin had cruelly described her.

Before, when Rutland had stroked her hair, and soothed her, conquering her fear of him, she had felt cherished by him; a feeling no other man had engendered in her. The males in her family had instigated feelings of powerlessness and inadequacy in her. A double first at Cambridge had been shrugged off as merely acceptable in her family. She had continually striven to excel, to prove herself to her males. Justin had originally flattered her into his bed but later cruelly demeaned her.

''Why did men have to prove themselves worthy by demeaning women,'' she asked herself?

It was her luck the man who raised her blood and had made her feel cherished was now the one who had called her a liar and a slut. Drakeman said to ignore him. He had suffered a hard life in the past and she wondered what he had meant by that and how it had framed the hard, severe man she now knew.

Rutland waved mockingly at her and went in to the hotel. She had wound him up again by looking at him and his adrenalin was pouring through his veins. He saw the receptionist who had encouraged him the first day in town. A soft needy woman was what he needed that night to take his mind off ravishing Kirsten. This girl would do if she was not engaged that evening.

She looked up from the computer she was working on and smiled, her eyes wide and opening, her lashes fluttering. This babe would suit him for the night, no complications, just hot sweaty energetic sex! She wore her uniform with a distinctive style, buttons opened just enough to hide her mystery but to encourage another look at the strategically placed pendant which slid between her breasts.

''Mr. Rutland. What can I do you for you?'' she asked, nibbling her bottom lip and running her tongue over her lips suggestively. *She could take tips for being less obvious*, he thought, thinking of Kirsten who could attract a man just by looking at him, needing no special tricks or artefacts.

''Damn it!'' he cursed himself. This girl was generously offering herself on a plate to him and he was criticising her, comparing her unfavourably with Kirsten. When would he rid his mind of that infuriating woman?

''I wondered if you are free this evening for dinner.'' He saw her eyes light up with pleasure and expectation. ''Certainly,'' she purred. ''I lodge in the hotel. Do you wish to dine here?''

''Might as well,'' he said unenthusiastically.

''It has the best cuisine in town,'' she added, appearing not to understand his indifference.

I had better stop acting the self-absorbed bastard. It was not her fault he was missing Kirsten's company already.

''That would be perfect. No driving and drinking. Reserve a table for us about eight o'clock, please. Shall I meet you in the foyer?''

''Sure. The band is very good as well.''

''I was here the second night of my arrival and experienced the music." He picked up his key and said, "See you this evening Ms?''

''De Vere. Danielle Kathleen De Vere,'' she stated, enunciating the syllables slowly and carefully. She matched her name; a slightly pretentious old Southern name, glamorous and with high expectations for a lowly qualified receptionist in a hick town. He hoped he would live up to her anticipation and give her a very good night.

He met her in the foyer. She dressed tastefully and he led her to the best table in the restaurant. She picked the most expensive dishes on the menu and talked garrulously about celebrities, giving him a headache. He reminded himself he was buying her dinner for her accomplishments in the bedroom not her conversational skills. He rarely found a bed partner on his intellectual level but it had not bothered him in the past at all as the liaisons rarely lasted more than a week.

''Can we dance?'' she asked. Rutland wanted to get to the main point of his evening, the bedroom but reluctantly took her on to the floor, grateful she no longer talked about the winner of the latest inane, reality talent show. She smiled, resting her head on his shoulder, inviting greater intimacy with her. Rutland felt uncomfortable with the intimacy but played along, dancing several dances until he whispered, ''I have a bottle of champagne ordered in my suite. Shall we go up now?''

She looked a little disappointed but he put his hand in his pocket and took out a small package and said, ''We can open your present upstairs if you want.'' Her eyes widened greedily and she moved faster than one could spin to the lift and up to his suite.

He opened the champagne while she opened the small jewel case. He always carried small presents of jewellery in case he met a woman he wanted to date and leave without any ties.

''It is beautiful,'' she said and turned around for him to put it around her neck. He loosened her mane of ebony hair letting it fall around her shoulders. He kissed her neck and undid her zip, letting her dress fall like a pool of silk around her feet.

Braless and wearing a thong she quickly disposed of her garments and it took only a moment before they reached the bed. He kissed her from her neck to the bottom of her spine where he found a tiny blackberry birthmark.

A few minutes later she was lying under him gasping and panting as he thrust deeply into her. She was a passionate woman, lithe but well-developed in all the right places and knew how to pleasure a man. Sated afterwards, he felt calmer but empty inside. He wanted more but didn't know or wouldn't admit to himself what he lacked.

Waking early in the morning he saw she still slept beside him. It had been a mistake to bring her back to his room when he wanted to leave early to go back to Miami. He had this awful feeling she expected to stay with him the weekend as it was her weekend off work. He would have to break his early departure gently to her. Taking his trunks, he went to the pool and whiled away an hour swimming lengths, giving her time to wake up.

Moving up to his room, he saw it was eight o'clock and she was still asleep. He should have left by now. He stroked her cheek gently and whispered, "Hi Beautiful, we have to wake up and breakfast. I must drive back to Miami this morning." Two sleepy blue eyes opened and looked blearily at him.

"So soon?" she asked. "I thought you were here for the court case of that murderer. She is heading for the needle you know!"

He scowled at her. He might doubt Kirsten's innocence but he disliked hearing this dim girl refer to her in that disparaging way. He no longer felt tolerant of her. "Alleged murderer. Her guilt is not proven yet. And I am no longer her attorney. Stop gossiping about her or you could lose your position." She sulked and said, "I didn't mean any harm."

He picked up the menu. No longer did he want her to accompany him in a public restaurant. She had served her purpose last night but now in his ruthless way he wanted rid of her, out of his suite.

"Choose your breakfast while I shower and then it will be your turn."

"I prefer a bath," she said ticking the menu boxes.

"I must leave in forty-five minutes Darlin. We drank too much last night and we overslept. Shower quickly, please!" She gave him a black look, he was no gentleman; but dressed quickly, by which time the food and beverages had arrived.

They ate in silence and picking up his cases and her jacket he led her to the door. Deciding to placate her a little he asked, "If I am here again, will I be able to contact you in the hotel so we can be together for longer?" The girl looked wary as if she didn't expect or want to meet him again but shrugging her shoulders she said airily, "I should be here but I may be moving to a bigger city."

He kissed her cheek and said, "I wish you luck. With your looks and manner, you will do very well somewhere more sophisticated." He gave her his business card. It was not her fault he was in a lousy mood and he was a bastard taking it out on her.

"If you want contacts in the hotels in Miami give me a ring and I will organise some meetings for you." She entangled her arms around his neck and kissed him full on the lips, a little mollified.

"Thank you for the dinner and the present." She then turned away from him and stepped into the lift.

He turned around and saw to his consternation Kirsten and Drakeman who had watched him come out of his room with the delectable but irritating Danielle. If her coming out of his room wasn't enough, her kiss and the thank you for the present told the onlookers their goings on the previous night. Kirsten got into the lift with him and said nothing, leaving the lift before him, turning in the direction of the breakfast room without uttering a word. Contempt was spelt on her face.

"I'll phone you when I reach Miami," he said to Drakeman.

''Goodbye Ms Gateman. I wish you luck with your trial. Mr. Drakeman will keep me informed of your progress.''

''Thank you,'' was all she said and entered the breakfast room.

''You've really screwed it up this time, haven't you?'' said Drakeman to Rutland's surprise and followed her, not giving him time to ask him to explain his remark. It was unlike Drakeman to criticise or condemn him, with his own morals never warranting inspection.

He got into the Aston and gunned the engine, enjoying the feel of the power in his hands. He wanted out of this hick town and its moralistic residents who had watched him on the dance floor last night; clearly condemning his one-night stand with its flighty receptionist.

He drove four hundred miles non-stop, not wanting to talk with anyone and at last dog-tired he stopped to break the journey in a hotel for a meal and a sleep. He stirred very late that afternoon after a restless night, bleary eyed and exhausted. He had woken through the night thinking of Kirsten's plight. He promised himself to try to wipe her from his mind. He didn't chase lost causes.

Unusually despondent, he checked his texts and found one from Drakeman sent hours before. ''Ms Gateman didn't want me to tell you before you left but we have evidence she couldn't have been at that restaurant. Ms Claremont has emailed to tell us the photos have been put through a lab and are thought to be doctored.

'We have enough evidence to show to the court she has been framed. I am working on the phone call and it may be worthwhile interviewing the perp in prison again. He may change his story if we present him with the information that contradicts his evidence.

'Kirsten doesn't want to tell you but the attorney we got at short notice is not up to this work. He is inexperienced and the Deputy's office are running rings around him.''

Rutland read this and groaned. He had been hasty and unprofessional; hurt by the lies he had believed she had told him. He was in two minds but he would go back and eat humble pie. If Kirsten would have him he would finish the case. There were a lot of loose ends needing tying up. Drakeman had named the attorney and he was good but lacked the knowledge to cut through red tape and the reputation and power to bully the Deputy. Kirsten needed an older more experienced attorney; she needed him!

He now regretted the night with the delectable Danielle. That night would haunt him in the future if Kirsten didn't forgive him. Danielle was like sugary syrupy molasses, wrapping him in a warm comfortable cocoon. Bored and feeling suffocated he missed the biting comments from the sharper minded acerbic Kirsten. She intrigued him and would never bore him.

He ate his meal and turned the car around and the Aston ate tarmac back to the hotel. He was wiped out. His night of swimming and vigorous sex and then a day burning up tarmac had exhausted him. He must be getting soft or growing old.

Drakeman heard the roar of the Aston in the car park and saw Rutland wearily haul his ass in again. He believed Rutland would have persuaded

Kirsten to enter his bed within the week were it not for the case and Kirsten's fear of dominant men. They had been like moths drawn to a flame, each watching each other when the other wasn't looking.

Rutland entered the Drakeman's hotel suite, where he saw Kirsten and Drakeman reading documents.

''What you do want?'' asked Kirsten.

''To help.''

''I have an attorney.''

''But not up to scratch, I have heard.''

Kirsten directed an angry look at Drakeman who merely shrugged. His shoulders were broad enough to stand a tirade from Kirsten if it meant she was proven innocent.

Rutland went to Kirsten who drew back a few steps. He stood in front of her, intimidating her with just his presence, he was such a forceful man. He spoke softly, stroking her cheek gently; no longer the harsh man who had accused her so recently. She backed off, distancing herself emotionally and physically from him.

He could no more resist touching her than he could have driven back straight back to Miami without helping her. He was 'surgically' linked to this woman. Something drew him back to her, some indefinable string which tugged him; made him want to become closer to her physically and emotionally.

''Face it, Sweetheart, you need me. I can wrap this up quickly and get you back to London.''

''No thanks!''

''I hear there is other evidence which proves you could not have been in the restaurant,'' he said. ''Can I see it?''

''No,'' said Kirsten but Drakeman thought this facing off had gone on long enough and was not getting them anywhere.

He intervened. ''It is on the cell,'' he said, showing him the photos he had taken of Kirsten.' 'She cannot wear a bikini now. We are having professional photos taken by police photographers but the judge has seen these and is convinced she has been framed.'

Rutland stood completely silent, reading the pages until he cried, ''Christ! I will kill the man who did this to you!'' His face was impassive but he was boiling over inside.

''You will be queuing up behind me,'' said Drakeman. ''Fancy a trip to London?''

''When you two have finished deciding to do justice for me perhaps you would stop interfering in my life. I will deal with Justin in my own way.''

''What do we concentrate on next?'' asked Rutland, ignoring her interruption. He had wasted a day of investigation. Their backs were against the wall and he needed all the information quickly before the trail grew cold.

''The phone messages and the perp's connection with Thirman. Want to come with me to the County Prison and destroy the scum's story?''

''Delighted,'' said Rutland, ''after I have a good night's sleep.''

''Wore yourself out, did you?'' asked Kirsten sarcastically, unable to contain herself.

''Jealous, were you?'' countered Rutland.

''Of what. A bimbo!'' cried Kirsten. ''You live in hope. I thought you would have better taste!''

''I wasn't after her brains, Sweetheart! She had ample of what I wanted and was very skilled as well.'' He liked this new passionate Kirsten. He wanted rid of the detached calm creature he had met in the past.

''You are just a lecherous inconstant bastard and a hypocrite calling me a slut.'' In truth, she had never felt so sick as when that woman had kissed him in the corridor. Her stomach had wrenched and she had wanted to punch her for touching him. Never had she felt such jealousy. Justin had always been the possessive, jealous one in their relationship.

''And you talk too much,'' he said grabbing her. "Phil, I would like a word in private with Ms Gateman."

''Please don't go Mr. Drakeman!'' pleaded Kirsten.

''I think I will make a bad third in this conversation. Five minutes only Joshua!'' The expression on his face and his hard eyes warned Rutland if he hurt Kirsten in any way he would deal with him himself. He had become fond of her, not in the way he felt for his lovely Elisabeth but in a friendly way. He felt almost as protective of her as Rutland did.

''Traitor,'' she uttered, still unable to move out of Rutland's grip, trying to push him away; trying to release herself.

He turned her to him. ''Listen to me for a few minutes. I apologise. I was hurt and felt betrayed and was unbelievably jealous of that man in that photo touching you. I take my words back. You are not a liar nor a slut. You are brave and honest and caring.''

She was taken aback. An apology from this confident, arrogant man, full of self-assurance meant a lot. He would not easily apologise to anyone especially a woman. It would be ungracious to refuse to accept his apology and bad mannered.

''Thank you. I accept your apology.''

''Will you let me help you?''

She hesitated but knew he was the best and she needed him! She must act rationally. She was not a schoolgirl! She had to control her own behaviour. This man had to merely order her about and her hackles rose. She rebelled like an adolescent cheeking her father. He brought out the worst in her!

Even Justin had not made her want to butt heads with him like she did with Rutland. It was if she was trying not only to save her independence but also her soul from him. If she gave in to him and let him know how he made her feel she would be lost to him. He reached something deep inside her that no other person had touched. She feared finding out how she could feel if she let him delve farther.

She set her conditions. ''Yes, but no more touching me and kissing me. Our relationship is purely professional.''

''Until the case is solved Ms Gateman, after that I cannot promise to leave you alone.''

''After that I will be back in London and you will be in Miami. Our paths will never cross again.''

''Don't be too sure about that Kirsten,'' said Rutland confidently. He wanted Kirsten Gateman and he usually got what he wanted.

''Damn you, don't you ever take no for an answer?''

''Rarely Sweetheart.''

''You are an arrogant bastard,'' she snapped, not mincing her words.

''I prefer the description confident,'' He asked Drakeman back in.

''One part of the puzzle Ms Gateman can try to work out is what the perps were looking for in her house. I don't think it is tangible as it hasn't been found yet.''

''Only two rooms were totalled,'' said Drakeman, ''we can go back and search again.''

''I would like to talk with Aunt Freja.''

''I will take you today,'' said Drakeman ''While Rutland works with the Deputy's office. Ms Claremont will be back very soon. She is worth her weight in gold having sorted the photos and verified the type of accelerant used and about the time the house was fired.''

After lunch Drakeman took her to her aunt. He sat with Michael Defoe asking him similar questions. Her aunt was totally lucid, no longer on pain control but she was still not out of the woods.

The nurse had taken them aside. ''Your aunt is not recovering as well as we hoped Kirsten. Pneumonia has set in. The next few days may be critical. The smoke inhalation damaged her lungs badly. Don't tire her too much with too many questions.''

She decided to make the questioning quick. ''Aunt Freja, the men must have been after something. Can you think of anything about the house that makes it valuable to an outsider? Did anyone famous or unusual live there?''

Aunt Freja looked puzzled. "Only a criminal who was found to be money laundering twenty years ago. He was involved in many criminal activities and there was a suggestion he had been involved in a gold bullion hoist."

"Was the bullion ever found Aunt Freja?"

"No.''

"That could be it!" she cried, enthusiastic at last. The days had drawn her energy, especially fighting Rutland, when they should have been working together. She had slept badly and dark shadows under her eyes made her look even more gaunt and thinner than before. She was eating better though, filling up on the calorie loaded Southern food. *To hell with a diet!* She was no longer with Justin.

Rutland said he liked a woman who enjoyed her food. She must try to stop comparing him with Justin. In her quiet moments, she acknowledged to herself Rutland always came out the winner in the comparisons of the two men. He might be obnoxiously domineering in his quiet way but he was more generous than Justin with his money, his time and his compliments, building up her self-confidence. If he didn't boss her about so much she could tolerate him but he could be so over-bearing.

''We now have to find the clue to where it is and the name of the criminal who went to prison.''

''It was Karl Grenman,'' said Michael from behind the curtain. Drakeman jumped up. ''I am phoning Rutland now with that name.''

''He was a merchant banker, a quiet man, a loner who kept himself to himself. Very few people knew anything about him which is probably why it took the authorities so long to link him with the crimes around here.''

''How long ago did this happen?'

'The bullion hoist about twenty years ago, but the other activities he was gaoled for, only ten years.''

''I will put this guy's name through the computer and we will dig up what we can about him. I am sure he is the answer to this puzzle.''

He observed the tired lines around the old lady's face. This interview was taking all her strength. She needed some peace and quiet. Her inner strength and fortitude made him forget that she had only just escaped death a few days ago.

''Ms Andersson, rest now please but think about this man tonight. Try to remember any peculiarities about him? Like his having unusual hobbies he could hide the clue in?''

He shook her hand and left her to sleep, her eyes already closing as he left the room with Kirsten.

''I think we are getting somewhere now. We must link Thirman and the other perp with this man.''

''My aunt is sharp. She will remember something if there is anything to find out.''

''She is like Michael. They make a good pair.''

''When I saw them first together I knew they suited each other; they are both as individualistic and cantankerous as each other.''

Like you and Joshua. They had both become quiet and fiercely independent loners who had pushed most people away; only allowing a very few trusted friends and relatives to pierce that armour they both wore.

"You can talk with her tomorrow while we men go to the prison to frighten the perp who said he overheard you in the restaurant.''

''You think you stand a chance?''

''I think put two ex-SEALS next to the weedy little creep and show him our evidence and he may change his story pretty quickly. The problem will be keeping Rutland under control. He is usually like a machine but you seem to have uncovered his emotional side. He really cares for you, you know.''

''He seemed to find succour in that lady pretty quickly.''

''She had come on strong to him since the first day and he was trying to forget you. I would probably have done the same to rid myself of your memory if I had felt betrayed by you.''

''Why Mr. Drakeman? Why should he have felt betrayed by me?''

''He was paying for your hotel, your aunt's treatment, for Ms Claremont's work and he gave his own time free. He thought you were lying and using him.

'It happened once before when a girl became engaged to him for the purposes of him gaining her a partnership in his firm. And earlier in the Navy he found his girlfriend in bed with another man. She admitted she would have married him for the security and his pension but she still loved her man and would have carried on the affair with him. It distorted his view of women for years. He thinks most women are after his money or are attracted by his power and lifestyle and he is usually right."

Kirsten thought back to her conversations with him and his obsession with making clear his relationships with her. He worked by establishing rules with his lady friends, clear guidelines, so no-one would feel cheated when the inevitable end came. He was covering his back all the time even in his non-business relationships. He clearly trusted no woman.

Getting back to the hotel she saw Rutland at the computer. He smiled and nodded to her but carried on with his work, frowning and cursing until he brought up the name he wanted.

''Got it,'' he exclaimed. ''The link between Thirman and the perp in the prison. They worked together for a mining company twelve years ago.''

''About the same time as Grenman was organising criminal activities. Where were they operating from?''

''Miami, Grenman also dealt with mining and oil companies, he organised their investments for them.''

''The picture is forming now. We need to find out what else he was put inside for. I will contact my friends at the FBI and make some enquiries.''

''I have arranged for us to visit the perp in prison tomorrow. Coming Phil?''

''Yeah. I will enjoy interrogating that bastard again. A more weasilish creature you will find difficult to trace.''

''Give Elisabeth the job of tracing Grenman's antecedents and Thirman's crime contacts. It will be good experience for her. She is too good to be a lab rat all day.''

''I was thinking of asking her to join my firm. We need good forensic investigators and her sharp mind would lend itself to more than analysing chemicals.''

''I thought your mind was working in that direction but do you really want to mix work with pleasure?''

''We have worked together well and I think we could do so again without muddying the waters.''

Rutland would have begged to differ, his own experience being different but he bit his lip and changed the subject. Drakeman and Elisabeth would sort their own life out. Whenever he interfered he made things worse and he was not the right man to give advice after his life had not panned out well.

Kirsten was sitting in her room watching an episode of Countdown. She remembered her aunt liked solving puzzles. ''I wonder,'' she said out loud.

''What?'' asked Rutland hearing her through the open door? What had set her thinking? He could almost see the cogs turning in her mind, so engrossed was she in solving their puzzle.

''I wonder if the answer to this mystery could be found in a puzzle. My aunt solves puzzles of all kinds. This man Grenman rarely left the house and was a loner; the sort who was intellectually challenged by puzzles maybe, if he didn't want to socialize much.''

Rutland did not underrate Kirsten. She was as sharp as needles when she was not wasting her time arguing with him. He had noted she was cool and calm with everyone except him.

Interesting that was!

He admitted she brought out the worst in him as well. Her challenges made him want to tame that spirit in her and dominate her, to make her submit to him.

He had to restrain the natural alpha male within himself and let her become her own woman but he was a natural leader and his macho instincts kept coming to the fore. If he dominated her too much he would frighten her off and lose her. Naturally impatient and driven, this would be the hardest test of his life, keeping patient until Kirsten came to him of her own free will.

''Check if he was in an internet gaming club or puzzle club. Something he could do anonymously from his own home.''

''I will ask Drakeman to put it on his list for Elisabeth to look at and talk to my aunt tomorrow about it.''

''I am on to it now!'' said Drakeman from the other side of the room. ''It is too important to leave to tomorrow.'' A few emails to a friend at FBI headquarters and he received the information he required two hours later.

''Grenman was a member of an online gambling club. Gambling was his Achilles's heel. He was in deep to the tune of ten million dollars. He was a socio-path, barely making friends, no partner nor family near, a lonely guy who wanted control over his life. His only release was this gambling and it took over his life.''

''Have you found links with Thirman yet, apart from his investments with the mining company?''

''No and Thirman seems to be a small cog in this wheel. Nothing indicates he is bright enough to have instigated the framing of Kirsten. Someone else who is much brighter is behind this. I'll bet my hat on it!''

''I thought that,'' said Kirsten coming in. ''My aunt described Thirman as a crafty property developer in the right place at the right time but not a brain.''

''He is a puppet. Somebody higher is pulling his strings, someone much more dangerous who must have connections with organised crime to pull off those photos and copy your texts. Keep digging Phil!''

''I want dinner and Elisabeth has just arrived,'' said Drakeman, his mind now occupied with more interesting things.

''I have another hour's worth of work,'' said Rutland. ''Eat dinner with Elisabeth now and Kirsten and I can dine later if she doesn't mind.'' He looked enquiringly at Kirsten. "In a public restaurant. No funny business, I promise. You'll be safer than eating with me in this suite," he joked. ''Straight to bed afterwards in your own room while I burn the midnight oil.''

''You must not over-tire yourself,'' said Kirsten. "You have had a long drive.''

''See you do worry about me,'' he mocked. ''I am growing on you.''

''Like mould,'' countered Kirsten, refusing to give an inch. After his insults and abuse of her he was going to have to work harder than this to persuade her to trust him unreservedly. She would trust him in a public restaurant but that was as far as she would go.

''An hour then and we will dine together,'' she said. ''No dancing though!''

''No dancing tonight,'' he replied, his eyes suggesting his promise would not last much longer. He was holding himself back but still making it clear he wanted her after their legal business was finished. He was like a shark hunting her, trailing her, until he was ready to gobble her up and she found herself wanting and waiting to be eaten by him.

After he had finished with her and was bored with her he would spit her out and forget her like that babe the night before. Kirsten had seen the hurt in the girl's eyes until he had turned on his charm and said something that had mollified her. She was brighter than that poor girl and had no excuses for allowing herself to behave like a pawn in his game. She knew what he was up to and should avoid becoming one of his toys.

Rutland had seen her withdraw mentally from him and wondered what he had done to cause her to mistrust him again. He was gradually showing his intentions, being totally truthful with her; telling her he wanted her but was ready to wait until after the case was over. Why did she still treat him like a barracuda?

He guessed it was because of that kiss this morning. She had seen him get rid of the girl in his efficient manner and thought she might end up in the same way. She had no idea she was unique, worlds apart from Danielle. She thought he likened her to that type, a babe, a beautiful plaything, able to be disposed of at his whim. His reputation was going before him again, his past fickleness coming back and biting him in the butt. He had to convince her he wanted her for more than a one-night stand.

Elisabeth came through the door and saw Drakeman waiting. He took her in his arms, case and all and kissed her as if he had not seen her for months.

''Well, Sweetheart, those photos you processed gave us the ammunition to persuade the Judge Kirsten is being framed. The Police Chief is also leaning on the Deputy and the warden of the County Prison to make them cooperate with us at last. It was like pulling teeth before.

'It was he who had also secured bail for Kirsten. A phone call to the Judge inferred something was not quite right in the Deputy's dept. Digging deep, his sources had found other complaints of due diligence not being followed and evidence being hidden.''

She kissed him back briefly but pushed him away. A Drakeman pushing the boundaries of their relationship at full pelt was too much for her. She had thought deeply about them while she was away and wanted to put the brakes on their relationship just for the duration of the case. He was too intense!

Drakeman recognised her reluctance to show her affections and put it down to her being in a public place. ‘‘Dinner?’’ he asked. ‘‘You can brief me and then you might want an early night.’’ His intense but tender gaze told her he wanted to spend the night with her. She had to make up her mind how far she wanted to go and not lead him on. She would not play the tease any more. It was not fair on him when he was being blatant about his feelings for her. He was too honest and decent to be played with.

‘‘Dinner in ten minutes after I have freshened up.’’

In the restaurant he said, ‘‘The fish was good yesterday as a change from steak.’’

‘‘Sounds good to me, with the mixed salad and baked potato.’’

‘‘With Balsamic dressing?’’

‘‘Please,’’ she said, delighted he remembered her tastes. Most of the men she had dated were so self-absorbed they could barely remember her birthday, let alone her tastes in dressings. He was refreshingly different, interested in her as a person. Her desire to keep their relationship professional was melting away again in his presence, he was so damned charming.

Drakeman felt something was wrong and kept the conversation going while she was unnaturally quiet. He couldn’t think what he had done wrong but something bad was in the air. He could smell it. She wanted to tell him something. They discussed business through the meal and then finishing after coffee he said, ‘‘A dance Sweetheart?’’ She looked as grim as she felt. He felt a black cloud descending over them. She got up and said, ‘‘Thanks but I am too tired. I really do want that early night.’’

She moved so quickly to the door he could only follow her into the lift. The machine started and he pressed the button to stop it mid-air.

‘‘What’s up?’’ he asked pinning her against the wall with his body. ‘‘What have I done to offend you?’’ She tried to push him away but he locked her in place standing there blocking her way.

‘‘You haven’t done anything. I just don’t want to pursue our relationship any further while we are involved with this case.’’

‘‘I am sorry I kissed you downstairs. I was just so pleased to see you. We can cool it if you wish.’’

‘‘That would be for the best,’’ she said disappointing him. A gentleman, he took his hand off the button and the lift started again. He hesitated, then he broached the topic he had wanted to open in the restaurant before she had clammed up on him when he tried to mention personal topics.

‘‘I had hoped when we finished this case you might want to work for me in Miami. Perhaps we could date and see where it took us.’’ He was opening himself up for a painful rejection but would not forgive himself if he did not take the chance and tell her how he felt. She looked even guiltier. Something was definitely up and he was going to find out or his name wasn’t Philip Drakeman.

‘‘Thank you for the offer but I have been offered a position in Paris, something I can’t refuse. I don’t think a long-distance relationship would work.''

''It works for others and it wouldn't be for ever. I share a private jet with Rutland and can come over frequently to you. We could have some weekends away together, somewhere exotic and private.''

''You are lovely and that is a wonderful gesture....'' She stopped mid-sentence. He took her hand and led her into her room shutting the door behind them.

''It is not the job that is stopping you have a relationship with me is it Elisabeth? Be honest with me. Why are you holding back?''

She cursed herself inwardly and said, ''I don't want any commitment just yet. It would be better if it we forgot about us!''

''Forget about us?'' she saw real anger and bitterness on his face. He was having difficult biting back the words he wanted to spit out. ''I will never forget you Lady but you clearly don't care enough about me to try hard and make it work.''

He pulled her toward him, impaling her with his eyes and punishing her with a brutal kiss. "I will leave you an email detailing what Joshua wants you to do tomorrow. We will be at the County Prison. You could also go with Kirsten to see her aunt. As for the rest, you can keep your own company now Sweetheart. I want no more to do with a tease.''

He stalked back to the suite and saw Kirsten and Rutland dressed for dinner. ''Elisabeth?'' enquired Rutland.

''An early night!'' snapped Drakeman, his terse manner telling Rutland she would be on her own. ''Her next engagement is in Paris. I am going into town and getting drunk. She has the work details on her computer. See you for breakfast tomorrow morning at 7.15. Goodnight Ms Gateman.'' He left them saying nothing else, shocking Kirsten with his brevity.

''Well that is one disappointed man.'' she said. "I thought everything was going well for them.''

''It was but Ms Claremont seems to have put the brakes on their relationship and he is taking it badly.''

''I will talk with her tomorrow and find out what is wrong,'' said Kirsten. ''I thought they were made for each other.''

''Let's make dinner now,'' said Rutland focusing on their relationship. He didn't want it to go down the drain before it had really started. ''Let them lick their wounds in private. I don't think either of us are wanted at this moment."

At breakfast, Rutland asked Drakeman if he wanted to accompany him to the prison. ''Thanks Man. Let's get this scum interviewed now and try to wrap this case up. I want out of this hick town as soon as we can,''

The interview room was like any interview room in any prison; white washed walls, hard backed chairs and plastic tables. Severe harsh lighting enhanced the coldness of the room and the perp sat looking nervously at the two men looming above him. Both tall, broad shouldered, muscled, hard looking men, they were slightly scarred on their faces and arms as though they had earned their scars in war. They looked menacingly at him and he gulped.

The man called Drakeman had already told him he didn't believe his story in their previous interview He would nail him to the floor if he could prove him a liar. He said he was gathering evidence and would come back when he could prove the woman's innocence. Was he armed with the evidence now?

He looked smug and satisfied but it was the other one who frightened him more. Dark haired and satanic looking he speared him with his emerald eyes that looked as cold as pebbles. This guy wanted his ass and didn't care how he got it. He was glad a warder was in the room. He would not put it past these guys to batter him to get the info they wanted.

They were raw energy, constrained under those casual clothes. Fit as a flea, each of them could make mush of him with just one hand. Their straight bearing bespoke a military background. Drakeman sat down and leant forward and the other man leant negligently against the wall. He felt as if they could turn into military machines, at any moment now, if given the order to attack.

"We now have lab evidence the photos were doctored and physical evidence the defendant couldn't be the one in the photo." He threw a photo of Kirsten's badly beaten back in front of the perp.

'She couldn't wear a bikini." The perp had the grace to draw in a breath when he saw her whip scars.

"Your choice Son! Tell us the truth and we forget everything or take your place on the stand and be proven a liar and get a longer sentence for perjury."

The perp was only twenty-two, lightly built and fresh faced; confronted by these hard men whose harsh faces wore their experiences. The dark one looked as if he was enjoying his uncertainty and confusion. He was the sort who would want to find a sore spot on him and press it until it hurt.

Crap! He was screwed! The man who had paid him hadn't told him all the circumstances or where his lies would lead him to. What had seemed easy money now looked like a trap with a longer sentence at the end. He now wanted out. If his lies were forgotten, he could be out of here in six months.

His only worry was the man who had organised the frame-up. He had not met him but Thirman's description of him had given him the shivers. He was bright, keeping out of prison while others were inside. Thirman had warned that if he let the man down he would be wearing a concrete overcoat if he was released. Even inside he was not safe. He shivered, unable to control his fear; a trip down the stairs and a broken spine or neck could easily be arranged. He needed to get out of the can as fast as he could.

Drakeman read the lad's mind. He looked scared to death. Drakeman had spent a spell in the Navy as a military policeman and knew how brutal prison life could be; any prison was run by the strongest and meanest bullies who intimidated a weakling like this boy.

"I have contacts in the FBI who will arrange a place on the Witness Protection Programme for you. A new identity, even a job will be set up for you."

"I'll take it."

As a convicted con, he would have little chance of getting a decent job or place to live in normal circumstances. He wanted a fresh start after the intimidation in this prison. Already, he had had his cigs stolen from him and his arm twisted behind his back to ensure he knew who really ran the prison. After his release, he would never go back if he could help it.

''Names and addresses and times now!'' said Rutland coming forward. ''Any lies and I will have your balls hung up and barbequed!''

''Hey Man, what's got up your ass?'' asked the boy, not understanding the pent-up tension governing Rutland's taut body. He was lifted up in the air by his neck and collar and a fist came close to his nose when Drakeman ordered curtly, ''Leave him be! He isn't the one we need to screw."

His arm pulled Rutland back. Rutland let the boy down and went outside for a break before he nailed the little shit to the ground.

I must control myself. Never had he felt this angry before but it was a long time since he had cared for a woman so much. Not since Vanessa.

''Forget that incident if you are sensible,'' said Drakeman.

''What's wrong with him? He is a freaking nutcase! I didn't do anything to him,'' said the boy rubbing his neck.

''Let's just say he has a personal interest in solving this case,'' said Drakeman.

''Oh, a woman!'' said the boy understanding.

''Names!'' demanded Drakeman closing the subject. ''Who is at the top? We know Thirman hasn't the clout or the intelligence to be the top man.''

''There is a man in Miami who is in finance and property and everything else that makes money. His name is Krussman. He is of East German and Slovakian descent. Second generation immigrant who won scholarships and became a financial analyst.''

''What is his connection with Thirman?' '

Rutland came in and the boy licked his lips nervously, watching Rutland carefully, waiting for him to make a move.

''Thirman worked for a company Krussman did work for. That is all I know but I can give you names where they hang out.''

''That's enough!'' snapped Rutland, still wanting to thump the little bastard who had nearly sent Kirsten permanently to prison. ''Who doctored the photos and sent the text?''

''A guy called Michael Burman, a tech whiz-kid. He can break into any computer or cell.''

''He has a record I presume?''

''Yeah petty crimes only. A spell of two months in the can when he was younger. Got a chip on his shoulder and now works for the hard men since he was in prison. Wants money quick!''

''I think we have enough for the moment,'' said Drakeman walking out with him. ''Ms Claremont can finish this off for us tomorrow.''

''If you want.'' said Rutland. ''I wouldn't want Kirsten to face that kid. I think a woman would be shown less respect by that piece of shit."

''I saw Lizzie with the Deputy the second time. I think she could hold her own with that inadequate in there. She is as tough as boots,'' he said rather sadly. Rutland fired the engine of the Aston, eating up the miles until they arrived at the hotel; neither man talking much, each absorbed by his own dark thoughts.

They met an excited Kirsten at dinner in the hotel. ''I think Aunt Freja may have worked out the mystery.'' She recounted her talk with her aunt that morning.

''Can you remember anything useful about Grenman, Aunt Freja?''

''He was a solitary man who watched games like Countdown or Mastermind. He enjoyed Sudoko and crosswords and entered competitions. He was so introverted no-one would have thought he would have masterminded a bank raid or other criminal activities.''

''We found he was an online gambler and owed a fortune. That was why he turned to crime to finance his gambling.''

''She always thought he looked and dressed poor for a merchant banker.''

''Did he leave any books or documents with puzzles in the basement?''

''No. but in the loft, there were crossword and puzzle books by the thousand. They should be untouched by the fire.''

''I think we may find the clues in the books.''

''Your Aunt Freja is a gem! Tomorrow, you Ms Gateman are going to look for clues in puzzles with Ms Claremont. Where is she anyway?''

''Eating in her room. She had a headache and intends to work and go to bed early.''

''Tell her I expect her at breakfast and dinner for briefings,'' ordered Rutland. He wanted no lovesick women avoiding meetings. She had to work with Drakeman for the next few days and lump it. Neither of them should have mixed business with pleasure and should have controlled their hormones until the case was over.

His own firm strictly enforced a no fraternising policy after his episode with his former fiancé. It worked and his love life was never brought into the office and work made messy or complicated. He was surprised Drakeman had hit on Elisabeth but that showed how much he thought of her by breaking his own no fraternising rule.

''She briefed me already and there is a report in your mail box,'' said Kirsten defending her new friend.

''Not good enough!'' said Rutland. ''I employ people not computers and like to know what they are thinking. I always talk to my employees when I work with them on a case, not expect to read between the lines of emails.'' Having tried to avoid Rutland herself Kirsten had every sympathy with Elisabeth but would pass on her message before he took out his ire on her.

''What did you find out at the prison?''

''Krussman, a second-generation East European immigrant is the brain child behind your frame-up.

'Grenman had links with his company and Thirman worked for a minerals and mining company which Grenman organised their investments for. They are all linked together in some way. The perp in the prison said he was frightened of Krussman who seems to be a big fish in the crime world.''

Kirsten seemed puzzled. He loved the way she wrinkled her nose when she frowned. She looked years younger than her real age, like a little girl puzzled by the world.

You're becoming a sentimental old fool. She just sees you as a bully! said the sensible side of himself.

The hopeful side reminded him how she appeared breathless when he got too close to her. He had not imagined the awareness in her eyes when he had kissed her before she panicked. She was attracted to him but was too scared to pursue it. He reminded himself he still had to be patient and win her trust. He ground his teeth and concentrated on the case, trying to put an image of himself kissing away her confusion from his wayward mind.

''I don't see why after all these years they are pursuing the loot, whatever it is. Why now? Why not try to get the previous owners to sell? Grenman was put inside nearly ten years ago.''

''That is a good point.'' She was a sharp as a razor, totally wasted in her job as a legal secretary working over the internet. He could find her stimulating work in his Miami office if she didn't want to be an attorney.

''Grenman must be the connection,'' she suggested, mulling over the problem. ''He or someone close to him must want the money and have asked the others to find it.''

''Why wouldn't Grenman just send the person to the place where he hid it? It doesn't make any sense.''

''No,'' she said. ''But Grenman is the clue.'' She threw the paper she was looking at down in a rare bout of impatience. Rutland smiled. He had only ever seen her irritated with him or the Deputy. Perhaps her unnatural calmness was wearing off and the passionate Kirsten was breaking out.

''Phil. Ask your contacts to find out if Grenman had any relatives and if he had recent contact with them. Something must have muddied the waters recently as Kirsten intimated.''

He took Kirsten's hand and said, ''We are getting cabin fever. Let's go for a walk in the hotel grounds. We need to refresh our minds.'' Noting her resistance, he said, ''I don't bite!''

''No, you kiss instead!'' she retorted. He smiled. She loved having the last word. He would have to break that habit or he would never win an argument with her. He would not take no for an answer and hustled her out of the hotel room into the corridor and into the garden.

Letting her arm go he walked beside her around the garden allowing her to keep her distance from him. He recognised she still needed her space but it irked him.

''You can be too independent you know.''

''And you are insufferably bossy!'' she retorted but he noted her resistance was only token now. Perhaps that wall she had erected around herself was slowly crumbling as she realised he could be trusted and would not harm her.

For Christ's Sake! He was giving his valuable time and spending a small fortune on her. When would she grasp that he was on her side? It was a new experience, knowing his money and power meant nothing to her, except to help keep her out of gaol. Her independence meant more than his money to her. Used to being chased by women for his money and power, it was a levelling experience for him!

''I know what losing my independence means,'' she said in a small voice, trying to explain her vulnerability to him. He listened patiently, waiting for her to continue. This was not the time to push her when she was opening up to him; really explaining who she was and how she had come to be in this position. He held his breath, hoping desperately that she was trying to build a bridge of trust with him at last. His hope was justified.

She stopped pacing and looked up at him with those blue green eyes that sparkled with tears. He felt he could look into her very soul when she directed that gaze at him; that spoke of sadness and hurt. She was delving deep into her soul, trusting him with memories she had wanted hidden for ever; making him understand what made her the woman she was now.

"I lost all my freedom with Justin. He got me my job with the firm he worked for, paid my salary into our joint account and paid all my bills. He gave me a small allowance. We had a housekeeper who reported all my movements to him when I was not at work and he was at meetings. I only had a small deposit account Aunt Freja had opened for me in another society. He didn't know about it. In the end, I saved every penny so I could get away from him.

'He gradually alienated all my friends and I only met with his colleagues and his friends. He even insisted we joined the same gym. He made me tired through trying to lose too many lbs. I would go to work and then the gym and then feel so tired I went to bed. I was becoming like a zombie until a female at the office noticed and encouraged me to go to a new gym. I could socialise with other women and not feel I was being criticised by Justin.

'The counsellor dealing with women's dietary issues said I was suffering from depression and was borderline anorexic. Justin was making me ill. He went mad when he found out the women's only gym I joined had a programme and instructors who encouraged me to put on weight. He hated fat women and always admired models, stick insects Aunt Freja called them. I was always slim but when I put on weight as I matured and my figure developed he said I was getting fat and ugly and goaded me to go to the gym and lose more weight.

'I loved my job but wanted to move out of corporate law. Justin would not hear of it. He first explained I had wasted time training in that area and would have to work hard to make up the time. Then he gradually became angrier, saying as his future wife I should support him and he was used to me working for him. I made it clear it was my career and he lost his temper.

'For the first time, he seemed out of control, as if my arguing with him made him so angry he saw it as a direct challenge and insult to him. He took me by the shoulders and shook me, holding me by my throat. I was terrified of him and said I would reconsider my decision to change my line of work to make him leave me alone. Later, I decided to talk with him and the seniors and say I wanted to move to employment law, my first love. One of the associates who specialised in employment was leaving and there was an opening for me.

'I was prepared to find another law firm if they didn't give me the position. It was the start of the decline in my relationship with Justin. To say he was angry was an understatement. I had an interview with another firm and was offered a position.

'I meant to tell him about the new job before he found out himself but a new receptionist from my future employer accidentally called me at home and he took the phone call. I had never seen him so angry; a cold anger, accusing me of being disloyal and a traitor, lying to him. He punched me in the stomach and left me sick and bruised.

'I was too scared to take the job and made an excuse to the new employer. I stayed with him because I could not escape him. He was taking me to and from work now and working more often at home with me, refusing to allow me to go to the women's gym or go out with my friends. My house became a prison and I withdrew into myself. Even whilst behaving passively and obedient I still incurred his wrath until I could not cope with the beatings any longer and fled after pretending to be sick while he was in a meeting.''

''What made you leave him finally?''

''The last two years he had changed. He was always dominant and he admitted he went to clubs, the sort in Soho you know where there were doms and subs. Leather collars and all that stuff,'' she said hoping he would understand. He nodded. ''He wanted me to join a club but I said I wasn't interested. He said it was very private, no-one would know but I rejected the idea and he grew angry saying I wasn't interesting in bed anymore and he needed an outlet to express his desires.''

Rutland's fists were clenched beside him. He felt a burning anger grow inside him. That inadequate perverted bastard had undermined Kirsten's self-esteem because she wouldn't play his games with him. He had been taken to these clubs by his friends but he personally found the idea of passive, doe eyed obedient subs repulsive. He was dominant in the bedroom but he liked a passionate woman who would stand up to him, who would challenge him like Kirsten would if she regained her confidence to sleep with men again.

''He began to be rougher in bed and used violence against me. He needed to choke me and do other things to have sex with me. When he started beating me I knew I had to leave. I couldn't think straight much of the time. I couldn't understand why I was so tired even when I cut down the exercise.

'One night I found a bottle he had thrown into the bin. I traced the bottle to the pharmacy he had bought it from. From the inquiries, I made of the pharmacist I think he had been drugging me for at least two years which explained the tiredness and my unnatural obedience to him. He started with a low dose but by the end I could barely summon up the energy to go to work at times, let alone defy him. A chemist at the clinic analysed the contents of the bottle and found it was designed to make me passive and obedient.''

Rutland felt his insides go tight at the thought of this woman tied to this malignant man, made passive by narcotics until she obeyed his perverted instructions. Everything Rutland wanted from Kirsten was the opposite of what this creep had demanded. He wanted an obedient robotic slave while Rutland wanted a feisty, argumentative woman who challenged him and made him win her over; the Kirsten who was gradually peeking from behind her icy mask and becoming the woman of his dreams A woman who gave herself willingly to a man; her self-esteem and confidence intact. Not a woman defined by a man!

''He beat me twice and the third time I left. I left with the clothes I was wearing in the office. Aunt Freja had sent me the ticket and met me in New York. She stayed near the clinic and saw me every day. The worst things were the withdrawal symptoms, sickness, delusions and fear. The psychotherapy helped and I had already set up the VSO appointment and left at the end of the two months stay.''

''Did the spell in Indonesia help you?''

''Yes, I was safe and it was tranquil. I had just my iPad to read. The local men respected the VSO workers. I could work covered up to protect my skin and no-one would question a Western woman who didn't want to uncover herself on the beach. When my skin healed, I found a private place to swim where no-one could see my scars. I also healed inside.

'I came home and lived in a hostel for abused women and took the internet law work until I can find another legal position under an assumed name. That is what I cannot forgive Justin for. He took my only source of income away from me as well as my self-esteem. He can still find me in England if he wants and Aunt Freja said her contacts in England say he is still looking for me. I still cannot escape him.''

''We can deal with that. Get a court order against him. You have the evidence of the doctor at the clinic.''

''Yes, I thought of that but I have no proof it was he who inflicted those wounds. The housekeeper hated me and was on his side. I told her he was violent but she ignored me.''

''It is enough that you fear him'.'

''I know. The drugs confused me. I could not think straight or I would have left him earlier and taken an order against him before.''

''Forget him for a while. Give me your hand. Let's sit under the trees and look at the stars.''

He knew talking about her problems was cathartic for her but she needed to relax now she had spilled it out. He sat down, pulling her down beside him and held her in his arms. She stiffened, taut as a wire, that feeling of suffocation overwhelming her again as she felt her weakness against the strength of him. Feeling her anxiety, he let her go and just rested his arm on the bench behind her, letting her get used to his support without any fear of being grabbed.

''Softly, softly catchee monkey,'' he whispered to himself.

''You can rest your head on my shoulder you know.'' She smiled and rested her head against him and he put his hand tentatively on her waist. She did not stir and he left it there as they relaxed in the warm night air, in harmony with each other for once.

After a while he stirred reluctantly. ''It is about this time the guy kisses the girl but we will forget that bit and go back to our rooms.'' He pulled her up but she stayed there strangely still, looking up at him. He didn't know what she wanted of him and was astonished when she stood on tiptoe and put her arms on his shoulder and kissed him gently on the cheek.

''Thanks for listening. Justin rarely listened to me.''

''May I?'' he asked putting his arms around her waist. She nodded and he took her gently into his arms and kissed her back, this time on the lips, a whisper of a kiss, just for a fleeting second. He held back his passion and she relaxed into his arms. For a moment, a wary look was still in her eyes; like that of a doe who has seen some danger and doesn't know whether to stay or flee.

He was the first to break away and say, "Let's get back to the rooms.'' Breaking away from her was one of the hardest things he had ever done in his life but they had made headway; she had instigated the kiss and was trusting him. He felt optimistic for the first time in days about his relationship with Kirsten.

Kirsten was confused. She had wanted to carry on the kiss. For the first time, she had seen him as a potential boyfriend instead of a bully or lately as a useful helper, a legal and financial saviour. Her fear was she hated sex. It had always been uncomfortable and later painful with Justin, he only taking pleasure quickly and not caring if she enjoyed it. Her university friends she had confided in had said she was with the wrong man and it could be enjoyable. They had great sex with their boyfriends and it was Justin's selfishness and lack of skill that made her dislike it.

She hadn't had any opportunity to test their theory with anyone else as Justin had been her only boyfriend but she wondered if she would enjoy it with Rutland. She believed she might. She had read about him on Google. The reports in the more sensationalist newspapers said women were queuing up to share his bed. He had a reputation for being a stud. The women were attracted as much by his reputation in bed as his money and power.

Back in her room she slept well for the first time since she had left Indonesia. Fear of Justin finding her had preyed on her mind these last few weeks and she had woken up sweating after nightmares. Being beaten and unable to run from Justin was a recurring theme in the dreams. Talking with Rutland had helped. She might be able to get a restraining order with the evidence of the doctor if he pestered her. She had been so drugged and wound up before she left London she had not been able to think straight but now she saw she had options and Justin could be put in his place.

She had talked to her father but he had told her she should not hurt Justin's reputation and he would have a word with him about being a bit rough with his woman. Justin had exploded when her father had reproached him and had pushed her against the wall and slapped her, warning her not to humiliate him by talking to her father again.

She had talked to a policeman she knew but he was one of Justin's friends and had disbelieved her. She was fearful of going formally to the police in case they broke confidentiality and reported back to their friend Justin. The 'old boys' network permeated the Bar Council and Police making a community which protected their own.

Now she might be able to practise law again in the future. Her job had been the love of her life and leaving it had depressed her mood. Her legal secretary's work was not demanding enough and the pay was adequate but not enough to pay her education debts. She needed a good job or she would be broke for years. She made a resolution. Justin would not stop her developing her career nor staying in one place and buying a house. She would fight him when she returned to London.

Strangely, the thought of returning to London was no longer pleasing even if Justin's power could be neutralised. She didn't particularly like the climate here but had enjoyed working in this tight knit team, laughing at the jokes and wind ups the men engaged in. She would miss them all. Elisabeth had become a good friend, shielding her when the men had become too pushy and she had felt suffocated by them.

Back in the suite Drakeman had received more intelligence during their walk. ''There is one child, an illegitimate kid called Valentina. A bright kid. Went to Harvard and studied Math and Finance like the father. She is now thirty years old and wait for it, was contacted by her father last year. Grenman is dying of cancer and probably wanted to pass on the information to his daughter.''

''Why didn't he just tell her the place where the loot was left?''

''Perhaps he wanted to hide the clues from prying eyes. I will fly to Miami to interview him before he creaks. He has a few months left still.''

''Where is his daughter now?''

''That is the odd thing. She left her well-paid job seven months ago and cannot be traced. I have traced her social security number but it hasn't been used for months. She could be around here but working under an assumed name.''

''Do we have a description?''

''Tall and slim but voluptuous with deep blue eyes and blonde hair. She takes after her Baltic ancestors in looks. A beauty from all accounts. We would easily recognise her if she hasn't disguised herself but that is unlikely.''

''Can you get a photo?''

''I am printing one just now,' he said. ''Hm, worth getting to know, this girl is!''

''Always thought you liked leggy blonds,'' teased Rutland. Kirsten slapped his wrist looking at Elisabeth whose ears were pricking up. Drakeman shrugged his shoulders nonchalantly. She had given him the push so what business was it of hers who he slept with. Mind, a bit of the old green-eyed monster could always reinvigorate a dying relationship.

Elisabeth bent her head and pretended not to hear their conversation but he could see her eyes had narrowed. She was very interested in what he thought of the woman.

To say the atmosphere between them was frosty was an understatement. She resembled an iceberg, maintaining an aloofness with him; in contrast to the warm jokes she shared with the other two people. He in turn made terse and biting comments to her, checking up on her work, criticising, making her grit her teeth and reply with barbed jibes back.

Rutland had put up with this war of attrition for hours and was tired of it. He would have a word with the pair of them and get it out in the open soon. Why the hell they couldn't just bed each other and see where it led them? The spark between them could light the room and their sexual frustration was turning them into bad tempered termagants, each wanting to snipe at each other the whole time.

''I am sure I know this woman,'' said Kirsten. "The shape of her eyes and nose seem familiar. But the hair colour is different as is the style'' She passed it to Elisabeth who screwed her eyes up and said, "I have seen her before somewhere.''

The blond had a short bob and her makeup was understated as expected in the financial world. Her eyes were almost hidden by wide framed large spectacles which didn't do justice to those beautiful blue eyes. It was as if she wanted to hide her beauty from onlookers in this photo.

''I wonder if she knew when this was taken she was going to change her looks and made herself look prim and proper, not the beauty she clearly was.''

''It would explain a lot,'' said Drakeman. "Let Rutland have a look at the photo as well.''

''Ask the lab to change the hair and take off the glasses,'' said Elisabeth. ''We might then have our lady.''

Rutland came in from the business centre and looked at the photo. ''She is familiar. Follow up Elisabeth's suggestion quickly Phil.'' He kept looking at the photo, expecting the name to jump up at him. Giving it up he said, "I have to talk with the Deputy again. I'll meet you in the restaurant for dinner at nine o'clock."

''We might be able to wrap this up soon. Elisabeth, did you and Kirsten have any joy in the loft today?''

''None, there are thousands of books of puzzles. The man must have been addicted to them,'' she said disparagingly.

"To each his own,'' said Drakeman. "Not everyone wants to spend their every hour in a lab."

"Was that a dig at me Mr. Drakeman?" demanded Elisabeth.

"If the cap fits!" he replied.

"If you are going to insult me do it openly and honestly," she snapped turning to him angrily.

"Right you two," said Rutland, "that's enough. Drakeman, you have been picking holes in Elisabeth's work and you Elisabeth have been bitching at him since you came back. Behave like adults or leave. I have had enough! I'll give you ten minutes to sort it out between yourselves."

As he went out the door he said, "And you want each other so badly why don't you just admit it for Pete's sake?"

Elisabeth looked at Drakeman and said, "He is right, we are behaving like children."

Drakeman came over to her and took her hands in his. "I think your work is great. That evening we sat together was so perfect I was devastated when you said you didn't want to make a commitment. You mean a lot to me Lizzie although we haven't known each other long. I know you feel differently but please give us another chance?''

"I don't feel differently. I feel the same as you but I am going to Paris and when my last relationship broke up it was so unpleasant I am afraid the same might happen to us."

"When do you go to Paris?''

"In three months' time. Not long!''

"Long enough for us to decide if we want a commitment. Will you give us a chance?'' He took her chin in his hand and he was looking so tenderly at her she was holding back her tears.

"Yes', she said, 'I will give us a chance but you must promise not to make a fuss if I want to end our relationship when I go to Paris.''

He was puzzled, wondering why she thought she lacked the ability to commit to him but he had three months to persuade her to stick with him. He was certain he wanted her in his future and he could make her want him to. It was a start at least. He took her in his arms and kissed her. Rutland coming in looked pleased to see them friends again.

"Thank God you are being realistic. I have never seen two people so into each other as you two are. You are made for each other!"

"We will see!'' said Elisabeth and pulled out of Drakeman's arms and settled down to work again. Drakeman raised his brows to Rutland and thought he would investigate her background and find out why she was so phobic about making a commitment.

Kirsten sat next to Elisabeth in the bar. Her friend was pensive. "Drakeman wants me to give us a second chance.''

''Don't let him force you into anything?''

''I agreed to give our relationship another go.''

''What is putting you off?''

''I was engaged to a younger man who pursued me for two years until I dated him. He put pressure on me to marry him. I was unsure but he was so eager I agreed but later I thought it was the wrong thing to do. I thought I loved him but I was wrong to accept his proposal, not being entirely sure.

'When I broke off the arrangement he kept coming around trying to change my mind. He finally tried to commit suicide! I have never forgiven myself for encouraging him when I should have stayed firm and discouraged him. He survived and had psychotherapy but he could have died and it was my fault. That is why I don't want to encourage Phil and let him down.''

''He sounded a trifle weak Elisabeth. Phil sounds nothing like him. He is a man but the other was a boy. Don't confuse the two.''

''I don't know Kirsten. Phil is so intense; he reminds me of David.''

''Elisabeth, Philip Drakeman seems to me to be the most confident man I have met excepting Joshua Rutland. No-one could dupe Drakeman. He is his own man. Too confident perhaps like Joshua. Let him make his own mind up. Your David was a boy infatuated with you but Philip cares, perhaps even loves you as a man does. It is not the same!''

‘‘I think you are right Kirsten but I couldn’t have another man nearly dying on my conscience! I still feel guilty about David.’’

‘‘What did you say to Phil?’’

‘I told him nothing but said I would give us another chance and he was satisfied with that.’’

‘‘Perhaps he deserves an explanation. It is only fair you know.’’ Kirsten believed Drakeman would find out for himself from his wide sources. He would have a reckoning with Elisabeth. Like Rutland he would not let a sore fester. He would want to drive the poison out.

‘‘And you Kirsten. What are you going to do with Joshua? He seems to want to pursue you! He doesn’t give up easily either.’’

‘‘He is like an avalanche, overwhelming me, pushing my objections away as fast as I make them. He has offered to deal with Justin for me in court if he comes after me. He has also hinted there could be a job for me in his office in Miami but that is like Justin again, wanting me in his office to control me.’’

‘‘He sounds nothing like Justin to me, merely like a strong man trying to help you find employment away from your bullying fiancé. How do you feel about him?’’

“Totally confused.

‘He irritates me and frightens me when he bosses me about but sometimes he is gentle and then I like him a lot. He has made no secret of the fact that he wants to bed me but is being patient and letting me determine the pace of our relationship, whatever that is.’’

‘‘Are you attracted to him?’’

‘‘Oh yes, but I take fright if he holds me tight. I feel sick and suffocated, my chest tight, if a man holds me too close. The psychotherapist said I can learn to accept that men are not all abusers but it will take time and a special man to overcome my fear.’’

‘‘Is Joshua special Kirsten?’’

‘‘I think so. He is very patient although I know it irks him to keep his hands off me. He has a reputation as quite a stud you know.’’

‘‘I googled him and Phil but Phil said the reports are vastly exaggerated!’’

‘‘They both seem to be very easy in women’s company. Look at Rutland with that receptionist. He even carries gifts with him to impress his casual encounters. He tried to pick me up in a hotel lounge and then in the plane. He is too used to buying his way into women’s beds. He doesn’t know the meaning of the word no!’’

‘‘Danielle is her name. She was coming on to Phil this morning. All breasts and batting lashes, a real babe. She hasn’t given up on Joshua either. She wants a ticket out of this hick town and sees them as it.’’

‘‘Is she local? I haven’t seen her in the past when I came to stay with Aunt Freja.’’

‘‘I thought she was local, but come to think of it her accent is more like that of girls from Miami. I will ask Drakeman to find out. He talks to the bar girls. They may know who has moved in from Miami recently.’’

They brushed up for dinner and the dinner was a civilised meal this time, neither of the former protagonists wanting to upset Rutland.

''Joshua, is Danielle a local girl?'' asked Elisabeth? ''Her accent seems less broad than the local girls.''

''Don't know. All she talked about was stars from reality shows and she said she wanted to move to a bigger city to get a job.''

''She doesn't dress like a local girl. I bet she has worked in a big city before now. City polish brushes off on one. She is too confident for a small-town girl.

'Those shoes are Jimmy Choo's and the ones last night were by Laboutin. You don't buy those on a receptionist's wage in a hotel in a hick town.'' She priced the girl's outfit she was wearing. ''That dress is Galliano and I bet the purse is genuine Prada. She didn't buy those on a receptionist's wage even in sales. She must have very generous friends or family.''

Trust a woman to price another woman's outfit to the last dollar. Rutland now felt as curious about the lovely Danielle as the two ladies. He remembered as well as talking about reality shows she had asked dozens of questions about him and the investigation in her seductive way but he knew almost nothing about her. She had given nothing away.

Most women liked to talk about themselves over dinner or in bed after making love but she was as tight as a shell, only wanting to pump him for information. His antennae were pricking. Ms Danielle De Vere could be less innocent than they had thought. She might not be the brainless babe she pretended to be.

''I am going to stay up a while and talk to the bar staff about the luscious Danielle,'' said Drakeman. ''She has piqued my curiosity.''

''Watch out you don't get stung!' said Rutland. 'Oh, and that woman has very expensive tastes. She chose the most expensive items on the menu!''

''We must make sacrifices in the line of duty,'' replied Drakeman, putting on his most seductive smile and going to the bar where he flattered the young girl into opening up to him.

''Her father lived here for a while but he never married her mother. She lived in Miami with her Ma but she met her Dad and speaks fondly of him. He paid for her to go to Uni.''

''Uni!'' uttered Drakeman surprised. ''What did she study? fashion or beauty.''

''Oh no. Something harder than that. She is quite bright although she pretends to be a babe. She studied science I think at Harvard.''

Drakeman's eyes widened. The co-incidence was too great. Substitute finance for science and she could be Grenman's daughter. He decided to risk incurring Elisabeth's wrath and went to where Danielle was sitting with other female staff.

''May I have this dance?'' he asked. Surprised because he had been rejecting her for days she smiled her wide seductive smile. ''I never thought you would ask. You seemed interested in your scientist friend.''

He looked contemptuously at Elisabeth and shrugged his shoulders negligently. “I was but she is too shy for me if you know what I mean. I like a mature woman who knows what a man likes, not an immature girl.’’ His meaning came across quite clearly to Danielle who threw a mocking look at Elisabeth who had heard every word and pretended to be outraged.

‘‘He is only pretending,’’ said Kirsten reassuringly.

‘‘I know he is trying to squeeze information out of her but does he have to be so damned insulting about me!’’

‘‘I think he is doing more than that,’’ said Kirsten. ‘‘I think he is trying to flush her out. That is Grenman’s daughter or my name is not Kirsten Gateman. She has the height and the baby blue eyes Drakeman described.’’

‘‘Where is Rutland?’’

‘‘He received a message and went to take a phone call in reception while you went to the powder room. He could identify her. He said she had a distinctive birthmark. Phil could check that against the FBI records.’’

Drakeman was making headway with Danielle. ‘‘You really dance beautifully and you have excellent taste in clothes, really sophisticated.’’

‘‘My Mummy always taught me to appreciate beautiful things and paid for me to have dancing lessons.’’

‘‘Are you a local? You don’t have the accent that the local girls have.’’

‘‘I was brought up in Miami but moved here for the job when my hotel closed. I can’t wait to get back. And you Mr Drakeman. How long are you going to be here for?’’

‘‘At least another month. If the old couple die we have no clues as to who fired the house.’’

‘‘I thought they were recovering last time I heard.’’

‘‘She had a relapse and he had a heart attack when he heard she was slipping away. She is hanging on for grim death, a fighter. He might survive but she is the one with the answers. He knows nothing but what she told him.’’

‘‘Has she said something useful?’’

‘‘Not much but she said something today which helped us and we are going tomorrow to ask her to expand on her information if she is well enough.’’

‘‘Poor sweet lady. She was always so kind to the staff when she lunched here with Mr. Defoe.’’

Drakeman blinked. He would not have described Freja as a sweet lady: fiercely proud, intelligent and cranky or cantankerous but never sweet and Rutland had said his Granddad wouldn’t touch the hotel’s over-priced food. This lady was sweet-talking him and lying through her teeth. He hoped the bull-shit he was feeding her about Freja’s state would make Danielle make a false move. They needed to flush her out to make real progress on this case. They were so close to the end now.

‘‘Is Ms Gateman still the main suspect in the case?’’

‘‘Yes, we tried to get the main witness to change his story but he is sticking with it. He claims he overheard her plotting with someone to intimidate and then kill her aunt.’’

‘‘That cruel woman, plotting to kill that old woman! I hear Ms Andersson was a little vague anyway. Was she after her money? She was a highly-paid vet you know before she retired.''

''We don't know why she is supposed to have done it although Ms Andersson would leave her the money and the house if she is not convicted of the crime.''

''I hear she is not quite all right in the head!''

''She had problems in London but she is recovered now and there was nothing seriously wrong.'' Drakeman wondered how she had found out about Kirsten's psychiatric problems and if she was passing rumours about Kirsten's fragile mental state around town. He had noticed a few women give Kirsten a wide berth and conversations had stopped when Kirsten passed the small groups of women gossiping on Main Street.

Thank God, he lived in Miami away from these small hick towns where no-one could keep their business to themselves. He liked the anonymity of the city life where no one knew his business unless the newshounds followed him about. A threat of an injunction or the offer of an expensive dinner or private story usually put a stop to unpleasant publicity about him. Here, everybody knew by lunchtime what he had had for breakfast.

He needed to get away to talk to Rutland. He looked at Kirsten who went out and came in a few minutes later and tapped him on the shoulder. ''I just went upstairs and there is an urgent memo for you. You need to reply immediately!''

''Thanks Kirsten,'' he said and kissed Danielle's hand apologetically. ''I must go now Sweetheart. It will take me forever if the memo is what I think it is about. I will try to catch up with you tomorrow night after dinner if you are free.'' He vanished through the crowded dance floor closely watched by Danielle.'

''Do you think she was convinced by what he was saying?'' asked Kirsten.

''I don't know but what she said made him run like a Jack Rabbit. He must be on to something. Let's have coffee and go upstairs and ask him.''

''I wonder where Joshua is,'' said Kirsten. ''He has gone a long time!''

They drank their coffee and made their way upstairs. Rutland had disappeared without trace. Kirsten telephoned Drakeman. ''Where are you?''

''At the hospital. I think Freja may have a visitor tonight.''

''Do you think they may try to hurt her?''

''Yes, I am getting her moved into another ward. I have a plan. Would you like to help me? Come to the hospital by taxi and bring your computer with you.''

''What about Mr. Rutland. He hasn't come back yet.''

''Damn it. Where did he go to?''

''Reception, to answer a phone call.''

''That sounds dubious to me. Ask them if he was sent somewhere else or met someone there and then phone me back.''

Worried now, they went to reception. ''I am sorry Ma'am there was no phone call but Mr. Rutland did receive a written message and drove off in his car somewhere.''

''Do you know where he went?''

''He threw the message in the bin. Ah here it is.' '

Elisabeth grabbed the piece of paper. ''Meet me at the old-School House if you want information about the arson attack,'' it read. ''Mr. Rutland left Mr. Drakeman a message in his post-box,'' said the receptionist. She took it before the receptionist could protest and read it.

''Gone to the old 'School House.' Follow me please Phil when you lose our Lady-friend. Not sure if the message offering me info is genuine.''

"I'll go to the School House and you go to the hospital,'' said Elisabeth. "I can shoot with my pistol. Like you I spent my holidays on a farm but it belonged to my Grandpa in Kentucky.'' They split up, promising to call each other when they had arrived safely at their destinations.

Chapter nine

Elisabeth stopped at the top of the narrow drive to the School House. She couldn't be seen from the house at the top of the twisty dark and unlit drive. She sat quietly in the car pensively, watching out for Rutland. She could barely see some faint lights in the house. She should be safe here until Drakeman arrived. She took out her revolver and clicked its safety catch on. She waited silently, alert for any movement in the shadows or from the house.

She heard a skid as a jeep careered up the road behind her and parked right behind her car, blinding her with its headlights.

This is trouble.

Shielding her eyes from the piercing light, she locked the windows, her heart in her mouth as two men each ran around the car to the front doors and tried to open them. She raised her gun, ready to use it against the men but they each pressed a gun to the window, pointing it at her.

''Open the door or we will break the window open,'' shouted one at top volume through the glass. She hesitated but the other took up a heavy wrench and smashed it against the window pane. She ducked as glass splintered. The window wouldn't last more than a few minutes under this onslaught and her face was already scratched by one of the splinters.

She unlocked the door. ''Put the gun down!'' ordered the first man. ''On the floor.'' She leant forward and placed it carefully on the floor and was then tugged out roughly by the second man.

''Move toward the house, Sweetheart,'' said the man, pushing her as he spoke. She pulled herself away from the detestable creep and drawing herself up to her full height she walked to the house, avoiding the ruts lit only by moonlight to where someone opened the door.

''Downstairs,'' said the man showing her the entrance to the cellar. ''Your friend should find you here soon. He is hanging around outside.''

He must mean Rutland. He would walk into a trap looking for her. How could she alert him? He didn't stand an earthly. Pushed to a rickety chair, her mouth stuffed with a dirty rag, her hands were tied in front of her and she had to wait for him to find her.

She heard a footstep on the stairs. "Mr. Rutland, your little friend will be dead in a few seconds if you don't throw your weapons down and surrender yourself immediately.'' Rutland stopped dead.

Christ Almighty. He had no room to manoeuvre. He had foolishly made a detour to get some things before he came here. These men didn't make idle threats. They would have killed Freja and his granddad in the blink of an eye. His delay might cause their deaths.

He moved to where he could be seen by the occupants of the room and slowly bent down and placed his gun on the floor, coming back up without any jerky movements that could make the men act violently. His knife was still in the back of his pants. He could use it on them later, silently, if his hands were unbound.

''Come in.''

He walked in his hands up. A goon searched his body roughly, easily finding the knife.

''Sit on the chair, hands together behind you.'' The gun didn't waver for an instant. These men were professionals and he was trussed up like a turkey. He hoped Drakeman would arrive soon and rescue them. His job was to keep the situation calm and find out what he could about Danielle's contacts.

''Are you ok?'' The pig untied her hands and took the rag out of her mouth enjoying a feel of her shoulder as he did it. She shivered at his touch but said, ''Yes, they did not hurt me thank you.''

''We are expecting your friends later. We are hoping they will lead us to the diamonds. Now we wait.'' He locked the door leaving them to their own thoughts.

Kirsten arrived at the hospital and went to Freja's ward. She was no longer there. ''She is safe, as is the old fellow. This is what I want you to do.'' Drakeman gave Kirsten her instructions.

''Does Grenman's daughter have the birthmark Danielle wears?''

''Yes. I think they are the same person in which case she is dangerous and knows more than she lets on. She was giving me the third degree about Freja's health and she implied both your aunt and you had lost your marbles.

'This night is going to be long. Here is some work you can put into the computer ready for sending to the FBI headquarters in the morning.'' They worked silently through the night only stopping for short comfort breaks.

The door to the hospital ward opened quietly and a head peered in. *No nurses, good,* the masked figure thought. A blond head was half under the covers but the plait was hanging outside and the sheet moved up and down as the patient breathed shallowly.

The figure moved closer to the bed where the drip and medicine were set up. It inspected the drip and took a hypodermic out and started to fill the drip with it. Finishing its job, it watched the liquid begin to slowly drip down the drip. It turned satisfied, but was stopped by a hand grabbing it tight and pulling its arm so hard behind its back it screamed with pain.

''Sorry, Ms De Vere but I need you to be very still,'' said Drakeman turning on the light.

Kirsten's colouring was the same as her aunts and she had convinced Danielle it was Freya in the bed. She sat up and dismantled the drip. The liquid had not come close to entering her arm.

''You Bastard, let me go!'' screamed Danielle but Drakeman merely put some cuffs on her hands and stuck a Band-Aid over her mouth.

"To the gaol with you I think,'' he said. ''I will ask Elisabeth to look at this before the Deputy's office gets near it. No chance of corruption then!''

He called the cop who was waiting in the corridor. ''This young lady is to be charged with attempted murder Officer. I saw her put something in the drip. I want the forensic investigation officer to look at it. This room is to be locked up until then.''

''Never did like this one,'' said the cop grabbing Danielle. ''She always hoity toity and too good for us locals.''

''It's Grenman's daughter,'' explained Drakeman.

''Explains it. He was an unfriendly character as well when he lived here. It must be in the genes.''

''They may both be sociopaths. Her records said she had few friends and neither did he. It would have been painful for her to mix with hotel clients and sleep with strange men but she wanted the loot. It must be worth a lot for her to change her behavioural pattern so much. She will tell us tomorrow.''

The woman's eyes darted fire at him, issuing a challenge to him. Then they changed to an icy blue and she smiled as if she held a secret from him. She sent a shiver down his back.

''Make that psychopath as well as socio-path. This one would enjoy inflicting pain on someone and enjoy watching them suffer.'' He couldn't wait to find out what she knew in the morning.

''She's horrible and we still don't know where Joshua is.'' Despite Drakeman being there Kirsten had begun to feel sick, an unnatural panic setting in. Rutland might be hurt somewhere. The damn man was haunting her now!

''Is Elisabeth safe?'' asked Drakeman. Rutland could usually take care of himself. He had been in far worse situations in Iraq or Afghanistan. A few mobsters would barely stop him.

''She texted a short while saying she arrived at the School House but he must be inside. She was waiting for us to go there with her.''

''Jesus! Is she out there on her own? I thought Rutland would be with her. Come on, we will catch them up now the officer has Danielle safely in the lock-up.''

Drakeman took the corners at break-neck speed requiring Kirsten to hold tight to avoid being slung across the car.

''Hold on Phil!'' remonstrated Kirsten. "I want to get there in one piece!''

''I want to find Elisabeth safe,'' he said and gave the car one more turn and skidded into the car park. It was a distance from the School House behind the trees, unable to be seen by those in the building. Unlit, it was eerie, the moon shining on the other vehicles there. Drakeman put the number plates of the two cars he didn't recognise in his cell and taking Kirsten by the arm he said, "Follow me and don't move unless I tell you. We want the element of surprise."

He had looked in Elisabeth's car but apart from her purse on the floor there was no other sign of a struggle. The windows were shattered. She had not left of her own free will. An icy grip took hold of his heart. His blood froze in his veins. His Elisabeth was probably in the hands of men who had already proven themselves to be willing to kill if the circumstances were right.

He looked in the windows of the School House and listened for sounds. There were no sounds of voices on the ground floor. He suspected if any foul play was intended it would take place in the cellars of this old building which were almost soundproof, their walls being ten inches thick.

He got through an unlatched window and helped Kirsten through. ''Wait for me here. If you hear anything upstairs come down for me quickly and alert me. I am going to explore the cellar. Use your gun if anyone threatens you. These men are not for taking prisoners!''

Kirsten felt a little calmer now she knew she could do something to help instead of twiddling her thumbs. She was like Rutland, a mover, driven to overcome problems and solving situations. Doing nothing made her nervous.

Her stomach churned and burned with the thought Rutland could be hurt. He might be an arrogant provoking sod but he had helped her time after time after she had rejected him. He was constant and caring. She realised she would be devastated if something happened to him. He was steadily making her want to rely on him, worming his quiet way into her affections.

Drakeman moved down the steep stairs, stopping at every corner and assessing the risks as he had been trained to do. He heard voices in the cellar. This was where the dudes were. He heard the voices of Rutland and Elisabeth and at last he could breathe normally again knowing they were alive. Peering around the corner, he saw Rutland tied to a chair and Elisabeth sitting with a man's hand resting heavily on her shoulder.

He had the desire to move forward and punch the bastard's daylights out but his military training set in and he took deep breaths and assessed the situation, wanting to get them out with minimum injury to all those in this room. A live witness who would squeal like a pig when questioned was more useful than a dead man.

Elisabeth saw a movement and her eyes widened expectantly. He put his head around the corner and nodded reassuringly to her and then drew his head back. Rutland had noticed that time but not the men. Their backs were facing him and he moved like a cat nearer them, silently, avoiding alerting them. There were three men all armed but only one pointed a gun at his colleagues. The man took his hand off her shoulder and moved back a little toward Drakeman. Rutland was tied up like a turkey but he could kick the men and a kick from Rutland was like a cannon ball hurtling at them.

He was close enough to hurt them now. Rutland said, ''You are dead men if I escape and find you,'' riling them, encouraging them to hurt him. The man with the gun dropped his firing arm and slapped Rutland on his face so hard his head snapped back on his neck but he then smiled a smile that did not reach his eyes. It was his turn to turn the tables on them.

Drakeman took his chance now the gun was not aimed at Rutland and swung around, kicking one man in the back so hard he spun across the room and head-butted the wall, collapsing in a heap. The other man reacted quickly but Drakeman aimed a slice at his throat, making the guy reach for it, coughing and kneeling on the ground until Drakeman chopped his neck and sent him unconscious to the floor.

Rutland kneed the man who had hit him in the groin and then kicked him even harder in the same place until he screamed with agony.

''Cut my hands Elisabeth!'' he ordered. She pulled the penknife out from the hidden pocket in her sweats and cut the bonds. Drakeman had by now cuffed the two men he had disabled and was holding Rutland's assailant by an arm twisted behind him. He cuffed him to the chair and then went to Elisabeth.

Kirsten ran down the stairs hearing the commotion. "Thank God you are all alive.'' Elisabeth moved to Drakeman whose hands were grazed from the blows he had made. She had never seen anyone move so fast. He must be a master of some martial art.

He was so light on his feet he could barely be heard as he had jumped and spun around, only the crack of the impact of feet and hands against flesh marking the silence in the room. He put his arm around her and they hugged each other as Kirsten went to Rutland and gave him a more restrained kiss on the cheek.

''Come on Sweetheart, I deserve more than that. I could have met my maker trying to solve this case.'' He pulled her into his arms and she didn't resist him, relief shining in her eyes.

''What would I do without you to irritate and annoy me?'' she said carelessly. ''Your ego hasn't been punctured then!''

''You do a good job puncturing that each day my love! Let's get these 'gentlemen' to the gaol for questioning. Then I can have a good night's sleep. You wouldn't like to rub some salve into my bruises? I fancy a massage from a willing woman.''

''You are incorrigible!'' she replied to this irrepressible man. "You are playing on your situation to get my hands on your body."

"Anytime, Sweetheart. Any excuse,'' he said winking at her and guiding her up the stairs. Drakeman had called the cops and he waited for them while the ladies went back to the hotel.

''Did you ever see anything so fast?'' said Elisabeth.

''I saw nothing!'' said Kirsten. ''I was coming down the stairs but Drakeman is a black belt and master of martial arts. He teaches some classes to kids in Miami; kids who are from hard backgrounds and need discipline and direction. Rutland says after being twisted to the floor and immobilised once by Drakeman the boys who think they're tough change their minds. Some have even joined the forces as a result of attending his classes.''

''He is certainly a tough guy!'' said Elisabeth, her respect growing for him by the moment.

''Don't try to compare him with David Lizzie. Drakeman is not weak at all. He just knows what he wants and goes for it and he wants you.''

''I think I may want him as well,'' said Lizzie relaxing, at last having made her decision to encourage Drakeman that evening. Kirsten smiled. Her colleagues deserved happiness with each other.

Now the case was nearly over she felt a little despondent. Would Rutland follow up his words and try to date her when it was solved or go back to Miami and continue his legal work without her? She castigated herself. First, she was pushing him away and then she was complaining if he left her. She was a pathetic confused fool who did not know her own mind.

Rutland's granddad glared at him through watery green eyes. ''Who gave permission to move us last night? Kirsten took a risk and could have been killed!''

''Phil and he was in control of the situation all the time. Elisabeth is bagging and recording the evidence and taking it to the Deputy and sending some to the FBI lab.

'Our good friend overrode the Deputy and gave her permission to do the work. To avoid a miscarriage of justice he arranged for Ms. Claremont to be seconded from the FBI and her bill will be paid from County funds. She is working officially for the County now and her information will be admissible in court.

'A mention of demotion and corruption made the Deputy acquiesce but his days are numbered in this town. I wonder how many other crimes he has overlooked deliberately to help rich and powerful men.''

''It is the way of the world boyo. T'was the same in the 'old country!''

''Well, it won't be any more in this town!''

''And what is happening to that young lady?''

''Kirsten?''

''Of course, Kirsten. You are like a cat on heat around her. Are you going to let her slip through your net?''

Rutland had the grace to look red. Despite his pretending he wanted to have a platonic relationship with her his Granddad was astute enough to enough to know he was more than attracted to Freja's niece.

''She still has business to finish in London, Granddad.''

''That Justin fella! He doesn't seem much of a catch. I thought she wanted rid of him!''

''She does but it might not be so easy. He may try to track her down and she may need an injunction to see him off.''

''A threat of a punch in the nose might be more appropriate,'' said the old man, his Irish temper showing. ''Aren't you wanting to sort him out young fellow?''

''Would that I could Granddad but he is in London not the Wild West. The law can sort him out and I am thinking of other ways that may be more painful to his pocket and keep me from being locked up for assault.''

''But not as satisfying though!'' muttered the old man maliciously.

''Let me have him in a dark street corner and my good intentions could dissolve,'' replied Rutland, his blood rising when he thought of what that creep had done to Kirsten.

''Will you follow her to London?''

''I hope I might persuade her to stay in Florida a little longer and have a vacation,'' said Rutland.

''So, you do have your eye on her! Does she feel the same way about you?''

''I think she is attracted to me but something stops her from letting me date her.''

''That low-life bastard has frightened her off men?''

''Think so. I have to get her to trust me but it is a slow process. I don't know if I have the time before she goes back to London.''

''I will ask Freja to persuade her to stay here. Freja would like the company and Kirsten will want to look after her while she is recovering from the fire.''

''I must go now Granddad. I must see the Deputy with Phil.'' He hugged his Granddad and said goodbye to Freja, who said, "Good luck young man,'' in her formal old-fashioned way.

He worried for her. Her breathing was laboured and her forehead hot. Her eyes were glazed and becoming vacant. Her speech was uttered in gasps as if every breath was an effort. She was sinking fast, only her indomitable spirit keeping her with them.

I am going to need it.

He went to the gaol. Drakeman was already there in the Deputy's office. Rutland thought facing Danielle was going to be a pushover, a quick wrap up job.

He was deadly wrong. The Deputy looked uncommonly smug and all Rutland's antennae rose. Something was wrong with the water here. He was too bloody pleased with himself. And Danielle looked quite happy for someone who faced an attempted murder charge. What was going on?

Drakeman had the look of a man who didn't want to be there. His face was grim, his eyes hooded. He wore the air of a man who was waiting to hear something he wouldn't like.

''Well Mr. Rutland. I have made a preliminary interview with Ms De Vere here and she has told me some interesting things we didn't know. She did help to instigate the arson attack and has made a full confession.''

"Good, then we can wrap this up quite quickly. Where is the clue to where the loot is buried? And satisfy my curiosity Danielle.''

''Ms De Vere to you.''

''Oh, after that steamy night together I think we are on more intimate terms than that,'' he mocked, not understanding why she smiled at his words. Something was very odd here.

''Well, Ms De Vere. Why collect the loot now and why didn't your Daddy pick it up himself earlier?''

''Joshua Sweetheart,'' she said, her voice reminding him of syrup and molasses as she bent closer to him, allowing him a generous look at her cleavage.

''You know his friend buried the loot and said he would tell him where it was so he could pick his share up later. The cops found out about his friend and sent him to prison.

'His friend had left the clue in a puzzle book but couldn't get a message out to him without the fear of the authorities finding out. He died but in his will left a codicil to Daddy in which he hinted there was a gift for him in the house. After Daddy was arrested his friend had entered the house and hid it there before it was sold.

'My Daddy wanted me to have the stuff now he was dying and that is why I left my job in Miami and came here to find the puzzle book but Freja would not acknowledge me. She thought I was a dim babe and I never got near the house.''

''I always thought Freja had good sense and taste,'' said Rutland scathingly.

''Better than yours. You took me to bed!''

''A mental aberration on my part which I regret deeply now. I usually have better taste!''

''You are just feeling sour grapes after we broke up in Miami,'' she said dropping her bombshell. ''I told the Deputy I was not the brainchild. It needed someone with more clout who had contacts in the FBI who could doctor photos and cut into phone records.''

Rutland began to understand the implications of what she was referring to. She was fitting him up!

''You lying bitch,'' he said getting up. By sleeping with her and calling her Sweetheart he had played into her hands. An arrogant, malicious bastard, wanting revenge for her treatment of Kirsten, his unsavoury sexual reputation had bit him in the ass.

''Down Mr. Rutland,'' said the Deputy. He was enjoying every minute of this interview. Rutland felt the desire to knock his teeth out but sat down to hear the rest of this fairy story. The worst was yet to come. Kirsten had come in and was listening. She had heard the last few words of Danielle and was fascinated and horrified by what she was hearing.

''Like to finish your story Ms De Vere?'' said the Deputy. "We are all ears. Ms Gateman take a seat. You may find this very interesting and informative. Mr. Rutland and Ms De Vere go back quite a long way.'

''I have never seen her before I came to this town to investigate this case.''

''Now Darlin,'' said Danielle. ''You know Thirman needed a contact with interests in minerals and mining who was rich and powerful and you were the man. Defoe Holdings made an offer to buy shares in the mining companies my Daddy had shares in and your company was rejected. If you could find the share certificates my Daddy's friends had hidden, you could get the control you wanted.''

''What company?'' asked Rutland.

''Reechman Inds.''

''I had a minority share ownership in the company but sold out years ago and have not made them an offer or made any other contact with them since.''

''Oh, but John Thirman acted as your intermediary. You stayed anonymous in the background as you so often do.''

''What has the puzzle book got to do with the mining companies?'' asked Drakeman.

''Nothing. It concerned some diamonds that were stolen in a jewellery haul and hidden somewhere. The puzzle book contains the location. Eighty million dollars of uncut jewels,'' she said licking her lips at the thought.

''This is all bullshit,'' exploded Rutland. "Innuendoes but no evidence.''

''Does your conglomerate invest in mining companies Mr. Rutland?'' asked the Deputy.

''Yes,'' he said ''but not that company. I diversified from property five years ago.''

''Unusual and rather unethical for an attorney to get involved in a dirty business, like mining,'' said the Deputy.

''I like to spread my investments widely in case of risk. Your pension is probably invested in that industry also. And for the record. I am a qualified financial investment trader as well so investing in companies is my trade and is perfectly legitimate. I keep my financial trading totally separate from giving legal advice to my clients. I work only for myself and my shareholders as a financial trader.''

. ''When he came to Devil's Creek I was quite shocked but he persuaded me to give him another chance,'' said Danielle. ''After all, he was involved in the planning and investment, so I thought it might work romantically this time. I didn't realise he began to fall hard for Ms Gateman here and muddied the waters. If he hadn't pretended to help her and brought our lady friend here we could have got clean away.''

Kirsten got up. ''I think I have heard enough. Please keep me informed of the progress of this case, Deputy.'' Without even looking at Rutland she left the room tears filling her eyes. Nothing made sense but that woman seemed to know a lot about Rutland.

''Kirsten!'' cried Rutland, trying to go after her but an officer stopped him with a hand on his shoulder.

''Steady Mr. Rutland, we need to ask you some more questions.''

Rutland gritted his teeth and sat down ready for the interrogation. Danielle had just injected enough distorted facts to poisonous Kirsten's mind about him. He would demolish the facts after Drakeman interviewed Thirman and clear his name but mud stuck and this would not help his firm.

''Phil, could you go with Ms Gateman and make sure she is ok?''

''In a minute, Joshua. I would like to hear what else Ms De Vere has to contribute,'' replied Drakeman starkly. He looked sceptical but sat there, arms crossed, waiting to hear more information.

''Of course, everything can be verified?'' the Deputy asked of Danielle.

''Of course,'' she said firmly.

What a bloody liar. She knew her story would fall like a pack of cards once it was investigated but she wanted to destroy his fledging relationship with Kirsten. He intended this bitch would go down for the maximum he could organise for her.

''You will enjoy our hospitality here tonight Mr. Rutland and then we will interview John Thirman,'' said the Deputy.

''Officer!'' He enjoyed watching the officer cuff Rutland and lead him out of the room.

''Delighted!'' said Rutland, just loud enough for him to hear. He was going down fighting this evening. He had been looking forward to a quiet dinner and dance with Kirsten who had been melting toward him. Now he had a hot uncomfortable cell with other alleged perps to share it with him. The evening had gone from bad to worse.

Drakeman said, ''I would like to interview Mr. Thirman tomorrow please. Is he in the County Prison? As I am close to Mr. Rutland I would like one of your officers to accompany me.''

''Are you an investor in Defoe Holdings Mr. Drakeman?''

''Yes, but a minority investor only and I never take part in any of the decision-making. I have my own businesses to run.'' He had invested monies in Joshua's businesses when his friend needed some quick finance but he admitted financial knowledge was not his strength and had let Joshua make the investment decisions, which companies to buy or sell. Thank God for that. He was already too close to Joshua for the Deputy's satisfaction.

He would chase up Thirman's story tomorrow. Something smelt around here. Danielle had the gleam of the fanatic in her eye, trying to trip Rutland up and enjoying every minute of it. He knew Rutland well and while he was a typical entrepreneur and attorney sailing close to the wind on occasion he was basically an honest guy, straight in his business dealings and well respected in the community. As for plotting to kill Freja and his Granddad by implication, it was farcical! Drakeman knew a stitch up when he smelt it.

Danielle had delusions of grandeur. Even with her Galliano dress and Jimmy Choo shoes she was outclassed by Kirsten when the other woman wore simple jeans and tee-shirt with flip-flops. Danielle was the cream on the top that enticed a man but Kirsten was the rich filling that made a man want to taste more of her. Danielle paled in comparison with her.

Kirsten had run out of the building, face pale and bloodless, leaving Rutland devastated. She had seen the horror on his face and his attempt to stop her but she could not stand any more suspense or stress. The look of triumph on Danielle's face when he had referred to that steamy night had made her feel sick to the stomach. It was as if she understood and knew Rutland intimately, much more than through one night of vigorous sex. Her stomach tied in knots, Kirsten felt like vomiting and reaching her hotel room she retched into the toilet bowl.

The Judge had already agreed to remove the charges against her. Calling a taxi, she told reception she was going to Freja's residence. She needed to find the puzzle book. The smoke had largely dispersed. The air conditioning had packed up but the bedrooms and kitchen were liveable.

Her aunt had left the key with a neighbour just as she had expected and the neighbour welcomed her.

''None of us believed you were implicated my dear. You always supported your aunt, particularly when she had to move for her health to the Creek.'' She thanked the woman and let herself in.

It felt like home. It might be a hick town but she had always felt Devil's Creek was home more than London. Its nosy but friendly residents had welcomed the niece of Freja, the old cantankerous but warm and generous woman they had warmed to over the last few years. Straight-talking was Freja but genuine, how the people of this small town liked folk to be. Not like that snobby aloof city-dweller John Grenman who had turned his nose in the air at ordinary folk and look what he had turned out to be! A thief!

She dragged herself up the stairs to the loft and faced the volume of books piled up across the floor. What books would interest a self-obsessed sociopath, more interested in figures than people? She gravitated toward Sudoko puzzles at first but there was a pile of puzzles that mixed financial crosswords and figure puzzles.

She phoned Elisabeth, offering her a pizza and bottle of wine to share. Elisabeth knew she needed more than a searcher to help her. Drakeman released her for the evening saying he would see her for cocktails later that night. Kirsten thought of Rutland in that cell with his companions. He was tough as steel and wouldn't be intimidated by the rougher inmates but he would be lonely and bitter.

''We are looking for a needle in a haystack!'' she said to Elisabeth. ''I hope you have fortitude. I picked some business puzzles out to start with.''

Two hours later she remarked, ''I hate financial puzzles but there seems to be a current theme. Shares in some specific industries targeted. Chemicals here but this one targets the mining and minerals industry. It could be relevant.''

''It has been filled in unlike some of the others. I think we might be on to something.''

''Strange. Only one puzzle was finished.''

''It is the same in this book.''

''There are five books pertaining to this industry.''

''All of them are filled in the same way. Just one puzzle!''

''Phone Drakeman and ask if there are any clues he may give, i.e. companies or minerals or even the diamond hoist.''

''The diamonds were stolen from a company called Eureka,'' answered Drakeman. ''Try to match it with one of the answers to the puzzles.''

''A Greek expression!'' cried Kirsten.

''Sounds as if he was a student of Greek as four more Greek terms were filled in the books,'' said Elisabeth.

'Take the first letter of the name of each and see if it makes a word or phrase.''

''Mount. Not enough. Take the second letter.''

''No joy!''

''Bloody puzzle!' said Kirsten 'I used to hate Countdown.''

''You are the lawyer, meant to be good with words and letters.''

''Reminds me of the 11+ entrance exams,'' grumbled Kirsten. ''I was glued to the desk with anagrams and word games. I hated them ever since!''

''Turn the letters round and use the last first.''

''Yes, it spells a word. Range. You are enjoying this, you unnatural child,'' teased Kirsten. ''Now use the middle letters.''

''Green. Put together it makes Mount Green Range. Does it make sense to you?''

''It is a golf club and I bet Grenman played there.''

''It was a friend of Grenman actually,'' said Drakeman answering their query. ''Now the obvious place is the locker room but is that too obvious?''

''There are still five books left. Let's work out those.''

Drakeman supplied another name linked to the hoist. Now they had the key it was quicker to solve the puzzles. The final word was bureau.

''Which bureau I wonder?''

''Can't be many there. I'll take you there tomorrow,'' said Drakeman learning their information. ''Send Elisabeth back now please,'' commanded Drakeman. "I have a job for her.''

''Watch it,'' said Kirsten. ''He is a man with a mission and I bet the job involves something to do with his bed.'' Elisabeth looked dreamy eyed.

''Enjoy yourself love,'' said Kirsten. ''He is a good man!''

''I hope Rutland is proven innocent for both your sakes Kirsten.''

''Oh, so do I,'' She was a fool but she was missing his teasing, irritating presence already.

Elisabeth arrived back at the hotel and Drakeman was waiting for her at the top of the elevator.

''You are wicked,'' she said poking a finger at him. ''What job have you for me?''

''More of a position really. My personal sex slave. I think you would fit the role to perfection!''

''You are blatant, aren't you?'' she said reeling from his bluntness.

''I prefer honest. Deception in relationships doesn't work. You don't want commitment so will a fling with good company and great sex do for a while?''

''What makes you think it will be great, the sex I mean?''

''Chemistry my love. That spark between us that you feel as well. When I touch you, I feel a thrill go through me. I can't wait to bed you.''

''You needn't wait too long then,'' she said drawing him into his bedroom and shutting the door. Drakeman moved toward her with purpose, pushing her gently on to the bed and undoing her dress slowly and seductively. He felt her tremble under her touch as he felt her silky skin. He took it more slowly, allowing her to enjoy every sensation as he stripped her, prolonging her anticipation of the final act. He intended Elisabeth Claremont to remember this night for ever and to want to come back for more.

The next morning Elisabeth woke up slowly feeling slightly sore. She remembered the night before and smiled at the man lying next to her. He slept the sleep of the dead. His fighting had made him taut with adrenalin and she had tried to relax him, with kisses and caresses.

''My beautiful girl,'' he murmured in his sleep. ''Lizzie, stay with me this morning.' '

She was surprised by him talking to her in his sleep but he had surprised her the night before, prolonging the foreplay until she was sated with pleasure and then and only then had he taken her and had enjoyed his own release. He was confident of his own sexuality and a generous lover, taking the lead but allowing her to take what she wanted from this love-making.

It was Monday and they had to work but she allowed themselves a little grace and let him sleep a little late until bleary eyed he woke up, flinched and said, ''We are late. I must go to the prison. Order what food you like while I shower. I will take mine to go.''

She looked a little disappointed and after nibbling her ear he murmured, "Tonight is an early night after I have taken you girls to the club to find this wretched loot.''

Through the window, she watched his exit as he tore up the miles in the borrowed Aston; a strong powerful man, enjoying the release of driving a supreme machine as powerful as he. He was nothing like David and it was wrong to compare the two. This man didn't need to stick like a leech to a woman long after the relationship was dead to feed his self-esteem.

He got to the prison without being stopped for speeding. He was faced with John Thirman. He didn't know if Danielle had made up the connection with Rutland on the spur of the moment or if it had been planned. He would let him mention it if the connection existed.

'Danielle told us the truth last night, what we are looking for. We have solved the puzzle in the puzzle books and are finding the hidden loot later tonight. We just have to fill in and confirm the details now. What was your role in this and who is the person organising it?'

Thirman was a harder nut to crack than the young perp. He was older and he had been paid well to keep his mouth shut and had no intention of serving a long period of time. He sat silently, insolently, waiting for Drakeman to start the questioning, no fear marking his countenance.

Drakeman's cell buzzed and he took it outside the room. When he came back in his jaw was set and he had a different look about him.

''You had better talk now Thirman. It is more than your freedom in jeopardy. It is your life. Freja Andersson died a half an hour ago, from pneumonia, lying in bed too long. The charge is now murder and attempted murder. At the least you will be going down for life.''

He enjoyed watching the colour fade from the man's face. Thirman's eyes bolted; a man who now knew his back was to the wall, who needed to cooperate with the authorities, he shrivelled in front of Drakeman.

''I didn't intend to murder the old lady. Danielle planned to get the books without hurting her but the old dear wouldn't cooperate by selling the house and she knew something was up when the house was searched. She was going to clear her house of rubbish and give the good stuff to charity. We could have lost everything so we arranged the fire.''

''Who is the brain behind the organisation?''

''Danielle and Krussman. Danielle runs the financial aspect and he runs the crime ring and organises the hoists. They rarely meet and work independently most of the time but they co-exist well and it worked for the last five years. Last year her Dad said he was dying and wanted to help her find the loot.''

''And your role?''

''I was the link between the companies and Krussman and Kirsten. No-one else met so the other two stayed anonymous.''

''Was there any other man or woman at a high level?''

''Yes, a man, a financier.'' Drakeman's blood ran cold. "His name?''

''Dave Clery. He works with an investment foundation in Miami.''

Drakeman realised he had stopped breathing so intent was he on hearing the name. He breathed at last with relief. Rutland was no part of it according to this perp. He looked at the Deputy's officer and the other man smiled, a satisfied smile. He was pleased Rutland was innocent. He had worked with Rutland and was clearly impressed by his integrity.

Drakeman drove them back to Devil's Creek. He was worried when the two girls were not there in the hotel. They went to the Deputy and the officer persuaded the Deputy to drop the charges against Rutland.

A rough looking unshaved Rutland was delighted to leave the cell. He smiled at the Deputy, a smile that promised retribution later and the Deputy seemed smaller, shrinking in Rutland's presence as if he knew his days in office were numbered.

You didn't cross a powerful man like Rutland unless you were sure of your facts. Pompous and intellectually inferior to Rutland he had overestimated his own capabilities and underestimated Rutland's ruthlessness. Rutland was not a vindictive man but he no longer trusted this man to remain impartial when enforcing the law. His was not the appropriate personality for such an office and Rutland intended he would be stripped of his tenure.

Drakeman observed his friend was as resilient as ever. "Have you had any breakfast or lunch.''

''Just some repulsive pap called cornflakes and off-milk. I could murder a burger or steak. The company was equally as stimulating. I had a drunk sleeping his whisky off, a petty thief and a bully in for battery.''

''Give you any trouble?'' asked Drakeman knowing the answer.

''The bully? Not after I warned him I would stuff his teeth down his throat if he gave me any grief,'' said Rutland grimly. "He seemed to believe me.'' Drakeman smiled. Rutland rarely lost his temper but his great height and broad shoulders and fierce expression in his eyes when annoyed would put the most aggressive perp off.

He then looked very seriously at Rutland. "I have some bad news. Freja died of pneumonia this morning.''

Rutland's first thoughts were of Kirsten and his Granddad. He wanted to be with them to give them support and to hug Kirsten. He felt her hurt. She would be devastated.

''We need to go back to the hotel anyway. Neither of the women were there when I got back.''

''No explanation or note left behind?''

''None. They found the clue last night and were pretty excited. The loot we are after came from a diamond hoist. They may be in a bureau in the Mount Green Range Golf Club. I am praying the ladies haven't taken off to find them on their own.''

''Did Thirman implicate anyone else?''

''Yes, there is another big wheel named Clery who could still be around and be dangerous.''

''I'll strangle Kirsten if they have gone on their own. That girl has a nose for trouble.'' Feeling the same about Elisabeth Drakeman pushed the car faster and it came to a skid in the parking lot.

''Remind me to drive next time,'' remarked Rutland dryly. ''Do you know how much these tyres cost?''

''Be grateful you are free,'' snapped Drakeman.' 'If I hadn't intervened and gone to the gaol your ass would have been on the line. You owe me a drive in the Batmobile.''

Sliding out of the sleek low machine Drakeman straightened and telephoned the women's cells again but they were turned off. Muttering something unprintable about difficult disobedient irrational women he stalked into the hotel now. He was boiling mad, torn between anger and worry about the women's safety. He could not believe they would go on their own after yesterday's fight in the School House. They must understand the danger lurking until all the gang were caught.

''I think we had better go to the golf club,'' said Rutland. ''The girls might be there. It is about thirty minutes' drive from here.''

''I still can't believe they would go on their own.''

''They are women. Since when do you understand what a woman does?'' said Rutland cynically. His opinion of women had never been high since his fiancé had cheated on him and his experiences with the girls who hung around the Navy camps.

What really pissed him off was the two women had gone off without leaving a message and their phones were turned off. What were they playing at? Elisabeth was still under his contract, in addition to working for the County and he was paying her well to be available and ready to carry out his orders. Kirsten was a different kettle of fish. He had learnt the hard way she was not to be given orders. He had to use persuasion with Kirsten to get her to work with him. She was her own woman.

The receptionist at the Mount Green Range Golf Club smiled at him. ''Ms K, Gateman and Ms E. Claremont. No, we haven't signed in anyone by those names today Sir. They might have gone directly to the Spa. There is a reception there. Shall I try the number for you?''

''Please,'' said Drakeman putting on his most winsome smile. The girl blushed and asked reception.

''No? Thanks.'' She turned back to Drakeman. ''No Sir. No ladies by that name or your description.''

''Well there is no point wasting our time while we are here,'' said Rutland. ''Please could you arrange a tour around the club facilities for us? We are thinking of joining with our ladies when we can find them.''

''Certainly Sir,'' said the receptionist ringing the facilities manager. A pretty girl arrived and gave them a visitor's badge each.

''Is there anything you would particularly like me to show you Sir?''

''I would need to do some work as well as play here so the business support area and the lounges would be useful.''

''The ladies can inspect the spa later,'' said Drakeman. *They could instigate a search as well as us.* They had managed to find the freaking puzzle books when they tried!

The men asked polite questions about the facilities, pretending interest. They went to the lounge and noticed a room off it. ''Is that a public area?'' asked Drakeman.

''No, that is locked. It used to be the office of the manager.''

''I would like to look at the fitness centre while my friend looks at the bar,'' said Drakeman. ''We really must get back to the Creek soon.''

He followed the girl to the fitness centre while Rutland took out some pass keys. They fitted easily and he slid into the office. There were two bureaus but only one was old and locked. He guessed this was the one which might contain the secrets. He set to opening the older one. A quick search and he found a false drawer at the back of it.

Bingo! He felt inside. A black velvet pouch was just within his grasp. He opened it and whistled. Some sparkling diamonds were winking at him. He had better get back to Drakeman and get these babies to a safe at the bank or Deputy's office.

He turned to go but felt hard iron poking in his neck, forcing his head down over the desk.

''Drop the jewels on the bureau please Mr. Rutland,'' commanded the quiet voice. Something made Rutland obey the order without a whim. The cool but deadly tone suggested his health was at risk if he didn't obey instantly. He put them down and waited for the man to say he could lift his head.

''Up and very slowly Mr. Rutland. Your hands spread across the desk.''

''Mr. Clery I suppose?'' enquired Rutland. He knew this man wouldn't let him live so to hell with it; he might as well find out who he was.

''Indeed. Our friend Thirman must have squealed. We will have to find a suitable punishment for him later,'' he said in voice that chilled Rutland to the bone. ''You know Freja Andersson died this morning? Collateral damage as you say in the SEALS.'' Rutland felt sick and a cold hand gripped his heart.

He did not show any compassion or care that the woman died. The bastard was as cold as ice. He then realised, *that is where the women are, at the hospital.* Their phones would have to be turned off. He and Drakeman owed both women an apology.

''What next Clery?''

''We walk through reception and across the range and I will dispose of you in an area where no-one plays anymore. *This is just like a Bogart film my Mom used to watch; where the hero is made to pass through the public rooms but knocks the gun out in the dark.* But it wasn't dark and this man could see his every move.

He moved slowly, his hands by his side and passed through reception. He saw Drakeman out of the corner of his eye and wondered if he guessed he was with this man under duress. Drakeman stayed there talking to the pretty girl, not grasping the realities of the situation. He was on his own with this psychopath who was clearly enjoying tricking him and trying to frighten him. The coldness in the man was reflected in his soulless steel grey eyes.

Rutland walked in front of him across the course to an out-building. It could not have taken more than five minutes to reach the old dilapidated building set behind some trees but it stretched out in time in his mind as he tried to find ways to avoid dying here. He had survived wars in foreign places and had fought in mean back streets in Miami when he was a tough kid but this man could be his nemesis if he didn't think fast.

''Open the door,'' said his tormentor and Rutland pushed the door. To his relief, it wouldn't open.

''It won't open. It is either locked or stuck,'' explained Rutland. "Try it yourself if you don't believe me!''

''Move out of the way to my side!'' said Clery. Rutland complied. You did not argue with a man who had death and hatred in his eyes. Clery rattled and turned the handle and pushed the door but it would not move.

''Shit!'' he cried and snarled, ''You're meant to be the Black belt. Kick it in!''

Rutland swore violently and fluently to himself but aimed one well-heeled boot to the door and the lock broke and it flew open.

''In!'' It was a simple order and he was given an unnecessarily hard shove which sent him sprawling head first into the seat of a rocking chair. He clawed himself up into a sitting position, facing the other man, not wanting him to think he was afraid of him.

''It will be over quick Mr. Rutland. I don't wish to prolong it although Danielle suggested I should make you suffer. Oh, you didn't know I spoke to her today then. I pretended to be her legal advisor and she said I should follow you.

'As you raced out of the hotel I thought you knew something about the diamonds and followed you. It wàs the right trail to follow. The women went to the hospital. Mr. Drakeman is being given an extended tour of the club. I bribed the girl to keep him a bit longer, telling her I wanted to discuss a business project privately with you.''

He pointed the Glocke directly at Rutland's head. No danger of missing his target. Rutland's brains would be blown out at that range even if he was a poor marksman and something told Rutland he was nothing of the kind.

My luck is running out, thought Rutland, his mind whirring, trying to find a way out of this fix.

The man's eyes narrowed on his target and Rutland closed his eyes expecting the worst but a quiet voice broke the silence.

''Put it down Mister or you will be dead faster than him.''

''You will take both of us then,'' said the man uncaring. "Ms Gateman, you would not want to kill your friend. You haven't got the nerve to pull the trigger if your friend could be killed.''

''Don't hesitate Kirsten,'' said Rutland. He spoke the words as he dived to one side as the man pulled the trigger. He was caught in the upper arm but saw the man slowly collapse in front of his eyes as the pistol in Kirsten's hand resounded with the bullet she had fired into the back of Clery's head.

''That was for Aunt Freja!'' she said and wrapped the pistol in a handkerchief and put it in her haversack.

Rutland was torn between relief that he was alive and anger at her risking her own life. ''What the hell are you doing here?'' he asked, grabbing her by the shoulders and shaking her. ''You could have been killed. We told you to stay in the hotel until we collected you!''

''Well and nice to see you as well!'' she said sarcastically. ''Get out of the wrong side of the bed, did you? We were at the hospital. We were arranging Aunt Freja's funeral.''

''My poor Girl,'' Rutland held her tight, establishing his possession over her. She was his woman and only his, and he wanted to comfort her.

'I know you loved her dearly,'' he said caressing her hair. She pushed him away and tore some cloth from her shirt and started binding his arm. He stood obediently, wondering how to charm himself into her good books again. Acting macho man had merely made her back off from him again, the stupid bastard that he was.

''We went back to the hotel and reception told us where you are and we followed you here. I followed Phil here and Elisabeth went to look for you. We did leave a message at reception but you didn't receive it.''

''Thirman has proven Joshua's innocence,'' said Drakeman finding him at last. ''The charges against him have been dropped.''

''Good!'' she said but still didn't go back into Rutland's arms ''I thought Danielle was trying to hurt you but the coincidences seemed too great.''

''She was clever, using just enough facts to trick us and I shouldn't have taunted her about our night together and called her Sweetheart. I trapped myself with my own words.''

''The cops are coming,'' said Drakeman who had been busy with his cell. ''They will want to interview Kirsten. Where did you learn to shoot like that?'' The distance and the angle she had shot at and the moving target would have taxed an experienced marksman.

''On my aunt's ranch but also at shooting parties with Justin at his father's country house. I hated shooting birds but did it to please him. I am not really a country girl. I prefer towns or cities.''

''That is over now. You can forget Justin,'' said Rutland.

''I must go back and confront him or I will fear his memory. I also want to get some of my wages back from him to help pay my tuition fees. I applied for some barrister jobs yesterday on-line.''

"I hoped you might stay here in Devil's Creek a bit longer,'' said Rutland.

''I would have if Aunt Freja had been alive but now I have nothing to stay for,'' said Kirsten sadly.

''I was hoping to change your mind,'' he said taking her chin in his hand as Drakeman made his exit.

''I would like you to come back with me to Miami for a vacation if you want to leave Devil's Creek.'' He guessed the town now only held bad memories for her.

''I can't Joshua. I can't give you what you want or any other man. I don't want a relationship with a man again.''

''I don't understand you,'' he said. "You enjoy kissing me. Why not a relationship?''

She pushed him away, exasperated she had to explain herself to him, something so private to her.

''I don't want to sleep with you or any other man Joshua Rutland. I hate sex. Do you understand now? And you are such a virile man. You ooze sex appeal.''

She went to the door and pleaded with him. ''Please leave me alone Joshua, listen to me. I am not good for you.''

''I am sorry I don't think I can. I need you and care for you Kirsten. I won't touch you unless you say I can but I will not stop hunting you and trying to persuade you to date me and then live with me.''

''Well I am sorry for you then because you are chasing a lost cause,'' she said walking away to Drakeman who had now been joined by Elisabeth who was encircled in his arm. She had heard the shot and had rushed to him to make sure he was safe.

''And you call us stupid, you two going after the jewels!'' She turned to Rutland. "Were the share certificates there as well?''

''Yes, I think so but I didn't pull them out to scrutinise them.''

Drakeman was enjoying being fussed over by Elisabeth even if she was scolding him at the same time. His mother had not been warm or cuddly, negligently leaving him to his older sister to look after while she hung around bars. She had looked for a perfect man to support her in the lifestyle she dreamed about after her husband left her to bring up three kids alone on child support. She had never found the man and had died embittered and poor while Drakeman was in the SEALS.

Like many other men, he had joined the forces as he had no wealth or future and little family life at home. His brothers were much younger than him and had grown up distant from him. His mother had constantly harped about her life and criticised him, driving him into the Navy. He had felt his unit was more than family to him than his own and had stayed longer in the SEALS than many men.

He had left the SEALS to support his two younger brothers when his older Sister married saying she had done her bit and wanted none of them anymore. She had taken herself off to San Francisco with her new husband and he hadn't heard of them since.

Drakeman had started studying during his period in the SEALS and later worked for a security firm whilst he took enough courses to get himself accepted into the FBI. His brothers lived with an aunt and he had paid for them to go through school and university. After he left the FBI he built a security business which had branches through America and then a private investigation business. He now had offices in several countries and had invested in Rutland's firms.

A wealthy man, he still felt lonely, feeling something was lacking. He was never given to navel gazing being a man of action but at thirty-nine he recognised in himself a lonely man who like Rutland needed someone to go home to; to welcome and love him and make his house a home. He had come to the age where he wanted a long-term partner and wife and maybe a family.

He thought Elisabeth might fit the bill. She was beautiful, spirited and confident and most of all intelligent. She never bored him like his babes before had done. It was just his luck, now he had met his almost perfect woman she didn't want commitment and was so independent. He had an upward struggle to change her mind but he was nothing if not an obstinate and persistent man. He had a reputation for getting what he wanted and he wanted Elisabeth Claremont in his life permanently.

The mood in the car was bleak. Rutland and Kirsten barely spoke, Kirsten distancing herself emotionally from Rutland in the corner. Rutland brooded, trying to think of a way of persuading Kirsten to stay. The funeral was in a week's time and then the next day she was to head back to London.

He was pleased she was regaining her confidence but the lawyer in him feared Justin would hurt her if she confronted him on her own. A man who would whip a woman, a professional woman, and try to dominate her until she became passive and submissive would not easily give in. He would try to regain his dominance of her. If she challenged him and argued with him he could easily use violence against her again.

She needed someone as strong as him to accompany her, a man like him or someone who would represent him if she would not accept his interference in her life. For the second time in his life he felt powerless to help someone he loved. He had felt gutted when he could not help his Granddad pay for his Grandma's ever rising medical bills. He had joined the SEALS and swore one day he would never be so poor he couldn't control his family's destiny again.

"If you must see that man let me come and meet him with you," he ventured over dinner.

"Thank you but no. It is of no concern of yours Mr Rutland.".

"No concern of mine!" Exasperated he bit out, "I care for you! It is my business! You are just so bloody-minded you won't recognise it! You are too independent for your own good!"

"That is my choice and my right Mr. Rutland. I can do what I want without any man to control me."

"And I have a first name. Use it," said Rutland. "We've kissed each other so we are hardly on formal terms"

He tried to regain control of the situation again. "Will you allow one of my men to accompany you? You can even pay me back later when you work? It will not cost much."

"No thank you. I have male friends from uni who will help me if I ask them."

Recognising his friend was up against a brick wall, Drakeman said, "May I make a suggestion?" Two pairs of eyes looked suspiciously at him but Elisabeth pressed his hand encouragingly.

"Both Joshua and I are experts in unarmed combat. I teach it back home to women who have been attacked. If you are going to face this guy, you should be prepared for a violent reaction from him.

'Men who abuse women don't take challenges from women without hitting back. I've met these types of guys before and seen the damage they wreak. They see a challenge from a woman as hurting their self-esteem.

'We could give you some lessons which would help you defend yourself at least while you shout for help. Think about it please. We don't want to see you hurt and this guy sounds a bastard toward women.''

Kirsten remembered how she had frozen when Justin had threatened her. Too scared to run or shout for help she had suffered his ill treatment when she should have hit back or run. She might do the same without preparation for their meeting and they might end up left on their own. He was manipulative, bribing people to change their plans to suit his purposes. If she was trained by these men she might be able to act appropriately if he threatened her with violence.

''I think it is a good idea. How much can you teach me in the next week?''

''Not a lot but enough to stop you freezing and give you time to run away and or shout for help.''

''I'll do it,'' she said. ''Thank you for your help.'' She bit back tears at the thought of these lovely people wanting to help her and moved quickly to the rest room.

Rutland breathed a sigh of relief. ''You cracked through that wall. I was getting nowhere.''

''You are too close to her. She cares for you or she wouldn't be trying to push you away,'' said Elisabeth. ''If she allows you to get too close to her she will give in to you and she can't do that while she is still so mixed up over Justin. She has to leave him behind and this meeting will give her closure.''

''She is not meeting him on his own. I will be there whether she wants it or not. Don't worry I will be incognito but be there just in case. I am not allowing her to face that monster on her own again. He could kill her this time.''

''You may alienate her by interfering,'' warned Drakeman.

''I have nothing to lose. She has already warned me off. At least I can do some damage to him. I have already asked my contacts to investigate his companies and find out if any are vulnerable. He will regret the fact he ever hurt Kirsten. I will destroy him financially by the time I have finished with him.''

''I thought he was a smart cookie when he comes to finance.''

''He started out inheriting from his father and took good advice in investing his monies. The smart asses are the ones who can get greedy and fall on their butts. I may offer anonymously a proposal that is too sweet to turn down. He will find out it is too good to be true when I have netted him and it is too late for him to escape.''

Elisabeth looked at him and didn't recognise this man sitting in front of her. Gone was the efficient, warm but detached employer. In his place was a cold machine, ruthlessly planning the destruction of a sworn enemy who had hurt a vulnerable woman whom he clearly loved.

Joshua Rutland had fallen hard for a woman for the very first time in his life. She could not return that love. He hurt and this way was the only way he could provide retribution against the bastard who had hurt her. God help the man when the force of Rutland's wrath finally hit him. It would hurt like hell!

•

Rutland tried harder to encourage Kirsten to trust him. It was Sunday and he wanted her to relax. She had spent her spare time clearing out Freja's affects and was quiet and contemplative, clearly remembering her beloved aunt.

''I think we need a day off. Elisabeth and Phil are working on some leads and don't need us. I have done most of the work I need to do here and need some r and r and so do you. I want to go horseback riding. Will you come with me? The dog needs a good run as well having been cooped up in the neighbour's house for days.''

Animals were a way of reaching Kirsten. She shared her aunt's love of all animals, furry, finned or feathered. He had collected his Granddad's dog, his Granddad's friend. Kirsten had met the animal the day before. A mixture of wolfhound and some other indistinguishable breed it had run from the doorway at ninety miles an hour howling at him. Jumping up at him it nearly knocked him over. Rutland had stepped back from the onslaught of over two hundred lbs of solid muscle, taking the force of the hairy animal head on; catching his great paws before it could reach him and wash his face.

Holding the giant creature away from him he spoke softly but firmly to him. ''Fury, I have had my shower today. Leave off will you.'' The dog howled again but subsided into a heap at Rutland's feet, his head rested on his paws.

"This is Fury Kirsten, an overgrown puppy who thinks he is still a baby. Granddad is still trying to train him but struggling. He was kicked out of a home for being too boisterous.''

''I met him before,'' she said kneeling and taking the dog's head in her hands and rubbing his head and back. The dog yelped with pleasure and rolled on to his back recognising a friend. She tickled the animal's tummy and the dog barked in ecstasy.

''You have made a friend for life there. He has good taste. Not everyone meets his approval.''

''He is handsome and I adore him.''

''The feeling is mutual. You have all males eating out of your hand,'' he said helping her up, leaving his hand in hers a little longer that was necessary.

''I have always wanted a dog or cat. Justin thought they were unhygienic.''

Justin sounds like a pompous bore who doesn't how to live life, thought Rutland, thinking of his own feline and canine delinquents in his condo who tried daily to wreck his home.

''If you think this guy is handsome you should see the horse I picked out for you at the stable yesterday. Can you ride?''

''Yes, but I haven't ridden for three years.'' She had loved riding but hated riding with the hunt with Justin, detesting hunting and field sports. She hated the country way of life and the city men's obsession with shooting anything that moved there. Like Rutland she was a city girl liking people around her. She was desperate to get back on a horse and wanted a cat when she went back to London; something loving and furry to greet her when she went home at night after work.

An animal made a home despite muddy paws and clawed covers. She wanted a home, not a palace to live in. Justin's house was always too clean and neat, full of porcelain and antiques; not a place for children nor animals to run about in making mayhem. It had always seemed too quiet and lonely for her when she was on her own or with his severe, critical housekeeper who wanted nothing out of place like him. Her mother had been the same, suffering from OCD, obsessing over any mark or mistake, wanting perfection always. Her house had felt like a mausoleum when Kirsten had grown up in it.

She had preferred her boarding school and had often spent the weekends and holidays away with her friends at their family and pet friendly houses. When she had been removed from school she had lost contact with her former friends and had become lonelier than ever. She had stood out with her refined private school accent and it had been difficult for her to make new friends. She had been driven into spending time at Justin's house, his family welcoming her as Justin more than liked her.

Rutland was waiting for her answer. He had been there when she wanted a shoulder to cry on; had been friendly without being excessively intimate with her during the last few days. She felt she could trust him not to pounce on her. What harm would it do to ride with a handsome, warm, kind amusing man when she would leave for London soon?

''Yes, I would love to ride with you.''

A smile lit up his face. He let a breath out as if he had been waiting for her to answer. He took her hands, gently covering them with his and said, ''I will ask the concierge for a picnic. A bottle of wine and salad and fruit and chicken and cake. How does that grab you Sweetheart?''

''Fantastic,'' she said returning his grasp. He removed his hand and put it around her shoulder as they walked amiably together, friends now; her suspicion of him steadily diminishing at last.

''Would you like a bike ride with me down the coast? Phil arranged for the Harley to be railed here. It would be a shame to waste it when we could have a cool ride in the evening or early morning.''

''I haven't been on a bike in years. One of the undergrads took me when I was at Cambridge before Justin and I became an item. It was fantastic. Can we do it one evening when work is finished?''

''I will arrange it for tomorrow,'' he said satisfied. A warm feeling penetrated his heart and made him go all gooey for the first time in his life. She liked the same things as he did, animals, nature, taking part in sports and her intellect matched his. She was his perfect match even if she didn't know it yet. He just had to make her appreciate him as her ideal mate.

His Granddad had said he would know when he found the right woman and she would be more important than anything in his life. For the first time in his life he was prepared to change his lifestyle for a woman. Previously, they had had to fit in with his workaholic life style.

He now admitted to himself for the first time that Vanessa had only been partly at fault in their relationship breaking down. Driven by his personal ambition and determination to succeed he had left her alone and lonely while he carved his path to career success. She wanted money but the man she loved was less intelligent but more human, sensitive and less focussed than him, having many friends. They had a balanced home life and family.

He realised his affection for Vanessa had merely been an infatuation. Vanessa had fitted his concept of a trophy wife, intelligent, beautiful and sophisticated; embellishing his image of being a successful financial and property magnet. He now wanted more than that; a woman to share his thoughts, ideals and be his soul-mate, not an elegant clothes-horse who would chameleon-like, charm her way through society events making the appropriate comments to his business associates.

Kirsten would not embarrass him but she was her own woman. Fundamentally disagreeing with him about the right to own handguns and hunting for sport she would defend her argument when she felt right was on her side. She was no pushover; this Ms. Gateman and he liked her the better for it, having met too many sycophants wanting him to gild their lily if they pleased him. She would irritate him, challenge him but never bore or disappoint him. For the first time in his adult life he would never want another woman in his bed.

The next day he appreciated her neat form dressed in old tight worn jeans and a tee shirt. She no longer feared him and dressed to suit her figure and mood. He lifted her onto her mount, enjoying the feel of her curves and her neat waist.

She was still too thin for his taste. Stick insects like many society dames or models always drove him away. Women who picked at their food were often difficult to please in other ways; never satisfied with their lot, demanding more clothes, jewels and cars and bigger houses to show off in. He also liked to feel a handful when he took a girl to bed, exploring a woman's luscious curves before he finally took her. He enjoyed boisterous sex with healthy energetic girls who had stamina.

Kirsten handled her horse as if she had been born in the saddle. "I rode at boarding school at the weekends," she explained when he complimented her on her seat. Her grey mare was gentle and had snickered when she had given her apples and a carrot. She had nudged her in the back and tried to pull Kirsten's plait which fell below her western hat. Kirsten had rubbed her head against the mare, accepting the growing affection from the animal, an affection based on simple caring and trust. This was a woman who enjoyed simple things; good weather, good food and good company. His sort of woman.

He rode with the natural authority and skill of a man who had worked on his Granddad's ranch with the horses for years, leading the way through the trees until they reached a river out of sight of prying eyes. It had been uncomfortable for them during the last few days. The press had heard of the fire and death of her aunt. The presence of a celebrity there had drawn them to the hotel where they were staying.

Kirsten unused to her celebrity status had at first found their attention suffocating. Cameras and microphones were pushed into her mouth the first day the press had arrived. She couldn't leave the hotel. She had felt wound up like a spring. After they had become intrusive Drakeman had acted as security guard, ensuring they had privacy when they left the hotel; his height, stature and intimidating manner acting as buffer between the press and their prey.

Rutland had pulled her against his shoulder. He covered her face and ushered her quickly through the small pathway Drakeman had opened for her. Ashen faced, she had felt sick when one of the press had demanded of her, "Did you come here to get your aunt's insurance money Ms Gateman? Did you conspire to kill her with Mr. Rutland?" Rutland had turned to them and with admirable restraint had said, "No comment Gentlemen. You will hear our version of the story later. Ms Gateman has suffered a bereavement and a night in gaol. She needs some space and time to relax."

''What about you two Mr. Rutland? You seem pretty close.''

Drakeman had intervened. ''Mr. Rutland has said all he intends to say. Leave them in peace now please." They backed off and tried to follow Rutland's car but the ex-seal had left them behind quickly. He knew which quiet back routes to take and was used to shaking off tails in his counter-intelligence ops in foreign countries. They did not stand a chance.

Rutland stopped his horse by a tree and left him to munch grass passively. He was a strong but well-mannered horse and knew who was his master. He had let the animal have his head as soon as he was assured Kirsten could keep up with him.

''Keep up with him,'' he smiled. She had ridden faster than him, a good head in front of him until he had caught up with her. She was a neck or nothing rider with a good horse under her, another example of her adventurous personality that had been oppressed by her fiancé. The real Kirsten was coming out of hiding when she was with him.

She looked down at him, cheeks flushed, hair blown out of her plait, untidy but full of health; the epitome of a strong woman who was enjoying herself. He had never seen her so confident or so beautiful.

''May I help you down my Lady?'' he asked bowing in a Southern manner.

''Thank you, kind Sir.'' She mimicked his tone, allowing him to lift her down, trying to ignore her body's reaction to sliding down his own. She felt relaxed with him but her body tingled when he held her waist and rested her against him; his arousal evident.

He moved away from her but she had felt the tension in him, his reluctance to let her go and his restraint as he held his emotions and lust tightly under control. He wanted her and had let her know it but had not hit on her at all. He led her horse to his own and let them feed together. He took the food out of the saddle bags and laid it out on a blanket, placing rugs for them to sit on.

He wanted her to feel comfortable and sat his back against a tree, allowing her to select another tree near him but not too close to him. He desperately wanted to hold her close and kiss her but he had promised not to touch her and would keep that promise. He wanted her to make the first move; to give him some encouragement.

Picking up the food she served him generous portions. He must have a fast metabolism to pack in the amount of food he consumed each day. He competed in veterans' swimming and martial arts competitions. He still built and restored houses when he had the time; the way he had originally made his first million before he had built his law firm to the level it had achieved now. He had the muscles of a man who enjoyed working physically with his hands.

She wondered what it would feel like if he ran his hands over her and caressed her. She had enjoyed his kisses until she had felt caged and suffocated. She guessed he would make a good lover; a generous lover who gave rather than took; the opposite of a man like Justin who only took and vampire like, sucked all the energy out of a woman.

He lay back against the trunk closing his eyes and enjoying the warmth but shaded by the tree. He took her hand and held it, saying nothing, just relaxing with her. He felt her nerves dissipate until she also lay back and drifted off. The smell of the flowers by the river was heavy and intoxicating. An hour later she woke up startled to see him sitting there watching her

''Wake up Sleeping Beauty. It is almost time to head back. Unless you want a swim?''

She looked startled. He had said the wrong thing. She was still too wary of him to remain close to him in just a swimsuit, nearly naked with him.

''I didn't bring a costume and I don't do skinny dipping,'' she said firmly.

''Shame, I enjoyed it whilst I was a teenager. The local kids always used the Creek for swimming. Cheaper and more fun than the baths.''

'When did you come here?'

'When my Mom died my Grandparents stepped in. They put me through High School and encouraged me to join the Navy and then the SEALS and later to study for law school. They also encouraged me to study martial arts to use my excess energy in the right direction instead of engaging in street fights. Granddad taught me to shoot as well as any sharp-shooter. The SEALS then recognised my expertise and sent me overseas.

'I hit lucky. They were better than my parents who had no expectations of me.'' He grimaced and then said wryly, "Without their intervention I would have joined a gang and become a bum. My friends in Miami ended up on the wrong side of the law and are in prison.

'Granddad taught me a real man works hard for his living and Grandma made me understand how a gentleman behaves. I was a ruffian who had a chip on my shoulder and could be violent when pressured or insulted by the other kids. They were gentle but firm and I had the belt at times from Granddad when I crossed the line but coming to the ranch was the best thing in my life.'

''Didn't you want to inherit the ranch and become a rancher?''

''No, the pace of life is too slow for me. It wouldn't stretch me intellectually and I like the buzz of the city.''

He turned to her and said, ''And what about Kirsten Gateman? Where is your home? And what stimulates you? Are you a country girl?''

''No. I like the country life for short spells but I prefer the museums, theatre and other city activities. I am a city girl and like to be near and work with people.''

''A girl after my own heart,'' he said. ''You see we have a lot in common Kirsten.''

''In another time and place, yes, we might have suited but I am carrying too much baggage Josh. Let me alone to sort out my issues please.''

''I can give you time Kirsten.''

Her face was now shuttered; staring impassively at him; she was raising her barriers to him. It was the time to back off. He collected the remains of the food, whistled the horses to him and lifted her up.

She felt a little sad having disappointed him. Hurting his feelings made her feel bad. He was worming his way into her heart with his kindness and gentlemanly ways. He was a man who could be relied on if she could trust herself with him.

They rode back in silence, she in a contemplative mood, he rather despondent but still remaining positive. He had hoped she would have invited him to kiss her but her eyes had still stared at him warily. He must tread carefully still. They were both glad when they reached the stables and could get into the Aston and reach the hotel in time for a briefing from the other couple.

The days went quickly after that. The next evening, they lent the Aston to Drakeman for a spin with Elisabeth and they sped off down the coast on the Harley. Leaning into his firm broad back, Kirsten felt completely safe for the first time with a man since she had left Justin.

He rode the bike like he rode the horse. Man, and bike appeared to meld together; a mixture of speed and constrained power until let loose. As the bike ate up the dust, this was the way this man let go of his demons. Her hair flowing behind her she felt free and liberated with him. He was a prime specimen of masculinity and he was hers if she wanted him.

Their bike had been followed by reporters but he had shaken them off, ignoring the speed limit. At the coastal restaurant, she took off her helmet and stood close to him, breathing in the salty air. She loved the sea more than the country and would love a second home in a coastal resort near to London.

She felt alive and excited for the first time in ages and knew it was because she was with him. He was an amusing, sensuous and stimulating partner. She still could not believe he was interested in her and thought her opinions interesting and intelligent. Justin had said she was clumsy in public; criticising her if she made what he considered inappropriate remarks to his associates. He made her nervous and passive and she was described as rather quiet by his friends.

She was not allowed to express her political opinions because they differed from the conservative attitudes of his friends and colleagues. Now she could not believe she had bowed to his opinion and had become so passive. It was as if she had been in a zombie state. Her friends had said she had changed and she had jumped if anyone came up behind her and spoke loudly to her. She had been a nervous wreck.

Rutland put his arm around her shoulder and led her to the deck at the back of a small restaurant. No-one was sitting there and he met her puzzled expression with a grin. ''I rented the whole restaurant for two hours.''

The advantages of having money. She had never been wealthy her father having spent his income supporting several families. She had lived on the breadline through her undergrad days at university, refusing to accept handouts from the loaded Justin. Only when she lived with him had she lived in wealthy circumstances; a nice townhouse and expensive dinners being the perks of living with a man from a wealthy and prestigious family.

Rutland jumped down on to the beach from the deck and lifted her down, his hands restrained on her waist. Then taking her hand and running with her down to the water they shucked their socks and shoes wading in, loving the warmth around their feet and the soft sand beneath them.

Like a big kid, he splashed her and lifted her around and around him in the air, swinging her until she felt giddy and begged him to stop. On the sand, she faced him, looking up at him, eyes meeting eyes, her heart tugged by the tenderness she saw in his emerald green orbs. This man meant what he said; he did care for her and worried about her. She was upmost in his mind.

She turned in on herself, cursing herself. She could not offer him what he wanted now. She was still damaged and scared of giving herself to a man. She could not act the tease and kiss him like she wanted to. He was too decent to be treated in this way. She had to be honest with him and show him he didn't stand a chance with her until she had had more therapy and could behave like a normal woman.

He saw her attitude and stance had changed. She had become detached and cold again, as if she was ready to tell him something. His heart sank. A coldness came over him as she took his hand and led him back to the restaurant and sat looking at the menu.

''What do you recommend Josh?'' she asked softly.

''The lobster and salad.''

He took her other hand and made her look directly into his eyes. He wasn't having any of this dissembling; he wanted to know what was up? What had he done wrong now? He had treated her as if she was glass; not making a move on her although it had nearly killed him to avoid touching her in any intimate way.

''Kirsten what have I said or done. You have that buttoned look about you again.''

''Nothing Josh. I was just thinking about going home. I will come back to make sure the house has been rebuilt to my instructions and then arrange for the sale and donate the rest of Freja's things to charity. After the trial, I will be able to leave this place for ever.''

Those words 'for ever' cut him to the quick. She was telling him in the nicest possible way there was no future for them. After they had enjoyed the picnic and had played like kids together in the sea she was still trying to pretend to herself she didn't want him. He was furious. His patience snapped. He didn't deserve a brush off like this.

Beside himself with anger and disappointment he took the menus from her and put his helmet on. ''Come on, let's get back to the hotel if you find my company so unpleasant and want rid of Devil's Creek so quickly.''

''I don't find your company unpleasant,'' she said trying to let him down lightly. It was for the best.

''Try again Sweetheart. You don't trust me and want to get rid of me. I get the message true and clear. Come on.''

He tugged her hand and pulled her toward the bike, lifting her on it and getting on it in front of her. He revved the engine noisily to the disgust of others on the beach who frowned at him. He gave them his best intimidating scowl and moved the bike along the road and ignored Kirsten for the rest of the journey.

Drakeman noted the black cloud that engulfed his friend. ''What back so soon? Something happen?''

''You could say that,'' snapped Rutland. ''I am eating in my room tonight. Goodnight Ms Gateman. Enjoy your own company.'' He stalked off and got his towel and trunks again and took his temper out on the water.

''What happened?'' asked Drakeman. ''I thought you were getting on very well!''

''I told him I would come back for the sale of the house and the trial but then leave permanently for London. He took it badly.''

Hardly surprising. Rutland was head over heels in love and the girl wanted no future with him. He was containing his temper when he clearly wanted to shake some sense into this girl. He was hurting badly but didn't know how to change her mind. The famous Rutland charm was failing him when he needed it most.

''Will you meet him if he goes to London?'

''Unless my therapist can help me, then no, I'm not making promises and raising his hopes.'' Drakeman saw the tears in her eyes. This woman was no flirt. She was a woman who cared for his mate and didn't want to hurt him anymore. His respect grew for her.

He took her hand and said, ''Keep in touch with Elisabeth and me in case your therapy works. Josh would wait for you if he thought there was any hope for you two, you know.''

''Thanks,'' she said hugging him. ''I will remember that but don't tell Josh.''

They ate in their own rooms that night while the Elisabeth and Phil took the Aston for a spin but the next few nights they ate with the other pair, acting like polite strangers, wary of upsetting each other.

It was finally time to say goodbye to Freja. Michael Defoe and Kirsten had each said something in the church and they had all thrown a handful of soil on the coffin as it was lifted slowly to the bottom of the grave. A few more flowers, white for hope, had been on the coffin. Aunt Freja had always been hopeful, never cynical about people and Kirsten wanted to learn from her. She saw Michael blink back some tears as Rutland put his hand on the old man's shoulder and led him away to the car.

Alone at the graveside, she allowed her tears to run down her cheeks, trembling until they could fall no more. Then she wiped her face dry and joined the others in the car. Rutland drew her hand in his and she didn't resist. Aunt Freja would have wanted her to have someone to hold at a time like this.

He had not tried to touch her intimately or talk to her privately since the bike ride. The strain was showing on them both as they tried to treat each other like colleagues or good friends, ignoring the chemistry that leapt between them. He had acted like a perfect Southern gentleman, hovering solicitously at her side, so unlike his usual forward self. She wondered how long he could maintain this façade before he reverted to his former behaviour. This restraint must be killing him with his ego and his libido.

At least Elisabeth and Drakeman were happy, Elisabeth was reconciled now to being his lover even in the short term and Drakeman was trying to make her choose him as her partner in life. He hadn't mentioned the longer term or commitment and Elisabeth had told Kirsten she enjoyed his company and would miss him when it was her time to go to Paris. Drakeman still hoped she would stay with him in Miami but had not pressed her. He still had several months to persuade her to change his mind and he was a very persuasive man.

It was their last night in Devil's Creek and Drakeman and Elisabeth wanted an early night as Elisabeth was leaving the next morning on an early flight. She was going back to FBI headquarters where she had a consultancy contract with the organisation for a few months. Drakeman could easily meet her at the weekends in the private jet he owned with Rutland.

Kirsten was sitting in the garden watching the carp swim by in the pond. She felt despondent. She gave herself a mental kick. It was stupid feeling sad she was leaving these people. They had become good friends and it was obvious she would miss them, their camaraderie and their teasing.

She heard Rutland's voice and she admitted to herself the cause of her despondency lay deeper than merely missing good friends. She would miss his chuckle and the way he teased her unmercifully. She had felt alive for the first time in years when he had kissed her passionately. If it wasn't for him being so virile and wanting her in bed she could have dated him but she would only disappoint him and make him resent her. She would be no good for him in the longer term.

Justin had convinced her she was not a sexual creature and could not perform happily with a man in bed. She was frigid. Even the thought of a man sharing her bed and touching her body made her feel freezing cold, unable to move and stricken with fear. The idea made her want to vomit and she closed her eyes trying to rid herself of the image of herself in bed with a man. The very thought made her think of Justin and those heavy arms holding her down and squeezing her throat until she begged him to stop and apologised for upsetting him and making him angry. Now she was angry at the way he had humiliated her but she feared she could never trust another man again.

She walked back past the pool on her way to her room. Someone loomed over her in the dark and she jumped backwards nearly into the water.

Strong hands encircled her waist and steadied her. She recognised the grip as belonging to Rutland, his aftershave tantalising her senses as he held her close to him. Dressed in trunks, water was dripping down him; the moonlight and the bare lighting around the pool outlining his severe features and his broad but streamlined figure.

She turned on him, angrily, trying to get out of his hold.

''Joshua Rutland, I could throttle you. You nearly frightened me to death. I nearly ended up in the pool. You should be ashamed of yourself coming up behind a woman in that way. Let me go!''

He had imbibed a little too generously that night and he was full of Dutch courage. Thinking irrationally, he had decided to chance his luck. He had forgotten in his inebriated state he had promised not to touch her without her permission. She was going back tomorrow and had not given an inch since their confrontation. He wanted to taste her once more before she left Florida.

''It was too tempting my lovely girl. You are so easy to tease.''

''And you are an egotist and a bully Joshua Rutland.''

''Guilty as charged Ms Gateman but a bully that loves you with all my heart.''

''This is nonsensical talk, the alcohol talking.''

''I am nearly sober Kirsten. Come and swim with me. I am not worried about your scars and can't see them in the darkness and the water.''

''No, that is a bad idea,'' she said trying to release herself. No man had seen her back in the flesh since her whipping.

''Well, I will have to do something drastic,'' he said, the alcohol making him mischievous.

Before she could complain he had picked her up in his arms and jumped with her into the pool. They plunged under the water, his weight taking them down. He kissed her underwater until they needed to breathe and came up for air. Kirsten coughed and spluttered, not used to breathing so long under water as him. She clung to him for stability while she recovered her breath. Her fine cotton top and wrap clung to her. He undid the buttons and slid the wrapper down her arms until her shoulders were bare and he touched her lightly on the shoulders.

Fear and shame were in her eyes as he looked at the top of her breasts and shoulders. He turned her round and disposed of the wrapper in the water leaving her back bare. He would not let her move, holding her in a light but crippling grip until he kissed her back lightly down to her top of her camisole; caressing her bare skin, kissing the skin which stood out where the weals had been cut.

She was astounded and seduced by his gentleness as he paid homage to her body. ''So beautiful. I care not for your scars. They are part of you and make you unique my Sweetheart. Don't hide yourself from me.''

He turned her to face him and lifting her chin he kissed her neck. Then taking her in his arms again he kissed her fully on the mouth as spellbound she looked in his eyes at the tenderness there. No other man had never shown her tenderness before, only roughness and pain. She could almost believe him when he said she was beautiful and he cared not for her scars; but he was nearly drunk and would feel differently in the morning when he could see the scars properly.

The scars would eventually become so faint they would be un-noticeable and she could have plastic surgery on the NHS as she had suffered emotional scarring as well. Until she could get rid of both her emotional and physical scars she could not face a man in bed again, even Rutland who she now believed truly loved her. She was not ready for any man yet. She must see her consultant and undergo therapy again until the touch and thought of a man in bed didn't terrify her.

''Joshua let me go!'' Through his drunken haze, he recognised the slight panic in her voice and let her go suddenly. She held the pool wall for support until she could calm herself again. Passion as well as fear had overwhelmed her. She had to leave the pool before she allowed her emotions to engulf her and she gave herself to Rutland wholeheartedly. She had never felt so conflicted, wanting to stay and yet to run.

This damn man tied her emotions up in knots. She had never felt so deeply about a man before. Her love for Justin had been immature compared with her feelings for this man but now she had to reject him and leave him. Life was unfair and she hated Justin with all her heart for forcing her into this hard place from where she was desperately trying to crawl.

She grabbed her wrapper and tied it around herself, not bothering to button it up. All she could think about was escaping from him before she gave into her emotions and admitted she wanted to stay with him.

''Don't follow me Joshua Rutland!" she ordered, despair making her angry with him. ''Stay away from the airport tomorrow.'' She kissed him quickly on the cheek and waded away from him, climbing up the ladder like the devil himself was after her.

''Very well, Kirsten, if that is you want,'' He stayed in the water disgusted with himself, the plunge in the water now having sobered him. He swum fifty lengths to overcome his frustration and then went aimlessly to his room. He would still pursue her in London.

He had seen the conflict in her face. She did want him and she had nearly given in to him but fear had stopped her at the last moment. He must persuade her to have therapy and recognise he was not a demon and wouldn't hurt her. She was a passionate woman under that cloak of fear and would love unreservedly once her fear was conquered. He thought her frigidity was purely mental in origin and therapy had helped other women in the past. He still held out hope for them in the future.

Kirsten made it to her room and shut the door behind her fast. Hyper-ventilating, she tried to control her breathing. She was tired of being afraid but couldn't face Rutland again until she had conquered her fears. He was too male, too masculine for her fragile state at that moment.

She packed her cases and went to reception. She took a taxi to the hospital. Michael Defoe had been allowed out of hospital for the funeral but was to stay there for another week until repairs were made to his home. Rutland refused to allow him to return home until the house was straight and then he wanted a nurse to look after him until he recovered fully. The old man grumbled about being treated like an invalid but Kirsten knew he appreciated his Grandson's kindness and his caring for him.

She sat holding his wrinkled and gnarled hand with its still strong grip. His eyes still twinkled emerald green like those of his Grandson's. She recognised where Rutland had inherited his strength and sense of humour from. Even sick and distraught over Freja's death he was still a force to be reckoned with.

He had looked her straight in the eyes and asked her, ''What has happened between you and my Grandson, Missy?'' Discomforted by this direct attack Kirsten gave herself a moment to think of a reply.

''I thought your Grandson was the smart attorney?'' she said flippantly, ''I see where he got his interrogation skills from!''

''I've never been a man to beat about the bush when the happiness of my family is concerned,'' replied Michael, pinning her with the same green fire in his eyes as Rutland's when he wanted to know something badly.

''I would have tried a career in the law if the opportunity had been there but it was difficult in my day.''

''It was as hard in England for a poor man to become a barrister forty or fifty years ago; the law was the province of the rich. I received a scholarship to pay my uni fees but have still to pay my College of Law fees.''

He was not going to let her off the hook. ''Josh has fallen for you hard and I don't want to see him hurt. It is years since I have seen him so smitten with a female, not since that devious lawyer baggage who nearly took him for a ride.''

Kirsten was obviously interested in the woman Drakeman had hinted at before but didn't think Rutland would want his private life described in detail. She was a private person like him and respected his need for privacy. Michael thought she needed to know more about his Grandson; to understand what made him tick so she could give him a chance.

His Grandson might be a playboy but at heart he was still the sensitive kid who had been hurt badly by his violent father and his vulnerable and weak mother who could not give him the love and care he needed. With the right woman, a woman like his late Grandma, Rutland could turn out differently; a good husband and family man. He had to find that woman and Kirsten just might be the one.

Freja had described her as proud and her integrity had shone through. She had worked hard on the farm with Freja during the vacations, uncomplaining and rushed to her aunt's aid when his darling Freja was in trouble. Freja had called her a treasure.

He did not know what his Grandson had done to offend her but he had always been driven and impatient and she clearly mistrusted him. He needed someone to argue his case for him.

''I have no desire to hurt your Grandson Mr. Defoe. I have not encouraged him at all but he chooses to chase me when I have told him there is no future for us.''

The old man's eyes crinkled for a moment in a frown as he considered her words.

''He is like his Granddad then. I chased his Grandma even when she said I was not the man she or her father wanted. I wore her down until she recognised my finer qualities and admitted she wanted me and we had forty years of happy life together.''

He pressed her hand gently. ''Joshua is a decent man. He would never lay a hand on a woman in anger unlike your former fiancé.''

''I believe that,'' she said. ''He is generous, tolerant and kind but he is not the right man for me. He is too domineering and manipulative. I must lead my own life, make my own decisions.''

''Josh may be a strong character but he is always reasonable and open to rationale arguments. He worries about you and is over-protective. His Grandma used to accuse me of being the same and I used to call her a stroppy, obstinate woman who wanted her own way all the time. We bickered constantly but making up was fun?'' he said winking to her. "My guess is that once Josh knows you are safe and relaxes with you he will loosen the leash and you will find he is a different person.''

''I need more space and time before I can consider a relationship with another man,'' she explained. ''Time to sort my career out. I want to develop a career, to be independent of any man for my financial needs.''

''Josh will respect that. That lawyer fiancé of his only wanted him for his money, a partnership for herself.''

''At least she wanted to work,'' said Kirsten.

''No, she didn't. She wanted the partnership for the money. She divorced the man who made her partner and took her share of the business he had built up and then went back to the secret lover she had slept with for years. Phil Drakeman warned Josh he should make her sign a pre-nup but Josh was too soft. Luckily, he found her in bed with the man in time to break off the engagement.''

''She sounds awful.''

''Simply poor white trash who had won a scholarship to study law and saw the main chance in Josh, an up and coming young attorney with a profitable property development business on the side. Too good to resist.''

''It must be awful to be in such a position. To have to sell oneself for a lifestyle.''

''Women of that kind think nothing of it. Josh found another at his naval base who wanted him for his pension and pay cheque. They both destroyed his confidence in women. He thinks most women now want him just for the security and lifestyle he can bring them and Josh is generous to a fault."

Kirsten couldn't deny that. ''He has certainly been generous to my family paying Aunt Freja's medical bills and my hotel account. I offered to pay him back slowly but he won't hear of it.''

''I would be astonished if he did. His Grandma was a Southern belle and installed Southern values in him, like looking after his woman.' '

''I am not his woman Mr. Defoe!''

''To him you are. You are the first woman he has met in years who isn't after his chequebook and he is learning to trust again. He has been let down and betrayed too often by women. Even his poor mother, my daughter was beaten to a pulp by his violent father and buried herself in a bottle.

'When her husband died, she made ends meet by whoring, leaving Josh to fend for himself, a latch key kid the neighbours tried to watch over. When he grew old enough to understand he was tormented by other kids in school about his mother's membership of the 'oldest profession.' He learned to defend himself with his fists and retreated inside himself.

'He came to us from social services after his mother died. He was in an unlit tenement block apartment for three weeks on his own, starved and thin, stealing from bins to feed himself and smelling of garbage; too scared to ask for help for fear he would be put into foster care. He had tasted that for a few weeks when his Mom was too sick with influenza to look after him and he vowed never to experience it again.

'It took years before he would open up and trust us with his thoughts and feelings. His Grandma broke through his armour and he was devastated when she died of cancer. She was the only woman he trusted. He lost the influence of a strong but gentle, caring and soft woman in his life; replaced by a series of cold, detached and heartless females.''

Kirsten thought back to the internet article from a celebrity magazine which talked about Josh Rutland's revolving bedroom door and the brittle beauties who serviced him. For the first time, she felt sorry for Rutland and recognised his insecurity for what it was. He entered short-term casual liaisons instead of risking getting hurt by engaging in real long-term relationships. How could he tell if a woman wanted him or his money? It was easier to assume she wanted the money and take what he could get from her in the short term rather than risking being hurt again.

She had come to realise he was a good, kind man who deserved better than the 'ladies' who would sell themselves for a dinner engagement, an exotic weekend away or a bracelet. That was why he was attracted to her. Money meant less to her than her independence and she was a novelty to him but a novelty which would wear off in time.

''I understand your Grandson now but I still think I am not the right woman for him. He wants a woman who can give herself unconditionally to him. I cannot give him that and will hurt him when he lives a less than fully satisfied life.''

''Hasn't he the right to make that decision, to decide to take you as you are regardless of the consequences?''

''I have the right to protect either of us from getting hurt Mr. Defoe!''

''So, you do care for him a little Kirsten?''

''Isn't it obvious?'' snapped Kirsten. "And that is why I will not offer him anything but a full relationship which I cannot give him right now. He has accepted that and so must you!''

''If you think that, you don't know my Grandson. Once he has got his bit between the teeth he will not let go!'' She saw the same hard determined light in his eyes his Grandson wore. So that was where he had got his tenaciousness from.

''For both of our sakes I hope you are wrong Mr. Defoe,'' she stated through gritted teeth. Kissing him on the cheek she left his room cursing the pig-headedness of the Defoe men. She was determined she would not give Josh any opportunity to try to pursue a relationship with her in the immediate future.

Having done her duty by Michael Defoe it was now time to leave Devil's Creek.

''A taxi for the airport please,'' she asked reception after picking up her cases.

''Now Ms Gateman? It's nearly midnight. We had you booked a cab for ten tomorrow morning.''

''I have changed my mind thank you. I am leaving now.'' She wrote a note of explanation for Elisabeth and Drakeman and got into the taxi, not looking back or she would have returned to Rutland's room and stayed the night with him. She was bailing out.

This was the safe way out. She needed safe until she sorted herself out. She didn't want to think of that powerful and virile man. She hoped he might leave her alone but knew Rutland was the sort of man who went after what he wanted. Even the Atlantic might not put him off. She had to hide herself away for a few months in a place of safety until she sorted her head out. It was aching as the stress of the past few days caught up with her.

She needed go back to London and face up to Justin. She now had the confidence to face him alone without Rutland. Home would be a hostel until she could demand some money back from him. Her rights were limited as a 'common-law wife' who had been living with him but she could try to get her salary back from him. She suspected the threating to go to her former employer and telling her story of his violence and intimidation would be enough to make him give her some money. He was always tight-fisted but his reputation meant more than anything else to him and she knew enough to destroy it. Now, she had made her decision she felt quite powerful. A new life awaited her.

She arrived at the airport and sat to wait the long night out. Rutland had booked her a complimentary pass for the executive lounge for the next morning but she had to wait in the public lounge until then. She took out her iPad and read it and drank water to calm her system down. Her stomach was still shaking and butterflies danced all over it making her feel sick. She couldn't take another confrontation with Rutland.

The psychotherapist said she would suffer physical reactions to any mental stress and she practised deep breathing to calm herself. Gradually her body responded and she relaxed but did not feel safe enough to sleep in a public place. Pickpockets had always lurked in these lounges waiting for the unwary travellers to sleep. In her present state of mind danger seemed to lurk everywhere. She needed to grab reality by the throat and ignore the irrational threats that seemed to overwhelm her.

At last she could show her passport and dump her cases. Wearily she left the public lounge and signed in to the Executive lounge where she could get a snack and fall asleep in safety. For three hours, she slept and then moved through security. Rutland couldn't follow her there without a ticket. For two hours, she gritted her teeth, waiting for him to arrive but he didn't and she sat in her seat on the plane and relaxed at last. Heathrow soon and then she would book into the hostel for a month until she could find a flat. She had a probationary period with a barrister's office in the suburbs of London.

She was back practising employment law, her real love; no longer working for financial barracudas like Justin in the back-stabbing environment of corporate law. After a month, she would have to find accommodation. She would no longer fit the criteria for living in the safe hostel for abused women. She might find a flat in a social housing complex, council or housing association.

She would contact her friends from Cambridge again. They were fun loving girls who had always welcomed her into their midst. Only Justin with his rudeness and standoffishness had driven them away, making them feel unwelcome in his house. Susan, a friend had warned her not to live in Justin's house.

''You need your own space or at least to own part of the house Kirsten. He is domineering and manipulative. He won't let you have your own life!''

She had been right but Kirsten had adored him since she was a young girl. He was the only person who had flattered her and made her feel worthwhile and treasured. An insecure teenager, skinny and tall, a late developer without any breasts; her fragile ego and personality had needed nurturing.

Her mother had fed her insecurity. She blamed herself for her husband's infidelities. An aloof, reserved cold woman with few friends, she had tried to be the perfect wife, making the house a perfect home but she had failed. Kirsten was not conventionally pretty. "She had to work harder," her mother said, "to make a man find her attractive." To conform with the ideal a man looked for. Justin fed her the attention she had craved. She had hung on his every word.

Kirsten realised that even then he had been grooming her, moulding her in the image of his perfect woman. At university, she had been immature and foolish, protected from other men by her concentration on her academic studies. Romantically and sexually she knew only Justin. Too late, she had found out Susan was right. She had given away not only her space but her liberty to run her own life. The compliments gradually gave way to criticism after he became her boyfriend at Uni.

Her clothes were not right. He insisted she wore sophisticated clothes to the legal and business dinners he attended but in private he liked her to wear clothes that made her look younger than her age, quite girlish. He hated a woman who wore make up and when she wore her hair up he said it made her look quite old and haggard. He thought it important for a woman to keep her figure and remain slim. He paid for a personal trainer for her to set and help her achieve her goal; to remain as slim as a reed.

Too often he came home from work a scowl on his face as he recounted his day; the idiots who kept him from achieving his goals. If she had not gone to work she would then face a barrage of questions about how she had spent her day, who she had met and talked with. Then, came the barbed remarks about her friends and their manners and their background; why she should be careful who she mixed with and how she should conduct herself and meet the right people to further her career. She had become a workaholic, working long hours, burying herself in paper and cases, to delay going home.

She fell short on all accounts excepting her natural beauty which he could not find fault with. A man at ill at ease in his own skin he had made her feel the same. She had realised too late she would never satisfy Justin's image of the ideal woman, no matter how she tried.

She gave herself a mental shake. No longer would he make her feel like that. She had a lot to look forward to. A new job, new home: a new life. She had rung the psychotherapist. If she could come to terms with what Justin had done and confront him she could become at ease with her own sexuality and she might have a future with another man. Joshua Rutland had raised her self-esteem and had encouraged her to demand more from life than Justin had offered her. She couldn't wait to start her new life.

Finally, she got off the plane and took the rail and bus to the hostel. She wanted to remain as anonymous as was possible and to make her money last longer. She did not want to think now of all the money she owed to Rutland. It would take years to pay him back but pay him back she must when she had stabilised her life and career. She would write to him in a few days and explain her circumstances.

Aunt Freja had spent a lot on her animals when she had run her farm as a rescue but the house insurance would allow it to be rebuilt and she could now sell it. That and Aunt Freja's insurances and her savings would allow Kirsten to buy a small house if she worked outside of London. The alternative was sharing a rented house in London and buying a property to rent to tenants outside the capital. That was if she could get some money back from Justin to pay back her fees or her aunt's money would partly go to pay back that debt instead.

Rutland had woken up and gone down to breakfast expecting to meet Kirsten with the others. Elisabeth, a grave expression on her face showed him the note Kirsten had written her.

"What happened to make her leave last night. What did you do to frighten her?''

''I was slightly drunk and invited her for a swim,'' he said rather shamefacedly.

''Was that splashing we heard last night something to do with that?'

''Ah yes! She had an impromptu swim with me."

''And you hit on her and frightened her; you an experienced man Mr. Rutland!'' She didn't care if he was her employer; he had behaved selfishly and frightened her friend away.

He scowled. ''It was my last opportunity to persuade her to stay here but I loused it up.''

He got up, pushing his chair forcefully away from him, breaking the peaceful atmosphere of the breakfast room. He was not here to be admonished by a young employee who did not understand his circumstances. He was angry with himself for drinking and becoming impatient, but for Christ's sake, he had waited a week and he still had not broken through that icy barrier Kirsten had rebuilt around herself after Freja's death. A man could be patient for only so long.

Elisabeth had jumped into bed with Drakeman when she felt like it after rejecting his friend. She had no right to criticise him. They had been like knife and fork all week, depressing him with their happy smiles and private jokes whilst Kirsten had been rebuffing him.

''Are you going to the airport, Joshua?'' asked Drakeman. ''She doesn't want you there and I would listen to her this time if I were you.''

Rutland stood still and said, ''I just wanted to wish her luck, that was all.''

''She'll be subpoenaed for the trial later. That scum Clery and Danielle are still saying she is part of the team who planned to hurt Freja. She will have to come back whether there is any evidence against her or not. Wait until then. She will have cooled off and be able to rationalise her position clearly.

'She told Elisabeth she has an appointment with a psychotherapist. A few months' treatment and she may see you in a different light. The poor woman has been abused for Christ's sake! That is as bad as the suffering we have seen from men in battle. She needs some peace.''

''I'll give her some space until she comes to Miami for the Federal trial,'' said Rutland reluctantly ''but I am going to London later and then we will have a reckoning. That woman wants me but is just too scared to admit it. I intend to make her give us a real chance.

'Oh, and Phil, I want you to set some of your hounds on to the fiancé. I have some information already about his financial relationships but I want to know his whereabouts and what he gets up to, his latest women and anything else I can use against him. He will be a dead man now; socially, financially and emotionally.''

''Be careful you don't destroy yourself in the processing of destroying him,'' said Drakeman. He had seen too many men take their finger off the pulse while trying to destroy their enemies. They had been too consumed by the taste of revenge to enjoy their life or run their businesses successfully and had ended up bitter sad men.

Rutland walked off to pack his case He was driving the Aston back, not wanting company while his mood was bad. Drakeman had promised he would visit Elisabeth. He was as much in the air as Rutland. She still intended to move to Paris. Together they were to be pitied; both in love with women who didn't return their love enough to make a commitment and it stank!

Chapter ten.

Kirsten read the letter requiring her attendance at the Court in Miami. She had expected this after she had heard Danielle still implicated her. She was happy in her new position and had worked there five months, advising dismissed employees of their rights and employers how to prevent cases going to tribunals by careful planning and communication with their employees. Her name was getting noticed in the legal world again.

The only blot on the landscape was Justin trying to make contact with her. She had met him once on the steps of her new place of employment. He was with another client of the firm and dared not cause a fuss. He had stared at her fixedly for a moment.

"I see you are back again Kirsten. We will have to meet for dinner again and take up where we left off.''

Dream on, you Bastard. To him she said politely, ''I am afraid I am too busy working, catching up on my reading to go out at the moment but thank you.''

''I am sure you can make time for old friends. I will call you.'' She ignored that last statement and went into the office. Looking back, he was still staring at her; a dark anger on his face and narrowed eyes that were as cold as a slice of ice. She felt as though they were drilling through her back, willing her to turn around. The shock on his face at her rejection of him was so palpable she could feel it.

An hour later she was asked to enter the office of her senior. "Please sit-down Ms Gateman. It has been drawn to my attention that you were uncivil to a close associate of mine. Justin Grayson has worked with us in the past and gives advice to us when we need it. His firm is bigger than ours and can carry specialist staff that we cannot afford to employ. We need to humour him, not alienate him Ms Gateman.''

She had been prepared for this conversation one day. Justin was respected in the legal community in London. No-one would want to offend him.

''I am sorry but I made it clear I did not have the time to have dinner with him. He tried to insist and I did not answer him. I was not rude to him but did not want to have to refuse him directly and cause a scene. He does not take rejection easily Sir.''

''Was that all you said?''

''Yes, I said I was too busy catching up on my reading at the moment. But Sir,'' she said firmly, ''in the office the firm and the seniors may tell me who I must talk with and associate with but when I am off duty I am entitled to choose my own dining partners.''

''You were engaged once I believe.''

''Yes, and I broke it off and left him and he hasn't forgiven me. He wants me back. He found out my phone number even though it is ex-directory and over the telephone he asked me to return to him. I told him no but that is when he persisted on the steps of this office.''

''I thought he was now an item with Ms Green. "

''I don't know that Sir. I have hardly socialised since I came back from

Miami but I want your assurance that no-one from this office will give my home address to him. I don't know who gave my phone number to him but I have changed it again. I would prefer it if the office contacted me only by my mobile now.''

''Surely that is over the top Ms Gateman.''

''I am leaving my present accommodation at the end of the week Sir. I aim to let no-one except your secretary have my address. My privacy is of utmost importance.''

He looked at her over the top of his glasses. She looked him directly, challenging him, but this boldness was belied by the fear in her eyes. Glassy and red-rimmed they showed the signs of a person who had had little sleep. She had joined the firm five months before looking thin and unhealthy but she had blossomed and looked happy until two days ago, when she began to appear withdrawn again and tired.

Something was worrying Ms Gateman. He had heard rumours about Justin and his lady-friends; some peculiar places he visited and complaints his former girlfriends made behind his back about his attitude toward women. He had closed his ears to the gossip. Justin was a good friend and very influential in his small world, a bad man to cross, but as this woman's employer he had a duty to protect her from unwanted advances from men at her workplace. It would look bad for God's sake if an employment lawyer was harassed at her place of employment. He could look away no longer.

''Ms Gateman if I am to help you, you must tell me what happened between you and Justin.''

She trusted him. She told him a potted version of her story, up to the point where she had to leave her job and her home. He still looked only partly convinced. She would have to ram her points home.

''I felt suffocated and told him I wanted to leave him Sir but he didn't take it well. I did eventually leave but felt I could not take another job because he would follow my trail. He was trying to find out where I had gone when I left for New York. He tried to trace me for a year although my friends were told to tell him I was safe.

'Sir, he deludes himself, he is unable to believe I no longer want him. I fear I will have to use an injunction if he doesn't leave me alone.''

He looked at her. The look she gave him spelt volumes. She was terrified of this man but was trying to hold back her fear and explain the situation rationally.

''I do not believe you have told me all there is to know my dear. What else made you leave him?''

''These Sir,'' she said opening her cardigan and sliding it down her arms. "He did this to me when I angered him and why I will not go back to him. I will be civil for the firm's sake but that is all.'' She covered herself up and waited for his reaction. None came at first. He did not know what to say. He was so shocked by her scars. No civilised man would do this.

The shutters fell from his eyes as he remembered situations he had preferred to ignore. The secretary who had left after she had worked only a week with Justin saying he was too friendly. The new girlfriend who had recently lost an enormous lot of weight and resembled a girl from a Biafra poster. With sunken eyes and deathly pale skin, she looked unhealthy but Justin had praised her for being slim and the girl's eyes had shone under his praise. Justin was repeating his behaviour toward Ms Gateman with this woman. He would make a few enquiries about his friend.

"I will tell Justin you are not interested in dating any men at the moment and my office steps are not the appropriate place to ask a woman to dine with him. You will be safe working for me my dear and we will keep your information secret."

She almost kissed him. He had a lot to lose being the head of a small firm. He would have to tread carefully for fear of upsetting his old friend. She left shaking, not out of fear of her new boss but out of fear Justin would find her home very soon. She was only obliged to give a week's notice and had done that the night before but she had to find a house to share again the following week.

She was living out of two suitcases, an itinerant's life, only keeping a few necessities about her. The therapist had explained why she had felt so guilty wanting to get the hell away from Justin, from that toxic house. She vowed never to be trapped again, never to be suffocated; unable to make a decision at home without another's permission. To never make the same mistake again; never to settle for something so cold and silent and still. Love wasn't meant to be a prison like that, trapping one with fear and insecurity.

The therapist said love was not what Justin felt for her, just a need to control the whole of someone else's life and personality, to subordinate that life to his. By stalking her he was controlling her life again. A few days in Miami would give her a break from the pressure of being hounded by this man. She must meet him in the future to gain closure but her therapist said it must be on her terms and when she was ready.

A street away a man was texting impatiently. He waited for the reply to his text and reading it he threw the phone angrily on his desk and walked to the window and back, unable to contain the raw energy that drove him. He wanted Kirsten but no one could find the woman, where she lived.

His only contact with her was at her place of work and his friend Andrew had just politely but carefully warned him from communicating with her there. He had been a friend at school but now made it quite clear the girl was in his employ and under his protection there; as if he Justin was a danger to her! He would not forget that insult! Andrew needed his help and contacts and would rue the day he had warned him off contacting Kirsten.

He would soon find her house. Now he had 12n so hard his pencil snapped. She had always had this effect on him. He had to have her again in his bed, passive and obedient, not challenging him like she had on the steps of that office.

He had been so angry he had allowed himself to take his anger out on Susan and he had seen the fear in her eyes, a fear he had not noticed there before but rather liked. He liked a woman to show she was a little afraid of him. It made her more willing to give him what she wanted without question. Susan had defied him in the past when he wanted to experiment sexually but after he had loved her more roughly than usual she had been more willing to try to please him. Some women responded more positively to harsh treatment than kindness.

Across the Atlantic, another man paced his office. ''He has started then, pursuing her!'' It was a statement rather than a question, made in a matter of fact way.

Drakeman answered Rutland honestly, knowing he would rile him. ''His contacts found her phone number and he has started to put pressure on her to dine with him. He met her on her office steps and invited her out. It is the latest on dit around the legal circles. They are betting on whether she will return to him.'' He stopped as Rutland slammed a book on his desk with such force he drove some papers off it.

''You will be pleased to know her boss has warned him off. She has someone on her side.''

''He will find her soon,' said Rutland negatively. 'His sort does. He is ruthless. She will have to go underground again and lose her job.''

''He has found another woman and listen to this. She has lost weight as well and someone noticed a bruise on her arm which she had tried to cover up. She looks pale and ill, another candidate for the psychotherapist. Our sources say she now looks as if she fears him and is trying to please him all the time and this is a professional woman who used to be self-assured.''

''What does she look like?'' asked Rutland dreading the answer but knowing what was coming next.

''Tall, slim blonde, not as pale as Kirsten, but with violet coloured eyes. A beauty. He certainly picks them well.''

''Is he taking control of her life yet?''

''She owns her own flat but is spending more time with him and he takes her to the gym after work. She still has her own friends though and close family who disapprove of him so he may find it difficult to suffocate her as easily as Kirsten.''

He has found a substitute for Kirsten but now he wants her back. ''She has a bruise, you said. When did the injury happen? Just after he met and was rejected by Kirsten?''

''Yes, you think he took his anger out on the new woman?''

''I'll bet my hat on it. Get your men to keep your eye on her. She'll be wearing new bruises in the next few days if he can't find Kirsten. His anger must be taken out on someone and she is the best candidate.''

''If my men think she is in any danger they can inform the police or her family if she is too involved with him to listen to sense.''

''Don't think she is brainless because she is acting foolishly. She is suffering from a syndrome. Seemingly intelligent women will allow a man to humiliate and hurt them because they think they are in love with these men. These men cocoon and suffocate these women until they lose the power to make their own independent decisions. The hardest one is leaving men of these types when their self-esteem is undermined continuously.

'She will put up with violence and intimidation even if it progressively grows worse, thinking her life will get better and by agreeing and serving this man's needs she will please him and earn his respect.''

He pondered the situation. ''When Kirsten comes here I may tell her about the girl and ask her to intervene.''

''It might bring his wrath down on Kirsten if he thinks she is interfering in their relationship.''

''It certainly will but I think he will soon be unable to contain his anger with Kirsten and may make his first move against her. We need to show she fears violence or is seriously disturbed by his attention. The police can act if we can show harassment and we can also get a civil injunction. If it were any other ordinary person it would be easy to provide evidence against him. Grayson is so tight with the police it was difficult for her in the past to persuade them he could be violent, such an upstanding member of the community did he appear to be."

''What about the whip marks?''

''Even if he says he did it he may say she accepted it voluntarily in a b.d.s.m relationship. She wouldn't be the first professional woman to become a submissive and submit to violence by a partner.''

''Are you willing to take the risk she might get hurt?''

''With your men tailing her she should be safe. Unless we can force his hand, we may not get the injunction, nor will she ever be free of him.''

''I am trying to find out if other women have suffered similar treatment during the period in which Kirsten was away from him. He may have groomed others.''

His friend turned to the window looking out. ''Thank God, Kirsten will soon be with us.''

He had black circles under his eyes. He was woken up sweating most nights by a recurring nightmare where Kirsten was beaten to a pulp. He had thought of moving temporarily to London and working out of a hotel but he knew she would regard it as an insult, suggesting she could not manage her own life. His fear was that she would underestimate that bastard and be injured permanently or mortality. Men like that could kill a woman when they finally lost control.

''She's arriving the day after tomorrow, isn't she? Are you picking her up from the airport?''

''I have arranged for David to do it. She wrote a very polite letter thanking me for my help and asking for the bill for my services and other costs I have incurred. She promised she will pay me back when she has worked long enough to earn some money. She offered to pay by instalments,'' he snorted angrily. ''As if I would take a penny from her!''

''I suspect she knows that but must make the gesture to satisfy her pride. Knowing Kirsten, she will send you an expensive gift when she has earned enough. She is not the sort of girl who accepts charity easily.''

''Too damned independent, she is,'' Rutland grumbled for the fiftieth time. Drakeman wanted to take his mind off the annoying subject.

''How did last night go?''

Rutland shrugged, barely caring. Drakeman had suggested he should start dating again as Kirsten had shown no sign of encouraging him. He had introduced him to several nice women recently.

''We had a nice dinner at Philippe's and then danced and she took me back to her place but there was no spark, little chemistry between us and we are not going out again.''

''Shame. I thought she might have suited you. She was your type; tall, busty and blonde.''

''She was my type and a lovely girl but I would have been kidding her and myself if I had taken her out again. We enjoyed a great evening together but agreed something was missing.''

''Still stuck on Kirsten, Man?'' asked Drakeman sympathetically.

''Will always be! I am going home to get very drunk. I was up at four working this morning.'' He left, his brows darkened and face scowling. Drakeman worried for him. A man who could easily hold his drink, he had drunk less than many SEALS, keeping fit for competitions, but now he seemed to find a friend in Jack Daniels most nights. He would not neglect his work which was his only real absorption now but his health could suffer although he still swam and trained regularly.

Drakeman felt no better. After the trial in a few weeks Elisabeth would fly to Paris to take up her new position. He had a box in his pocket but was fearful of showing its contents to her. It would either prove she wanted a commitment or it would frighten her off. He feared the latter.

She loved him he was sure but not as much as he loved her. Why else would she want to leave him and finish with him for good for that is what she had intimated? She didn't want a long-distance relationship. His own investigation of her had dug up the dirt about David and he understood she feared a clingy boyfriend. He had given her as much freedom as she wanted, often not calling her for fear she thought he was checking up on her. She would have to make a decision soon.

Justin sent her letter, this time to the hostel. She had fled the refuge that night after talking with her boss. She had escaped just in time. She had to open it in case it might provide evidence in a case against him. Gingerly, she opened the corner, wary of what she might find. He had played practical jokes on her before with live spiders and tormented her afterwards about her phobia. Nothing crawled out but what she read on the paper contained inside made her feel sick. The paper contained a photo of a riding crop with blood on it and a picture of her back with bloody wheals on it. He had taken it the one time he had beaten her with the crop and had obviously kept it as a sick memento of the incident.

Her head spun and she nearly blacked out as she remembered too easily the fear which had gripped her as she had frozen, her blood chilling, unable to move or escape him. Sick to the stomach she dumped the envelope and the paper onto her desk and ran to the bathroom to vomit into the basin. To her surprise, she felt purged and angry instead of terrified. She wanted to fight back against the bastard. Her therapy was working. Her reaction was natural after remembering her pain and fear.

She now determined to face him after her court appearance in Miami. She wanted closure. No longer would she live in this depressive malaise and allow him to dictate how she lived her life and whom she would love. She was recovering her mental health and her pride and had a future to look forward to if she confronted him and won her money back.

She arrived at the airport. She saw a man with a card labelled Ms Gateman waiting for her. A man dressed in a chauffeur's garb could only have been sent by Rutland. The man anticipated everything. Smiling a thank you, she climbed into the car and was astonished to find she was alone. Rutland was staying away from her.

"Mr. Rutland asked me to take you to his office to meet your attorney Ma'am."

The Mercedes rolled up to Defoe Holdings. She looked up and saw the glass fronted skyscraper facing her. It dominated the horizon, like the man who owned it. She knew he was a wealthy and powerful man but just how much he had achieved so young now hit her. For a powerful man, he had been modest. Only the Aston Martin and his casual approach to spending had indicated money was no object to him.

The chauffeur whose name was David took her to a private lift. He left her with a secretary who offered her coffee. The older woman looked like a wise owl, assessing her, noting her tiredness.

"Would you like some refreshments Ms Gateman? Airline food is always so poor."

"It was excellent thank you. Just some water and coffee please."

Another thing she owed to Rutland. Coming to the gate she found she had been upgraded to Club Class. She was sure Rutland had paid the extra. Arguing was no point as it already been paid. She had settled back into the comfy seat so different from her last flight. She slept through the journey, only worry waking her up several times. The scrutinising judge had inferred there was no case to answer by her but she would be glad when the case was over.

She had two cases with her, the same two cases that contained all the clothes she owned. The rest she had left with Justin when he had fled his house. She wanted nothing more to do with them; he had dictated her fashion taste. Most of her clothes were now office wear suitable for court or jeans and tee shirts and cardigans and fleeces. She might be poor in clothes terms but her liberty was worth much more.

Kirsten walked into the office and saw Rutland there with an older man.

"Now I am accused formally as well as you I should not represent you or myself. Peter here has been briefed by me and will undertake the role. You should only need be here for two days if all goes well and Danielle's evidence is thrown out as the pack of lies it is."

Kirsten relaxed as Rutland's manner was now so professional, but her attorney started asking her questions and she saw him out of the corner of her eye. He was as wound up as a tight spring, awareness of her showing in his hooded eyes. His hands were gripping the top of the chair so hard his knuckles whitened. He ran his eyes down her body, mentally stripping her, making her aware of him waiting silently for Peter to end his questioning so he could have her there on his own.

She shivered in anticipation of being alone with him. She might curse his interference but he still excited her just by looking at her. The man had inflamed her passion with his kisses in the pool and she wanted more of them. In a moment of self-searching before she had got on the aeroplane she had admitted she had missed him and had felt sad and deprived when he had respected her wishes and hadn't phoned her. She had changed her cell but he could have got her phone number easily from Elizabeth. He had held back and the saying, 'absence made the heart grow fonder,' was truer than she could have believed.

She had missed his sharp wit and black humour. They had indulged in legal discussion over their dinners. His military background and republican politics had coloured his interpretation of Federal cases. He disagreed bluntly with her and they agreed to disagree; but he still took pro bono criminal defence cases when an underprivileged person had otherwise been deprived of legal representation by in his words, 'an unjust justice system which favoured the rich and privileged.'

He had not forgotten his deprivation amongst the hard streets of Miami. He had defended the drug addict Kirsten had met in jail, giving his legal services free of charge. He had found her a place in a rehabilitation clinic he had financed after a relation had nearly died of drug addiction. She intended to start college, a new life.

She might curse his overprotectiveness but she still thought him the most stimulating man she had set eyes on and wanted him by her side. He treated her like porcelain and made her feel like a lady, something Justin had always failed to do. The damned man had gradually eroded the high barriers she had erected by his kindness and caring nature. He was melting the ice around her heart and she no longer felt in danger from losing it to him.

Peter sat and ran through a mock interview pretending to be the prosecuting and defence counsel until she was sure of what was expected of her. After hours, she was drained and Peter said on leaving, ''Tomorrow is the real thing. Joshua will take you for an early dinner and then you should go to sleep.''

Rutland said, ''Sandra has arranged for us to have our meal in my condo prepared by my housekeeper and then you go back to the hotel.''

He saw she would have refused the offer but he put a finger over her lips to silence her. "You are perfectly safe. The press vultures will be after you if we go to a public restaurant. This way I can talk to you without us being hounded.''

''I could eat in my hotel room.''

''That would be miserable for both of us. I miss your company Kirsten. Please give me the pleasure of your company for the nights you are in Miami.''

He took her hand and kissed each finger. She pulled her fingers back as a shock passed between them. She could not deny the chemistry that sparked between them and electrified the room.

Why not enjoy a meal with this handsome charismatic man? "I like your company too,'' she said, admitting it to him for the first time. She saw his face light up.

''Sweetheart, that is the nicest thing you have said to me. Come let's go get dinner.'' A broad grin split his face and he took her hand and pulled her through the door and into his private lift.

His secretary had smiled at them. ''She likes you. She is not easy to please so be gratified.''

''Does she usually arrange your social appointments?'' asked Kirsten, not willing to admit to herself why she was interested.

''Yes, some of them but if she meets them and disapproves of them she freezes them out. Since I have no mother, she thinks she has taken on the role. Some women she never meets. She is too easily shocked. I have an address book and diary she has never seen.''

He changed the subject. ''The vultures will be outside my office block. They have an inkling I have the hots for you and want to know if there is a romance between us.''

''A dinner in your condo will only fuel the fire,'' she protested.

''No more than if I were to eat with you in your suite. And no, you are not going to eat alone in your room. Let's face the fire,'' he said pushing her through the crowds, one hand on her arm and the other placed possessively on the small of her back, guiding her to safety.

"Is there any truth in the accusations against you Mr. Rutland? Did you and Ms Gateman hurt her aunt to get the shares and the diamonds?''

''Are you and Ms Gateman lovers Mr. Rutland?''

''No comment,'' was all he said. ''You can read my story when I give it to the press and not before. The proceeds will go to Amnesty International and another charity after my costs are paid.''

To Kirsten he explained, "You see you don't need to pay me back nor Phil. Our story will cover the costs and possibly some of your tuition debts.''

''I hadn't thought of that.''

''Some celebrities have sold their wedding stories to Hello and donated the proceeds to charities.''

''I didn't know you were so famous.''

''Infamous my dear. My exploits in the courts and my success in business has made me newsworthy and the press have an unnatural interest in my rather boring love-life.''

His car entered an underground car park. He showed her to the lift and they moved up quickly to the penthouse he owned. Entering the apartment, she looked around her. It was the apartment of a man who loved art, original masters decorating the walls. Impressionists and Pre-Raphaelites added colour to the stark cream walls in the lounge. Sculptures were hidden in the wall scones and the hues of Mexican style furniture were enhanced by warm rugs in rich red and brown hues. This was the habitat of a very private man whose stark clinical facade hid a warm passionate inner self in love with shape and colour.

''Would you like to look around before we eat? The bathroom is in there if you want to freshen up. Feel free to look in all the rooms. I'll put the food out.''

She nodded, wanting to know more about this secretive enigmatic man. He showed a different person to the outside world than the one he was showing to her; a more sensitive person in his own home where he felt comfortable. She suspected he rarely brought strangers to this apartment; only those who he trusted well would see him as he really was. She felt honoured being allowed in here.

She found the bathrooms were filled with glass and huge tubs and outsized showers. Someone had filled the rooms with robes and luxury shampoos and soaps as if they expected a lady to visit. She wondered if Rutland would try to persuade her to stay there. It was tempting to hide away from the prying eyes during the very public trial but he might want more than she was prepared to give at that moment.

Her sessions with her therapist were proving helpful. Once, if a strange man had come behind her suddenly she would freeze and her heart rate would rise dramatically and uncontrollably. Now she could even anticipate Rutland hugging and kissing her with pleasure but if he tried to take their relationship any further she could easily freeze and withdraw from him again. She wasn't ready to share his apartment with him yet for even a few days. It would be too intimate. She even feared the intimacy of this shared meal.

The rest of the apartment was filled with contrasts of cream and colour but the bedrooms surprised her. She peered around the door to the master bedroom. It was surprisingly tidy but she remembered his military career. Most military men were tidy by necessity, barrack rooms' inspections being a regular affair.

Instead of the dark heavy furniture she expected of this very masculine man he had used light chestnut wood for the dressing table and drawers. Cream and burgundy drapes matched a cream and burgundy striped comforter on the bed. The bedroom lead onto a wide balcony overlooking the garden and potted plants decorated it. The overall affect was light and airy, a bedroom she could relax in, not dominated by a masculine presence. His clothes were folded neatly on the chair.

The guest bedrooms were equally light and decorated similarly but in blue and green. The lounge and dining kitchen had patio windows opening onto a balcony which revealed a view of the bay. Vines were running up the outside walls. This was a man who loved nature and natural things.

''What do you think of this place?'' he asked carefully, as if her opinion really mattered.

"It is one of the most beautiful apartments I have ever been in. You have an artistic eye,'' she said and watched a smile spread over his face. He was proud of his home and was gratified she liked it.

''I spent hours making it a home. I didn't want an interior designer making a show home.''

''It is beautiful but homely.'' She heard a thud and a furry cat landed on the floor from its sunny spot on the windowsill. "That is Solar,'' he said as the cat stretched and then sat in front of Kirsten, watching her until she had made up her mind about her. She got up and jumped on to the sofa where Kirsten sat and curled next to her into a little ball. "She has decided you are not going to eat her and she is safe. You are honoured, she only comes to Phil and me normally.''

''Perhaps she doesn't like women.''

''You are the first woman who has come here other than my P.A. and Housekeeper,'' he said with meaning in his words. "She knows you're special!''

A knock came on the door and as he opened it a huge hairy dog bounded through it pulling its handler. Rutland took the overgrown monster and pushed it back when it tried to jump up him.

''Down Charlie!'' he said to the curly head which tried to lick him to death. ''I have had my wash today,'' he cried to the over-enthusiastic labradoodle. The animal looked as if it had had a perm which had gone wrong but bounced about declaring its Labrador heritage, still trying to knock them over.

''Right! On the balcony,'' he said to her and despite her straining protests he lugged her to the door and locked her out until she settled down and lay mournfully watching them with sorrowful eyes. The cat watched her disdainfully, washing a paw and irritating the imprisoned mutt.

''Sorry!'' said Rutland. ''They are both rescued animals. Solar is a thief and Charlie was kicked out of her home for being too boisterous.'' He clearly adored them. This severe man's heart softened when he stroked his feline and canine delinquents.

''I will have a cat when I get a permanent home.''.

''A house is not a home without pets.''

''The food is ready now,'' he said deftly putting out the dishes from the oven on to the table. "Please help yourself. I asked my housekeeper to prepare the dishes you ate in Devil's Creek.''

She ate with enthusiasm the prawns and jerk chicken and spiced rice and salad. He noted she had put on a little weight and didn't pick at her food. Her cheeks had colour in them and her eyes no longer looked anaemic. She had energy, walking briskly instead of rather tiredly as she had when he had last seen her.

She dipped a strawberry in chocolate and cream and ate a delicious mouthful, savouring its sweetness, licking her lips with the tip of her tongue.

''Christ, Kirsten!'' said Rutland jumping out of his chair and walking to the window. He was clenching his fists and when he looked back at her his eyes were full of lust. ''That was the most sensual thing I have seen in weeks. I am having difficulty in keeping my hands off you and then you go and do that. You would tempt a saint!''

She did not know what to say. She had never considered herself a temptress, rather the opposite! Justin had said she needed to train and lose weight to be sexy. Sexy, she associated with babes in nightclubs or on the beaches they went to, not with a barrister who wore suits.

''Come here!'' he ordered. ''If you care even a little for me show me by letting me kiss you.'' He looked so serious, with so much tenderness in his eyes; something broke within her. Tears flowed in her eyes and she ran across the room and flung herself into his arms and let him hug her. He still did not hold her tight and kissed her on the lips, first with feather-light kisses, then with his finger-tips he traced a pattern down her neck and over her shoulders moving her pashmina out of the way.

''You have beautiful skin my love. Your scars are not important to me. I loved you before I saw them.'' He kissed her again, this time more passionately on the lips, then he rested her head against his shoulder when he allowed her to come up for air.

''Look no hands,'' he said when he felt her discomfort at being held so close.

''You idiot!'' she said and standing on tiptoe she put her arms around his neck and kissed him back passionately this time. She felt truly safe with him.

Putting her away from him he said, ''We had better get you back to the hotel before I lose self-control. You will soon be in my bed Kirsten Gateman; I promise you that! I am going to make you want to bed me!'' She now shivered in anticipation rather than fright. This gorgeous, sexy man wanted her.

''I am still scared of sleeping with you but the therapist says I am improving. Soon she thinks I will want and enjoy sex with a man.''

''No woman could kiss as passionately as you and not enjoy love-making with the right man,'' he said. ''That bastard hurt and frightened you and you associated pain and fear with sex.''

''That is what the therapist said!'' replied Kirsten as they walked down to the car.

''The bloody vultures are still here,'' snarled Rutland as he drove out past the reporters.'' Tomorrow's papers will have us having an orgy up there.''

''I don't care providing my Aunt Freja's killers are caught.''

''That's my girl. Full of pluck.'' He shielded her as they passed the newsmen when they arrived at the hotel.

''Will Ms Gateman move into your penthouse after the trial Mr. Rutland? Is there any truth in the story about your engagement?''

Kirsten turned and said to the reporter who had asked the last question. ''No, I am not sharing the apartment nor are we engaged.''

As he pushed her into the foyer she said, ''I had to answer that question. Justin is pursuing me and if he knows I am seeing another man it could push him over the edge. I have to confront him but not until I am ready. My therapist said I need a little more time.''

''Where are you living now?''

''I have no fixed abode at the moment,'' she said grimacing. ''Justin found out my number so now he must know my house. I am fixing a house share for when I go back home. I have two cases and some books to my name. I left my other things with Justin when I left his house and I don't want them back. He chose my clothes for me when I moved into his house.''

''You can't go on evading him. If you want, I could share a house with you in London on a purely platonic basis. He would not touch you then for fear of what I would do to him.''

''That is kind of you but no.'' She thought it was impossible. No longer was it he she mistrusted. She mistrusted herself when she was near to him. She was steadily, irrevocably falling for this lovely man who was prepared to uproot himself temporarily to guard her. Perhaps she needed to compromise a little with him, show that she more than liked him if he would give her space to develop without suffocating her.

''I am going to set up a meeting at a solicitor's office with him in one month's time. I intend to ask him for some of my money back. I can then pay some of your costs.''

''I will get angry if you insist on paying me. You would have done the same for me if you had been in the same position.'' He moved to the door. "Now love, David will pick you up and take us to the courthouse. Elisabeth has arrived and Phil will take her.''

''She wrote to me. She intends to move to Paris.''

"Phil will be gutted. I think he intends to pop the question. I have never seen him so animated by a female.''

''She told me she doesn't want to become engaged at the moment. She thinks she is too young to marry and have children and Phil seems ready to settle down and wants a family.''

''I think Phil will be disappointed and she will leave for Paris. They are the right people at the wrong time sadly. I just hope I can be there to pick up the pieces.''

Drakeman picked up Elisabeth and took her to the courtroom. The atmosphere in the Mercedes was icy as neither of them would broach the topic that was on their minds. He ushered her into the courthouse and sat her next to Kirsten.

''Soon it will be over,'' said Elisabeth. ''You look very well.''

''I feel good and positive. Justin isn't going to poison my mood Lizzie. He is old news. And you?''

''I am looking forward to my role in Paris!'' She felt cold suddenly. Eyes as hard as steel pierced her. If looks could kill she would fall dead at Drakeman's feet. When would the damn man realise he didn't own her? She was a free woman, entitled to do what she wanted. She concentrated on the case, being a material witness who was soon called and cross-examined.

Her evidence over she could breathe freely and Drakeman said, "You are finished now.''

"I can fly back tomorrow then.''

''We are having dinner tonight,'' said Drakeman curtly. "I will pick you up at seven from your hotel.''

''Thank you for your gracious invitation Mr Drakeman,'' snapped Elisabeth, his attitude riling her. He was on his high horse again, issuing orders to her as if she was a schoolgirl! She hated him when he was in this mood.

''Cut the crap Lizzie!'' snapped Drakeman. ''We have things to discuss. I will see you at seven,'' and he walked out of the courthouse, a dark mood enveloping him.

''He has got one on him,'' said Kirsten.

''He has been like this since picking me up at the airport.''

''You can't keep him dangling in the air,' said Rutland. 'He is not that sort of man. He needs to know where he stands.''

''I have been quite honest from the beginning Mr Rutland. He knew I would leave and go to Paris but he can't accept that we have no future together.''

''The bloody man loves you Lizzie. And they say men are heartless!'' His name was called and he entered the stand.

''Mr. Rutland, Counsel for the accused have said you organised the search of Ms Andersson's house and the fire. You wanted the shares and the diamonds.''

''That is not true Sir. I have never expressed interest in owning a dominant share in that mining company.''

''But your company owns shares in mining companies and you had a minority share in it.''

'Yes, but the management changed. I found the company was badly managed and had made poor investment decisions. It would cost too much to turn around so I didn't buy or offer to buy any options in the company over the last seven years. In fact, I sold out of the company five years ago.''

''You didn't send a Mr. Graham on your behalf to make offers to the defendants for their help in securing the shares?''

''Not at all. I would have been overstretched.''

''And that would not be a good reason to want the diamonds to sell, to get your company out of trouble?''

''That is hypothetical and irrational. My companies were not in trouble. Anyway, my investments were heavily in construction at that time. After the property bubble burst, I bought more property while it was dirt cheap, a much better bet than minerals at that time when the price of gold and minerals were fluctuating.''

''You did not meet Mr. Graham on the 15th of October of last year?''

''Not at all; nor did I communicate with him at all. I was out of touch in China in a meeting with government officials. I was not allowed out of the hotel nor to communicate with anyone outside.''

"I ask the jury to peruse evidence for the defence, no. fifty-seven which supports my client's statements. He could not have met the person in question being holed up on an island with the Chinese government officials.''

''Did you have a relationship with Ms Danielle De Vere?'' Rutland thought carefully, a pained expression on his face.

''Not a relationship but a one-night stand. I dined and danced with her and slept with her and left for Miami the next morning. I also gave her a bracelet as thanks for her time.''

''You treated her like a prostitute then Mr. Rutland?'' accused the counsel for the defence.

''No, the gift was thanks for an enjoyable evening.''

''Do you often give your one-night stand's gifts of jewellery?''

''Yes, I usually do. I make it clear I am not interested in a long-term commitment with them and a gift usually keeps them sweet,'' said Rutland feeling sick; acknowledging what sort of person he was to the world in this courtroom. Even to himself, he sounded like a self-absorbed bastard, a player who used women.

"You did not have an affair which lasted a year but was terminated by Ms De Vere and then try to start the affair again that night you claim you slept with her just as a one-night stand?'

''I did not. I didn't know her until I met her at the hotel where she was a receptionist at Devil's Creek. I found her attractive and asked her to dinner and one thing led to another. She had intimated she would like to dine with me on several occasions.''

''You may leave the witness stand Mr Rutland.''

''Call Ms Gateman.''

Kirsten took the oath and stood there. The Counsel for the defence had to shake her and make her seem an unreliable witness.

''You have had a relationship with Mr. Rutland since you arrived in Florida?''

''That is not true!''

"You were seen cavorting with him in the hotel pool and kissing him.''

''He was a little drunk and he pulled me into the pool and he did kiss me.''

''Had he kissed you before?''

''He kissed me a few times but I was not interested which is why I think he slept with Ms De Vere. He was acting on the rebound.''

''And you did not go to his apartment today?''

''Yes, I did. His housekeeper had cooked us lunch and we could avoid reporters if we were there. I was only there an hour.''

The attorney pursued his line of questioning, determined to make her out to be Rutland's lover.

''So, you can say you definitely have no romantic feelings for Mr Rutland and are not committing perjury to help him.''

Kirsten looked at Rutland across the courtroom. He gave her back, stare for stare, hardly breathing, willing her to tell the truth irrespective of the consequences for their trial. He realised her feelings for him were more important than his freedom now. He needed this girl like he needed oxygen in his body. She was vital to his existence!

The seconds ticked over in her head like hours. She could read the emotions traversing his face, hope and fear intertwined in one. He wanted her to tell the truth and to hell with the consequences. She could not lie to him or herself. She was in too deep. Her absence from him had shown how imbedded he was in her psyche. She had missed his interfering and his caring. She wanted to be by his side. She was not sure if this was love but if it wasn't it was a close imposter, pretending to be its twin.

''Ms Gateman,'' prompted the attorney, determined to reach the truth. Kirsten took a deep breath and chose her words very carefully.

''I rebuffed Mr Rutland when I was in Devil's Creek and wanted nothing to do with him romantically nor sexually. He was persistent and wanted to follow me to London but I rejected him, thinking I had no feelings for him except as a kind, brave, decent man rescuing me from my legal problems.

'I was wrong! I missed him while I was in London and realised I do have some romantic feelings for him; how deep I am not sure but we have not slept together nor have we dated at all.''

She looked at Rutland and saw him breathe a sigh of relief and then a wide smile split his face. He was overjoyed at her honesty. He knew how painful it was to bare one's soul when the press would share this gossip to the whole world.

''Thank you for your honesty Ms Gateman. You have put us in the picture. The jury can decide themselves if you are telling the truth.

'Do you know Mr. Thirman Ms Gateman?''

''Only by name and reputation.''

''Did you meet him in the café or text him?''

''Not at all. Someone is trying to implicate me in the murder of my aunt.''

''Why did you come to Devil's Creek recently?''

''My aunt told me John Thirman was trying to intimidate her into selling him her house. I was investigating him and his contacts and then she said someone was searching her house and she was afraid. I heard from the hospital Aunt Freja and Mr. Defoe were injured and so I came to find out how I could help them and visit Aunt Freja.''

''Thank you, Ms Gateman. You may leave the witness stand.''

Rutland collected her and took her to her to a very select restaurant open only by invitation of the chef and then after that to the theatre. After her admission in the court room he intended to push his advantage as much as he could but didn't want to scare her off.

"I will miss you tomorrow when you leave for London.''

''I will miss you as well. Perhaps you can visit London in the future when Phil visits Lizzie in Paris.''

''I would love that,'' said Rutland. At last she was giving him some encouragement. ''Let's not go back yet to your hotel. I have a private pool on the roof-top, one of my other luxuries. Would you come for a swim with me? I promise not to pull you in this time."

''I enjoyed it in the pool although I was shocked at the time. I was afraid of getting too close to you, physically and emotionally.''

''Come with me. The pool is fantastic at night. We can swim under the stars.''

Kirsten was tempted. *Oh, what the hell. What harm can it do?* His arm around her, she nestled against him as they walked to the car. She ignored the flashlights as the press recognised them.

''They know we are an item so we had better humour them,'' They stood for the photographers to take some shots. ''Hey Guys give us a break! Ms Gateman goes back tomorrow. We wanted a relaxing night together.''

''Are you two an item Mr. Rutland?'' Rutland looked at Kirsten.

''Mr. Rutland was trying to persuade me to date him in Devil's Creek,'' said Kirsten for the first time, ''but I wanted just to be good friends. I missed him in London and decided today I wanted to be more than good friends with him.''

''I guess we are an item now,'' he admitted ''but it is a very recent decision." He kissed her on the top of her head and a reporter said, "That will make a good spread tomorrow Mr. Rutland. The hard, womanising lawyer has fallen for a woman at last!''

Rutland grimaced and pushed Kirsten into the car. He gripped the wheel tightly and took his exasperation out on the car as he sped along the freeway.

''Your previous reputation doesn't bother me Joshua.''

''I took a woman out recently but I couldn't forget you Kirsten. When we are together I want us to be mutually exclusive, no other lovers. I can wait for you Kirsten. I am a very patient man when the prize is worth waiting for.''

''I went out with no-one but I didn't expect you to be celibate Joshua. I had pushed you away from me.''

''Let's just swim again Kirsten and be kissing partners only but when I visit you in London you may wish to revise the terms of our relationship." 'He squeezed her hand and stopped the car, ushering her into the lift and up to his penthouse again.

He took her up to the rooftop garden where a long pool lay hidden surrounded by vines and potted plants. It was magical with lily pads and subtle lighting like a fairy grotto. Solar sat by the pool near a pond watching some fish float by.

''It is magical, like an island up here,' she said. 'The pool is enormous!''

''My company built this apartment block and I trained here and swum in competitions earning some good money. I have only lived here the past few years when I wanted privacy. It was a good money earner for years.''

He dived into the pool and swum a few lengths, cruising without any effort. She admired his style; power without using much energy.

''Come in before I get tempted to pull you in,'' he said wickedly and she hustled her robe off before he could make on his threat. She swam to him and he splashed her. She responded and they were totally soaked until he dived under the water and pulled her under, holding her and kissing her until they had to come up for breath.

''I only promised I wouldn't pull you into the water.''

''You are a cheat,'' she said spluttering but didn't let him go. He tightened his grip and ran his hand through her hair holding it tight.

''I can't let you go Kirsten. I must have you soon. You are too good to lose. I am a different man when you are here, at peace and content. Without you I feel alone.''

''I felt strange in London without you. Normally I like my own company but I kept wanting to telephone you and chat with you. I miss your distorted sense of humour.''

''My black humour you mean. That woman I went out with was too nice. She didn't challenge me. I wanted my acerbic Kirsten back. You tell me when I am getting too authoritarian. Your independence and risk-taking nature worries me however. I want to look after my Woman.''

''My Woman.'' Those words should have rung warning bells in Kirsten's head, a man wanting to look after and control her. Instead Kirsten felt a warm feeling of being secure and wanted and protected, not suffocated or cocooned until she shrivelled and died inside. She wanted to be this man's woman!

''Swim a few lengths and get dressed and I will take you back now,'' he said reluctantly, determined to keep his word. He desperately wanted her in his bed but he was prepared to wait until she was ready. Her passionate responses to his kisses and caresses indicated she was nearly ready to be there. He need only wait a little while.

They arrived back at her hotel and he checked her room was safe for her. ''I am flying out of Miami earlier than you tomorrow Kirsten. Drakeman will ensure you and Elisabeth get to the airport safely but I will contact you in London and make a date to visit you.''

Kirsten drifted into to her room in a dream. She had wanted to stay in his arms during the night and she thought he knew it but being a gentleman, he hadn't pressed her. She would invite him to London and their relationship would progress from there. For the first time in years she thought she might want a long-term relationship with a man; a strong man who would give her enough freedom to be her own woman but still protect and love her. She was beginning to think Rutland was that man. Her Aunt Freja had liked him and that was a good testimonial in her mind. Time would tell.

Elisabeth felt uncomfortable. She resented Drakeman pushing her around but she had to set the record straight with him. She asked him to come for a pre-dinner drink. ''I thought we were dining together,'' he said, wary. She sat stiffly opposite him as if something was worrying her. Lizzie was not a worrier. Carefree by nature she took each day as it came, only serious when it came to her work.

"I want to dine in my room Phil and have an early night. I have a bad headache coming and need to get up early tomorrow.'' He didn't believe her. She was making excuses but he would not put pressure on her. He felt the box in his pocket. It was clearly not the time to discuss their future. She was clearly putting a stop to their relationship and he had to give her space.

''When do you leave for Paris?'' he enquired.

"Next week. I must pack and clean my apartment. I am renting it out.''

"I would like to visit you. I can use the private jet.''

"That would be nice. I will call you when I have settled in.'' Phil recognised a brush off when he heard it. She was telling him in the nicest possible way they were finished. She got up and put her share of the bill on the table. He immediately placed the note back in her hand and she shrugged and kissed him on the cheek.

"Bye Phil. I will miss you.'' He was left sitting there desolate but knew she would hate him following her and making a fuss. He would follow her later to Paris and make her change her mind.

She made for the stairs. She hoped he would not follow her to Paris and make it harder for them. She would bury herself in work and try to forget him.

She went back to her room. Kirsten arrived later looking dreamy and contented.

''I saw the news. You have finally decided to become an item.''

''They had guessed anyway. This way they only print the truth. Joshua will feed them the information he wants them to know.''

''You love him then!''

''I think I do but haven't told him yet. He will come to London and we will see what happens. And you? What happened between you and Phil? He seemed serious in the courtroom.''

'We had a drink and I dined alone in my room. I tried to put him off but he still wants to meet in Paris. He won't take no for an answer."

'Joshua thinks he wants to settle down.''

''I don't want to settle down. I am too young to marry and have children. I saw my mother suffocated by her marriage and don't intend it to happen to me.' She picked up her purse and kissed Kirsten on the cheek. I will ring you when I get back home and of course from Paris. Good luck with your new job.'' Kirsten recognised the subject was closed and let her go. She was sure her friend was making a bad mistake and watched her walk sadly to the lift. She and Phil would have to sort their own life out. She went to bed relaxed and feeling positive for once.

Chapter eleven.

Kirsten had settled into a dreary studio flat in an old converted warehouse. The warehouse was being converted by a women's group. It was guarded by a burly ex-commando whose own sister had been beaten up and abused. Some of the flats were still damp and mould was on the walls. Kirsten could bear the scruffy rooms and broken furniture donated by the charity. One bed, desk and chair and sofa plus a cupboard and chest of drawers was all she had. She had no car, going by bus or tube everywhere, but she was happy as the lark that sang outside her window each morning.

Her previous house sharers had passed on her letters and she sat in her office at work reading them. She opened one and froze, a sickening feeling in her stomach. 'There was a photo of her and Rutland with the caption, **'Love at last. Rutland and Gateman an item. Their own words. The hard lawyer falls hard at last for another legal eagle.'**

Kirsten's eyes widened at the hard, black line drawn through their faces as if cutting through them. The word **'No'** was drawn in black ink across the words, **'love at last.'**

A typewritten note accompanied the newspaper photo. There was no name, he was too clever for that but the message was clearly from Justin.

Kirsten's mind whirled. For an instant, she panicked, then her legal mind set in and she started to think her actions out. She had a number she could ring if something like this happened. She made an urgent appointment with her boss leaving him a copy of the contents of the envelope. He knew Justin's phone calls had become more frequent even when she changed her number regularly.

Justin was more powerful than she had thought if he could find out information about her so easily. He must have an investigator working for him all the time, checking up on her. She was certain he now knew where she lived.

Inside her flat she felt safe, the burly marine or another always there acting as concierge, looking after his ladies. Rutland had sent a man to pick her up from work in an unmarked car. He would not take no for an answer. The same car picked her up in the evenings from her flat and took her to her gym and self-defence classes.

He had arranged through Drakeman's London office a man she could ask for help. He was still looking after her from a distance. This is what he meant when he said she was his woman and he would protect her. She rang the man and left a message for him to contact her.

Rutland was by his pool working on a legal case. A buzz notified him of a call. Instantly his mind was on red alert. It was a phone number known only by a few friends of his and Kirsten.

''Rutland,' he answered then his tone changed. ''Kirsten, what is the matter?'' His heart hammered, knowing she was in deep trouble. She was not the sort of woman who would interrupt his work for social calls.

''I was sent a photo of us crossed out in black pen.''

''Tell me what he wrote.''

''He typed, 'your betrayal will be your last Kirsten. You promised once you would be mine and only mine.' The reporter had written 'love at last,' and he wrote 'no' over those words.''

''Where are you now?''

''In my office at work. I have arranged an appointment with the boss. He will support me when he sees the newspaper cutting.''

''Have you spoken to Drakeman's man?''

''I left a message.''

''The bloody man is supposed to be on call,'' he exploded, infuriated he was not there to be by her side.

''It was ten minutes ago, Joshua. Be reasonable.''

"I want you to stay there while I make some calls.''

''I have no intention of moving. I have files to process.''

''If anyone calls you and asks you to leave the office for any reason I want you to go into the admin office and wait there. Do not leave your place of work. You understand?''

His voice had become harsher, authoritarian, as he gave the order to her. To hell with her sensibilities; this was not the time to tread gently. Her life was in danger and he needed to act quickly and impress on her how dangerous this man might be.

''I understand,'' she said and he cut the call, instead calling Drakeman. His Mate's P.A. said, ''He will be in a meeting for twenty minutes Mr. Rutland. He asked not to be disturbed.''

''To hell with his meeting, dig him out immediately, this is urgent!'' snapped Rutland impatiently, drumming his fingers on the desk until Drakeman came to the phone.

"If I didn't think this was about Kirsten I would tell you to take a jump Asshole, bullying my P.A. What's up?''

Rutland explained the situation. ''I am taking the jet in two hours and will sort out this bastard myself for once and for all. Did you want to come?''

''Yes, London is near Paris. I may drop in on a certain young lady afterwards while you are courting Kirsten.''

''Is it wise when she has told you in no uncertain terms to push off?'' asked Rutland, not wanting his friend to be hurt yet again. The last two months had been spent by Drakeman in a haze of beer and scotch. He was recovering his good sense at last and starting to go out with Rutland instead of girls he had used for one-night stands.

''A man can only get told no,'' said Drakeman. ''I would regret it if I didn't try. I'll meet you at the airport in ninety minutes. In the meantime, I will contact my man and find out what the score is.'

''I want her in my hands by tomorrow night. Where we took the other girls!''

''At the moment, she is at work and a private car collects her to take her to the flat which is guarded by a man.''

''You can handle one man, can't you?''

''I think it would be better to stop the car. A driver in a car is easier to take out.''

''Do so then. I will be at Latham Lodge by eight o'clock tomorrow night and will expect her then.''

''Now she has seen that newspaper cutting she may have taken more precautions,'' the second man warned this angry intimidating man who impatiently gave out commands.

''I wanted her to be scared, to feel we were crowding in on her. When we finally meet again I want her scared out of her wits.''

''You don't want her to run to someone who will guard her.''

''This American, Rutland, already has some tails on her and sends the car each day. You can bet she has contacted him already.''

A third man said, 'She is going to the same banquet tomorrow as you Justin. You could meet her there and then she might disappear on her way home. It will only delay her coming to Latham Lodge by a few hours.''

''That isn't a bad idea. She won't make a fuss in public. She hates scenes. It will appear she wanted to get back together with me again. When I have finished with her no-one will believe she didn't come with me to the Lodge voluntarily.'' He smiled maliciously and drove his Bentley back home thinking of the shock he would give her the next night.

Kirsten had gone home and was reading a file in front of the fire. A stray cat had adopted her and she was scratching its ears. ''I will keep you, old girl, if I can buy a house to live in permanently.''

The cat widened green eyes at her and pawed her, asking her for more attention as she had stopped scratching her momentarily. Undertaking her duty to the feline again she was rewarded by a deep purr. Kirsten felt this flat was home for the first time ever. Her job was rewarding and Rutland rang her several times a week, still pursuing her. She felt lucky and happy for the first time in years.

Bored with the files she took up an invitation that had been sent to her. It was to one of the banquets the legal profession organised each year and for her career's sake she should be there. She had sent letters to Justin outlining her demand for some money from him but had received nothing from him by way of answer.

She would meet him at the banquet tomorrow and the fear of meeting him in person was rearing its ugly head again. She would have to face him. Tomorrow she would ask him for the money in person and warn him she would take the case to court if he didn't co-operate. She had hated scenes in the past and avoided them like the plague but she was a different person from the submissive woman who had shared the townhouse with him. If she had to make a scene to win her money so be it.

She looked at the dress a friend had lent to her. Ashamed of showing her scars she would wear a sea green and blue silk dress with a low neckline but a fine floating shawl collar covered her bust and shoulders. The skirt ended in a train. She looked like a sea witch and she wound her hair into a loose bun with wavy tendrils flowing from it. A sophisticated but romantic look, she was satisfied she looked good. She wished Rutland could see her in it. She was missing him badly, each day looking forward to his phone calls.

She had spoken to Lizzie promising to visit her when her finances were sorted out. Lizzie was no-nonsense as usual. She loved her job, Paris was exciting and the French men dreadful flirts but fun. She had no regular boyfriend yet and reading between the lines Kirsten thought she wanted none. She detected a wave of despondency under her friend's gay laughter and attempt to seem cheerful. Lizzie was missing Drakeman dreadfully. If Kirsten mentioned his name Lizzie changed the subject, a sure sign that he occupied her mind all the time and her attempt to forget him was failing.

Rutland found out Kirsten's whereabouts the following night and a few calls gained him and Drakeman tickets to the banquet as honoured guests. *'There were advantages to being well known.* Freja's case was coming to an end. The jury had found the defendants guilty. All that remained was for them to be sentenced.

Rutland was pressing his counsel to ask for the harshest sentences. He was afraid they would be let out too soon. Danielle was vindictive and could try to hound and hurt Kirsten. The court psychoanalyst had found she was a psychopath with sociopathic tendencies, moving about from job to job.

She gained malicious pleasure from hurting people. Unfortunately, her sociopathic tendencies meant like her father it had taken years before she was found out. A bully at school and at work she had intimidated her school and work colleagues, inspiring fear in her weaker, gentler victims.

Unlike his daughter, her father had showed no evidence of having psychopathic tendencies but his former partner, her mother, had been committed to an asylum and Drakeman suspected if her mental records were examined she would show similar traits to those her daughter exhibited.

Kirsten was taken to the banquet by her boss. She had explained she intended to challenge Justin if he approached her. He knew it took a great deal of courage for her to enter the ballroom knowing her fiancé was there. In the past, Justin had been able to shrivel her with a curt remark or hard stare. Many of her fellow students were there and greeted her like a long-lost friend. They had heard of her sudden disappearance and welcomed her back into the legal community.

Happy, she stood there relaxed, until suddenly she saw a movement out of the side of her eye. She froze. Her therapist had talked her through this occasion but she was still not ready for the reaction when she saw him coming toward her. He stopped to talk with others, a social chameleon, oiling his way through the room. How she could have thought he was attractive she did not know but she had not met Rutland then!

He was handsome in a traditional sort of way, his height dominating over other men in the room. It was his eyes that gave him away. A pale grey, they had no depth to them. They were as grey as a dull day, steely but lacking warmth. He stared at her and she felt impaled on them. He smiled knowing the affect he had on her, knowing he terrified her just by his stare. The bastard was enjoying every minute of the time it took for him to walk over to her.

She moved across the room to another group of friends. She was not going to wait for him to choose his battleground. Her boss was there. "Steady Ms Gateman! I am here if you want me to intervene."

''Thank you, Sir. I will speak to him alone but I will not go into any other room with him. Anything he says has to be in public.'' He stood a little away from her with some others, allowing Justin to come over to her. Neither Justin nor Kirsten saw the two men sitting in a corner out of sight of most of the diners. They had been watching the proceedings with interest.

That's right, Kirsten choose your place to meet and fight him, thought Rutland. His knuckles were white, he held his glass so tight but this was her fight and he had no right to intervene.

"She looks as if she has her emotions under control,'' said Drakeman. He looked at his friend. Rutland looked as if he was fighting to retain control over his own feelings.

''I thought you wanted to keep this bloodless. You look dangerous!''

''I do for Kirsten's sake and my reputation. I don't want the police called for a case of assault but that doesn't mean I wouldn't like to throttle the bastard if I had the opportunity.''

''If we get the opportunity to get him down a back alley on his own I will help you knock his daylights out,'' said Drakeman, his own bad humour needing an outlet. He had texted Elisabeth telling her he was in London but he had not got a reply. He would fly to Paris and surprise her in a few days.

Justin now stood in front of her. He was surprised; when he took a step forward Kirsten stayed put.

''Good evening Justin,'' she said putting out her hand for him to shake.

''Very formal Kirsten,'' he said shaking it. ''We had such intimate dealings in the past!''

''The past is over Justin,'' said Kirsten. ''I just want to tell you that I expect my salary to be refunded less reasonable expenses. I am going to give you one month and then I will take legal action.''

''Oh, and how will you finance that Kirsten? With help from your lawyer boyfriend?''

''Think Justin. How would it ruin your reputation if our story got around? I will tell anybody of consequence about your perverted ways.''

''Perverted ways. You have such a vivid imagination my love.''

Kirsten's eyes screwed up at the use of that endearment. She hated him calling her that. There was no love on his side, just the desire to manipulate and control.

''One-month Justin. We have said all we have to say and now I am going back to my friends.'' She turned to go away and he said quite softly, "We haven't finished at all my love. You will come to Davan Hall this weekend and resume our relationship''

''You never listened to a word I said Justin, but listen carefully now. I want nothing from you except my wages you owe me.''

As she moved away she was jerked sharply back, his hand gripping her arm firmly. Trying to move without causing a scene she bit back a cry as his cruel sharp nails dug into her arm.

''You will come with me at the end of the evening Kirsten, just as we used to go home together.''

''In your dreams.''

''You were always neurotic,'' he said in a loud voice which carried over the ballroom, causing people to turn to listen to his words.

''That is why I kept such a tight control on you when we were engaged. Your father said you lost control very easily and needed to be guided. 'A brilliant brain but temperamental,' he said, 'always trying to look thinner and making yourself ill.' You needed a strong man to help you.''

''Did I hell?'' she said pulling herself free. ''You are not strong. You are weak!'' He grabbed her shoulder this time and held her in place, not realising that others were watching and he was causing a scene.

Rutland had had enough and was moving through the tables, sweeping past the couples standing chatting. He stood at the edge of the ballroom floor, waiting for the right moment to intervene. Kirsten pulled away and tried to prise Justin's hand off her but as she did some buttons ripped and the shawl collar slipped down, revealing her neck and shoulders.

Her scars were visible to all who stood near to her and some people gasped and others stared. Justin now fearful of public opinion moved closer to pull up the collar. Kirsten embarrassed but emboldened asked him coldly, ''Don't you like to see what you did to me Justin? A weak man has to hurt women.''

Justin moved forward again and said, "Come with me Kirsten. I have a car waiting for us.'' His eyes seemed glazed as if he didn't understand fully where he was and the implications of what had happened during the last few moments. Rutland moved between them and said, "The lady said she doesn't want to come with you. Please leave her alone.''

Kirsten was shocked and pleased to see him appear out of the blue but wasn't surprised. She had been amazed he was going to let her go to the ball alone.

''What is it to you Rutland?'' asked Justin. To Kirsten he asked, ''Is this your Irish immigrant boyfriend Kirsten? Tell him your fling with him is over.''

''If you are going to insult me, please be accurate. I was born in Miami. It is my Great-Granddad who was the immigrant.''

''Same difference. Filthy Irish scum!'' retorted Justin. ''I really am amazed at you Kirsten, associating with such low-class trash, but you always did like to associate with rubbish.''

''He is worth ten of you Justin,'' said Kirsten but Rutland dragged her away saying, ''Thanks for the compliment but he is not worth arguing with. You have said your piece. It is now time for legal action. He will not act reasonably. He is irrational.'' He put his jacket over her shoulders and with Drakeman following they said goodbye to their shocked hosts and went back to the car.

''The hotel,'' he told Drakeman. "She needs looking after. No arguments, Sweetheart. You are with me tonight. I have a large suite, too large for just me.''

He cuddled her as she started trembling, the shock of confronting her fiancé just hitting her. "You were fire and ice, just as I expected. You gave him the shock of his life standing up to him.

'It is a shame everyone had to see your scars and hear you accuse him but once he had pulled your collar off we were past the point of no return. His name will be black in legal circles. Most of his best work will decline now.''

''I don't care as long as he leaves me alone,'' she said, trying to control her trembling voice and her tears.

''You don't need to worry about him anymore.''

Drakeman pulled into the underground car park of the hotel. He morphed automatically into his role as security adviser

''The press will have a field day with this. There were photographers and reporters in that ballroom. Take her upstairs and I will deal with the others waiting outside.'' He walked through the foyer and out on to the pavement.

''Hey guys. You're too late tonight. Mr. Rutland has gone up to his suite. You can read what happened at the banquet in the morning.'' He then walked back into the hotel. He wanted this case over with so he could go to Paris. He would have one last try to persuade Elisabeth to give them another chance.

Rutland pulled Kirsten out of his car and carried her in the lift to his suite. It was at the top for increased security and privacy. Kicking open the door, he carried her to the second bedroom and dropped her on the bed.

''Stay there while I run you a bath,'' he said. He poured her a brandy.

''I don't drink spirits,'' she protested.

''It will calm your nerves.''

''You are bossy.'' she said, as he pushed the glass in her hand.

''And you need looking after. Take your dress off and take a bath. I am in the next room tonight, although it may kill me!'' She undressed and made it to the bathroom on shaky legs. He yelled out through the open door.

''Are you hungry or do you just want to sleep?''

''Sleep please!'' she replied, the stress now draining out of her. Exhaustion was now taking its place. She wrapped herself in a robe after soaking in the deep scented water. He was sitting on her bed looking as sexy as hell and serious.

He kissed her cheek and whispered ''Good night Sweetheart. I am dealing with the bogey man. No need for bad dreams'' He left her as he anticipated his restless night thinking of the long legged blond beauty in the next bedroom.

''Not much longer Rutland,'' he said to himself ''and she will be yours!''

He fell asleep hours later but woke up suddenly hearing screams coming from the next room, piercing the silent night. He jumped out of bed fearing the worst. Had Justin got to her through his security? He saw thankfully she was huddled up in the bedclothes in the foetus position crying in her sleep.

''Kirsten love, wake up. It's Josh.'' He shook her gently, frightened by the terrified look in her now open eyes. She hit out at him but he held her still. Her pupils were focused on him, wide and dark, like that of an animal caught, waiting for its prey to tear it apart.

She gradually came back to reality. ''Hold me tight!'' she pleaded with Rutland.

''Gladly!'' he replied and opened the bed and got in with her. He was only wearing his boxers but making love with a terrified woman was not on his mind that night. Comforting her was the only thing he wanted to do.

''Sleep Kirsten. We will discuss everything in the morning,''

When she looked into his eyes he could see absolute trust there. As she fell asleep in his arms he could relax his hold on her and gradually drifted to sleep himself until the dawn chorus woke him and he stretched. Kirsten had flung her leg over him and was nestled up to him.

I could get used to this, he thought contentedly.

He got out and showered. Peeking in at Kirsten he saw she was fast asleep but lying relaxed this time, her flaxen hair spread out on the pillow. How he wanted to run his hands through that hair and kiss her senseless but he shoved his lustful thoughts back where they belonged and put on some running gear.

He was still used to running each morning if he didn't swim; after years of fatigues the habit was hard to shift. Kirsten was in her underwear but a quick phone call and he had clothes delivered for her to wear that morning. It was Saturday and smart casual was appropriate. He knew she liked wearing sweats and trainers when she was off duty and some chinos and tee shirts and cashmere sweaters would suit her style.

He set off down the street at a fast pace ignoring the looks of female pedestrians watching him. He always attracted the looks of females. It went with the territory of being well above average in height and more than a little good looking. Add a natural assurance to that and women were drawn to him. His wealth and power meant he could pick his ladies like cherries off a tree but all he wanted was Kirsten, happy and safe.

After his run, he would talk to his contacts at Drakeman's office and find out what else Grayson was up to. He had already found out two of his companies were over-extended. Rutland had asked his finance division to audit those companies. At the base, they were good businesses which he could turn around. Grayson had recently bled the companies dry.

He was building a mansion to show to his contemporaries his wealth but where the other money was going it was difficult to find. Rutland believed Grayson had his finger in other pies, some of which he suspected were illegal. He was now buying stock in Grayson's companies at a low price, aiming to take them over. The real pleasure would come from seeing Grayson's face when he was forced to sell them at a low price to him.

He had run his six miles and was heading back to the hotel when he realised a black limo was closely following him down a back street. He recognised it as a car he had seen for the last half hour wherever he had run. He stepped up his pace, wanting out of the lonely street. The car pushed past him up the curb slowing down and a partially open door hit him hard in the side.

He doubled up as two men came from the back and front of the car. As he stumbled to his feet he felt a prick in his arm. One man held him by the hair, dragging his head back, while the other punched him in the guts.

He moved as if he was in slow motion as the drug slowed his movements, dulling his senses. Kicking at them he hurt one but another man kicked him in the back. He doubled up, his kidneys crucifying him as the car moved forward and they pinned his arms to his side until they could handcuff them in front of him. *Amateurs.* He was pushed into the car still kicking until he gradually fell into unconsciousness.

Kirsten woke up at ten o'clock feeling refreshed and relaxed for the first time in months. She saw a note pinned on to her pillow with a rose. ''Gone for a run. Shower and we will have breakfast. Fresh clothes are in the bathroom. Joshua.''

Looking at the clock she was astonished Rutland wasn't there. She knew he was an early riser and his run couldn't have taken very long. He must have been delayed by something.

She waited until eleven o'clock and then phoned his cell. No answer. It was turned off and she couldn't even leave a message. This was weird. He would always leave his phone turned on for her texts. Breakfasting in her room, she phoned reception but no messages were left there. The doorman said Rutland had gone out for a run but had not returned yet.

Now alarmed she phoned Drakeman. Just back from the hotel gym he picked up the phone and snapped impatiently, ''Drakeman!''

'Phil, Joshua went out for a run four hours ago, and hasn't come back. He was supposed to come back for breakfast. He isn't answering his phone. It is switched off which is unlike him.''

''You have asked reception. Of course, you have. I'll be there in five minutes.''

After a hasty shower, he grabbed his phone, briefcase and gun and knocked on Kirsten's door. He went in and checked the phone and then Rutland's room and cases. Nothing explained his prolonged absence.

''He didn't wake you?'' She shook her head. ''Here is the note.''

''I am going down to the doorman and to walk around the streets. I might find someone who might identify him and trace his last movements. I know where he runs. We ran together yesterday morning but I thought he might be occupied this morning and went to the gym alone.''

Kirsten blushed but said nothing. She was as reserved as Rutland when it came to discussing her private life. Drakeman got up.

''You stay here until I come back. I will phone you when I want you to answer the door but otherwise you don't go out.''

She nodded but soon became bored. She took her notebook from her haversack and started keying in detail about Justin. She was sure he was connected with the disappearance of Rutland and wanted to find out anything about Davan Hall. Justin was going there and so he might take Rutland.

She hated the place. Dark grey Victorian stone, it had always been gloomy and damp when she had stayed there. She had heard he was turning it into a plush country home but she could not forget the cellars he had made her visit when they had stayed there.

He had some peculiar delight in making her go down to a badly lit cellar to get wine and laughed when she said it gave her the creeps. He had locked her in one night and refused to open the door until she had pleaded with him to let her out. She had sat there frozen in fear as the floor was covered with spiders. Webs covered the steps leading to the door.

It was like the scene out of an old black and white horror movie. She had pushed her way through the silken, sticky web, the fibres clinging to her head while she hammered on the door. Wriggling legs caught in her fine hair and she had screamed, stumbling down the stairs until she sat at the bottom, tearing at them until he had finally released her trembling and sobbing. It was the week before he had started hitting her and she had begun to discover his cruel sadistic streak.

As she suspected Davan Hall was being renovated at great expense but he had not renovated the outbuildings yet. There was a lodge still in disrepair about a half a mile from the main house. She texted a photo and address to Drakeman and wrote, ''Joshua could be there.''

''I am on to it,'' said Drakeman. ''I will send a man there immediately. It is the best lead we have yet.'' He had been digging into Justin's background and was finding some unusual trails to follow.

''Kirsten, was Justin involved in any sex gangs or did he belong to any bondage clubs?''

''I think he belonged to the latter. He tried to get me to go along to one.''

''I will follow that up,'' he said. ''Kirsten, he may have been involved with under-age girls like the ring we heard about in the news that operated in Belgium many years ago.''

Kirsten remembered top rank government officials, businessmen and other high-profile figures had been netted by the police. The ring had operated across state boundaries. Huge monies had been passed to take young children and keep them in secret houses for the enjoyment of older men. The oldest girls were fourteen but some of the children were only eight.

She could only imagine the fear these young kids were subjected to. Surely even Justin could not be involved in something as evil and perverted as this. She then remembered his eyes when he had described the club he had wanted her to join. They glittered and gleamed and he looked happy for the first time. At other times he always looked as if he were searching for something to make him content.

Thinking back, he had always been hanging around the children at parties and enjoyed dancing with the teenage girls at dances they attended. She had thought he was being kind, a sophisticated man paying attention to the raw young girls. One parent had suggested to her he paid too much attention to his daughter but he had laughed when Kirsten had said it would be wise of him to leave the girl alone. He had called her jealous, scared of losing her youthfulness.

She had retreated in the face of his anger as she had always done if he argued with her. His anger was too unpleasant to be stirred up. He was a different man when angered. Gone was the pleasant easy-going man who charmed women and men alike. In its place was a cold, harsh, god-like creature who always thought he was right and had to be obeyed. Yes, Justin could be involved in the evil that dominated this gang. She had only touched on the danger that he represented to the world; the evil that was in him, the ability and desperate desire to corrupt.

She texted Drakeman telling him about the parties she had attended and the name of the man who had complained about him. He might know more than he had let on to her. She then remembered some of his business contacts. One Jason Deepham had been convicted for possession of heroin but also had been cautioned for attempting to solicit women. That on its own would not have even raised an eyebrow in her world but the girls involved were barely sixteen. There were hints of grown men grooming under-age girls but it had been whitewashed over. Deepham's family were rich and powerful and the charge had been dropped.

Kirsten remembered Deepham at a party at Justin's parents' house. He had run his hands down the back of her deep-cut halter-necked dress, making her cringe. She had wondered why Justin had not objected as he was her boyfriend. Perhaps he liked sharing women even then, as she suspected he did now. She speculated whether he and Deepham had taken young girls to Davan Hall to be abused. She sent more details about Deepham to Drakeman.

"Want to change career?" he texted back. "You are doing me out of a job."

"No thanks. Your work gives me the creeps. I prefer legal work any day. It is tidier."

"Yep, my work is dirty most of the time. Makes it interesting though."

"What have you traced about Josh?" she asked, fear really beginning to take hold of her now. Just as she had found a decent man with integrity, who was as sexy as sin, he had been taken away from her. Her bad luck was following her again.

"I ran the same way we did yesterday and some people remembered him, mainly women as you would expect. Josh always attracts attention when he runs."

Kirsten remembered him in his singlet and shorts in Florida; deeply muscled legs pounding the ground, his massive chest heaving and arms pumping and his green eyes sparkling. Of course, women would watch him. He was a prime example of raw masculinity. She would have if she had been there.

"The last person saw him quite close to the hotel when he must have been running back. A few delivery men saw him being followed quite slowly by a black limo. No plates to go on but I have a marque and the time. They gave descriptions of the driver which all match. I can only assume he has been snatched which surprises me as Josh can usually take care of himself."

"How can you trace him?"

"My men will soon be at Davan Hall and may find some connections with his kidnappers there. Stay put. If this Justin is as arrogant as we think he may contact you about Josh and use him as a bargaining tool to make you meet him there."

He broke off. Another text was coming through on his other phone.

Yeah, there was a tall blond man who had connections with a club which specialised in finding very young girls for mature men. The age limit started from eighteen but the police had targeted this club when informants said some of the girls who passed across the threshold were barely into their teens.

So far, they had never been lucky. The raids had only found older girls. Most brothels used girls from the age of sixteen but there were many madams who were less fussy and the police turned a blind eye, finding bigger fish to fry; thinking cynically, the young girls were safer in the brothels than walking the dangerous streets.

He now wondered if his men should look at girls who had suddenly disappeared and runaways who had not been found. It would be like looking for a needle in a haystack in London but he had to try. He also needed to find out who Justin's pimp was and the managers and owners who ran the bondage clubs or others who dealt in the more dangerous games he played. He thought, *Kirsten and I are in for another long boring night at the computer.'*

They waited anxiously but next day in the late afternoon Kirsten received a call from reception. ''Ms Gateman there is a note for you. I was asked if you would collect it from here.''

''Go down but don't leave the hotel Kirsten. I will be near you,'' said Drakeman. *At last,* he thought. Josh would be kicking himself for getting into this mess. They must have surprised him. He had taken eight men out once single handed with his bare hands.

Kirsten took the note from the receptionist. It was typed again and the sentences were quite explicit and concise.

''You leave for Davan Hall at ten tonight in the car which will be waiting outside for you. You will come alone. Your boyfriend will await you there.''

Her first thoughts were Justin was an idiot giving his game away so soon but then she had seen the mania in his eyes last night. He had made a scene in front of influential people. This man was not the man she had loved since she was seventeen. It was a man who had changed; an irrational man, an egotist who considered he was above the law. An insane man!

She texted the info to Drakeman who was sitting reading a paper in the lounge.

''Upstairs!'' he ordered and followed her to her room again.

''He is not thinking clearly,'' said Kirsten.

''I think his needs are overwhelming his common sense. He is no longer acting rationally. We will catch him easily.''

A knock came on the door and a very thin tall blond woman came in. Drakeman recognised her as Susan, the girlfriend of Justin. He had texted her suggesting it would benefit them if she talked with him.

''Can we help you Ms Green?'' asked Drakeman.

''Did Justin beat you up and give you those scars?'' she asked Kirsten. Kirsten noted she was wearing a high-necked jumper on such a hot day.

''Yes, he used his fists and then finally a riding crop and a whip. I knew it was time for me to leave. He wants me to live with him again.'' She didn't want to hurt this girl who was clearly fond of Justin but she wanted her to know the truth, what kind of man he was, for Susan's own protection.

''He visited me after the banquet last night and he did this to me.'' She pulled her collar down, showing the livid red and purple marks on her throat that were turning black. ''And these,'' she said, pushing her sleeves up to show the bruises and burns on her arms

''You must leave his house,'' said Kirsten, ''before he injures you badly.''

''I have evidence he seriously hurt a woman before,'' said Drakeman. Pages of papers were coming through his printer telling the man's stories. ''Disabled her. She walks now but it took years for her to recover full function in her legs. He paid her off so she did not take a legal claim against him.''

''I don't live there with him. I only keep some clothes there and sleep there regularly.''

''Leave them. They are not worth it. Don't go back to his house or yours. He may know you have come to this hotel.''

Susan nodded looking frightened. ''I will go to my Sister in Scotland. I am owed a fortnight's leave and was going to take some.''

''Please leave the address. Contact me by your cell only. Take a hired car to the nearest station and then a cab there please for your own safety.''

''Have you been to Davan Hall?'' asked Kirsten curious.

''No, he wouldn't take me which was unusual as I thought he had taken other women there. He said it was being renovated.''

''Who did he take?''

''I don't know. I saw some pictures in his study of girls in low cut dresses at a party I suppose but he told me to leave the study and not go back in there again. He was nasty about it.''

''I bet he was,'' said Drakeman. ''How young were these women?'

''Pretty young, about fourteen or fifteen.''

''I would go now if I were you,'' said Drakeman. ''I will send a man with you to Scotland if you want.''

''No, I will wait in the lounge. My Brother is meeting me and I will ask him to take me.''

''Good luck,'' said Kirsten and hugged the woman noticing how thin she was. "Look after yourself.'' She recognised herself in that woman years before when Justin had encouraged her to starve herself but had not beaten her badly yet.

Drakeman was on his cell again. "Scotland Yard please, Vice dept.'' He had a contact there who would be very interested to know that their enemy had pictures of young girls in his study. If the girls were very young a search warrant might be gained to search his home and computers as well. Susan had given them the evidence they needed to get a warrant.

Kirsten waited anxiously, butterflies fluttering in her stomach. Drakeman had decided on a plan he had outlined to her. ''You will go in the car as Justin wants. I will bug you with a tracking device and we will follow you at a distance. Pack for a few days. He will expect it.''

''What about Josh.''

''My men reported a limo being parked near the outbuildings you described but they haven't been able to discern who is in the building.''

''Where is Justin? I know him. He will want to be there if he intends to hurt Josh.''

In her darkest moments, she knew Justin would not stand for being humiliated by either her or Josh as he had been last night. Her psychotherapist had indicated his latent narcissism would not allow his ego to be damaged. He must be right all the time. His need to punish and humiliate, to prove himself in the right, would mean he would want to hurt them until they cowered in front of him and begged him for mercy.

''He has not left London yet, He will get to Davan Hall about eight if he drives. I am going to try to detain him. A problem at work that will take a little time to solve.''

She took a deep breath holding down her panic. *Thank God for small mercies. Josh would be safe for a while yet.*

She carried on researching for anything that might help them find Josh safely and neutralise Justin's power and influence. He had diluted his stock in two companies recently. The money was being poured into Davan Hall but the expenses on that didn't cover the amount of money he had realised from the sale of his stock. Where else was he putting his money?

She searched until it was nearly time to meet the car outside the hotel. Just when she was giving up she searched the Land Registry and found Justin had bought land in Lancashire. Rightmove told her it was another old pile which needed doing up in the middle of nowhere.

What the devil did he want another old house for? It was of no historical significance with no influential neighbours to impress. Justin had always impressed on her the importance of showing his peers he was successful, to pave his path to even greater success.

''Phil. He has bought another pile in Lancashire. Look at it when I am gone.''

''I will,'' he said, ''but not for long. I want to follow you. Josh would never forgive me if I left this job to my men.''

She hugged him and went down to reception and out to the car. She recognised one of Drakeman's men talking to the doorman and knew he would take down the number plates and text them to Drakeman.

The suited Chauffeur did not speak to her but let her into the car. When the doors locked automatically she panicked for a moment, but took deep breaths and calmed herself. Her yoga classes were helping her cope with panic attacks these days. She felt for the bug in her bra and took comfort from it being there. Would Justin guess she was being followed and had been bugged? He was no detective but was a clever man and knew Rutland's men would be investigating his disappearance.

''Where are we going?''

''I am sorry I am not at liberty to tell you, Madam.'' She settled down for a longish journey knowing how far Davan Hall was. She dozed and felt disquiet when she woke after only an hour and the limo stopped outside electric gates. They opened and the car progressed down a very long tree-lined drive and stopped outside a house she didn't recognise.

She felt sick now, knowing Davan Hall was not their destination. It had been a decoy, designed to put anyone wanting to trace them off their track.

'What was the point in stopping here? Drakeman would wait outside until we moved again?

''Please get out Madam,'' said the chauffeur in a tone that sounded polite but made the request sound like a command.

''Where am I?'' she asked playing for time.

"Madam!'' he repeated, this time firmly grasping her arm and moving her out of the car. He ushered her through the open door into the house and down corridors until they got to the garden doors.

Bright lights shone through the French windows. She was temporarily blinded as she was pushed down a path until she stood blinking before the vehicle parked there.

Oh Christ! she thought as her sleeve was pulled up and she felt a sharp prick. She was aware for a few minutes of her environment and what awaited her and then blackness enveloped her.

Drakeman sat in the trees hidden away from the cameras near the gates. Everything was going wrong. They were in the Home Counties and the house had recently been bought by Justin's mother.

Why would he come here when it was obvious the car could be followed?

He racked his brains for answers and then one of his men said, ''Look Sir,'' as a helicopter rose above the garden walls and took off at speed. ''Follow the fucking thing,'' said Drakeman pulling his cell out and telephoning his friend at the Yard. ''Keep him in your vision and if you start losing him tell me the direction he is taking.''

Thank Christ, they had a Landover. "Go across country. I don't care if we are trespassing. Just keep the damned thing in sight.'' They were heading north and he kept his contact informed of their location. The copter was losing them fast. They must be going to that place Justin had bought in Lancashire. He put the destination in the Tom and settled back for a while.

''Brian, he has planned this. He knew we were after him and doesn't care for the consequences. He is totally focused on getting Ms Gateman.''

''There is a helicopter waiting at an airport near you. You will only have lost about 30 minutes and police will be waiting at the destination to support you.''

''Thanks Man. I owe you one.''

''We have been waiting to net these paeds for a while. This may be our chance Mate!''

He read another text. Josh had been moved from Davan Hall and his car was moving in a northerly direction as well, obviously to meet the copter there. When Justin finally arrived at Latham Lodge he would have some surprises waiting him. Tom had sent a team to his townhouse and they had searched his computer.

There were graphic photos of very young girls with him and others in interesting positions. They were enough to send this guy to prison for a long while if added to charges of kidnapping and g.b.h. Kirsten said she would press charges against him for beating her without her consent.

Justin was clearly using his Lancashire base for his nasty activities. Drakeman's London contacts had revealed a few girls who had serviced Deepman and Justin had disappeared. A wall of silence had faced his men initially when they had questioned the madams and some of the friends of the girls who had vanished.

His man had seen fear in victims before but rarely as devastating as that on the face of one girl. She was as thin as a rake, her blue veins showing painfully through her unnaturally pale skin. She shivered and trembled as if she were frozen, despite the central heating belting out in her flat. Her eyes were clouded, the result of substance abuse but despite her unnatural lethargy she managed to exude a hysterical fear when Justin's name was mentioned.

''I don't know nuffing!'' she had cried and tried to slam her door in his face. His foot stopped her closing it and she shrunk back, cowering with fear.

''Ms Treetham. You have nothing to fear from me. We think Mr. Grayson is connected with the disappearance of your friend and that of other girls.''

''I don't know nuffing!'' the girl repeated, a stubborn negativity clouding her face as if a shutter had come down.

''There is a very large reward for the person who gives the police help in convicting him. My client has offered it.'' He mentioned a sum which made her gape.

''My client is richer and more powerful than Justin Grayson and he will be destroyed and put in prison for a very long time.

'You will be put under a Witness Protection Programme. A new identity and enough money to live comfortably wherever you want and payment for any rehab you need.''

''What do the police know about him?'' she asked, her avarice warring with her natural fear.

''He beat both his fiancé, a Ms Gateman and his present girlfriend. The former will press charges against him. Add that to kidnapping my client Josh Rutland and assault and battery, and stalking Ms Gateman. You may have seen Mr. Rutland on the news. He is the man who is putting up the reward.''

''He's a wealthy geezer?'' said the girl her eyes narrowing sharply. She had watched the news and had seen where he had been staying, one of the most exclusive hotels in London. This flash bloke reeked of cash. Perhaps she had a chance to get out of this rotten life.

''We also think he has abused and raped under-aged girls. Intercourse with an under-aged girl constitutes statutory rape,'' he said.

''Huh, all the girls here would be able to say they had been statutorily raped,'' she mocked, disbelieving him.

''It is true but we think he may have hurt these girls and they have disappeared. They may have died as a result of their abuse. The police have found pictures of abusive acts between him, his friend and young girls. There is a warrant out for his arrest as we speak so you see he will not get off this time.''

He saw a look in her wary eyes as the last words registered. ''He was reported to the police then before but was let off?''

''He's got friends among the filth. A girl thought she was safe reporting that pair to the police but he found out and got off and she was beaten up so badly she couldn't work in this business anymore. They scarred her face.''

''What did they do to you?'' he asked pitying this young girl who was barely sixteen. Used to showing men her body she took off her top and showed a knife scar down her back. Red and livid, it was recent and must still hurt like hell.

''They also made me use this stuff until I was hooked?'' she said showing the needle marks on her arms

''Where does he get the girls?" He had broken through her resistance. She wanted out so much she was prepared to risk her life. A severe heroin addict, she knew her life expectancy would be short unless she entered a clinic soon. Her pimp would offer no help.

''Through my pimp who supplies girls to the Power and Control House, a bondage club. That's its nickname. He picks up runaways, usually orphans running from foster care.''

''Where does he take them?''

''To a place, he has got in the North somewhere, although he often starts them off somewhere in London. I don't know the address Mister,'' she said, honesty shining in her eyes. ''He has another of my friends, a young fifteen-year-old kid. I don't want her to be hurt like my other friends. Can you help her?'' she pleaded. "I don't have many friends!''

''You may have saved her life. Now pack. I want you out of here. I may have been seen coming in here. Mr. Rutland will pay for you to stay somewhere safe.''

After she packed he had parcelled her off to a police station well out of London where she would be found a 'safe house' for the future. The police would protect her if her evidence could bust this vile gang that was likely to be linked with narcotics as well as prostitution.

Chapter twelve.

Rutland's head ached like hell and he felt like shit. Thumped in the stomach, nearly strangled and drugged, all he wanted was to drink a bath full of water and fall asleep. The drug still tried to drag him back into unconsciousness but his conscious mind told him he had to wake up.

If they had him they could make Kirsten come to find him. He was certain now she loved him although she had not expressed her love for him. He knew she would trade herself for him if she thought it would save his life. He had no illusions about what Justin would do to him if he could get his hands on him in his present state, trussed up like a freaking turkey.

Thank Christ, Drakeman would stop her heroics and manage his rescue and that pervert's arrest.

If his kidnap could be linked to Justin, that and Kirsten's beatings could send him down, plus more time for any other things he was mixed up in. Money could only extend so far and once the man was indicted the men who protected him would withdraw their protection and vanish. His power and insidious influence would dissolve.

He opened his eyes. He was being transferred from an old Victorian building to a car.

''Change of plan,'' one man said to the other. ''We are taking him to Latham Lodge. This place is too well known to his friends and enemies. Only a few people know about that place.''

''I wish he would make up his bloody mind. We have hours of driving left!''

''Our friends are taking the woman to Latham Lodge by helicopter and then sending it for us. We are meeting it at a disused airport near here.''

Rutland shook himself awake. It was twelve o'clock. He must have slept on and off for hours. Justin must have tricked Kirsten and Drakeman. He was not afraid Drakeman would lose their trail. His contacts extended into the British police and armed forces. He interfaced with Interpol while he worked for the FBI and knew many friends and associates he could call on for help now. Rutland only feared Drakeman's help would come too late. His blood ran cold when he thought of what Justin could have in store for Kirsten.

He was dragged, half carried to the car and pushed in, banging his head against the window. As he saw stars he speculated maliciously what he would like to do to these men when he got himself free and his mangled brain cleared itself. He would not try to escape yet. He would go along for the ride and rest until he needed to be fit to fight and help free himself and Kirsten.

Unsurprised and on the attack, he could demolish these thugs one-handed. They were big and muscular but portly and unfit. A few hard kicks would take them out. They had only been able to take him out because the bastards had used a needle on him.

He slept until the car stopped. A copter waited for him. He squinted at the watch on one of his captor's arms It was past one o'clock. He needed to delay this trip as long as possible. He was certain he would be used as a pawn by Justin to make Kirsten cooperate with him.

Justin would use the time with her to frighten and humiliate her but he would save any violence against her for him to see and vice versa. In his mind, he thought all the nasty things he would do to Justin if the police didn't arrive too soon. Before the copter could start he bent over. He was pushed aside after vomiting over the man's pants

''You filthy bastard!'' said the man and half-dragged him out of the copter as Rutland fell to the ground vomiting. He had always been able to vomit at will, a function that had got him out of school many times until his Grandma had wised up to his prank. These men were not as wise as the old bird and pulled him to a seated position and thrust water down him until he nearly choked.

''Feel sick,'' he said feebly. ''Don't travel well.'' One swore at him but carried some travel sickness pills. He fished them out.' 'You're worse than my kids,'' he said but gave him one. Rutland pretended to take one but spat it out into his hands during another coughing fit. He didn't want to become drowsy.

''He needs 30 minutes for the pills to work.'

''Ten minutes should be enough.''

''He didn't puke all over your pants,'' said the first man grumbling, wiping his pants with the water and a handkerchief. Ten minutes later Rutland was pushed into the copter again and began his next stage of the journey.

An hour later the copter landed in the grounds of another Victorian house but in much worse shape than Davan Hall. He jumped out of the copter enthusiastically now, wanting to settle this matter once for all. He stumbled through an old dilapidated building that looked as if it could barely stand on its own to a courtyard, the men enjoying pushing him and watching him trip over the uneven floors.

Wait, you filth! I am going to enjoy kicking your brains in. Out went the sophisticated man of law. In its place was Rutland the fighting machine, ready, totally focused on destroying the men who could harm the woman he loved!

In the middle of the courtyard was a drain cover which was pulled up. Peering down he saw a ladder with rusty rungs still complete.

''Down,'' said the man he had vomited on. Rutland was pleased he still smelt of puke. He could still get some malicious pleasure from irritating the man. He slid and slipped down the rungs. He heard Kirsten's voice and his heart lurched at her familiar tones.

He reached the bottom and was moved through a doorway into another room which was much bigger than the first. He noticed Kirsten was sitting unbound, unhurt thankfully but rather tired, still feeling the effects of the drug.

''Hi Sweetheart!'' he greeted her. Her head shot up and she beamed a smile at him that made his heart leap. She saw his blackened and bruised throat and got up to reach him.

''Josh, are you hurt?'' She was pulled back and made to sit down and she looked indignantly at the ape who roughly held her down. ''He may need medical help,'' she snapped.

''No chance Darling. Just a few bruises. He won't die yet!''

Her eyes clouded at those last words but she held herself together. She needed to stay strong for Josh to help him if he needed to fight his way out of there. She knew his reputation as a fighter now and trusted him to save them if the police couldn't get them out of this hell-hole.

''That's right, Baby,'' said Josh reassuringly. ''Nothing to worry about. I am as fit as a fiddle. Where are we by the way?''

''In rural Lancashire near the borders. I think this is a recent acquisition of Justin's. Even his girlfriend had not heard of it.''

''Sit down,'' said the ape motioning him to a chair. Rutland sat although his limbs ached from sitting still so long. He looked around him and saw fear in Kirsten's eyes. They drew him to a wall covered in instruments some of which he recognised but the functions of others he didn't know or want to know. They could all be used for hurting a body seriously badly.

She must be scared shitless after being beaten in the past by Justin.

These thugs were clearly waiting for their boss but he didn't want to wait his arrival now. He wanted Kirsten out of there fast. If Kirsten knew the location of this place, then so did Drakeman and the police might be outside even now.

It was time to disable these thugs and free himself. They didn't appear to be carrying guns although a knife glinted at the belt of one of them. He needed to get Kirsten out of their way. He didn't want her used as a hostage.

''I need to puke again!'' he said. ''Quickly! Those pills didn't work very well. I didn't take them in time. A bucket for Christ's sake!'' he cried, the urgency in his voice evident to the thugs, one of whom moved out of the room.

One had stayed in the courtyard to Rutland's delight. ''Do you have a handkerchief please.'' The man found a rag from the corner and pushed it into his cuffed hands. In response Rutland raised his fists and bloodied his nose. As the man grabbed at his face to stem the blood running down his body he kneed him in the groins sending him to the ground doubled up. A chop to his neck rendered him unconscious.

''Thank God, they acted like amateurs handcuffing his hands in front of him.'' The other one had heard the noise and came rushing in; holding his knife ready to use it on Rutland. Rutland had the element of surprise, sending the man to the opposite wall with a kick that resounded with the man's head hitting it. The goon crumpled to the ground, blood gushing from his head, temporarily dead to the world.

''Keep him alive Kirsten. Find the keys to these cuffs for me please.''

She searched hurriedly through the ape's pockets, then undoing his cuffs with the keys, she enabled him to cuff the one who he had chopped. Kirsten mopped the blood off the ape's head and bound it with a strip of her tee-shirt.

''We want him to turn Queen's Evidence,'' she said. ''He may squeal if he knows he is going down for a long time.''

''I want to get that clown upstairs in the courtyard. Is there any way out of here?''

''No. There is one other man who chauffeured me here and locked me in.''

''Is he armed Kirsten?''

''I don't think so but he is pretty tough and strong.'' She came to him and kissed his cheek. ''Be careful! I don't want to lose you now I have found you, Josh Rutland.''

Reading confusion on his face she explained; "The real Josh Rutland I mean, not the hard-bitten lawyer or tycoon but the kind gentle man who protects me and whom I adore.''

He hugged her and said, ''I should get up there, Love. Keep your fingers crossed they don't hear me. Thank God, the cover was left off.''

''No wait Josh. They must keep me unhurt but they might hurt you badly if they see you. Let me go first instead.''

''Not a chance! I am trained for this type of situation.''

''Sorry!'' she said, ''I am right this time,'' and started to climb up the ladder nimbly, faster than he could have imagined. He went to grab her and pull her down but what she said made sense to even his over-protective mind.

He smiled to himself. There were some advantages to being with an independently minded woman. He had a great view of her tightly rounded ass which even her loose sweats couldn't disguise. She had a great figure, even better now she had put on some extra pounds. He couldn't wait to get her to safety and have her in his arms. *Later I will enjoy you Kirsten Gateman.*

She peered over the top. ''It is all clear.'' He was now coming right behind her.

''Get out quickly and move to the right where there are shadows. I am following now.'' She dived to the right under an archway, thankful no-one had seen or heard her yet.

He climbed out and ran with enormous speed for such a big man and joined her. His arm about her he growled, ''Honest to God Kirsten, I will throttle you if you give me a fright like that again. Wait for me next time.'' She just gave him a mischievous look which sent his heart racing again. He had to stay in control. He was losing it around Kirsten. He was so scared of her being hurt.

He directed them to the main house. Moving silently like ghosts they moved through the corridors, checking the rooms for any men. They heard a voice. Rutland put his arm behind him stopping her.

"Look in the other rooms and if they seem empty see if there is a gun cupboard. Break it open and bring some weapons to me please. I will deal with this guy alone. You will only distract me and could get hurt. Please Kirsten.''

''Keep safe.'' She vanished in the other direction. Rutland could focus on his objective now he knew she was out of immediate danger. He thought there was one man in the room. He wanted him alive to provide information about Justin and any incriminating paperwork or photos or computer discs that might help them indict him. It was easy disposing of the man on the phone. Rutland took off his trainers and crept forward without making enough noise to disturb a mouse.

He waited until the man put down the receiver. A head-lock silenced the man as he struggled to breathe. Rutland pulled his other arm behind his back until he heard it break and the man would have cried out in agony if his face wasn't covered by Rutland's big paw.

He trapped the man's good arm behind him and said, ''The other one is next if you don't cooperate. I am going to take my hand away from your mouth and then you had better start talking. Nod if you agree.''

The man nodded and he removed his hand from his face and allowed him to breathe. The man gasped deep breaths of air but looked terrified. Rutland didn't care if he was in pain. Kirsten had bad bruises on her arm where this moron had held her too tight.

''When is Justin Grayson arriving and by which means of transport?'' The man stuttered, he was so desperate to cooperate with Rutland but then he spat out the required information.

''He was delayed in London so the helicopter went for him and he will arrive in about forty minutes.''

''Where does he keep his papers or computer software?'

'Here in this room. Over in that filing cabinet and desk?''

''Is there anyone else here other than the men in the room under the drain cover?''

''No, just me and the woman.''

''Kirsten,'' Rutland yelled. ''Here.''

Kirsten appeared.' 'Couldn't find anything useful in those rooms.''

''Everything is in this room according to this guy. Get the ropes off those drapes and bring them here.

He tied the man's arms behind him to the chair, ignoring his cries of pain. ''What is wrong with him?'' asked Kirsten.

''I broke his arm when I subdued him,'' said Rutland negligently.

She grimaced. She was becoming accustomed to this different Rutland; the sophisticated lawyer being superseded by a harsh and violent fighting machine. Focused on his objective he ignored all other distractions and concentrated his energies on getting the job done. Gone were the wicked sparkling emerald eyes that looked tenderly at her; replaced by dark green cold orbs that looked as hard as stones and lacked humanity.

''We can search this place now. I put the cover back on the drain and locked the other men in. We have a half an hour before Justin comes. You look in the filing cabinet and I will take the desk. The cops will confiscate the computer.''

After ten minutes, they had found what they wanted. He phoned Drakeman's number.

''Hey Man. Where are you? Kirsten and I are at a place called Latham Lodge and we are both safe. I have four goons disabled and locked up here. Justin is arriving by copter in about half an hour and I might need help then if he has brought others with him.''

''We are about five minutes away hidden behind the trees. I've got a car of cops next to me. Scotland Yard have an idea this Justin has abused and tortured and disposed of very young girls and is a part of or the mastermind behind a paedophile gang.''

''We need to wait until he comes here for the police to catch him red-handed with the stuff we are digging out now. Kirsten has found some computer discs that look promising and I have found some incriminating photos.''

''I'll send the cops in five minutes after he has landed then.''

''Give me ten and I want Kirsten out of the way. The bloody girl wants to get involved all the time.''

"She has got spunk.''

''Too much!'' said Rutland but he loved the new version of Kirsten; not wanting the withdrawn creature he had first seen at the airport. He could envisage banging heads with her continually in the future but would enjoy the making up with her. Make up sex could be great sex!

He put the phone down and said to Kirsten. ''I want you out the way when Justin comes. He is very dangerous if he has taken these risks. He is clearly out of control.''

''Tough!' 'she said. Her jaw jutted out as she stubbornly held her ground. ''If he confronts me and tells me what he wants to do with me we have evidence against him. I can be a witness in court against him.''

''It is too dangerous.''

''Oh, come on Rutland,'' she said. ''Stop treating me like a kid. I shot that other criminal. If it were any other barrister or witness, you would let them get involved. I can get you the evidence we need.''

''You are not just any other witness. You are my Woman,'' he said holding her shoulders and making her look into his emerald eyes. She saw concern there and something else she couldn't identify but it made her heart sing.

''And you are my Man, Josh Rutland and I love you,'' she said, ''but you must let me help you. I need to be able to face Justin to get closure and forget what he has done to me.'' Rutland beamed. It was the first time she had said she loved him. He could have jumped for joy. He had broken through that emotional icy cage that had surrounded her heart.

He took her in his arms. ''When this is over Kirsten my love, I am going to kiss you senseless, seduce you and marry you in that order!'' She did not argue with him but just pulled his face down to her and kissed him until they were both breathless.

''I can hear a helicopter. If you must take part in this episode then this is what I want you to do. Sit by the desk and wait for him to reach you. I will be in this room with you but behind the window drapes.''

He took the guns she had found and gave her a pistol and he took a pistol and several rifles. He had filled them with cartridges and had clicked off the safety catches. He took his place behind the heavy velvet drapes.

She heard Justin come in. Another man was talking with him in a hushed voice. ''The lady was left in the room under the drain cover Sir. Rutland should be with her by now.''

''I need to do a little work on the computer and then I will go and visit them. Bring some sandwiches and coffee to my study please."

Justin proceeded to the study and walked in. He saw a slight figure at his desk outlined by the dim table light and enveloped by shadows. He took out a gun as the figure swivelled around to face him.

''Kirsten,'' he said shocked. She was waiting silently as if she expected him, not worried at all that he was there. He had expected her to be frightened out her wits, imagining all the worst things he had store for her. He had stored that thought in his psyche during the helicopter trip, relishing the look on her face when he confronted her.

Now she looked calmly at him, unworried, as if she was not his prisoner. *Where are my men? How come she is in my study instead of in the room under the drain cover?*

''Hello Justin!'' she said. ''You do look foolish with that gun pointing at me. I have read some of your discs and seen some of your photos. I knew you liked little girls but not in that way?''

He shrugged. "I needed some release when you would not give me what I wanted Kirsten. It would not have taken much for you to have joined that club.''

''Don't blame me for your perversions Justin. Some of these girls are children. Where are they now?''

''They were expendable, only street trash I had picked up at the station, runaways. The younger ones were sold to us by their parents. Large poor families often find their children an unnecessary expense. They are gone now.''

His slate eyes seemed flat, devoid of all emotion and he shrugged when he talked about the little girls. She shivered as a chill went through her as she thought of the terror those little girls had felt.

''Us?'' she enquired.

''Deepman and Grentcham and Olivier,'' he said coming forward as if he were in a trance, still aiming the gun at her.

"Your inner circle,'' she said. ''Tell me, why not stick with adult women? You said I was not experienced enough in bed and you wanted mature women who would service you better and understand your needs. Surely young girls would have even less experience and knowledge.''

''Indeed but no woman could replace you Kirsten and you underestimate the pleasure a man can get from watching the faces of those young girls when they understood what was in store for them.''

She felt like vomiting. Holding out a photo of a young girl of about eleven years she said, ''Like this?''

He focused on the photo of the girl and smiled; a smile that did not quite reach his glazed eyes as he tried to remember something. ''Ah that one, a pretty young thing, wasn't she?''

The photo showed the girl's horror as she faced the camera. She appeared to be pleading with a person in front of her as someone else held her head back to face the lens. She was naturally of olive complexion but the blood had drained from her face and her eyes told of her pain and agony; screwed up, as her hair was pulled tightly by the man behind her who showed just his hand. Her hands were in front of her as if she were begging or praying.

''She begged for mercy Kirsten as you will.''

''How many girls were there?'' asked Kirsten. She guessed they were all deceased by now. He was too thorough to leave loose ends.

''About twenty-four over the last few years. They enjoyed suffering pain Kirsten, as you will.''

''In that room beneath the drain cover?'' she asked, thinking she had most of what she wanted now. The police could finish his interrogation at headquarters and tie up the loose ends.

''Yes, that lovely room I had altered for my needs. De Sade had a room just like it you know!'' Kirsten knew of the reputation of De Sade. Sadists had been named after that evil man who had corrupted and tortured women in France. She had heard enough. He was sick in the head. While living with him she had had doubts about his sanity. His sexual tastes had become more peculiar but she had never envisaged how narcissistic he had become.

Justin was on a high. He enjoyed talking about his young conquests. His ego needed to be fed and his power grew when he saw Kirsten was revolted by the photo she had shown to him.

He felt like an emperor when impoverished, uncared for young girls gushed at him when he bought them presents. Delicate young lips and hands caressing him and almost deifying him had made him feel godlike. He knew what the Roman Emperors had felt like with their slave girls. They would do almost anything for him until the things he asked frightened them and hurt them emotionally and physically.

He had the power of life and death over them in his special room and it made him feel complete in a way no other women could make him feel. The void he felt when the last breath disappeared out of them could only be filled by the usage of replacement girls. His need was accelerating and was almost uncontrollable.

He blamed Kirsten. When had been able to beat her, and make her cower before him he had felt in control and satisfied, if not sated. When she left, he had needed to find another outlet.

He had already joined bondage clubs and the managers had suggested he might want to try younger models to experiment with. After her disappearance, he had increasingly found younger girls more enjoyable to tame and now he had a taste for children.

He still wanted Kirsten. He had wanted her since he first set eyes on her when she was only seven, a slight flaxen haired child with innocent blue green eyes that looked at him as if he were a god; he appearing to be the only one who liked her amongst her family and their friends.

When she became his lover, he had tried to keep that waiflike creature who had adored him by making her diet and look thin like a lost young girl. Sadly, she had resisted him and developed physically, looking more woman-like, until he had tried to make her obedient to his needs in a more physical violent way.

''Come with me Kirsten,'' he commanded, putting his hand out to her to take his. His trance-like state had intensified.

''Where are you taking me?'' she asked, getting up as she saw Rutland put his head around the curtain and shake his head.

''We are going to my room. My playroom. You have been bad and must be punished Kirsten. You left me and put on weight. You no longer look like my little girl. You were such a pretty little girl when I first met you and I wanted you to stay the same; a little girl, never growing up. You always did what you were told then Kirsten. Not now; which is why you must be punished. I am your master and you my little girl!''

Realisation hit Kirsten. She had looked so young when she was a thin A level student and then an undergrad. Her friends joked about her ability to get in the cinema for a child's price but Justin had nearly caused her to be anorexic in order to keep her looking a child. He had not loved her as man to woman but as man to child.

She saw Rutland creep forward. She must keep Justin talking and give Josh a chance to disarm him. ''I don't want to come with you Justin. I have found another man who doesn't see me as a child but as a woman.''

''You are still child-like Kirsten. You came when I asked you to. You wanted to come. You haven't grown up.''

''You are wrong Justin. I love a man now. I felt a foolish infatuation for you but what I feel now for Josh Rutland is a real love, an adult woman's love.''

Rutland was creeping closer, now only a few feet behind the almost zombie-like Justin whose gaze was fixated on Kirsten now; his eyes running from her flaxen plait to her trainer shod feet, mentally stripping her, making her feel denuded and dirty as he had done in the last few years she had lived with him.

Suddenly, Justin woke as if from his sleepy state and spun around to meet Rutland. A loose plank had squeaked giving Rutland's presence away. Rutland stood still as the aim of the gun was directed his way. Just two feet and he would have nailed the bastard.

Now it was up to Kirsten. She had her guns behind her. He raised his hands away from his pocket where his gun was. The rifles were by the drapes. This guy was a psychopath and out of control. He had to humour him, keep him talking until Drakeman came or Kirsten could use her weapons.

''Mr. Rutland. I thought you could have done better than this even if you rejected me Kirsten. Immigrant scum from the gutters of some slum in County Cork. His Great-Granddad was a labourer on building sites. He only got to university because of scholarships and his service in the military.''

Rutland's hands clenched at these insults to his Great-Granddad. This ignorant moron had been born with a silver spoon in his mouth and had been to the best private school and universities and had walked straight into an excellent job which had taken him to the top of his profession.

He had the audacity to insult his Great-Granddad who had worked so hard to provide for his children he had died of a heart attack when he was only fifty-six. He had been loved and mourned by his family and had the satisfaction of knowing his children would have an education although he was himself illiterate.

What would Justin leave behind him except money and estates and a hated reputation? No-one would mourn him when he died. Many wished him dead already. If he wasn't such an evil bastard, he would feel sorry for him.

Justin stood between them. ''Kirsten walk in front of Rutland. We are going to go to my room and have some fun.'' Kirsten walked past him to Rutland. He wondered if she had the gun stuck down her capacious track pants.

''Move ahead one after the other in single file please,'' he said, enjoying commanding them. Rutland remembered Drakeman's words. The cops should be moving in on them by now. He heard some movement outside and blue lights flashed. Christ! He hoped Justin wouldn't panic and shoot someone by accident. He might want to die a martyr.

Justin listened and ordered, ''Quick to the back.'' He pointed to a curtained alcove. Opening the curtain, Kirsten saw a studded door with a wooden knot carved into the relief.

''Turn it to the right twice.''

Christ, this was like a Boris Karloff film. The door opened and a passage was revealed.

''Down,'' said Justin.

''You know I don't like dark spaces,'' said Kirsten. ''I get claustrophobic.'' She looked terrified.

''Move quickly!'' was the only response. Rutland put his hand on her shoulder to comfort her but it was knocked off by the gun in Justin's hand.

Come just a little closer, you bastard and I will nail you, thought Rutland rubbing his smarting fingers.

Kirsten shivered as a rat scuttled by but then she stopped dead still.

''I can't,'' she said frozen to the spot. A spider web, thick and full of black legged spiders was swaying across the ceiling and partially covered the passage.

For a moment, she was overwhelmed by a deep irrational fear. She would rather face Justin's gun than the spiders! A particularly hairy creature fell on to her hair and she screamed and moved back stumbling into Rutland. He backed a little, his heavy chest cushioning her fall but Justin didn't move fast enough backwards.

For a moment, he was close to Rutland, close enough for Rutland to spin around and hit the gun from his hand. His enemy disarmed, Rutland head butted him into the wall and then kneed him in the groin making Justin double up in agony and try too late to fend off the next kick which sent him to the ground screaming. Rutland pushed him on his front and sat on him, his weight holding him down, his enemy's arms pinioned behind him.

''Kirsten get something from the room to tie him up with.'' Kirsten ran like the devil was after her through the passage to the study then tore a thin curtain from the alcove. Running back, she gave it to Rutland.

''Aim this pistol at his head,'' he said whilst tearing up the curtain into strips which he used to bind Justin's hands. He pulled the little rat up by his collar and pushed him ahead of him. The man was still half doubled up, stumbling in pain until they reached the study.

The police were swarming over the building and Drakeman saw them through the doorway.

''Got the little rat then I see. Those photos on the desk look interesting. The cops are going to go through all his desks and cupboards. They already have his computer.''

''He has helped to kill several dozen girls and enjoyed abusing and torturing them. He blamed me for not attending his bondage clubs. He accused me of driving him to those places and to the younger girls. He still thinks of me as a little girl he wanted power over. Those girls were substitutes for me.''

''We have commandeered his helicopter,' said Drakeman. 'Take her back to London while I sort out things here. I know these guys and will help them process the work faster than you.''

''I will take you up on that and we will make our statements to the Cops tomorrow.'' He then thought of Drakeman's other reason for coming to London. ''And what about Paris then? Are you considering going still?''

''Yeah but I am worried. Elisabeth hasn't answered my texts. When she left, she said she would still text me regularly to say she was ok.''

Rutland wasn't particularly worried. His opinion of Elisabeth had fallen since she had cruelly dropped his friend. She hadn't lead him on. She had told him she didn't want any commitment and would leave for Paris but Rutland thought she shouldn't even have dated him when she went back to FBI headquarters.

She had given him hope when she should have dashed his hopes immediately. He had felt like slapping her when he saw how devastated his friend was. Kirsten had said she had good reasons for not wanting a commitment but he still thought she had acted like a tease and Drakeman was a fool chasing after her. He was heading for a harder fall.

Rutland could breathe steadily now. He had never feared Justin would win that night but he had worried Kirsten might be injured. The cops now had enough information to bang him up for life without much chance of early parole and even longer if they could prove he was insane and he could be held at her Majesty's pleasure.

''I didn't know you had a phobia about spiders."

''I didn't until Justin locked me up in a cellar with hundreds of them at Davan Hall. There was no light and they crawled into my hair. I had nightmares for months but he laughed at me. Said I was a coward.''

''I think you are one of the bravest woman I know facing him after what he has done to you.'' He helped her into the helicopter and rested her against his shoulder. ''Sleep baby, you deserve it. You gave the performance of a lifetime back there in that study.''

''I wanted him to convict himself by his own words. I still can't believe he could become such a monster. He was so kind when I was very young.''

''Well that monster is going away for a long time and can no longer harm you.'' He played with a wisp of hair that was escaping from her plait and watched her fall asleep.

When the helicopter deposited them on the outskirts of London they had a police escort to speed their way to the hotel. He carried her to their suite despite her protests. One reporter was still 'hovering' there. Rutland said, ''I will make a press statement in a few days Pal and it will be worth waiting to hear my news.'' He was more concerned with making sure Kirsten was relaxed and had no more nightmares about Justin. She was fast asleep when he undressed her to her underwear and put her in his own bed.

He fell asleep beside her but this time when he woke up she was already awake. She smiled sleepily at him and kissed him on the cheek. He turned over on his side and took her plait, playing with it in his hand. He pulled her to him with it and undid it, spreading it over the pillow.

''I prefer it loose, my blue-eyed witch,'' he said, running his fingers through it. She was no longer shy with him. She grasped his face with her hands and pulled him to her for a kiss. Not a man to turn down an invitation he kissed her passionately until he broke away breathless, looking carefully at her; trying to assess if she wanted to progress their relationship further or merely kiss.

Kirsten was no longer afraid of him and wanted him to know it. Her therapist had examined with her loathing of sex and she had admitted it was due to Justin's approach to sex. He had not made love. Sex was merely a rough way of satisfying his desires and it had gradually become more painful.

She knew Josh would not merely want sex but would want to make love, to make it as good for her as for him. She ran her hands over his hard pecs and then lower down over his abdomen and his narrow hips. They explored his well-defined swimmer's legs and rested on his waist.

Her touch had electrified him; the chemistry he knew had always existed between them nearly exploding.

''Kirsten?'' he asked, strangely hesitantly for him, the renowned player of women. He did not want to hurt her or frighten her by rushing their relationship but he knew women well and could read their moods and subtle body language.

Kirsten was sending out signals she wanted to make love and now. She undid her bra and took off her pants slowly, watching him enjoy her every movement. No longer was she imprisoned in her body by her terror, her distorted and damaged psyche. She was a woman who recognised her own sensuality and her power over the man she loved,

''Love me Josh. We have waited too long!''

"At your service, Ma'am,'' he whispered and flipped her on her back. He started slowly, kissing her neck, intending to pay homage to her body, every nook and cranny he could discover. After her neck, he decided her shoulders were being neglected and then her breasts. *I could spend hours on those breasts,* he thought, sucking her nipples until Kirsten cried out with pleasure.

In turn Kirsten ran her hands between his groins, rubbing him, caressing him, making him gasp and his breathing turn harsh and sharp. He responded by rubbing her between her legs, opening her folds and sticking a finger in gently, moving it rhythmically until she was overwhelmed by sensations, orgasmic pleasure she had not experienced before. He took her over the precipice three times until she grabbed his buttocks and said, ''Now Josh, I need more!''

She heard the rustle of foil as he prepared himself. Taking the weight of himself on his elbows he opened her up and with a strong but gentle thrust he finally entered her. Long slow but powerful thrusts entered her warm heat and she relaxed, less tight now.

She moved with him slowly, her hands gripping him tightly as he pushed her over the edge, time and time again, into a vortex she hadn't known existed. She came down again as he exploded within her and then lay beside her, both sated. She recovered first and curled next to him lying within his arms.

''That was not just sex Kirsten. We made love. I was attracted to you in some indefinable way when I first saw you in that lounge. I was drawn to you despite your rejections of me which hurt my ego no little.''

''Your ego couldn't be damaged if I tried,'' she replied, tracing her fingers down his hips, making him go hard again. ''You were always certain you would have me and I knew it as well.

'Even when I tried to push you away, I wanted you, needed you too, at some subliminal level. When you pulled me into that pool I was torn between kissing you and murdering you for breaking down my barriers.'' Whilst on the surface her rational mind had told her to reject him her sub-conscious had screamed out to invite him to kiss her.

He pulled himself up and leant across the bed to the corner table where he delved into the set of drawers.

''Close your eyes Sweetheart!'' She closed her eyes and he held out her right hand, putting a ring on her third finger. ''Open your eyes, my lovely girl.'' Her eyes filled with tears when she saw the sapphire and diamond stoned ring.

''Will you marry me Kirsten?''

''Oh yes, you mad, bad man.''

''You make me happy when you are with me?''

''As you do me? I have been lonely in London without you to boss me about and torment me.'' She looked a little sadly at him. ''I wish Elisabeth would change her mind about Phil. They seemed so happy together. I am sure she is missing him.''

''I think he is better off without her. She has dangled him on a string. He is going again to find her in Paris. He is still mad about her.

'She is as tough as old boots. You are more sensitive, Honey.''

''I had no-one to turn to for help. I told my father and mother about the abuse but mother hid her head in the sand as usual and father told me to grow up. He thought I was being melodramatic and refused to believe me. He thought women in a relationship should be passive and obey their husband or partner's every whim. They wouldn't listen to a bad word about Justin.''

Rutland could still see the remains of fear in Kirsten's eyes. It would take years to finally eradicate that fear even if the cause of it was locked safely away. It was up to him to make her feel secure and forget him. Another bout of passionate love-making followed.

''You have nothing to worry about Justin anymore,'' he said later when they were ready to sleep.

''Justin who?'' she said snuggling up to him content and fell asleep.

The End.

ABOUT THE AUTHOR

This author studied history and politics and then business and law. She became a law and economics lecturer in Higher Education and later left to start her own tutoring agency. She has since run a guesthouse and lives with her husband and two crazy Birman cats in a restored cottage near to a canal in Knowle in England. Many of the novels derive from the cases she read during her teaching career.

She enjoys Zumba and yoga. She loves art and illustrates her own book covers. Her current passion is making succulent and cacti bowls for her gazebo where she likes to write in the summer.

She also writes historical romance novels under the name of Alexie Bolton and books for children under the name of Dawn Bolton.

Proof

79348108R00113

Made in the USA
Columbia, SC
23 October 2017